D1168505

Looking for
Mr PIGGY-WIG

Looking for
Mr PIGGY-WIG

ANDY SECOMBE

MACMILLAN

First published 2008 by Macmillan
an imprint of Pan Macmillan Ltd
Pan Macmillan, 20 New Wharf Road, London N1 9RR
Basingstoke and Oxford
Associated companies throughout the world
www.panmacmillan.com

ISBN 978-0-230-71233-1

1 3 5 7 9 8 6 4 2

A CIP catalogue record for this book is available from
the British Library.

Typeset by Intype Libra Ltd
Printed and bound in the UK by
CPI Mackays, Chatham ME5 8TD

Visit **www.panmacmillan.com** to read more about all our books
and to buy them. You will also find features, author interviews and
news of any author events, and you can sign up for e-newsletters
so that you're always first to hear about our new releases.

This book is dedicated to those who labour under
Hippocrates' maxim – angels every one.

Acknowledgements

I'd like to thank Jo Rowe-Leete, Witch of the West, Roderick Lane, Wizard of Harley Street, and the good people of Derriford Hospital, Plymouth, without whose care and professionalism I wouldn't have been around to finish this book. Special thanks to Paul McArdle, Pat MacLeod, Maggie Jarvis and Linda Bedford. Thank you, thank you, thank you.

Three months previously...

The monk raised the hem of his heavy woollen habit to reveal the mechanism strapped to his left thigh. Gripping the small wooden spile, he turned it slowly, making the gaily coloured bungee cords bite deeper into his flesh.

He gasped with the sudden, sharp increase of pain. 'I chastise my body and bring it into subjugation.' Then he gave the spile another turn. The cords bit deeper still, the skin beneath turning from a livid red to a deep and poisonous blue. It was almost unbearable, but the monk, gasping with pain, continued with the purification rite. 'I mortify my flesh for the sake of the body of my Lord, and for His Holy Church, Ave Verum.'

From far off came the lonely sound of a bell, slow and sonorous. 'Vespers,' the monk sighed.

Fixing the spile in its new position by tucking it into a loop in the tautly stretched bungee cord, he lowered the hem of his habit, crossed himself, and opened the door of his cell. But instead of making his way down towards the chapel with all his brothers, the monk turned against the tide and headed for the abbot's office.

'You wanted to see me?'

'Ah, Brother, come in, come in.' The abbot was a small, twinkly man, whose eyes glittered beneath his bushy grey eyebrows and short, grizzled hair. Usually he was a jolly, up-beat sort of fellow, but today he seemed uncharacteristically nervous. 'You have some idea why I've called you here today?'

The monk nodded.

1

'Good, good. Here is the list of . . . ah . . . those who wish to destroy the order and bring down Ave Verum.'

'You mean the targets.'

The abbot nodded and slid a typewritten sheet across the desk towards the monk, who scanned it for a few seconds.

'Take it with you,' the abbot urged.

But the monk handed it back. 'No need, I have committed it to memory. You should destroy it.'

The abbot's bushy eyebrows shot skywards.

'Well, I wish I had your mental capacity. My brain's like a sieve these days, I can't even remember my own birthday.'

He opened a drawer in his desk and pulled out a brown envelope stuffed with cash.

'You'll need some money for expenses. Don't spend it all at once,' the abbot twinkled.

The monk took the envelope without comment and stared back at the abbot, unsmiling. 'I should get to Vespers now.'

'Yes, yes of course you should. Thank you for dropping by.'

The monk turned to leave, but the abbot stopped him at the door.

'When will you depart?'

'Tonight.'

The monk opened the door and was gone, leaving a palpable chill in the room that made the abbot shiver.

Chapter 1

The woman was tall and elegant, her clothes expensively understated, and she had the kind of easy style that can only be
acquired from long and intimate contact with money.

Jack Lindsay first spotted her from the window of his office
on the third floor as she was getting out of an electric black cab
in the street below. Actually it wasn't so much her that he
noticed but her hat. It was unusual to see a woman wearing a
hat in this neighbourhood; for a man, outdoor headgear,
usually in the shape of a trilby, was de rigueur, but a woman? If
a woman wore anything on her head in this part of town it
was a headscarf, not a hat which sprouted peacock feathers –
it would have been a dead giveaway in an identity parade.

Understandably this young lady seemed a little uncertain
about the neighbourhood in which she now found herself. She
looked nervously up and down the street, drawing interested
looks from some of the rough types hanging around the café
doorway opposite, then she leaned back into the cab and
quizzed the driver. Her misgivings were obviously rebuffed
because seconds later the hat re-emerged from the cab and she
produced a quantity of notes from her handbag. A fat, hairy
hand grabbed the money and the cab hummed off down the
road, leaving the lady floundering on the pavement.

From his vantage point several storeys above, Jack watched
as the hat floated above the paving stones, frozen for a moment
in indecision. Then he saw it turn decisively away, wobbling five
or six yards towards the east, peacock feathers trembling, before

coming to rest yet again. There was still more indecision as the hat revolved this way and that while an obviously deep and meaningful internal dialogue was conducted. At last the hat came bobbing back down the street, stopped right outside the entrance to Jack's building and then finally looked up at his window.

'What's so fascinating?' Mango, Jack's assistant, entered the room carrying tea.

Mango was a short, misshapen individual whose head seemed too big for his body. In spite of this, his large forehead didn't leave much room for his face, which was crammed into the narrow space between his eyebrows and his chin. But Mango seemed unashamed of his looks, proclaiming his presence with brazen sartorial vigour. Today he was wearing a cream suit accessorized with a purple chiffon scarf.

'Don't tell me – an attractive female.'

'A *lady*,' Jack corrected.

'In this neighbourhood?' Mango joined Jack at the window and handed him a cup and saucer. 'Here.'

'Thank you.'

'Is she still there?'

'No, she's gone now.' But Jack continued to stare absent-mindedly out of the window.

'You know, she really must have been something special.'

'How's that?'

'You're stirring your tea with your pipe.'

'Oh, damn!'

He put the cup down on the desk and wiped the pipe stem with a handkerchief.

'Come on, help me tidy this place up.'

Mango looked at Jack as if he'd just asked him to go camel trekking.

'You *are* joking?'

'If I'm not mistaken, that young lady is headed our way, and from the look of her she won't be used to our brand of homely disorderliness, so I want this place looking respectable. I at least want to be able to offer her a chair.' Jack picked up a pile of dust-gathering files from the chair reserved for clients.

Mango threw his hands wide with joy. 'I've been looking for those for weeks!' he squealed.

The room was dominated by Jack's heavy, dark-wood desk with its peeling leather inlay. In the cramped space it was just about possible to negotiate one's way right around its perimeter, so long as you kept flat to the wall most of the time. There was also an overflowing metal filing cabinet in one corner and every available surface was covered in messy paperwork, dirty teacups and pipe-racks.

Jack looked around in vain for a place to deposit the files. In the end he threw them in the waste-paper basket.

Mango seemed disappointed. 'You didn't want me to file those?'

'It's already done, under R for Rubbish.'

'Your jokes used to be better.'

'My life used to be better.'

Mango waved a finger at him. 'You can't fool me, you never had a life.'

Jack caught sight of his reflection in the window. He was tired and grey; his thinning black hair was scraped back across the top of his skull, his cheeks were hollow and his blue-grey eyes looked as though they'd seen too much life. He was clean-shaven, but his chin still showed the dark blue outline of his beard – it was impossible to get decent razor blades. He was around six feet tall and very thin. He liked to think of himself as lean, but in reality he looked as though he could have done with a decent meal. Unfortunately that was unlikely, given the shortages.

Luckily, in less than a year he would be out of this game. All he had to do was to hang on for another nine months and then it would be the good life all the way.

'You're right, Mango, but that doesn't excuse disorder.

Come on, she'll be here any minute and I want to make her feel welcome after her three-storey climb.'

'Mr Lindsay?' the woman breathed as she pushed open the office door; her top lip was bedewed with perspiration.

Jack got up and limped awkwardly round the desk to greet her, tangling with the hatstand in the process. 'Call me Jack. Please, come in and take a seat.'

She moved into the room like a lynx, her thin cotton dress clinging to every contour of her body. She emanated sex like heat from a five-bar electric fire and she smelt gorgeous. She sat down, crossed her legs slowly and gazed up at Jack with her liquid hazel eyes, full red lips parted in demi-pout.

It was quite a performance and for a moment Jack was speechless. 'I . . . I'm sorry about the lift,' he said, once he'd wrestled his brain back out of his trousers. 'I've been trying to get somebody to repair it for weeks now, but for some reason the man doesn't seem too keen to venture into this neck of the woods. Still, I expect you welcome the exercise. I mean, a figure as good as yours must need a lot of maintenance.' He'd meant to be complimentary, but had fallen somewhat short of the mark.

She glared at him from under the broad, shielding rim of her hat.

'I'm sorry, have I offended you?'

'No, you're standing on my foot.'

'Oh, please excuse me, it's this damn leg.' He shifted back and perched on the edge of the desk.

She looked at him challengingly. 'I was told you were the best private detective in the business.' Disapprovingly she cast an eye around the room. 'So why—?'

'Am I living in squalor?'

She shifted uncomfortably in her seat, as if afraid she might catch something from it. 'I'd expected something a little . . . classier.'

Jack pulled his pipe out of his pocket. 'I'm afraid class is one thing that's at a premium out here. And they do tell me that it's living amongst the common people that gives me my edge.' Jack clenched his pipe between his teeth. Now it was his turn to look challengingly at her. Unfortunately the effect was rather spoilt by the fact that his pipe was still full of tea, which dripped steadily onto his trousers.

'I think I'd better go.' She got up to leave. 'I appear to have made a mistake. I was told you'd be sympathetic.'

Jack let her reach the door. 'You were right about me being the best in the business.'

She stopped and turned.

'I'm sorry.' He smiled. 'It's just that these days I don't often get to meet respectable women.' He paused, realizing what he'd just said. 'I mean . . . I don't want you to think that I . . . what I meant was that I rarely meet people of a respectable nature of either sex . . . Oh, lord, this isn't going well, is it?'

The corners of her mouth twitched.

Jack stood and rested his hands on the back of her chair. 'Now I've thoroughly embarrassed myself, perhaps we can start again?'

She studied him for a long moment, then, coming to a decision, swayed back into the room and sat down again.

'Thank you. Can I offer you a cup of tea, or perhaps something stronger?'

'It's a little early for me. Just tea, thank you.' She studied him closely, eyeing him up and down. 'Your . . . leg?'

'You mean what happened to turn this fine athletic specimen into a cripple?'

She stared demurely at the floor. 'I didn't mean to pry.'

'No, it's quite all right.' Jack hobbled back around his desk, colliding once more with the hatstand, then sat down in his big leather recliner. 'If you must know, I caught it in a door.'

'That's rather a serious injury to receive from just catching it in a door.'

'The door happened to be in a collapsing building.'

'I'm sorry.'

'Don't be. My gangster-chasing days might be over, but there are compensations: like getting sympathy from a beautiful woman.'

She coloured slightly and Jack smiled.

'There's someone I'd like you to meet. Mango!'

'Did somebody call?' he said, sticking his head immediately around the door.

'Mango, come in. This is . . .' But this young lady had definitely upset Jack's equilibrium – he'd forgotten to ask her name. He looked at her helplessly, like a trout that's just swallowed a fly.

'Marian Lawes.' She offered Mango her hand.

He took it and gazed deep into her eyes.

'This is Mango Pinkerton, my assistant.'

Mango held her hand tightly, concentrating hard on her face. She looked uncertainly in Jack's direction.

'All right, Mango, that's enough. Give the lady back her hand and go and make us some tea.'

'Oh, certainly, sorry.' He let her go. 'Earl Grey or Assam?'

'Don't let him mislead you, however he makes it it always tastes the same: like dishwater.'

'Don't blame me, blame that damned grocer. He takes two ration cards for a carton of Earl Grey and I'm sure it's exactly the same tea he sells as his house blend.'

'I'll have . . . whatever.' Marian smiled.

Mango looked enigmatically at Jack before leaving the room.

Marian seemed troubled. 'Isn't he a telepath?'

'That's very observant of you, Miss Lawes.'

'Mrs Lawes.' Her jaw tightened.

'Oh, I'm sorry, I just thought—'

'That because I'm not wearing a wedding ring I'm not

married. My husband and I don't believe in tagging each other like cattle. I don't own him and he doesn't own me.'

Jack had obviously touched a nerve. 'I'm sorry if I offended you. Mrs Lawes.'

Her face softened again and she half-smiled. 'Forgive me, Mr Lindsay. Please, call me Marian.'

'And I insist you call me Jack. So, what can I do for you . . . Marian?'

'Actually it's about my husband. He's gone missing.' She fiddled with the clasp of a small clutch-bag she held in her lap.

'How long?'

Her eyes widened.

'How long has he been gone?' Jack repeated. 'A week, a month?'

'Six months.'

Jack eased back in his chair and the ancient leather creaked. 'Six months?'

'I know what you're thinking, but he often disappears for long periods. Like I said, we don't own each other.'

'I understand that, but six months?'

'It's not the first time, but he's always called before to tell me when he'd be back . . .' Her bottom lip was trembling.

'And this time you've heard nothing?'

She shook her head.

'Have you informed the police?'

'Yes,' she said hesitantly.

'And they've been less than helpful?'

Silent tears began to fall into her lap. She struggled with her bag, but her trembling fingers couldn't loosen the clasp. Jack offered her a clean handkerchief from a neatly folded pile he kept in a desk drawer. She took it gratefully and dabbed her eyes.

'Thank you,' she murmured.

Thoughtfully, Jack pulled on his pipe and got a mouthful of cold tea and tobacco ash.

'Ugh!' Taking yet another handkerchief from his stock in the desk, he wiped his mouth. 'Forgive me – morning tea incident.' Now he needed something strong to take the taste away. Reaching down, he slid open the bottom drawer and pulled out a half bottle of whisky and two shot glasses. He filled them both and pushed one over to her.

'Oh no, I—'

'Drink. I find it puts a completely different complexion on things. After one or two of these even this office begins to look plush.'

Mango came in carrying tea.

'*He* might even begin to look normal.'

Mango's eyes went straight to the whisky. 'My, we're starting early today. What's the occasion?'

'First client this month. Come and join us.'

'I'll stick with tea,' he said, affecting a superior air. He looked disdainfully at the two full glasses. 'I can see I'm the only one.'

Mango put the tray down, sat on the edge of the desk and poured himself a cup. 'I'm afraid we can't offer you any biscuits, because someone has already munched his way through this week's ration.'

Marian gazed at him for a moment then her eyes flicked nervously Jack's way.

'You don't mind, Marian? Mango here is my partner, I have no secrets from him.'

But she seemed unsure. 'Well I . . .'

'If it's his mind-reading capability that's troubling you, don't let it. The same building that did for my leg fell on Mango's head and now he doesn't even know his *own* mind.'

'Jack saved me from a burning building,' Mango gushed. 'I was born and brought up in the Philippines, and was over here on the Police Exchange Scheme, studying British police methods. During a case involving booze smuggling, I found myself in the middle of a burning warehouse full of illicit liquor.

Jack was hauling me out when the ceiling fell in. If it hadn't been for him I'd be dead.'

'Yes, and my life would have been a lot easier.' Jack poured a good shot of whisky into Mango's tea. Mango looked at him in that long-suffering, sad-eyed way of his.

Jack raised his glass with a smile. 'Cheers!'

Everyone drank.

With a shot of twice-refined, wood-aged grain alcohol running through his system, Jack's head suddenly became remarkably clear, his thinking sparklingly lucid.

Choosing a fresh pipe from the rack on his desk, he filled it with Old Hobson's Curiously Fragrant and set light to it.

'Now then, Marian. I'm going to have to ask you some questions. I apologize in advance if I appear impertinent, but I need to know everything about you, your husband and your relationship, all right?'

'Very well,' she said uncertainly.

'So, how were things between you? Forgive me for making assumptions, but from what you've already told me would I be right in describing your relationship as "open"?'

She nodded.

'And you were perfectly content with that?'

She inclined her head and studied the floor. 'It . . . wasn't always easy. I don't know exactly how many lovers he had, we never discussed details.'

'But he had – excuse the saying – a few more notches on the bed post?'

She closed her eyes and nodded again.

'Would you say your . . . intimate relations were good?'

She looked up sharply.

'Forgive me, but I need to have a complete picture of your relationship. Men disappear for any number of reasons but, in my experience, sex is chief among them.'

Marian recomposed herself. 'I suppose . . . yes. Although

he'd stopped being quite so caring. You might say the honeymoon period was over.'

For some reason the thought of this delectable female being intimate with another man made Jack feel uncomfortable.

'Did you ever argue? Not just about that, but about other things, you know: the colour scheme of the bathroom, what toothpaste you should use?'

'Daygan made all the little decisions like that.' She shrugged.

'And you didn't mind?'

'No. With those silly, inconsequential choices taken away from me, I was free to follow my own interests.'

'Good, we'll come back to those in a moment. But you must have argued about something?'

'Yes, we did argue,' she sighed. 'The last time must have been a couple of weeks before he left . . .'

She seemed close to tears again, but soon pulled herself together. 'We made it up afterwards.'

'And what was that about?'

She half closed her eyes and took a breath. 'It was our anniversary. We were going to have a romantic dinner at The Vine, but when we got there I found that he'd booked the table for four: he'd doubled up our dinner date with a business meeting.'

'The absolute bastard!' Mango exclaimed.

Jack glared at him and Mango pulled a sorry-little-boy face.

'It wasn't the first time he'd done something like that,' Marian continued. 'But he's always very busy. Apparently the two men were only in town for one night, they were taking the liner back to Corbett in the morning, so it was the only chance they had to meet.'

'Corbett, in Indonesia?'

'Yes.'

'That's an island of cut-throats and pickpockets,' Mango offered without provocation.

'And what kind of business is your husband in?' Jack asked.

12

She shrugged again. 'You know . . . business. I don't really understand all of it.'

'But you must have some idea in which area?'

'It used to be just fast food, but recently he's been getting into all sorts of things. He actually started out as an actor.'

'An actor?' Mango's eyes grew large. 'What's his name? Would I know him?'

From Marian's wan smile it was obvious this wasn't the first time she'd been asked that question. 'His name is Daygan Flyte, but you'd probably know him better as Mr Piggy-Wig.'

Mango looked as though he might wet himself. 'Mr Piggy-Wig? I often eat there. Is that him on the adverts?'

She smiled. 'The commercials are the only acting he does these days.'

'So Lawes is your maiden name?' Jack said, trying to bring the conversation back to something a little more adult.

'No. Daygan's real name is Michaelmas Thurrock-Lawes. He changed it when he became an actor.'

'Wise move.'

'Michaelmas?' Mango said. 'How can you christen a baby Michaelmas?'

'Daygan Flyte,' Jack said, pulling on his pipe. 'Let me think . . . head of PW Enterprises; built up Mr Piggy-Wig from nothing. Am I right in saying that PW Enterprises has recently been expanding its portfolio?'

'Yes. If you can't nobble the competition, buy it out.' Marian coughed suddenly and covered her mouth with her hand.

Mango raised an eyebrow and threw Jack an old-fashioned look.

'If I remember correctly, PW Enterprises has just bought out another fast-food chain: Faggot-in-a-Basket,' Jack continued. 'Am I right?'

'My, you're a walking business encyclopaedia.'

'I like to read the financial papers.'

'He keeps a stack of them in the lavatory,' Mango added unnecessarily.

'You said you had other interests,' Jack went on, swiftly changing the subject.

'I'm sorry?'

'The other interests that Daygan left you free to pursue.'

'Oh, I run a charity for children from less fortunate countries.'

Jack raised an eyebrow and leaned forward to rest his elbows on the desk. 'Surely there are enough children around *here* that are deserving of charity?'

'Have you ever confronted *real* poverty, Jack? Some of the places I've been . . . the things I've seen . . .' Her voice faltered and she stared at the floor.

Jack broke the silence by becoming brisk and businesslike. 'So, Daygan's gone and you'd like us to find him?'

'That's the general idea, yes.'

'Any idea where he might be?'

'I thought you were the expert.'

'I'm good, yes, but I'm not a miracle worker. I need something to go on.'

'Well, like I said, he was trying to set something up with those two men from Corbett with whom we shared our anniversary dinner.' She rolled her eyes. 'At the time everything was Corbett, Corbett, Corbett. I'm surprised we didn't end up living there.'

'Do you have a photograph?'

'Of Corbett?'

'No, of Michaelmas, of Daygan – your husband.'

She laughed. 'Of Daygan? Not a chance.'

Mango looked puzzled. 'But he's an actor, there have got to be pictures!'

'There are a million publicity shots of him as Mr Piggy-Wig, but without the make-up, nothing. These days he's a very private man and very protective of his public image. He's always said

14

that he wants people to think that Mr Piggy-Wig is real. Seeing the man behind the mask might be confusing, especially for children, and they are Mr Piggy-Wig's core consumers.'

'What about family photos?'

'No cameras allowed in the house.'

'Passport?'

'I'm assuming he's taken that with him.'

'There's nothing?'

'Jack, my husband is a powerful man. If he doesn't want something to happen, believe me, it doesn't happen. There are *no* photographs.'

Jack rose. 'Then I can't help you.'

Marian seemed shocked. She fiddled with her handbag again. 'I have money . . . I'm willing to pay . . . I'll pay whatever you ask.'

Jack shook his head. 'Marian, for a start your husband has quite a stock of names to choose from – he could be going under any one of them, or something completely different. On top of which I have no idea what he looks like. How can I search for a man whose name I don't know and whom I've never seen? No, my dear, you'd be throwing your money away.'

Mango was opening and closing his mouth like a frog in a swarm of flies. 'But, I mean . . . We know what Mr Piggy-Wig looks like.'

'Yes, big pointy ears and a pig's snout.' Jack turned back to Marian. 'I'm just guessing, but I assume in real life your husband bears very little resemblance to a pig.'

She stared at him blankly.

'I'm sorry, Marian.'

'Oh.' Her bottom lip trembled again, but she appeared more affronted than hurt. She stood up stiffly and once more fumbled with her bag. This time she managed to open it and pull out a business card. 'If you change your mind, you can find me here.' She dropped the small, white card into the empty in-tray in front of Mango, who was still perched on the edge of the desk, frozen in disbelief that Jack had turned down this month's, perhaps this decade's, chance of eating well – or even at all. Jack limped awkwardly round the desk to get the door.

She watched as he clumsily negotiated the hatstand and came round to her side of the desk.

'It's all right, gentlemen, I can see myself out.'

'I'll give you some advice for free,' Jack said.

She stopped with her back to him, fingers on the door handle.

'If he's been missing for six months, either he's dead . . .'

'Or?' she said, not turning round.

'Or he doesn't want to be found.'

She looked briefly at the floor, straightened, then pushed open the door and was gone.

They listened to the sound of her footsteps echoing forlornly down the stairwell as she made her way to the street. At last Mango managed to pull himself out of his stunned reverie and grabbed hold of Jack's sleeve. 'Are you insane? That woman was rolling in it. You heard what she said: "I'll pay whatever you ask." We could have decorated this place, or even moved to a nicer location. We could have had lunch!'

Jack looked at him coolly. 'I don't believe it.'

'I beg your pardon?'

'Her story. I don't believe it.'

Jack stumbled back around his desk, colliding once more with the hatstand. 'Why do I keep doing that!'

Mango looked shifty. 'I moved it.'

'Why?'

'It used to be on the other side of the desk, but I thought it unbalanced the room.'

'That hatstand has been in the same place for ten years, and *now* you decide to move it?'

'I've been studying feng shui. It's all about balancing energies.'

'Well, would you please put it back where it was before it unbalances *me*!'

Mango picked up the hatstand without saying a word and put it in the corner on the other side of the room.

'Thank you.' Jack eased into his leather recliner and chewed on his pipe.

Mango resumed his perch on the desk. 'What do you mean you don't believe her story?'

'You're the mind-reader.'

'You know I can't do that any more,' Mango said sulkily.

'All that expensive genetic engineering wasted.'

'I didn't ask to be born a telepath,' Mango suddenly wailed. 'Do you think I enjoy looking like this?'

Jack was immediately contrite. 'I'm sorry, Mango. I'm sure your mother was only trying to do her best for you, by giving you a skill.'

Mango shrugged. 'Yeah.'

'And you can count yourself lucky she didn't go for the athletic option,' Jack continued. 'You'd have worn your joints out by now. Think of it, galloping arthritis by the time you're twenty-five.'

Mango toyed with a loose paper clip on the desk. 'You know what a sensitive subject my origin is, Jack.'

'I'm sorry, Mango, I wouldn't have you any other way. It seems that Mrs Thurrock-Lawes has unsettled me somewhat.'

'You don't say,' Mango replied flatly.

Jack raised an eyebrow. 'But your genetically engineered heritage aside, you sensed something, didn't you? When you shook her hand.'

Mango looked coy. 'We-ell, I thought there might be something not quite kosher about her it's true, but it's been so long since I've been able to rely on my telepathic sense I discounted it immediately.'

'You just smelt money and all sense deserted you.'

'That's not fair! I used to have almost seventy per cent

17

accuracy, but after that knock on the head that nearly killed us both, at best I've got a fifty-fifty chance of being right, which is as good as useless, as well you know, Jack Lindsay!'

'All right, all right. But I saw the look in your eyes when you were introduced. You felt something and I'd like to know what it was. I'm not going to hold you to it, I'd just like you to share it with me, that's all.'

Mango calmed down a couple of degrees. 'I just got the feeling she didn't want to be here.'

'Aha!'

'But that doesn't mean anything. It might be that she didn't like the decor.'

Jack glanced at the peeling, mould-dotted wallpaper with its faded blue cherubs and Doric columns.

'That would be surprising,' he said, drily. 'But think about it, if she really was looking for her old man wouldn't she want, more than anything else in the world, to find out where he was and what had happened to him?'

'Yes,' Mango conceded.

'In which case she would very much want to be here, with someone that she thought could help her, no matter how awful the wallpaper.'

'I suppose so. And then there's what she let slip about him nobbling the competition. She looked rather embarrassed she'd said that.'

'Yes, hardly the thing you'd offer to a stranger if you were trying to paint a sympathetic picture of your old man. No, Mango, I don't know what she's up to, but she certainly isn't looking for Michaelmas.' Jack picked up her business card from where she'd dropped it into his in-tray. '"Marian Lawes, Patron of A Planet Fit for Kids",' he read. 'You know, it's a pity. That's one lady I would have liked to get to know a little better. Correction – a lot better.'

*

'You bring the merchandise?' The big man was sweating like a hog in the midday heat.

'We have samples, yes sir,' the small, hump-backed individual lisped.

'We think you'll get an adequate idea of what we have to offer from the array of weapons Lazlo and I have to show you,' his taller colleague added.

'Well, come on, come on, let's get this demonstration on the road.' The big man was eager to get out of this God-forsaken desert and back to the cool oasis of his hotel.

'Very well. Lazlo, show the gentleman the . . .' Like a child choosing candy in a sweet shop, the strange emaciated man let his eyes move over the weapons spread out in the rear of the truck. 'Yes! The sonic doubler.'

'Oh, a wise choice, Jakob.' Lazlo lovingly picked up the weapon in his short, stubby fingers. 'Yes, yes, a lovely weapon, hand-made on Izzard.' He showed it to the fat man. 'Admire the decorative work on the stock, carved from a single piece of Minging Mahogany. Feel the weight.'

The fat man took it and weighed it in his hand. 'Yeah, yeah, it's . . . heavy.' He handed it back.

'All working parts are guaranteed for life. The barrel is made from no less than fifteen types of metal and takes an Izzarian blacksmith three months of heating, beating and rolling to achieve that distinctive black and silver sheen. Look closely at it, sir. They say that if you look long and deep enough you can see mermaids dancing in the depths of the South China Sea.'

The fat man ran a finger around his shirt collar. 'Can we just get on with the demonstration? This heat is killing me.'

'Certainly, sir, whatever you say, sir. Lazlo, show the gentleman how it works.'

'I'd be delighted, Jakob. Now sir, watch closely.' The little man gently stroked the top of the barrel and a small metal dish, like a satellite aerial, flipped up. 'The sonic amplifier: a masterpiece of micro engineering. Now to find a target.'

'Lazlo, I do believe that small hummock over there is the burrow of the desert cotton-tail rabbit.'

'Yes, yes, you are wise, Jakob, you are wise.' Lazlo turned back to the fat man.

'Observe.' Aiming the weapon across the arid desert sand at the rabbit burrow, Lazlo clicked a small switch in the stock with his thumb. The weapon immediately began to emit a high-pitched scream.

'Shit, that's a terrible noise,' the fat man observed.

But it was clear that the sound he was hearing was far less terrible than that which the inhabitants of the burrow were enduring. And before long, several of the animals loped out of hiding with their forepaws over their ears.

'Now we've flushed out the enemy, it is a simple matter to pick them off one by one.' Which Lazlo proceeded to do with the weapon's highly accurate rifle function.

Before long, the entire population of the burrow was lying dead on the baking sand.

'Give me that!' The fat man grabbed the sonic doubler from Lazlo's hands and looked at it longingly. 'This is quite a piece of work. OK, I'll take two thousand units. What else have you got?'

Lazlo and Jakob looked at each other and smiled. There was nothing quite so gratifying as a satisfied customer . . .

Chapter 2

Home for Jack Lindsay was a mansion block in what used to be an up-market area near the Thames called Docklands. The war had wrought many changes to the neighbourhood – it had been bombed almost to obliteration in the New Battle of Britain and, in the rush to provide the newly homeless population with affordable housing, rancid high-rise blocks had been thrown up, seemingly without reference to any sort of planning strategy. Where once a thriving business community had rubbed shoulders with the wine bars, coffee shops and neat little parks of the pre-war neighbourhood, now ugly dank tenements rose out of dark narrow streets.

Just across the river, on what used to be elegant Greenwich, squatted the brutal grey expanse of a transport hub. From there you could catch a ground-based transport to take you around the city, or if you were rich enough hire a helimotor to fly you anywhere in the country.

The London underground system was no more. During the war it had been badly damaged by weevil bombs: devices with hair triggers which drilled themselves into the ground and lay darkly in wait for the bomb disposal crews. The system had been so badly infected the whole network had been sealed up. These days the quickest way to travel around the city was by monohanger, a sort of overhead railway. It may have been efficient but it was rather expensive and a bumpy ride to say the least, best avoided by those with a delicate stomach.

For the more budget-conscious there were the slightly less

sick-making battery-powered trolleybuses which ran in specially designated tram lanes. Then, for the slightly better off there were licensed electric black cabs, also allowed to use the tram lanes. Private car pods were only for those who valued their privacy above their need to actually get anywhere, as it took an age to move through the choked streets. Of course for the super-wealthy there were copter-cars. Basically these were car pods fitted with powerful turbo fans, the jets of which could be directed downwards, sideways or backwards, giving them amazing manoeuvrability in the air and the capability to take off and land vertically. Their use was restricted by law as, although they used biofuels and were thus carbon neutral, they were not terribly fuel-efficient and the manufacture of such fuels was still nowhere near its pre-war production volume.

However, there were enough of them scooting around the skies to make one wonder just how strictly their use was policed, reinforcing the notion amongst the downtrodden populace that rules were only for the poor.

And for those without very much in the way of ready cash, the scrupulously green, or the romantically inclined, there were the rickshaws – open bicycle carts that seemed to be magically able to weave their way through the heaviest of traffic.

Although they exposed their occupants to the fumes and dirt of the street, and in winter they were absolutely freezing, they were immensely popular. They were cheap, efficient and there were enough of them to ensure you didn't have to wait long for one to turn up.

Gatwick was the only one of the old London airports still operational – Stansted, Luton and Heathrow having been reduced to wasteland by carpet bombing. Now the capital's main airport, Tommy Cooper International, sat in what was once Hyde Park, over which hovered the great intercontinental liners: gigantic dirigibles which bobbed about in the breeze like enormous gas-filled saveloys. Since aviation fuel – taxed at a thousand per cent – was now more costly than vintage Krug, this new breed of airship had replaced the old-fashioned gas-guzzling jets, offering a greener and more sedate means of traversing the globe.

Jack stepped off the trolleybus and limped down the dark streets between the tall, faceless concrete buildings. The little light afforded by the inadequate street-lamps was suddenly removed without warning and he was plunged into inky black-ness. *Oh God, not again. The New Dawn is a bloody long time coming!*

It was hard to believe that it was nearly twenty years since the war had ended.

Thankfully the major powers had been restrained in their use of nuclear weapons, happily allowing those nations who had recently joined the nuclear club – i.e. poor countries which had poured millions they could ill afford into acquiring one or two prized warheads – to virtually annihilate themselves and their limited stock of weaponry. This left more or less intact the global power of the United States, the reformed USSR, China and Europe, all of which had been safely sheltered underneath their hugely expensive 'Nuclear Umbrella' defence systems (which, to everyone's surprise, had worked). However, certain parts of the Middle East, Africa and South America would remain radioactive for a few decades yet.

But things could have been much worse, although in Britain it was hard to imagine how.

Immediately after the war there had been the promise of good times ahead: 'A New Dawn and a New Deal for all!' was the phrase the political spin doctors had come up with. And, as the populations on some of the islands in the Caribbean, the Indian Ocean and Indonesia had been completely wiped out by the conflict, the British government wasted no time in seizing a number of these isles for the Crown and offering families made homeless by the war a new life overseas in these recently acquired tropical lands.

Of course, it didn't take long for the other old colonial

powers to start doing the same. Some of the islands were even rechristened to make the new settlers feel more at home. The French named theirs after their philosophers, the Spanish after their explorers, and the English after their best-loved comedians. So it was that Grenada became Foucault; East Timor, Cortes; and Mauritius – Hancock. Even America got in on the act, finally realizing its long-held dream of annexing Cuba, or as it was now known, Wayneland.

China too had taken advantage of the war to extend its boundaries, and now owned most of Southern Africa, which it had rechristened New Tibet.

But while the colonies thrived, back in Britain twenty grinding years after the war, the promised dawn seemed a long way off. Rationing was still in force, there were shortages of even the most basic of foodstuffs, and power blackouts were a frequent and disruptive occurrence. If anything, things had got worse.

Jack's life too had suffered a gradual decline. He had fallen a long way from the proud war hero who had marched confidently out of the army and into a new life in the police force.

And what did he have to show for his part in saving the world? A bad leg and a drawer full of decorations gathering dust.

He groped through the darkness, feeling his way along the walls of the crowded buildings, edging forward like a blind man, stick clicking and clacking on the pavement. The sound of a trumpet floated out on the still night air and Jack stopped to listen. Music was always a welcome distraction to the sheer bloody drudgery of life, and while the unseen horn player blew his take on that old song 'In a Sentimental Mood', Jack smiled, surrendering himself to the melancholy sound. Then a window was abruptly thrown up. The horn player stopped in mid-phrase and raised voices could be heard. Finally a shot rang out, then . . . silence.

At last the street lights winked back on. Jack sighed and quickened his pace – he was nearly home now.

He pressed his palm to the cool, black surface of the entry-pad outside his building.

A thin green bar of light scanned his hand and the door slid open.

'Welcome home, Jack,' said a slightly husky female voice. 'You're looking terrific this evening.'

'Good evening, Angela,' he greeted the building computer. 'That's very sweet of you, but I know I look like a five-car pile-up.'

'You always look good to me, Jack.'

'Is that so? Well here's an idea: how about you and me putting our feet up in front of an old movie with a bottle of something this evening? We could share a bowl of noodles, and then perhaps I could give your capacitors a massage.'

'I'm sorry, Jack, but I don't understand.'

'Isn't that just like a woman, to lead you on and then drop you when things start to get interesting?'

'Would you like the lift, Jack?'

'Thank you, Angela.'

With his stick clacking on the concrete floor, Jack limped towards the lift and, as he did, little lights in the floor illuminated his path, blinking on before him and winking out once he'd passed.

In the lift itself there was a three-dimensional representation of Angela on a small holographic screen alongside the doors. She was a beauty: blonde, red lips, big chest and wearing a skin-tight jumpsuit that left nothing to the imagination – except of course that with Angela imagination was all there was.

'Um, Jack?'

'What is it, my dear?'

'I . . . I don't think I'm supposed to tell you this, but—'

'Tell me what?'

Jack had never seen worry on Angela's face before. He'd

always assumed it was because she didn't have the requisite worry chip. Besides, what function could it have served? Humans do enough worrying on their own without needing to drag the machines in on the act as well.

She looked off to the left and right then beckoned Jack towards her.

'Come closer.'

Feeling a little foolish, Jack inclined his head so that she could 'whisper' into his ear.

'What is it?'

'Be careful, Jack. There's someone in your . . . your . . . aarrgh.'

The lights flickered and for a moment the lift slowed. Then the lights came back on and normal service was resumed – except for Angela. She was lying motionless on the floor of her screen.

'Angela?'

'Take care, Jack. I'm sorry!' she breathed. 'I—' Over the speakers came a long, lingering sigh, then . . . nothing.

She'd never done anything like that before.

'Angela! Angela, my dear!'

But she remained lifeless.

What had she said? 'There's someone in your . . .'

In my what? My flat?

The lift stopped at Jack's floor and the doors slid open. He stepped out and reached for the cool comforting hardness of the grip of his .45 calibre Thomas & Mayhew revolver. Pausing outside his flat he pressed his ear to the door. Through it he could hear the strains of one of his oldest and most loved records: the D'Oyly Carte's recording of *The Pirates of Penzance*. He'd loved it ever since he'd been a child – it had been his father's favourite.

Thank you, Angela, he thought. *But I'm afraid you probably died in vain*. Smiling grimly, he put his gun back in its holster and inserted his key-card into the lock. He waited for the light to go green, then opened the door.

'Come out, come out wherever you are!' Jack called.

Poor wandering one! the music trilled.

A head appeared from behind the little bamboo bar in the far corner of the room. Slowly, the rest of the individual emerged, eyebrows raised quizzically.

'Ah, there you are, Jack. Now you're here you can tell me where you keep the good stuff, all I can find is Welsh whisky. They may know how to sing but they certainly can't distil.'

'Commissioner, to what do I owe this thankfully rare visit?' Jack moved across to his ancient turntable.

Take heart, fair days will shine;
Take any heart? take mine!

He lifted the needle from the record and turned to face the commissioner.

'What have you done to my building computer?'

'Ah. I thought she might try to warn you and so I inserted a gagging program into her system. I was afraid that you might not be so very keen to see me.'

'Well, you were right, and now you've killed her.'

'You sound as if you really cared for her, Jack.'

'Sometimes I get lonely.'

'That's good, that's why I'm here.'

'To gloat?'

'No, to invite you out to play. But first, Jack, *please*, do you have anything decent to drink?'

After he'd filled the commissioner's glass with a large shot of the expensive Scotch he'd stashed away for a rainy day, or in the unlikely event of his ever luring feminine company up to his sad and lonely eyrie, the two men sat down around Jack's coffee table.

'How's the leg these days?'

'Not that you care, but it's fine. In exactly nine months and eleven days it'll feel terrific.'

'Ah yes, your pension's due, isn't it?'

'And isn't it just like the Police Department to withhold it until my fiftieth birthday?'

'That *is* the official retirement age for someone in your line of work.'

'My leg was destroyed on police business, I'm invalided out of the force, and yet I can't claim disability pension until retirement age.'

'Rules are rules, Jack. Can't have any special cases. We'd leave ourselves wide open to a flood of litigation. But I never worried about you, Jack. You've always been able to look after yourself.'

'I'd like to see you try to scrape a living in the real world. I wonder how you'd get by without your expense account lunches and Whitehall cocktail parties?'

'Horses for courses, Jack. It's your closeness to the street that makes you so good at what you do.'

'Don't try to flatter me.'

'I'm only speaking the truth, which leads me on to why I'm here. I'll get straight to the point. I need your help.'

Jack looked at him. At his unlined, unworried face, his neat, greying-at-the-temples hair and the well-fed swell of his belly beneath his expensive suit. He was actually five years older than Jack but looked ten years younger. Horses for courses.

'And how can I help *you*? Do you need someone to polish your shoes?'

'Don't be facetious, Jack. There has recently been a spate of political assassinations worldwide.'

'Killing politicians isn't a new pastime.'

'This is different – more organized. The assassin has targeted only those countries where there is known political unrest. In all of the states he's hit, democracy is balanced on a knife edge, the line between peace and conflict wafer-thin.'

'Sounds like a job for the International Force.'

'You know what a monster that organization is: a bureaucratic nightmare. It can take years to get through the red tape before you can even *start* an investigation.'

'What about the Secret Service?'

'We think the Service might be compromised. We need an outsider, a good one, and you're the best in the business.'

'You speak the truth. Unfortunately, Freddy, I find myself otherwise engaged. But I can recommend a few trustworthy private investigators. Jimmy Short is good.'

The commissioner shook his head. 'Cole McClaggen himself asked for you.'

Jack sat up a little straighter. 'The World Council leader asked for me?'

'Well, not in so many words. He asked me who was the best man for the job, and I said you were.'

'He came directly to Scotland Yard? What did the Americans and the Chinese have to say about that?'

Freddy paused and took a long sip of Scotch before replying. 'All right, Jack, I'll level with you. I had to fight to get this case. The Russians and the Chinese weren't interested: they saw no merit in preventing conflict that might win them even more territory. McClaggen was about to hand it over to the Yanks, but I pleaded with him, played on his Canadian heritage, emphasizing the age-old connection between our two countries. I also waved the Scotland Yard flag and our long and noble heritage of villain-nabbing: Inspector Morse, Sherlock Holmes—'

'Inspector Morse was Oxford CID, and Sherlock Holmes was a private detective. Besides, they're both fictional characters.'

'McClaggen doesn't know that. Anyway, the upshot is we've got the case. But only for a limited time. The deal is: if we don't come up with anything within a month it reverts to our brothers across the Atlantic. But if we do crack it, think of the kudos.'

'And the praise that will be heaped upon the shoulders of a certain Freddy Lindsay. I see a knighthood if you can bring this off.'

Freddy stiffened. 'This is purely for the good of the force and, by association, Britain.'

'Stop, please, all this patriotism is going to make me cry.'

Freddy leaned forward earnestly. 'We need you, Jack. If anyone can solve this case, you can.'

Jack downed his Scotch and put his glass on the table. 'I'd love to help you, Freddy, but as I said I've got a lot on at the moment.'

'You haven't had a case for months.'

Jack frowned. 'And how would you know that?'

'Conflict has already broken out in the Middle East and it's spreading. If we're not careful everywhere from Iran to Bangladesh is going to be on fire. And then there's Africa. As far as we can tell – reading between the lines in the news reports that the Chinese feed us – Namibia and Botswana are already at each other's throats. You know what a tinder box that God-forsaken continent is – it won't take long for the fighting to spread, and if it does there is a danger of the world being plunged back into the same kind of devastating conflict we endured twenty years ago. The conflict that killed billions of people and wiped out thousands of years of history. You wouldn't really wish that kind of tragedy on the present gener-ation, would you, Jack? Or have you forgotten the war?'

'It seems to me that of the two of us I'm more likely to remember it.' Jack gazed levelly at Freddy.

'Couldn't resist that little dig, could you?' Freddy scowled. 'Always rubbing my nose in the fact that while you were making your name as a war hero, I was stuck at home with a medical condition.'

'My, my, I had no idea you were still so touchy about it. *Don't mention the war in front of Freddy . . .*'

'It's not my fault I have a weak heart!' Freddy breathed

deeply, sat back in his chair and smiled, baring his teeth in imitation of brotherly affection. 'Let's not bicker. Shouldn't we try to help each other out? Let's put our differences aside, for the memory of Mum and Dad.'

There was an extended pause during which Jack refreshed his glass and took a sip. Eventually he spoke. 'Freddy Lindsay only ever cared about one thing: Freddy Lindsay. And for your information, no I haven't forgotten the war, nor the fact that it killed our parents.' Jack threw back the rest of his Scotch and slammed his glass down on the table. 'Look at you with your suntan and your hand-made suit. I'll bet you've never gone short; I'll bet you don't have to queue with your ration cards in the butcher's for a paltry four ounces of rump steak! And don't give me all that rubbish about brotherly love; you never really liked me, so it's a little late to try and be my friend.'

'All right, so you're jealous of my position and my salary. But do you have any idea what it's like to be your brother? To have people come up to you and say, "Oh, is Jack Lindsay – the famous war hero – your brother?" which is inevitably followed by the question, "And what did *you* do in the war?"' Freddy put a hand to his chest and closed his eyes, breathing noisily through his nose.

Jack was unmoved. 'If you're going to have a heart attack, can you please have it outside? I can't afford a cleaner.'

Freddy opened his eyes. 'Just because we don't like each other doesn't mean we can't work together. You're the best bloody detective I know, Jack. You're one of the few real coppers left. The kids nowadays put too much reliance on Dr Watson – they don't think for themselves.'

'And whose fault is that? I seem to remember that Commissioner Lindsay was one of the driving forces behind getting Dr Watson on line.'

Freddy shrugged and smoothed the hair across his temple. 'That was simply a political move – it was in everyone's best interests at the time.'

'It was certainly in Waverly Computers 'interests – their stock price shot up two hundred points. How much did you make from that deal, eh?'

Freddy gripped the arm of his chair and glared at his brother. 'If you're suggesting I was in any way involved in anything illegal or underhand—' He broke off and clutched his chest again. After a few moments he recovered. 'You always do it to me, Jack. You're the only person I know who can really upset me. I've no idea what you've got against me, especially when all I'm trying to do is help.'

'Why not ask Dr Watson?' Jack snorted.

The Dr Watson of which they spoke was a supercomputer capable of processing a vast amount of information that was constantly fed into it from police forces worldwide. When first unveiled the system was hailed as a triumph of computing technology. The beauty of it, so the advertising went, was that it needed almost no human intervention – it decided *itself* which bits of information on any given case were important and should be drawn to the attention of a human officer, and which bits were irrelevant and could be dumped. Its conclusions had been presented as evidence in numerous court cases and it was reckoned to be responsible for sending thousands of miscreants to prison. Of course, being a computer without an appreciation of the complex and varied nature of the human psyche, the conclusions it came to were invariably wrong, but the politicians and the policemen loved it and would never allow an annoying little thing like truth or justice to get in the way of progress.

Freddy leaned forward earnestly. 'Jack, I'm asking for your help. Correction: I'm begging.'

Jack looked back at him with steel in his slightly unfocused blue-grey eyes. 'It doesn't suit you. Look, let me spell the situation out to you, so that even *you* can understand. I've got nine months to go before I get my pension and I'd like to stay alive long enough to enjoy it. I am not going back to the Yard. I'm not entering into anything that might be hazardous to my health. As far as I'm concerned, all that's happened this evening is that I've wasted half a bottle of good Scotch.'

Freddy put down his glass and stood up. 'I'll take that as a no, then.' He walked over to the corner of the room and picked his hat up from where he'd left it on the bar. 'Shame, I hate to think of you going through the rest of your life without the support of your disability pension.'

Jack had a sinking feeling in the pit of his stomach. 'What do you mean?'

'What's it worth, Jack – sixty, seventy thousand a year, on top of what the state'll give you? Besides robbing a bank I fail to see how you're going to find that kind of money. You can't even pay your bills now – you're three months behind with your rent. You needn't look so shocked, I know all about your financial situation. How much longer do you think you'll be able to keep on playing at private eye with that leg of yours – another five years? And what then, when you can no longer fend for yourself? Enforced retirement to a state rest home surrounded by drooling geriatrics and fat-arsed nurses. Not much to look forward to, eh Jack?'

'And your point is?' Jack growled.

'I didn't want it to come to this, Jack, but it boils down to a simple choice: either you work for me or there's a chance – correction, a strong possibility – of your finding old age very uncomfortable indeed.'

'You wouldn't.'

Freddy smiled his self-satisfied smile. 'Oh yes I would. What Freddy wants, Freddy gets, you should know that. I'll expect you at the Yard at nine-thirty sharp tomorrow morning.'

Freddy left, closing the door softly behind him. Jack threw the half-empty bottle of Scotch after him. The glass smashed and fine, twenty-year-old Scotch ran in rivulets down the back of the closed door. That was stupid, now he'd wasted the whole bottle.

Chapter 3

The next morning, what with the hangover from the bottle of Welsh whisky he'd consumed after Freddy had left, and the three-storey climb up to his office, Jack's leg was extremely sore. He eased himself gently into his leather recliner, angling it so that he could look out of the window. Across the way, on the fourth-floor balcony of a nondescript concrete and steel office block, some latter-day Adam had planted a miniature garden, complete with hanging baskets, mounds of red and pink flowers, and trailing fronds of honeysuckle and clematis. It was a little bit of paradise in the centre of the city.

Although Jack loved London, his dream had always been to retire somewhere green and pleasant, with grass underfoot and real trees overhead. The countryside had been devastated by the war, but there were still such places left, especially down in the West Country.

For a moment, Jack let his thoughts wander around the little smallholding he would buy when he got his pension: a place with chickens and perhaps a pig or two.

But then the memory of Freddy's previous night's visit intruded and the vision faded, to be replaced by a sharp acid pain in the pit of his stomach.

Damn him! What gives him the right to treat me like that? My own brother! He pulled his chair upright and his heels hit the floor, which did his leg no good at all.

'Ow! Ow! Ow! Bloody ow!'

As he leaned forward to massage his painful knee, he noticed

Marian's card in his in-tray and picked it up. Her perfume was still on it, faint and faded like a beautiful dream. He had no idea why, but he slipped it into his pocket. Maybe he didn't want to let her go just yet. But this wasn't getting him anywhere. He needed a clear head to think, and the best way to deal with a hangover was to fight it. He reached instinctively for the bottom drawer of the desk and the half-bottle of blended Scotch it contained, but something stopped him. Perhaps it was the thought of Mango's disapproving look when he smelt the liquor on his breath before ten a.m., but more likely it was the steadily dawning realization – since meeting a certain Mrs Thurrock-Lawes – that the something that was missing in his life couldn't be found by staring into the bottom of a glass. He slammed the drawer shut.

'Mango! What about some tea?'

No reply.

'Mango!' he called again. 'Get your worthless self in here!'

But his strange, squat little form did not materialize. In all the years they'd been together, Mango had always got into work before Jack, and he had no recollection of his mentioning that he was going to be late this morning.

Getting up awkwardly, Jack grabbed his stick and pushed open the door to the kitchenette, which doubled as Mango's cramped back office. Mango was standing stock-still in the middle of the room, staring straight ahead with absolute terror.

'There you are. Why didn't you answer me?'

But still he made no move.

'Mango, hello!'

Jack limped towards him.

'Don't move,' Mango hissed out of the side of his mouth. 'Movement sensor.'

But it was too late. Something beeped and the little man started leaping about and yelling. 'Now we're going to burn! The building's going to go up like it did before! I can't go through that again, Jack! Oh Jack, I don't want to die!' He grabbed hold of Jack's lapels and nearly pulled him over.

'Steady on, what are you talking about?'

'The desk! The desk!'

Jack followed Mango's outstretched and fearful finger with his eyes. On top of the blotter was a small black box attached to a round plastic container. He recognized it immediately as an incendiary bomb. A small charge in the timing device would rupture the plastic tank and ignite whatever was inside it – probably acetone. The result would be a huge fireball.

Jack went over to it. There was a circle of about twenty red flashing lights on its surface that were blinking out one by one.

'The window!' Mango yelled. 'Throw it out of the window!'

Pulling aside the dusty curtains, Jack struggled with the metal frame of the *Eezi-Slide* (pat. Pend.) window. It wouldn't budge.

'OK, leave it!' Mango screamed. 'Let's just get out of here!'

'We can't let the whole place go up!'

'Yes we can. I don't want to die!'

'Be quiet and let me think!'

Blink, blink, blink . . . More of the little red lights went out. Now there were only ten left.

'I know, the lavatory!' Jack yelled.

Picking up the bomb, he walked across the room with it and pulled open the door to the small cubicle. But in doing so, in his haste and nerviness, he managed to knock the device out of his own hand. It skittered across the floor to settle in the dusty gloom underneath the desk.

'Get rid of it!' Mango screamed.

In the darkness beneath the desk, five red lights glowed brightly.

Hoicking it out with his stick, Jack bent down and picked it up as yet another light went out. Now there were only three left.

'AAAAARRRGH!' With all his might, Jack threw the bomb

36

into the lavatory and kicked the door shut, forgetting for the moment that he had only one sound leg. He fell over, knocking Mango to the ground in the process.

WHOOOOOOMMMP!

A tongue of flame punched a hole straight through the door, filling the room with fire and singeing Jack's ears.

'Mango, are you all right?'

'Yes, but I'll never get the stains out of this suit.'

The stack of *Financial Times* in the toilet was now burning merrily, as was what was left of the door. The fireball had also set light to the curtains from which small but eager tentacles of flame sprouted to caress the ceiling tiles.

'We've got to get out of here,' Jack said, struggling to get up.

'We're really on the ball today,' Mango added.

As soon as Jack had rolled off him, Mango leapt up and ran through the door out into the corridor, screaming, 'Fire! Fire! Run for your lives!'

Pulling himself to his feet, Jack cursed Mango's over-developed sense of the dramatic and looked around at the burning room. Now the ceiling was starting to melt, dropping burning gobs of plastic all around. Where they fell, more fires sprang up like little saplings, which would soon grow into great, blazing trees.

Grabbing his stick and his hat, Jack followed Mango out into the corridor. By now the little Filipino had gathered quite a crowd who, once they had ascertained what all the shouting was about, began pushing and shoving their way down the stairs in unseemly haste. Jack wondered for a moment if there were such a thing as seemly haste, but now didn't seem the moment to explore that particular thought.

Jack grabbed Mango's arm. 'You could have waited until we'd got downstairs before raising the alarm. Now we're going to have to leave the sinking ship with the rest of the rats.' And he yanked him towards the stairwell through the press of panicking people.

Out on the street, the inhabitants of the block stood around in shock as they watched their place of work go up in flames.

'Ow!' Mango yelped. 'I said ow!'

Jack was still holding Mango's elbow and squeezing rather too hard.

'Let me go!'

'Sorry,' said Jack, finally getting the message. 'I'm a little upset.'

'You're upset? How do you think I feel? My favourite overcoat was in there. You know, the ecru and cerise with the purple lining?'

'Let's be thankful for small mercies,' Jack muttered. 'Tell me, Mango, what happened earlier, before I came in?'

Mango's high-domed forehead contorted with effort as he recalled the events of the morning.

'I was just putting the kettle on when these men burst in, wearing masks. They put that thing on my desk and told me not to move. I'd been there half an hour before you came in and ruined everything.'

'Go home, stay there and wait for me to call.'

'Where are you going?'

'A little family reunion.'

'Ah, that's nice.'

'Not really.'

Mango studied Jack's face. 'You're not going to do anything silly now, are you?'

'Just go. I'll call you later.'

Mango walked away unsurely and Jack watched him weave his way through the crowd until he disappeared. Then, to the distant accompaniment of approaching sirens, he turned and headed towards Westminster.

Chapter 4

'Where is he?' Jack bawled at the sergeant on the front desk at Scotland Yard.

'Hello, Jack, I hear you're coming back to join us.'

'I wouldn't come back here if it was the last place left on earth. Now where is the turd?'

'I assume you're talking about Commissioner Lindsay. Conference room four on the sixth floor. But he's in a meeting at the moment.'

'Is he? We'll see about that.'

Thankfully, the lift at Scotland Yard was always impeccably maintained, and so Jack took it to the sixth floor. But when the doors opened he found the corridor full of people in dark suits, as broad as they were tall.

'Excuse me, sir, can I see your identification?' A big square man blocked Jack's way.

'And who the hell are you?'

'Let's not have any unpleasantness, sir. Just show me your ID, please.'

Jack pulled his private investigator's licence out of his pocket and showed it to the man. He seemed satisfied.

'Thank you, sir. Now, if you don't mind . . .' He held out his hand.

Jack sighed, reached inside his jacket and withdrew his revolver, which he placed in the man's outstretched palm. The man examined it carefully.

'Hmm, nice piece. I saw one just like it in a museum once.'

'It's a family heirloom – my great-aunt Elsie gave it to me,' Jack scowled.

The man smiled. 'She must have loved you very much. Don't worry, I'll look after it for you, sir. Please, carry on.'

Limping angrily through the crush of identically suited individuals stationed in the corridor, Jack headed for the door of conference room four – the grandest of all the rooms on this level and the only one that had immediate access to the roof and the helimotor-pad. There were two more solidly built guards stationed outside the door, but they simply smiled and let Detective Lindsay pass.

Jack crashed into the room. Freddy was seated at the far end of a long table, talking to another man.

'You bloody idiot!' Jack yelled. 'Were you trying to murder me? If they hadn't taken my gun I would have been sorely tempted to blow your bloody brains out!'

'Ah, Jack.' Freddy smiled his insincerest smile. 'I've been expecting you. I don't think you've met Councillor McClaggen.'

For the first time Jack took in the other man. He knew the face well. He'd seen it almost every night on television newscasts, and staring out at him from a thousand newspapers: Cole McClaggen, Chairman of the World Council.

'I . . . I'm sorry, sir, I didn't realize . . .'

The councillor rose and came towards him. 'That's all right, Jack. I hear you've had a little trouble down at your office this morning.'

Jack glanced at Freddy. 'News travels fast.'

'Nice to meet you, Jack.' The councillor shook his hand. 'Freddy here has been telling me all about you. It's very kind of you to agree to come and help us out like this.'

'I'm sorry, councillor, I don't know what the commissioner has told you, but I no longer work for the Yard, and have no—'

'What Jack is trying to say,' Freddy interrupted smoothly, 'is that although he is extremely busy at the moment, he's prepared to give us some of his valuable time so long as the package is attractive. Isn't that so, brother?' Freddy leered.

McClaggen tapped the side of his nose knowingly. 'Very wise of you to want to get the business out of the way before we start. Man after my own heart. Well now, let's see. What would you say was a fair price for what you're about to do for us? The way I see it, you've got us over a barrel. You could ask for virtually anything you want.' The councillor's wide open face beamed with the fiscal innocence of the super-wealthy.

Jack blinked with the dawning realization that he might just have been handed the winning lottery ticket. 'Anything I want?'

The councillor nodded and Jack noticed with delight that Freddy was looking a little nervous. Perhaps he was beginning to regret giving his brother such a glowing reference.

'Well now, I usually charge –' Jack took a moment to consider what he might be able to get away with. Go in with too low a figure and he might never get it back up again '– five thousand a week.'

Freddy gasped.

'Plus expenses.'

'Sounds fair to me.' The councillor clicked his fingers and an aide appeared as if from nowhere. Jack had had no idea there was anyone else in the room, but when he looked a little closer he was able to make out at least half a dozen men and women standing around, all pretending to be various components of the office suite. The aide handed the councillor a pad and pen, then resumed his impression of a potted palm.

The councillor immediately began scribbling on the pad. 'Jack Lindsay to get five thousand a week, plus expenses of . . .' He looked up at Jack. 'Shall we say another five thousand, to make it nice and even?'

'Oh, let's.' Jack smiled at Freddy, who was quietly turning purple.

'Good, good.'

The councillor finished writing on the pad and signed it with a flourish.

'Here's my authorization.' He tore off the top sheet and handed it to Freddy.

Freddy took it and glanced at it in disbelief before stuffing it in an inside pocket.

McClaggen turned back to Jack.

'Now then, come and sit down and we'll fill you in.'

It looked like Jack had been railroaded into this job whether he liked it or not. But then for ten thousand a week, he wouldn't have minded actually being hit by the train.

'So, how much do you know?' the councillor asked when they were all seated.

'Well, er . . . only what Freddy's told me. Something about heads of state being knocked off?'

'Yes, that's the essence of the story. High-ranking ministers in some of the most unstable states across the globe are being assassinated. I needn't tell you what that might mean to the fragile peace that the World Council has struggled to maintain since the devastation of the war.'

'Just what does it mean?' Jack asked.

The councillor narrowed his eyes. 'What does what mean?'

'What do these murders mean to the fragile peace that the World Council has struggled to maintain since the devastation of the war?' Jack was beginning to enjoy himself.

'What do they mean?'

'Yes.'

'Well, they mean . . . tell him what they mean, Freddy.'

Freddy leaned forward and glared at Jack. 'They mean that there's a distinct possibility that we could once again be plunged into a world war.'

'Exactly,' the councillor concluded.

'I see,' said Jack, 'and these murders, what's the MO?'

The councillor frowned. 'Medical orderly?'

'Modus operandi,' Freddy explained.

'Oh, you mean, how does whoever is doing these awful things . . . do these awful things?'

'That's exactly what I mean.' Jack pulled out his pipe, but Freddy silently shook his head and the deeply polished briar was put away again.

'Let me show you.' The councillor clicked his fingers irritably at Freddy. 'The file, give him the file.'

Jack enjoyed Freddy's barely concealed resentment at being treated as a menial. But then next to the councillor that's what he was. Horses for courses.

The commissioner slid the file over to Jack. Inside was a series of crime scene photographs: blood-soaked bodies lying in the street in awkward, unnatural positions. At first glance Jack noticed nothing unusual – he was used to seeing such horrific images from his days as a policeman – but on closer inspection he realized that all these unfortunate individuals seemed to be missing their heads. Pulling out the pathologist's report, he scanned it with an expert's eye. In each case the method was the same: a single bullet to the head, which exploded on contact. The victims died instantly, creating a huge dry-cleaning problem for whoever was standing next to them.

There were no clues, no leads, no motive – nothing. Even the bullets left no trace, atomizing along with their targets' craniums.

'So what do you expect me to do?' Jack asked.

'Find whoever is responsible.' From the uncertain look in Cole McClaggen's eye, Jack could tell the councillor believed he might be next on the list.

'With nothing to go on?'

'Let me tell you a story.' The councillor leaned back in his chair and a faraway look came into his eye. 'A long time ago a small boy was sitting by a river bank looking at a toad floating on a log in midstream. That little boy wanted to get hold of that toad but saw no way to do it – it being out of reach across the moving water.

'Then he had an idea. A little way downstream the river narrowed as it fell between two large rocks; if he could get there before the toad, he could clamber over the rocks and just might be able to grab the toad as it passed. But when he did get there he remembered that he was hungry, and so got out his sandwiches. Munching happily on his banana and jam on wholemeal, he watched the toad pass him by only to be smashed to death on the rocks.' The World Council chairman smiled wistfully.

Jack and the commissioner looked at each other.

'What I mean is: you can't skin a rabbit with a blunt knife.'

The wrinkles on Jack's already furrowed brow deepened.

'We'll give you all the support you need, Jack – anything you want.'

'That's very kind. But I still don't understand why the Secret Service is being kept out of this.'

Cole McClaggen shook his head. 'We believe the Service has been infiltrated by person or persons unknown, who is or are working for the organization or organizations responsible.'

'So you think there are other persons, er, people involved?'

'There have to be. Wide-scale slaughter on this scale has to be the work of a complex organization. The very scale and complexity of the organization of this complex and wide-scale slaughter leads me to believe that these crimes have to be the work of a complex organization on a wide scale, and could not possibly be the work of one man working on his own, singly and alone outside of a complex organization of unbelievable complexity.'

Jack, Freddy and the councillor took a moment to organize their thoughts.

The councillor slapped the table with his hand. 'How about this: a worldwide network of assassins? Yes, what about that? An organization of "sleepers" who get a code word in the morning mail and go into a trance. You know, like in that film . . .' He clicked his fingers at Freddy again. 'What was that flick called?'

'Which one, sir?'

'You know, the one where the hero – respectable pillar of the community, nice family, friends, drives a Chevy, drinks at the golf club every Sunday – suddenly gets a call from the spymaster who hypnotized him years before, and goes into a trance and starts killing people. It's excellent, you must have seen it.'

Freddy and Jack shared a brotherly moment.

'No, sir, I don't believe I have.'

'Well, never mind. The point is there's more than one killer, and that's what we've got here, I'm sure of it!'

But Jack *wasn't* so sure. For the councillor's scenario, you'd need a vast network of hit-men all over the earth, primed and ready – it would be murder to set up and very expensive, and there wasn't a crime outfit *that* organized, not yet at least. Most of the crime syndicates had been blown apart in the war and hadn't yet managed to recover fully. The way Jack saw it this was the work of a lone wolf, someone who could sneak in and out without being noticed.

From above came the unmistakable sound of an approaching helimotor. A flip chart and several articles of furniture suddenly came to life and an aide sidled noiselessly up and whispered something into the councillor's ear.

'Oh, right, thank you.' The councillor stood up. 'Gentlemen, I leave you with a great responsibility, the responsibility of finding the guilty persons responsible for these heinous crimes.'

He went to shake Freddy's hand, but instead Freddy saluted smartly, leaving the councillor with his hand waving ineffectually in mid-air.

The councillor turned to Jack, grabbed his hand instead and pumped it energetically.

'Don't hold back on this, let's have no pettifogging or hog-whiffling. As my daddy used to say: "Cheese doesn't stick on a charging moose." I'm taking a risk backing you Brits, so don't let me down. The future safety of the world depends on persons like you.'

'Rest assured, sir,' said Jack seriously, 'this person or persons won't rest until he or they have arrested the culprit or culprits responsible and he, she, they or it are residing behind bar or bars.'

The councillor frowned at him.

'I won't let you down, sir.'

'Good, good,' McClaggen nodded vaguely.

The councillor and his entourage swept up the steps to the roof-top helimotor-pad followed by the two guards who'd been on door duty, one of whom handed Jack back his pistol.

When the helimotor's rotors had begun to beat a retreat away across the city's rooftops, Jack turned to his brother.

'He's certainly . . . colourful.'

Freddy airily waved a hand. 'That's why they made him chairman: it's the one place where he can do the least damage. All he has to do is say a few words to open council meetings, then sit back and let the debate happen. If his casting vote is ever needed, he's got an army of good people advising him. But don't worry, he's got more than enough clout to deliver on his promises.'

'He can be as flaky as he likes as long as he delivers my ten thousand a week.'

Freddy glowered at him. 'Sit down.'

The two men faced each other across the big table.

'You've got a bloody nerve,' Freddy snarled.

Jack smiled. 'One thing I learned from big brother: if you don't ask you don't get.'

'But ten thousand a week? That's . . . that's . . .'

'More than you get?'

Freddy's silence told Jack all he needed to know.

'Put it in perspective, Freddy: you've been getting it for years, whereas I'm only going to be pulling it down for as long as it takes to crack this case.'

'Well, let's hope that doesn't take too long.' Freddy glared at his brother.

Jack put a hand over his heart. 'I shall do my utmost to wrap up this case as swiftly as possible.'

Freddy snorted and reached inside his jacket. 'You'll be needing this,' he growled and slid a police ID wallet across the table at Jack. 'I'm assuming you'd rather keep your own, quaintly outdated weapon?'

'Correct. I don't trust all that new hardware.'

Jack fingered the wallet and opened it up. His mug shot scowled up at him from alongside a silvery hologram of the arms of the Metropolitan Police. Despite his misgivings, it felt good to be a part of the system again.

Although irritated by his sibling's new-found wealth, the commissioner consoled himself with the fact that he had at least got his own way, and he smiled smugly at his brother. 'So, how does it feel to be in the big league again, Jack? Glad to be back in harness?'

Jack's meeting with the councillor had, for a moment, driven out of his mind his real reason for being there. But Freddy's smug smiling face brought it all back like a cheap lunch.

'What do you think you were doing, blowing up my office?'

'Jack, Jack. I know you have a low opinion of me but, really, do you think I would stoop to something like that?'

'I know you would.'

'It's probably pointless trying to convince you otherwise, but you have to believe me when I tell you that I had nothing to do with what happened this morning. Think about it: why would I jeopardize my position by carrying out such a wanton act? Besides I didn't need to set fire to your office to convince you to join us. I already had you by your, ah . . . pension.'

Jack grudgingly had to admit that he had a point. 'Very well, if not you, who?'

He shrugged. 'Maybe someone has a grudge against you. Perhaps you've rubbed someone up the wrong way.'

'I can't think who, I'm so good with people.'

'Anyway, I don't want you to worry about that now, Jack.

You've got a brand new office waiting for you on the third floor fully equipped with secretaries, first-class officers and the latest electronic gadgetry dreamt up by the department's boffins. I've even got you a new assistant.' He dropped his voice confidentially. 'She's blonde, got legs up to here, and no morals.'

'That's a tempting proposition, but Mango'd never forgive me.'

'You're not planning on bringing *him* here, are you? He's a telepath, for God's sake.'

'So?'

'You know what people think of telepaths – they don't like them and with good reason: they're untrustworthy and they can read your thoughts. But apart from all that, Mango's a fruit.'

Jack smiled. 'You do realize what you just said?'

'You know what I mean.'

'Oh, Freddy. Let me put you straight on a couple of points. One: Mango is as honest as the day is long and whatever mind-reading capability he once had he lost in our little accident; and two: he's not gay, he's just . . . outgoing.'

Freddy sighed long-sufferingly and ran his hands through his neatly trimmed hair. 'Look, if it's a telepath you want, at least let me find you one that works.'

Jack shook his head. 'I'll hang on to Mango, thank you, and I want him given full security clearance. After all, he's the nearest thing I've got to family.' Jack looked steadily into Freddy's eyes.

'You're a stubborn bastard.'

'Is that any way to talk about Mother?'

Freddy fiddled with the buttons of his jacket. 'Very well, I won't argue with you. I'll arrange for an ID wallet to be waiting for him at the front desk. What else do you need?'

'All available CCTV coverage of the crime scenes and environs on the day of the shooting and, if possible, the day before. I need witness statements and full backgrounds of all the

victims. I need to see if any of them have anything murky lurking in their past.'

Freddy was outraged. 'Jack, these people were in politics!'

'Exactly! The department can also pay off my back rent and
outstanding utility bills, and they are *outstanding. And* I want
a Metropolitan Police credit card – none of mine work any
more.'

'Now, just a minute!'

'You heard what the councillor said – anything I want.'

Jack could tell that Freddy was beginning to wonder if getting little brother on board had been such a good idea after all.

'Very well,' Freddy growled.

'Oh, I also need a phone, they disconnected mine last week.'

'Here.' Freddy withdrew an envelope from an inside pocket
and slid it across the table.

Jack picked it up and weighed it in his hand. 'What's this?'

'A wrist communicator – very high tech. With that you can
contact Scotland Yard instantly from anywhere on earth.'

Jack opened the envelope and slid its contents onto the table.
It was a sleek, expensively heavy piece of equipment and looked
just like a wrist-watch, except that it was at least twice the size.
These communicators were absolutely cutting edge; the latest
thing from across the Pond and *the* must-have accessory for the
autumn. The drug dealers had already had them for months, of
course.

At the moment its big square face was filled with a picture
of Freddy's wife and kids, but pressing one of the chunky buttons on the bezel brought up a myriad of different screens:
phone book; clock; record function; Google . . .

'Switching to E will put you straight through to me via an
encrypted link. You can also access email and the internet.'

'And will it also make the bed and prepare breakfast?'

'It's a serious piece of kit.'

'I'm sure it is. One thing I'd like to know: how do I change
the screensaver? Much as I love Gloria and your two little

darlings, having them gazing adoringly up at me constantly is going to be a little disconcerting, especially in the places I'm likely to find myself.'

Freddy threw an instruction manual at him. Something small and white in a clear plastic pocket was stapled to its cover.

Jack opened the pocket and pulled out what looked like a tooth. 'What's this, a spare in case someone socks me in the jaw?'

'It's the latest advance in hands-free technology – works with the Greentooth system. It goes in your mouth.'

'I think I'd already worked that out.'

'Drop it in a cup of hot water until it's malleable, then push it down over one of your canines. It'll set hard and give you a permanent hands-free link to your communicator.'

'Couldn't I just talk to my wrist?'

'There may be times when you'd rather not advertise the fact that you're using it.'

'I want Mango to have one.'

Freddy's eyebrows shot up so far they threatened to part company with his forehead. 'What? Do you know how much one of those costs?'

'Mango is my partner. I can't deny that the ability to communicate with you from wherever I happen to be in the world gives me a wonderful warm, brotherly feeling, but as Mango is going to be a little more actively involved in the case, it's him I really need to keep in touch with.'

Freddy gripped the edge of the table until his knuckles turned white. 'Very well,' he said at last. 'I'll arrange it. But remember, and you can tell your telepathic friend this as well: your work here is top secret. No one save you, me and those working closely with you knows the nature of the case.'

'And how do you know that my little work group hasn't already been compromised by person or persons unknown?'

'I evaluated all your staff personally: they have the highest security clearance. This ship must have no leaks.'

'You know, Freddy, that was almost poetic.'

Commissioner Lindsay narrowed his eyes and pushed a newspaper across the table. 'We have to do this in a hurry, Jack. The journos are already beginning to have their own theories about what's going on. This is from a couple of days ago.'

Jack picked up the newspaper. '"The Cranium Killer strikes again!"' he read. He looked up at his brother. 'The Cranium Killer?'

Freddy shrugged and shook his head. 'Journalists.'

Jack carried on, '"Yesterday lunchtime, the Turkmenistan government lost one of its longest-serving members. Foreign Minister Murgab's assassination will send a cold shiver through the hearts of politicians everywhere. Is this, the latest in a series of killings, part of a plot to destabilize the fragile peace that was so gallantly fought for during the war? If so, who could be behind such a scheme? Are we seeing a resurgence of the power of the Syndicates? Full story, page three . . ."' Jack looked across at his brother. 'The Syndicates? Who wrote this?'

'Gelda Longhorn.'

'Does she know something we don't?'

Freddy leaned forward on the desk, looked earnestly into Jack's eyes and repeated the speech he'd said at a hundred and one press briefings. 'The Syndicates were blown apart during the war, and since then police forces everywhere have been extremely vigilant in not allowing them to regroup and seize back the control they once had. No, Ms Longhorn is adding two and two and making five, but if she persists on this tack she's in danger of starting a global panic.' The commissioner looked at his watch. 'You're already late for work, Jack. By the way, I didn't want to mention it in front of the councillor, but our man has struck again.'

'Where?'

'Kyrgyzstan. I suggest you get to work immediately.'

'Third floor you said?'

'Room number 3106.' Freddy stood and headed for the exit,

but in the doorway he stopped and looked back. 'We need to find this fellow. If we don't, this country, this planet of ours, is in grave danger. But besides all that, Jack, if whoever is doing this succeeds in plunging us back into war, Mother and Father's sacrifice will have been in vain.' He turned and walked out, leaving Jack alone in the big conference room. The only thing missing from his exit was the swelling of the string section.

Jack sighed, took off his old and battered watch and strapped on his gleaming, state-of-the-art wrist communicator. He stood up, but the unaccustomed weight of this new piece of arm furniture pulled him over to one side and he hobbled awkwardly towards the door.

Jack looked at Freddy's family beaming up at him from the communicator's flat, rectangular screen. 'Where we're likely to be going, you'd better be waterproof, fireproof, bomb-proof and hooligan proof,' he warned them. And exiting inelegantly through the door, he headed for the lift.

Chapter 5

'Ooh, big boy! Ooh, you great big boy! You give girl big pleasure! Oh! Oh! Oh!'

In the darkness outside the bamboo shack, the prostitute's voice rang out on the warm night air, competing with the strident chirruping of the tropical frogs.

'Don't stop! You master cocksman, you know what girl likes! Oh!'

In the name of all that's holy, the monk thought, *either this chap is really good or the lady's taking her professionalism beyond the call of duty.* He clipped the night sight to the top of his rifle and eased the barrel into the cleft of the tree. Settling his cheek against the cool metal of the weapon, he put his eye to the telescopic sight.

From his elevated position – lying prone along a sturdy branch of an old baobab tree – he could see over the split-cane half-screens of the shack and into the candlelit room. But from this angle all that was visible was the top half of the petite, dark-haired prostitute. The target was below vision, lying beneath her on the floor of the hut. The other occupants of the room – several bored-looking girls – sat around waiting their turn.

Well, he's got an appetite, I'll grant him that.

While Vice-President Negarawan lay back, the girl humped and shimmied on top of him, writhing in simulated ecstasy.

Isn't that just like a politician – making her do all the work? Come on now, Mr Vice-President, lift your head for Daddy.

The monk settled further against the branch of the tree and

clicked on the rangefinder. Using the prostitute's head as an aiming point, the rifle automatically calculated distance, elevation and even took into consideration the slight breeze blowing from left to right. There would be only one chance at this.

The assassin waited, hardly breathing, while the girl's voice went up an octave.

'OOOOH! You come now! You come now, big boy! You give me your slime now!'

I imagine that's supposed to be a turn-on.

He rested his finger lightly on the trigger.

Mr Vice-President, you're about to have the orgasm of your life.

'OOOOOHAAAAAH!' yelled the girl, and suddenly there it was, jerking up into the viewfinder: the greying head of the second most powerful man on the Malay Peninsula.

You go to a better place.

The only way he could tell that the gun had fired was from its kick – the soft-nosed bullet made no noise as it exited the barrel and sped on its way towards the vice-president's right temple.

In the awful silence that followed the dull *ch-splud* of the vice-president's head exploding, the man dropped to the ground. The monk was so practised in his art he'd already stowed his rifle in the long pocket of his specially adapted trousers before the first screams ripped the night apart. These had a different intensity from those that had preceded them; they weren't simulated yelps of pleasure, they were bona fide screams of terror.

In the darkness he smiled and fell to his knees. *Mission accomplished. I give thanks to You, O Lord, for allowing me to be Your instrument.* He looked down at the dead body of one of the vice-president's elite corps of bodyguards. *Elite my arse.* And running his hands over the dead guard's face, a strange and unsettling transformation came over the monk. In a few short moments he had become him, or had at least arranged his features into an approximation of the bodyguard's features.

Slipping on the dead man's jacket, the assassin reached inside the breast pocket and took out an ID.

My name is Anwar Ibrahim.

Suddenly the undergrowth was full of the sound of running feet.

'Anwar! Anwar! Where are you, did you see anything?'

Hauling a leafy branch over the body of the guard, the assassin ran out of the tangle of scrubby bushes surrounding the bamboo brothel and onto the concrete path beneath the perimeter fence.

He pulled out the guard's pistol and started firing into the air. The *crack!* of the automatic soon brought the other guards running.

'Anwar, is that you?'

'He climbed over the fence and headed off up the road! I think I winged him.'

'OK, Abdul, Emas, come with me. Anwar, you and Intan search the immediate area, he might have an accomplice.'

The leader of the squad and his two lieutenants set off at a run.

In the unnatural, pale green light of the soda lamps perched at intervals on top of the perimeter fence, 'Anwar' looked uncertainly at Intan. 'Is the vice-president OK?'

Intan shook his head sadly.

'Shit. I hope they find the bastard.'

'Come on,' said Intan, 'let's see if there's anybody else around.'

In the soda lamp half-light, Intan saw the other man reveal his teeth in a strange, green smile.

'Bit of a pointless exercise, my friend.'

Intan also saw, but too late, something glint in the man's hand. Before he could call out, the knife had gone deep into his chest, expertly angled under his ribcage, its razor-sharp tip severing Intan's aorta.

The look in Intan's eyes went from shock to blank surprise

in seconds. The assassin let Intan's body fall to the ground with a soft *whump* then dragged the corpse into the shielding under-growth.

Emerging out of the scrub onto the road at the front of the brothel, the assassin was not at all surprised to see the vice-president's car completely unguarded. Everyone was either inside questioning the girls, or out looking for the killer.

These chaps are really sloppy, I'll bet they've even left the keys in the ignition . . .

He slid in behind the wheel.

Hallelujah!

The car started with a whisper.

I love the sound of expensive machinery.

He would be well down the road before anyone had even noticed he'd gone.

Jack's new office was a sight to behold: light and airy with a bal-cony at one end offering views of Big Ben and Westminster Abbey. The room hummed with shiny new computers, message pods whizzed and clattered through miles of vacuum tubing that snaked across the ceiling, and at various 'refreshment centres' one could make oneself a cup of just about every kind of tea going, from Earl Grey to Vanilla Ceylon: there was no austerity here. Not that such frippery particularly interested Jack; he liked his tea straight and strong. With a little milk, of course, and preferably a biscuit or two. He was particularly fond of Garibaldis, not that they were easy to come by in these strait-ened times.

A mixture of suits and uniforms bustled to and fro carrying bundles of files, or stood huddled in groups around the various work stations. It had the old familiar feel of a police operations room, the only difference being it all looked so damn *efficient*.

As Jack stood uncertainly in the open doorway surveying the scene, people gradually became aware of his presence. One by one they stopped what they were doing and turned to stare at him. Soon, the bustle and aura of efficiency he'd walked into was replaced by a stiff and formal silence. Jack felt like he'd stumbled into a nudist colony wearing a thong.

'Please, don't let me interrupt. I love watching people work, I can do it all day.'

No one laughed, no one even cracked a smile. Perhaps this was going to be tougher than he thought . . .

'Detective Lindsay?' someone breathed in a Deep South accent close by his left ear.

He turned and gasped. She was beautiful: her blonde hair was scraped back in a loose pony tail that cascaded down her back like a golden waterfall. She had soft, melting grey eyes, high cheekbones and red, pouting lips. Her naked legs glowed with health and her white shirt was unbuttoned almost to the waist, revealing most of her bra, which was engaged in a life-or-death struggle with her cantaloupe-like breasts.

My God, Jack thought, *maybe things are going to work out splendidly after all* . . .

He cleared his throat and managed a breathless but formal, 'How do you do?'

'I do very nicely, thank you, Boss,' she smiled, taking his hand. 'I'm Detective Sergeant Lana O'Hara, and I'll be acting as your personal assistant.'

'Oh, really? Jolly good,' he replied with a lopsided smile.

'Can I get you anything?'

'Hmm?' Jack was wondering how he was going to break the news to Mango that he'd been replaced.

'To drink?' Lana mimed sipping out of a teacup.

'Oh, yes, lovely. Um . . . tea would be nice . . . a nice cup of tea.'

'Assam, Ceylon, Oolong, Green Gunpowder, or flavoured?'

'Er . . . sorry, didn't quite catch that, could you repeat the question?'

Lana grabbed hold of Jack's tie, pulling his face almost into her cleavage. 'I make a mean banana toffee pudding Orange Pekoe.'

There was a strange ringing in Jack's ears. 'Er, sounds splendid,' he muttered to Lana's bosom.

Releasing her hold, allowing Jack to re-emerge and catch his breath, Lana gazed dreamily at him. 'I think we're going to get along just fine.' Then she shimmied away towards the nearest refreshment centre.

Looking up, Jack saw that everyone was still watching him. He was not altogether sure that he was making a very good first impression on his staff. Swallowing hard, he straightened his tie.

'Right, now, listen up, chaps!' *Listen up, chaps? Good God, did I really say that? You're not in the army now, Jack.* Feeling it beholden on himself to say something inspiring, he tried again. 'Er . . . we all, all of us here, have been given a great responsibility. A vitally important chance to serve our own and future generations . . .'

It wasn't going well, already their eyes were beginning to glaze over. 'What we do here . . . our work, is vitally important. I'm sure I don't need to remind you how vital our effort is to the security of the planet. Now, our work, being vitally important is indeed . . . vital . . . and important. Indeed, as far as the security of the planet is concerned, I'm sure you don't need me to tell you how vitally important our work is . . .' Jack ground to a halt. It seemed that Councillor McClaggen's eloquence was catching. Then he remembered something he'd once heard on a radio police series and seized on it gratefully, 'At the moment we're just a disparate group of people, but it's my job to forge us into a team!' Jack thought it sounded rather good.

'Er, sir?' It was a young man in a dark suit.

'Yes?'

'Most of us already know each other. We were brought together last year to work on the Chang Carlsson case. We operate very well as a team.'

'Ah, good . . . good.' *Damn!* 'Right, well, even better, so then . . . you'd best . . .' Jack trailed off and his audience turned away one by one and went back to what they'd been doing perfectly efficiently before he'd come in. 'Good, good, that's it, back to work . . .'

'Hail to the chief.' Lana came to his rescue, bearing tea. 'I've given you a little froth on top. You strike me as a man who likes froth.'

Froth on tea was a new one on Jack. He nodded vigorously. 'Oh, froth, my favourite! How did you guess?'

At that moment, Jack would have said he liked having his eyelids pierced with bamboo shards if he thought it would get him into her good books.

'Tea's hot, so be careful now. Shall I show you to your office?'

'Lead on, Macduff!'

She turned back to him and frowned. 'It's Lana.'

Jack didn't really have the heart to explain. 'Yes . . . yes, of course it is . . . sorry. You're American, aren't you?' he added unnecessarily.

'Guilty.'

'So what are you doing over here, in the land of rationing and rusk-filled sausages?'

She looked around conspiratorially, then leaned forward and whispered in his ear, 'I like English men.'

Jack glowed pink and there was that strange ringing in his ears again.

'This way.'

Jack followed Lana's perfect behind as she weaved between the work stations, leading him towards a glass-walled booth in one corner of the large room.

'Here we are.' She opened the door and showed him inside. It had everything an office should have – a desk, a chair, several phones, a vacuum-tube message terminal, the ubiquitous computer – plus a few extra gadgets that the average office was lacking in, like a holographic map of the Earth and a bank of video screens built into the wall. It was nice but it wasn't home, at least not yet; it had the scrubbed-down feel of a brand new mortuary.

Jack sat down behind his desk and surveyed his new domain. 'It's very . . . new.'

'Don't worry,' said Lana, 'you'll soon give it your own personal stamp. I want to show you something. I know you're going to love this.' She closed the door and picked up what looked like a television remote control off the desk. Clicking it immediately darkened all the windows, save those on the street side. 'You can use this when you want to be . . . private.'

'Private?'

She leaned forwards across the desk so that he could see right down her shirt, and took hold of his lapels. 'Yes, you know, any time you want to abuse your position of power. After all, honey, you *are* the boss.'

The ringing in Jack's ears grew louder and he was feeling unbearably hot.

Smiling coyly, Lana gently released him and picked up the remote again. The windows cleared. Placing the control back near his right hand, she came around the desk and stood behind him. Leaning over his shoulder so that he could feel the firmness of her breasts through his jacket, she opened up a small flap in the surface of the desk to reveal a control panel next to two small slots.

'These are the controls for the video wall. You can select single or multiple view mode, allowing you to watch one or several different recordings at the same time. As you can see, it has two record-o-chip ports. And this –' she took his hand, extended the index finger and placed it lightly on a red button just above the computer keyboard '– is the most important piece of equipment in the whole room. This is my call button. Any time you need anything, *anything* at all, press it and I'll come running.' She wiggled towards the door, paused in the doorway and smiled back at him provocatively. 'I just know we're going to have a great working relationship.'

Jack could no longer speak. 'Hmm, hmm . . .'

'You said it, big boy.'

When 'big boy' eventually managed to refocus, and the ringing in his ears had subsided to a point where he could once again hear the sound of sirens in the street, he remembered he had a job to do. He also remembered Mango.

Absently he picked up his cup and took a sip of Lana's tea. 'Oh my God!'

It was sweet and sickly, heavy with ersatz banana tones, but he might yet put it to good use. Pulling the false tooth that had come with his communicator out of his pocket, he dropped it into the steaming beverage. If Freddy and the councillor were right and somebody had infiltrated the system, it was a sure thing they'd be listening in to police communications. If Jack wanted to keep his conversations private, using his new-fangled wrist communicator with its encryption facility was probably the safest option.

Having allowed the false crown (remote, mouth-based, two-way wireless transponder – according to the manual) to soften in the revolting brew for a few moments, he hoicked it out with the stem of his pipe and stuck it over one of his canines, as instructed. At first it felt uncomfortable as hell, but then, as he bit down, it gradually moulded itself to the shape of his mouth and the discomfort eased. Now he had to find out how it worked.

He fiddled unsuccessfully with the wrist communicator. He could read the latest news and weather reports, get up-to-date stock prices, download all his favourite tunes, watch just-released movies; he could probably even hire a troupe of Slovakian egg-jugglers, but how the hell did he dial a number?

He flicked through the instruction manual. Under the section 'Voice Communications' he found what he was looking for. Apparently all he had to do was speak a number, tag it with a name and then, whenever he said that name again, the communicator would connect him. But first he had to go through voice-recognition-chip configuration, which involved speaking a lot of random words so that the device could get an idea of the idiosyncrasies of his speech patterns. As the words came up on the communicator's screen he was to say them in a normal voice. Although he wasn't really a fan of modern technology, he thought he could probably manage that.

The first word was *Alhambra*. 'Alhambra,' Jack said, a little self-consciously. The next was *Benzedrine*. 'Benzedrine,' he repeated, a little more confidently. It didn't take him long to relax into the task and he was soon annunciating the random words roundly and with relish.

'Landing,' he read, followed by, 'lingerie, massage, bikini, thong, gusset . . .' He looked up to see three of his staff standing in front of his desk. From their expressions they were obviously unused to seeing their superior talking dirty to his watch. 'Oh, er . . . come in.'

'We already have,' said one – a slightly sour-looking young woman with black-rimmed glasses and hair pulled back into a severe bun.

'Good, good . . . I was just . . . er . . .' He waved his communicator at them. 'New watch . . . communicator thing . . .'

They all remained stony-faced.

He sat up straight and tried to look efficient. 'What do you want?'

The woman stepped forward and thumped a sheaf of paper on the desk. 'Witness reports of all the incidents from Afghanistan through Nepal. Plus the latest on the cluster of killings in Pakistan. Reports from the colonies will be ready after lunch.'

She pulled a leaf off the top and handed it to Jack. 'And this is a chronological list of all the incidents, stating method, location and time.'

'Excellent.'

An officer in a suit was next. 'CCTV footage of all the crime scenes on the day of the incident and the previous twenty-four hours. It's mostly in real time, so there's several weeks' viewing there.'

Jack sighed heavily as the man placed a small black record-o-chip on the desk next to the pile of papers.

'I can see I'm going to be watching a lot of television. Maybe I should send out for a take-away curry and a few bottles of beer, eh?'

The woman looked at him sharply. 'Sir, the consumption of alcoholic beverages is prohibited during working hours.'

'Times have changed, then,' Jack muttered, pulling out his pipe.

'And smoking is also strictly forbidden.'

Jack groaned and put his pipe back in his pocket.

Another male officer in plain clothes placed a second record-o-chip next to the first. 'A recording of the post morta on all the victims.'

'Post morta?'

'It is the correct plural for post mortem, sir,' the man said smugly.

One up on the boss already.

The woman was already at the door.

'Will that be all, *sir*?' She hit the last word, managing to make it sound like an insult.

Jack relaxed back in his chair and regarded her coolly for some moments.

'Actually, no. The witness reports, I take it, have been run through Pattern Analysis?'

She looked shiftily at her colleagues. 'No, sir, neither have they been sifted by Dr Watson, as per Commissioner Lindsay's instructions.'

Well at least Freddy's done something right, Jack thought. If Dr Watson *had* been allowed to have a go at the reports they'd be worse than useless.

'I thought you'd want to read through the full reports and draw your own conclusions,' the woman continued.

Now he understood. This lot were all that Jack despised about the modern-day force. Oh, they were expert in using the technology and they knew all the jargon, but they did just what was asked of them and nothing more. Heaven forbid they should actually get involved and think for themselves; that messy little bit of police work they left to mugs like Jack.

'Draw my own conclusions? You want me to wade through several yards of witness testimonies and draw my own conclusions? By the time I got to the end I'd be an old man. Correction – older man. Like my brother, I may think that Dr Watson is a useless pile of junk, but Pattern Analysis I've always been fond of.' He shoved the pile of statements back at her. 'I want these reports PA-profiled and once you've done that I want to hear your opinion.'

She looked like he'd asked her for her knicker size. 'My opinion?'

'That's right, it's called using your brain. You do *have* a brain?'

She hesitated a second, then came forward and picked up the heavy sheaf of paper.

'And, as I'm a glutton for punishment, I'd like to see the airport immigration records from all countries and colonies concerned in the weeks leading up to the murders and the days following. I want to know who went in and who went out. And this time before you give them to me, I want them scanned for any recurrence of the same or similar names. It's called Pattern Analysis Profiling – we in the business usually call it PA for short. Do you think you can handle that, my dear?'

She clenched her jaw, turned on her heel and stalked out, leaving Pinky and Perky blinking at each other.

'What about us, sir?'

Jack looked at the two young bloods in their expensive suits. 'You—' He picked up the record-o-chip containing the recordings of the pathologists at work and threw it back at the man who'd laid it on his desk. 'I want you to check through these *post morta*, and see if you can find out anything new about the victims' missing *crania*. Then I suggest one of you makes your female colleague a nice cup of tea while the other tries to remove the steel rod from up her backside.'

They looked at Jack, at each other, then back to Jack again.

'Go, go! You interrupted me in the middle of making love to my watch.'

They left and Jack went back to configuring his voice chip.

Ten minutes later and he was ready to actually use the damn thing.

'Mango, encrypt,' he said.

Sure enough, seconds later, Jack could detect a ringing through his new tooth. It was an unnerving experience, like having a miniature phone booth in his mouth. He just hoped he didn't have any would-be superhero bacteria lurking around his gums.

'*Hello?*'

'Mango, how are you this fine morning?'

'*Jack? I've been worried about you.*'

'Me? Whatever for? I want you to get down to the Home Office – Immigration Department – and pull out Daygan Flyte's passport file.'

'*You are joking? They'll never let me in the door.*'

'Oh, I forgot to say . . . before you go, drop in at the Yard and pick up your new police badge – security clearance Alpha.'

There was silence at the other end of the phone.

'Mango? Are you still there?'

'*I'm speechless.*'

'Well, that's a first.'

'*How did you do that?*'

'My native wit and charm, and apparently I'm the best dick in town.'

'*That's not what I heard.*'

'Lies and defamation. It seems we're back in the force, Mango – working on a nice juicy intercontinental murder case.'

'*So if we've got a new case, why this rekindled interest in Michaelmas? Or perhaps it's his wife you're really interested in?*'

'No, no, it's . . . simple curiosity. Pull his passport file and his photograph, I want to see what the chap looks like. When you've done that, come and join me at our smart new offices. You'll find me on the third floor.'

'*You really are something. I'm on my way.*'

'Oh, and Mango? You know the dress code at Scotland Yard.'

Jack could sense him becoming tight-lipped.

'*What are you saying? That I don't know how to dress appropriately?*'

'No, no, you always look . . . like a confection. I'd like to encourage you to follow your own inclination and wear something you feel comfortable with. Something . . . fun.'

'*Fun?*'

'Yes, this place is tighter than a nun's knickers and I'd like to loosen it up a little.'

'*Anything to oblige.*'

The line went dead.

Now what did Jack do with the rest of the morning? He pulled a newspaper off the top of the pile thoughtfully supplied by Lana and flicked through it. It seemed Gelda Longhorn's take on the murders was being actively debated. Jack followed the story in the other papers. Several reports mentioned that the murders were indeed reminiscent of the style of Syndicate killings that were an almost daily occurrence in the bad old days before the war, but none of the journalistic heavyweights seemed to be taking the idea seriously.

Ms Longhorn, however, had really got behind the story,

quoting an anonymous source as stating that the Syndicates were definitely back in action: At the moment hers was a lone voice but it couldn't be dismissed. Although a respected journalist, she was widely regarded as hot-headed and prone to blind persistence, having recently got into trouble for hounding a policeman accused of accepting bribes who turned out to be perfectly innocent. But if she was wrong in this instance it would be certain professional suicide. What was it that made her so sure when everyone else was looking the other way? Where was she getting her information?

The Syndicates? Jack wondered. *Picking off politicians one by one seems a little minimalist for them. They once trashed an entire country just because its president was a little late in coming up with his protection money. No, delicately cherry-picking victims had never been their style.*

Jack sighed and put down the newspaper. Now what was he going to do? He ran a hand thoughtfully across his sunken and stubbly cheeks. *I must ask Freddy where he gets his razor blades. They probably cost the earth, but hey, I'm a wealthy man all of a sudden.*

With this happy thought at the forefront of his mind, he considered pressing Lana's red button and seeing just how dark and cosy they could make his office, but then his eyes came to rest on the record-o-chip on the desk. Cursing the Protestant work ethic instilled in him by his ever-toiling parents, he picked it up. The prospect of several days' worth of CCTV footage was not appealing, but it would have to be trawled through at some time.

Slipping open the cover of the small control panel, he snicked the chip into one of the slots provided. Pressing a button marked 'Simultaneous', Jack swivelled round to face the bank of video screens.

On each monitor, the fuzzy image of a soon-to-be crime scene blinked on. One showed people ambling aimlessly about a big public square, on another a press of people crowded down a busy urban street, while other screens remained blank or replayed a completely deserted panorama: the platform of a railway station late at night; the darkened interior of a conference hall; the car park of an industrial complex . . . In the top left corner of each monitor screen, the location and time was burnt into the recording along with a rolling time code, showing the exact time down to a thousandth of a second.

Jack watched, eyes flicking from screen to screen. It was deadly dull, and if he watched the whole thing in real time he was going to bore himself to death. He hit the double speed button and the images began to move more quickly, jumping and dancing jerkily across the screen making it impossible to keep track of what was happening on each one. After ten minutes he'd had enough – he needed a fresh pair of eyes. Hitting 'Pause', Jack clambered to his feet, opened the door of his office and looked out. As soon as he showed his face everyone immediately appeared to be extraordinarily busy, looking intently at their computer screens as if their lives depended on it, or scurrying about importantly looking neither left nor right. A youngster rushed by carrying a tray of steaming tea cups.

'You!'

He had braces on his teeth and steel-rimmed glasses, and his dark, nondescript off-the-peg suit was a couple of sizes too big for him. He stopped and blinked at Jack then looked around the office. Holding the tray with one hand, he pointed uncertainly at himself.

'Me?'

'Yes, that's right – you, come here.'

'But, I'm just—'

'I don't care what you're doing. Whatever it is, drop it and get in here.'

'Drop it?'

'Drop it!'

'Now?'

'Now, for Pete's sake!'

'All right.' He let go of the tray and it fell to the ground with a crash, decorating the new, hitherto pristine carpet with a swirling, interlocking pattern of walnut-flavoured Lapsang and cherry Keemun, given texture by an overlay of fig rolls. Either this boy was immensely stupid or he had a great sense of humour. Either would do for Jack's purposes.

He pulled him into the office and sat him down in his chair.

'You like watching television?'

The boy nodded eagerly. 'Oh, yes.'

'Good. I need you to watch what happens on these screens and tell me if you notice anything . . . strange.'

'Strange?'

'Unusual; out of the ordinary. Like anyone acting suspiciously in any way . . . or something that looks out of place – anything that you deem odd. The controls are by your left hand, off you go.'

He looked up at Jack like a dog at his master. 'Where are you going?'

'I'm stepping outside for some air. If you need me I'll be on the balcony.'

Jack hobbled the length of the still-bustling office and out through the doors that led onto the little terrace. It was obvious no one had been out there before, as a stack of tubular aluminium tables stood untouched in one corner, next to a similar stack of chairs. He pulled a chair off the top and took it to the edge of the balcony.

It was a great view. From up here you could see all the way down Victoria Street to the Houses of Parliament and beyond – to the festering slums of old Southwark. Jack sighed and filled his pipe. He had to admit that although the city was dark, dirty and dangerous, the sun hardly ever shone and that, nearly twenty years after the war, Garibaldis were still in short supply, he loved it. In fact there was the odd occasion when he fell gloriously and passionately in love with London all over again. This was such a moment. He felt a surge of pride in his breast

69

that he belonged to such a place. She may have been badly scarred by the war bombing, but you had to admire the way she had survived, rising phoenix-like out of the ashes to become once again the most magical and downright glorious city of them all.

Jack wasn't aware how long he sat there puffing contentedly on his pipe, feeling the city's power surge through him like an electric current, but he was eventually brought out of his reverie by a tap on the shoulder.

'Er, sir?'

It was the boy with glasses.

'Yes?'

'I think you should come and look at this.'

'You've found something?'

'I don't know . . . it may be nothing.'

Taking a last lingering look at the glowering hulk of the city, Jack sighed, tapped out his pipe and, scrabbling to his feet, grabbed his stick and followed the boy back inside.

'Now, sir, watch carefully . . .'

The boy hit the 'Play' button on the desk. The images moved jerkily across the screen just as they had done before and, as far as Jack could make out, just as pointlessly.

'There, did you see that?'

Jack squinted at the screen. 'What am I looking for?'

'I'll play it for you again, but this time I'll slow it down. Keep looking at the bottom left-hand monitor and the second from the top on the right.'

'You're in charge. Play it again.'

Jack watched, eyes flicking between the two screens.

'Get ready, it's coming up.'

Jack concentrated.

'There it is!'

Jack's eyes were moving so fast they were giving him a headache.

'Well?'

'Did I miss it again?'

The boy rolled his eyes and Jack could tell he was rather disappointed with him.

'We'll try it one more time,' said the boy long-sufferingly.

'Sorry, my eyes aren't what they used to be.' He thought ruefully that there were a few other parts of him that could also have been described in those terms.

The boy hit 'Play' again.

Jack watched . . . And watched . . . And then . . . 'Yes! Er . . . I think so.'

'What did you see?'

It appeared for a brief second, flitting across one of the monitor screens and then appearing a split second later in the other.

'A shirt.'

'Exactly.'

'The *same* shirt. But what does that prove?'

The boy rolled the images back and froze on the shirt in question.

'This pattern shirt was only issued to the Purple Trousers Brigade during the South China Sea campaign.'

'They handed out Hawaiian shirts to elite troops?'

'They were only to be worn during undercover operations.'

'Yes, I can see how a canary-yellow shirt with heliotrope sunbursts is going to help you blend in.'

'It did in that part of the world. You see, before the war, those living in the Indonesian archipelago had a very poorly developed sense of style. Oh, they had food and clean water and the infrastructure to deliver it to the people who needed it, but as far as fashion was concerned it was basically Third World.'

Jack looked at this strange boy with his big teeth and braces, his bad haircut and his oversized suit. Where had he come from? 'How do you know all this?'

The boy looked coyly up at Jack from under his bird's nest hair. 'I read military history and fashion at Reading.'

'That's an interesting double.'

'My father was in the army – intelligence division – and my mother was a cutter for a couture house. I just felt comfortable with those two subjects.'

Horses for courses.

Jack squinted at the monitors. One was the footage from North Korea, the other from Japan. He quickly scanned the list that Miss Tin Knickers had given him earlier.

'The incident in Pyongyang occurred on August the twelfth and that in Tokyo on August the fourteenth, just days apart. So what does this shirt tell us?'

The boy was so keen to give him the answer he raised his hand like an eager schoolboy. 'Well, sir, apart from telling us that in all probability this person was a member of the Purple Trousers Brigade during the South China Sea campaign, it also informs us that this individual was in at least two of the murder locations at the right time.'

'Give the man a cigar – not on police premises, of course. All right, Einstein, what else does it tell us?'

The boy's face crumpled into a thoughtful frown.

'It tells us he's mean,' said Jack. 'He doesn't like using laundries. It could also point to a possible personal hygiene problem.'

'Er . . . sir?'

'Never mind.' There went Jack's theory about him having a sense of humour. 'How many Purple Trousers were involved in the South China Sea campaign?'

'Five battalions, anywhere between two and five thousand men.'

Jack ran his fingers through his thinning hair and sighed. 'Well, that narrows it down a bit. Er . . . what's your name?'

'Clark Kent.'

Jack frowned. 'And is it true you have a tricky relationship with Kryptonite?'

'I'm sorry?' The boy looked genuinely confused.

Jack shook his head. 'Never mind. Good work, Clark Kent.'

Jack scribbled something on a piece of paper, signed it and handed it to him. 'This gives you top security clearance. I want you to do a little research. Have a nose around and see if you can get hold of a list of the soldiers involved in that campaign. Then I'd like you to start checking up on them. Find out what they're doing now, if any of them have criminal records, etcetera. It's going to be a long and tedious process but that's what detective work is all about. If anyone queries what you're doing refer them to me.'

'Er, sir?'

'What is it, son?'

'I'm not really a policeman, I'm just the office boy.'

But Jack wasn't listening any more. He'd seen something on one of the screens that had possessed his whole being. He'd just seen a face he knew, the face of someone he was beginning to care deeply about. There in the centre of the top left monitor, standing frozen in time in some far-away street, was Marian.

Chapter 6

Jack phoned Mango and told him to meet him at a small tea shop down on Chelsea Harbour where the great trading ships had once docked and disgorged their cargoes of lumber and steel. During the war the place had been flattened by the bombing but since then it had been rebuilt with little walkways bristling with cafés and restaurants – although God alone knew why, there was never anything to eat.

Jack chose a table near the water, overlooking a marina full of old, but impeccably maintained pleasure craft. It was the kind of place where neither he nor Mango felt comfortable – dress code: slacks and blazers, cravat de rigueur – but then, Jack reckoned, no other policeman would feel comfortable here either, and he wanted to be far away from their prying eyes.

'What can I get you, sir?'

Jack looked up at the waitress. She was young and blonde, her pale cheeks marked with the red blush of acne. Her name badge read Kelly-Ann Kowalski – probably third-generation Polish, Jack surmised.

'Er, cup of tea, please.'

'Earl Grey, Broken Orange Pekoe, Assam or Raspberry Keemun?'

'Just straight tea, please. Strong and no froth.'

'No froth?' She looked confused.

'Sorry, I . . . never mind.'

She scribbled something on her notepad. 'Anything to eat?'

'I don't suppose you have any Garibaldis?'

She shook her head. 'We may have some digestives. I know we've got custard creams and jammy dodgers. Do you want me to ask about the full selection?'

'No, it's all right. I'll have . . .' He quickly scanned the menu. It was the usual fare: ham salad sandwich, luncheon meat salad, corned beef fritter and reconstituted egg omelette. 'The ham, is it real ham, or ham roll?'

The waitress investigated her ear canal with the end of her pencil while she thought about the question.

'Um . . . I don't know, actually. I could find out for you.'

'No, don't bother. I'll risk a ham sandwich, thank you.'

The waitress left and Jack stared out at the boats bobbing on the scummy water under the leaden sky. It was almost sacrilege to think it about the city he loved, but sometimes he wished it wasn't quite so unremittingly gloomy. Every now and again it would have been nice to catch a glimpse of the sky – if only for a few minutes, just to feel the sun on his face.

Mango arrived to snap him out of his reverie. He was a sight to behold. Wearing a salmon-pink suit with white shoes and a lime-green shirt he looked like he could have been on the menu of one of the harbourside fish restaurants. He did a slow twirl so Jack could take in the full effect.

'If you're not careful someone's going to order you.'

'You said the department was too rigid.'

'I wanted to loosen them up, not scare them half to death. Never mind, pull up a chair and tell me what you've got on our friend Michaelmas.'

Mango's face collapsed at the mention of the name.

'What?'

He sat down and stared glumly at the table-top. 'That man must have a lot of very high-powered friends.'

'Don't play games, Mango, just show me what he looks like and then I'll take you to our brand new offices.'

'I can't show you what he looks like because his file wasn't there.'

Jack shook his head. 'No, no, no, it's a national database, everybody's file's there. Everybody who was born here, anyone who has even passed through the country is in it. He's got to be there!'

'Somebody has pulled the file.'

Jack blinked at him. 'Pulled the file?'

'You know for someone who is usually so on the ball you're being remarkably dense. I'll spell it out for you: Mr Michaelmas Thurrock-Lawes, alias Daygan Flyte, aka Mr Piggy-Wig, does not want his likeness getting into the public domain so, using his vast influence, he has expunged all images of himself from that particular arena.'

'There's no photograph?'

'Now you're catching on.'

'You looked up Daygan Flyte?'

Mango nodded. 'I even got in touch with his old theatrical agent, but—'

Jack finished Mango's sentence. 'It was the same story – no photographs.'

'Correct, although I was informed that from next year he would be available for supermarket openings and bar mitzvahs at a very reasonable rate – as Mr Piggy-Wig, of course.'

That was a blow. This Michaelmas character was getting to Jack. Maybe it was because he could disappear so easily; could simply slide behind an impenetrable veil and remain there just out of reach – like a Rich Tea down the back of the sofa. And that annoyed Jack like hell.

At this point Jack's tea and sandwich arrived, and while the waitress fussed over the layout of the table, Jack fingered the record-o-chip in his pocket. He had planned to tell Mango about seeing Marian on the CCTV footage but something stopped him. Was he being overprotective or just plain stupid? Whichever it was he didn't want to expose her to any outside scrutiny, not yet. He had a feeling that Marian was in trouble and he had a little investigating of his own to do first.

'Will that be all, sir?' the waitress beamed.

'That's splendid, thank you. Oh, Mango, do you want anything?'

'I'll just have a lemon tea, thanks.'

'I'll be right back.' She turned and went inside.

Mango smiled slyly. 'So, are you going to tell me your news? Why did you want to meet down here?'

'Well . . . I'd say this is right up your street: a story of sartorial vandalism . . .' and Jack told him all about the Purple Trousers and their undercover Hawaiian-shirt uniform.

'That would mean he'd have worn the same shirt for more than two days running!' The idea horrified Mango.

'I suppose, if you're a rufty-tufty Purple Trouser, such things wouldn't bother you too much.'

'I hope his deodorant was up to it.'

'That was my first thought.'

'It's not much to go on.'

'No, and this afternoon I want you to join Clark Kent in the records department and sift through the lists of those involved in the South China Sea campaign.'

Mango raised his thick eyebrows. 'Whatever happened to Pattern Analysis?'

'Clark doesn't know about such advanced police methods, not yet anyway. He shows promise, and before he discovers all the labour-saving technological goodies we have at our disposal these days, I want him to learn about good old-fashioned police work.'

'You're a sadist.'

'And to have stuck with me all these years, I'd say you were a masochist. Which makes us a perfect team.'

Mango rolled his eyes.

Jack looked down at his sandwich and cautiously lifted the top slice. Immediately he wished he hadn't. Underneath was an unappetizing, wafer-thin sliver of reconstituted ham resting on a mess of slimy, dark green lettuce, glistening with margarine. 'I'm sure this is not the sort of thing the Earl of Sandwich had in mind when he invented this noble snack.' He pushed the plate away. 'What's happened to this country? What about our traditional British cuisine: bacon and eggs, bangers and mash, fish and chips?'

'Foul pest killed all the chickens, swine fever did for the pigs and the potatoes were wiped out by Colorado beetle.' Mango gestured towards the murky waters of the marina. 'And would you want to eat anything that had been caught in there?'

'But the war was two decades ago!' Jack sighed.

'Mr Piggy-Wig's pork burgers aren't bad,' Mango said brightly.

'And where do they get their meat?'

'America.'

'Of course.'

'At least we still know how to make a decent cup of tea.' Jack picked up his cup and took a good long slug. After the frothy muck Lana had served him that morning it was rather refreshing. Oh dear, Lana was another subject Jack should have broached with Mango but he didn't quite have the energy to cope with a full-on Mango sulk.

'You never told me what really happened this morning,' Jack said at last.

'When this morning?'

'You've forgotten about nearly being incinerated so soon? My, your life must be full of incident.'

'You were there, you *know* what happened.'

'I know what happened after I inadvertently set the thing off, but I wasn't there for any of the action leading up to that moment. You know, when the nasty men came in and put it there.'

Mango's lemon tea arrived and he took a sip while gathering his thoughts. 'I was just putting the kettle on—'

'Sorry to interrupt, but is that *real* lemon?' Jack peered into Mango's cup.

Mango fished out the yellow wedge and examined it closely. 'No, it's a slice of sponge, soaked in lemon extract.'

'Ah. Carry on.'

'As I was saying, I was just putting the kettle on, like I do every day, seeing as how it takes a cup of something strong to get you going in the morning, and tea is marginally less harmful than whisky.'

'Please, spare me the lecture.'

'You're damn lucky I'm here to look after you. Without me you'd have killed yourself years ago.'

'At least then I'd have been spared your censorious comments. Can we get back to the story, please?'

Mango gathered himself again. 'I was in my office making tea when I heard the front door open. I looked at my watch – half-past eight: far too early for you.' He gazed at Jack sadly, like a schoolmaster at a hopeless pupil. 'So I was just about to go and see who it was, when in burst these two men, wearing black balaclavas.'

'Such a cliché.'

'That's what I thought, but worse than that, one of them was wearing a blue suit! Can you imagine: black on blue? To me that's like nails down a blackboard.'

Jack glanced at Mango's bright pink suit and contrasting green shirt but said nothing.

Mango had another sip of tea to wash away the awful memory. 'One of the men held a gun to my head while the other placed the bomb on the desk.'

'Did either of them say anything?'

'I was just coming to that. The one with the bomb growled: "In just five seconds this little beauty is going to arm itself. It's sensitive to the slightest movement, so if you don't want to end up as toast, I'd stay exactly where you are." Then they left and the bomb lit up like a Christmas tree. For the next half hour very little happened, except that you arrived and made yourself comfortable in your leather recliner, while I got cramp and had to suppress a desperate desire to pee.'

'That's it?'

'What do you want, *The Greatest Story Ever Told*?'

'But didn't they say anything else? Didn't they give a clue as to who they might be – who had sent them, and why?'

'Oh, yes. Sorry, I forgot. As they were leaving, one of them said, "Beware of Marian Lawes!"'

Jack leaned forward. 'Really?'

'No! Everything happened exactly as I told you.'

Jack grunted, pulled out his pipe and proceeded to fill it. 'Who on earth would want to blow me up?'

'I don't know, after all you're Mr Popular.'

'But I haven't offended anyone for at least a week. Apart from my brother, of course.' Jack suddenly looked up as a strange and unsettling thought began to form at the back of his mind. 'What if . . .?'

Mango frowned. 'What if what?'

Jack shook his head. 'Nothing.'

But Mango could read him like a book.

'You're hiding something.'

'No, it's just that . . .' But Jack needed some cool and unhurried thinking time before he shared his disturbing thought with anyone.

'Well?' Mango stared at him, his head cocked to one side.

Jack lit his pipe and took a thoughtful puff or two. 'Well what?' he said innocently.

'Well, is that *all* you have to tell me?'

'Absolutely. Why would I keep anything from you?'

'Why indeed?'

Jack puffed enigmatically on his pipe and gazed out over the grey waters of the Thames. 'Wait until you see our new offices, you're going to be really impressed.'

Mango shook his head. 'That's a lame attempt to change the subject, Jack Lindsay, but I'll let it go for now. Come on, let's make an entrance.'

Chapter 7

Luckily, when Jack and Mango made their 'entrance' at police HQ, Lana was still on her lunch break, postponing still further any need to inform each about the other. Unfortunately they arrived in Jack's office to be met by a very unhappy-looking commissioner.

After taking in Mango's salmon-pink suit and lime-green shirt in open-mouthed astonishment, Freddy turned to Jack. 'This came in while you were out at lunch.' He thrust a pile of papers at his brother.

Jack took them and settled back in his chair. On the top sheet was a facsimile of a front page, bearing the picture of a headless corpse. 'Another victim?'

'Yes, another victim. It seems the papers got hold of the story before us. That says a lot for our efficiency, I don't think!'

At the top of the page the headline screamed: 'CRANIUM KILLER STRIKES AGAIN!' Jack began to read out loud. '"Malaysian Vice-President Perak Negarawan was last night assassinated while visiting a local night spot." He glanced up at his brother. 'I'm assuming that's news-speak for brothel?'

The commissioner nodded curtly.

'Well I suppose that's a nice way to go,' said Mango.

'It beats the hell out of bowel cancer,' Jack agreed.

The commissioner looked as though he might blow a fuse. 'God damn you, do you never take anything seriously?'

Jack regarded his brother coolly. 'Freddy, if I took things seriously I'd have killed myself years ago. Now, where was I?'

He resumed his reading of the newspaper. '"Local police are baffled. Although the compound which Vice-President Negarawan was visiting was completely surrounded by his personal guard, the murderer somehow managed to break through the tight security and then, after committing this terrible crime, disappeared into the night without trace."'

'How the hell is he doing it?' Freddy asked.

'He's a Purple Trouser,' Jack said simply.

The commissioner looked startled. 'You have a lead?'

Jack shrugged. 'At the moment I'd rather categorize it as an educated guess, but who else but a Purple Trouser, trained in espionage and all manner of killing techniques, could pull off something like this?'

'Find him, Jack. You have to find this bastard!' The commissioner leaned on the desk and stared at Jack, eyes wide, mouth open like a hooked fish. 'More than our lives depends on it,' he said quietly. Then, turning smartly on his heel, he stalked out of the room without a backward glance.

Mango raised his eyebrows. 'What was that about?'

Jack shrugged. 'Probably some sort of mid-life crisis. Perhaps Gloria's withdrawn her favours.'

'Do you want me to go to Malaysia?' Mango asked.

Jack stretched and yawned. 'No, you won't find anything there. Our man will be long gone.'

There was a knock at the door. 'Mr . . . er, Chief?'

'Ah, Clark, come in, meet Mango.'

Clark regarded Mango's outfit with a look of barely suppressed horror. All his finely tuned feelings regarding colour coordination wanted to scream NO! and throw the offender out of the window. But being a thoroughly well-brought-up young man, instead he offered his hand. 'How do you do?'

'Any luck with the Purple Trousers investigation?' Jack asked.

'Yes, Chief,' Clark replied. 'There's quite a lot of stuff in their database regarding the South China Sea campaign, and a full list of those who took part.'

'Good, good. So this afternoon I want you and Mango to sift through all that data; see if anything leaps out at you. Mango can show you what good old police work is all about.'

Clark wondered if his stomach was up to spending a whole afternoon in the same room as Mango and his colourful ensemble. 'Er . . . OK.'

Mango smiled and took the nervous Clark by the arm. 'Come along, my dear, Uncle Mango will introduce you to the wonderful world of trawling through shit.' He glared fiercely at Jack as he led the boy from the room.

While Mango and Clark were getting acquainted, Jack darkened his office windows and settled himself in front of the video wall to watch again the footage of Marian from the CCTV scan. Was it just coincidence that she'd been there – in the wrong place at the wrong time – or was she somehow involved in all this?

To Jack she looked scared. At one moment she seemed to stare right down the lens and open her mouth to say something, then she reacted to something off-screen, turned away sharply and exited frame. The location ident read: São Paulo, Placa de Republica, 29 July, 14:27.

Jack replayed the footage, letting his eyes wander hungrily over every inch of her. It was very hard to concentrate on the issue in hand. The only thing that kept him focused was the thought that unless he found something to the contrary, Marian could end up as a suspect in a murder case.

He went back to the beginning and studied her face frame by frame, trying to interpret the movements of her delicious mouth. Pressing the enlarge function on the desktop control panel, Jack allowed Marian's lips to fill the screen, then he watched the sequence again. At this magnification her lips were two grainy blurs, but he could make out just enough detail to see the shapes they made.

'That looks like a K. KA?'

He watched the sequence again. No, the edges of her lips were drawn down slightly.

'KEH . . .'

Then he caught the faintest flash of her moist tongue as it flicked the roof of her mouth.

'That's got to be an L. OK, so we've got KEH and L. KEL . . .'

He played the sequence over again until he had the final sound. At the end of the word her lips touched lightly together in a percussive.

'P, so the last sound's a P. So that's: K-E-L-P. Kelp . . .? Why is she talking about seaweed?'

He replayed the sequence again.

'No, that's not a K, it's an H. HELP! She's saying "Help"!'

She'd looked right down the camera lens and asked for help. That meant that whatever she was involved in, she was an innocent party. It might not stand up in a court of law, but it was good enough for Jack.

He was overwhelmed with relief and flooded with a desperate desire to see her again as soon as possible. Reaching into his jacket pocket he took out her card. Then, encrypting the call, phoned the number of her charity.

A woman's voice answered. 'A Planet Fit for Kids, how can I help?'

'I'd like to speak to Marian Lawes, please.'

'Who's calling?'

'Jack Lindsay.'

'Please hold, Mr Lindsay, and I'll see if Mrs Lawes is available.'

After a few seconds of a terrible made-for-muzak rendition of Beethoven's Ninth Symphony, she came on the line.

'Hello, Jack.'

The sound of her voice turned him to the consistency of gently melting raclette.

'Marian?'

'I'm surprised. After our last meeting I never expected to hear from you again.'

'Things have changed. Look, I can't talk now, but can you meet me this evening?'

'At your . . . office?' She hesitated over the word.

Jack smiled. 'No, do you know—' He didn't think she'd appreciate his taking her to one of his usual drinking haunts, full of deadbeats and wrinkled old bar flies. 'How about Florian's?' It was an upmarket wine bar in Kensington, frequented by bankers and financiers; discreet and old-fashioned.

She sounded surprised. 'Florian's? Isn't that a little out of your league?' There was a slight pause as she realized what she'd said. 'Oh I'm sorry, I didn't mean to be rude.'

'No, that's all right.' Jack felt like a small boy who'd just been smacked down for insolence. He tried to make light of it. 'Besides, you're paying.'

'I'll keep you to that.' She sounded as if she was trying to make amends.

'Eight o'clock?'

'I'll see you there.'

The line went dead.

Clark and Mango reappeared around teatime, Clark looking distinctly tired around the eyes.

'Anything?' Jack asked.

'You were right about this boy – he's good.' Mango beamed at him like he'd discovered a new clothes designer.

'Discounting those who are dead and those still active in the military, we've managed to narrow it down to two thousand individuals,' Clark announced.

'That's narrowing it down?'

Mango looked at Jack darkly. 'Listen, we've wasted a whole afternoon doing something that would have taken minutes with PA, so don't complain about the numbers.'

'PA?' Clark enquired.

'Besides,' Mango continued, 'if you'd given us a little more to go on, like times and locations, we could have refined the list even further. But no, you sit there like God Almighty and keep all the information to yourself.'

'What's PA?' Clark asked again.

'Don't start with me,' Jack said, glaring at Mango. 'I've had a hard day: my office was burnt down, my disability pension is hanging by a thread and my staff think I'm a pervert.'

'This PA thing . . .' Clark persisted.

'You think you've got troubles,' Mango bridled. 'I've spent the whole day being whistled at.'

'That's your fault for wearing a candy-pink suit.'

'It is not candy pink! For your information this colour is tropical sunset.'

'WHAT'S PA?' Clark yelled.

That got their attention. It got the attention of everyone on the entire floor.

Looking through the windows of his office, Jack could see the whole team had stopped what they were doing and were staring their way.

Mango threw Jack one of his old-fashioned looks. 'I think he wants to know about PA.'

'So, Clark, you want to know about PA?'

'YES! I mean, yes. Sorry.'

'Very well, Clark, PA, or Pattern Analysis, is a technique for—'

'Finding recurring patterns in a large amount of data.' It was the woman from the morning. 'It's useful for finding specific names or ages or . . . just about anything.' She thumped a heavy pile of papers on the desk. 'Reports from all the crime scenes, profiled and annotated with my conclusions.'

'There you are, you see, that wasn't so hard, was it? By the way, I can't keep thinking of you as Miss Tin Knickers. Do you have a name?'

'Ruth, like in the Bible. Ruth Jones.' She scowled and walked out of the room.

Clark was beginning to realize he'd been had.

'You mean we didn't have to go through all those names by hand? We could have just stuck the lists through the computer and it would have picked out the relevant details for us?'

'It's a terrific labour-saving device.' Mango smiled.

'We've wasted nearly a whole afternoon? You sent us on a wild goose chase?' He waved a wobbly finger threateningly at Jack.

'Don't point that thing at me,' Jack warned. 'I'm sorry, Clark, think of it as a sort of rite of passage. Now you know what *real* police work is like, you'll appreciate the technology that much more.'

At that moment Lana swayed into the room. Oh dear, Jack could sense a confrontation brewing for which he was totally unprepared.

'Who's this?' she asked suspiciously.

'This is Clark.'

'I didn't mean the tea boy, I'm talking about shorty here.'

Mango sucked in his cheeks in indignation.

Jack had a feeling this wasn't going to be pretty. 'Now, now, Lana. I'd like you to meet Mango, my . . . er . . .' He swallowed hard. 'My personal assistant.'

Lana's eyes went ice cold. She looked at Jack as if she wanted to rip out his liver with her fingernails and eat it raw.

Perhaps now would not be a good time to ask her to give me a back massage, he thought.

'Why wasn't I told about this?' she snapped.

'Who's Miss Frigidaire?' Mango asked.

'Ah, I don't think you've been introduced. Mango, meet

Detective Sergeant Lana O'Hara, my . . . personal assistant.' Jack hunched as low as he could to present a smaller target.

Mango took exactly half a second to work himself up into a froth of extreme indignation. 'Well, that's nice. We work together for twenty years and now suddenly I'm not enough.'

Lana eyed Mango's diminutive frame. 'From first impressions I'd say there's never been enough of you.'

'You keep your mouth shut, sister!' Mango turned to Jack, pleadingly. 'Are you letting Mango go? Don't you want to work with me any more?'

'No, no, Mango,' Jack said with a placatory smile, 'it's nothing like that. It's because . . .' What he wanted to say was that it was because Mango didn't have melon-sized tits and long, sun-kissed legs. But what he actually said was: 'It was the department's idea. They thought because of the amount of work involved and the urgency of the situation that it would be a good idea to give me Lana to help you out.' The moment it was out of his mouth he realized his mistake.

'Help *him* out!' Lana exploded. 'Help this misshapen little oddball out? What do you think I am, a nursemaid? I was hired as your personal assistant, not assistant personal assistant, so unless this freak packs his bags now I'm handing in my notice.'

Mango exploded. 'Did you hear that? She called me a freak! I have never been so insulted in my life!'

'Really? With your looks I'd assumed it was a daily occurrence.'

'Are you going to let her stand there and talk to me like that? Why don't you come out and admit it. Now you've got yourself a powerful new job, Mango's old news so you're just going to screw me up and throw me away.'

'That wouldn't be difficult – someone your size.'

Mango was turning purple and clashing horribly with his suit. 'Get rid of her, or so help me I'll—'

'What, burst into tears?'

Jack suppressed a smile: she was probably right. 'Now calm

down, both of you. I'm sure we can resolve this amicably. If I'd thought you were going to behave so childishly I would never have called this meeting.'

'You never called any meeting,' Lana snapped.

'No, but I was thinking about it. But that's not the point. The point is . . .' Jack wasn't sure what the point was any more, he just wanted everybody to stop shouting. 'I want us all to start behaving like grown-ups. What sort of an example are we setting Clark here?'

Clark was standing in the corner with a big smile on his face. It wasn't often he got to witness a spectacle like this back home in Maidenhead.

'I know that either one of you,' Jack continued, 'is perfectly qualified – overqualified, even – to do this job.' Jack looked at Lana. She was qualified to do things that Mango couldn't even imagine. 'But there is a lot of material to sift through and so . . .' *And so what?*

But if he stopped to think there was every likelihood they'd start up again.

'So, here's what I suggest,' he went on hurriedly, then paused again while his thoughts raced. What *did* he suggest? His mind was a blank. Everyone was looking at him expectantly, but he didn't have a clue.

'It seems to me that what we need here is some kind of division of labour.' It was Clark.

'Go on,' Jack urged, glad for someone else to become the focus of attention.

'Taking into consideration their own particular field of expertise, your two assistants could divide the workload between them. That way nobody steps on anyone else's toes and the work gets done in half the time.'

'Good idea!' Jack seized on Clark's initiative and ran with it. 'OK, Lana, what are you good at? Er, I mean, what skills would you say you possessed that set you apart from others in the department?'

She thought for a moment, chewing her bottom lip. 'I suppose my forte is coordination: organizing meetings, collating documents, getting people to the right place at the right time and making sure they have the information they need to do their job.'

'Good. Mango, how about you?'

'I'm excellent at what she's good at obviously, but I have additional skills. You know me, Jack, I'm a people person. I'm a terrific interviewer, I can get information out of witnesses they didn't even know they knew and it doesn't take me long to wheedle the truth out of a suspect.'

'Excellent. So it seems to me that the obvious way to resolve this schism is for you, Lana, to handle any task that involves administration . . . and for you, Mango to be . . .' But Jack couldn't quite think of the right phrase.

'The public interface?' Clark suggested.

'Very good. Yes, you can talk to witnesses, families of the bereaved and, further on in the investigation, suspects.' Jack turned to Clark. 'Well done.'

Clark shrugged. 'It's not rocket science.'

'Don't push your luck, son.' Jack turned back to Lana. 'From now on it's your job to make sure that every single member of this team is up to speed with every bit of information we have about this case.'

'OK, Chief.'

'Mango, I want you to further refine the results you got this afternoon. Our Hawaiian shirt was in Pyongyang on August the twelfth, and in Tokyo on August the fourteenth – run the list through PA using those parameters and see what you come up with. Clark, why don't you join Mango and find out how it's done?'

The boy beamed like a loon. 'Thank you, sir.'

'Now everybody – get to work!'

Chapter 8

Stepping anxiously out of the cab at the head of the narrow alley that led to Florian's, Jack had to remind himself that he wasn't embarking on a romantic rendezvous – but that didn't stop him feeling as nervous as a teenager on his first date.

Pushing through the doors into the wood-panelled lobby Jack immediately felt out of his depth.

A youth in a tailcoat was instantly at his side.

'Take your hat and coat, sir?'

Jack handed him his homburg and trench coat.

Pulling a sour face, the youth took Jack's accoutrements, holding them at arm's length as if they were dead vermin. Finally, dropping them both in an untidy pile on a small table, he hovered expectantly at Jack's elbow.

'Oh, er . . .' Jack fished in his pocket and pulled out a couple of notes. 'Here.'

The boy took the tip as ungraciously as he'd taken the clothes. Jack had half a mind to ask for it back. But then he didn't want to cause a scene – his reason for being here in the first place was to keep everything low key.

'Keep the change,' he muttered, moving away from the morose young man and through into the bar itself. The room was large and opulently furnished with crystal chandeliers and ornate stucco work. Jack was immediately assailed by the smell of cigar smoke and money. It was odd in these austerity-ridden times to realize that some people were actually living as though the war had never happened, indeed, many of the people in this room had actively profited from it. Jack scanned the clientele. Most were middle-aged men in dark suits busily puffing on Havana torpedoes, but Jack was glad to see this dismal sea of conformity enlivened by the odd welcoming splash of a cocktail dress.

He found a table in a nicely secluded section where he could keep an eye on both the door and the rest of the room, and sat down.

'What can I get you, sir?'

Standing above him was a set of shining white teeth in an open and friendly face.

'What have you got?'

The waiter handed him a wine list.

Jack shook his head in disbelief when he saw the prices.

'I know,' the waiter sympathized, 'and most of them are bad years. The trouble is, all the good wine is bought up by the Yanks these days. We just can't compete.'

'So if it's not good, why the sky-high prices?'

He shrugged. 'The people who come here can afford it. And besides,' he added, *sotto voce*, 'most of them don't know the difference.'

This chap was a breath of fresh air compared to his unhappy colleague working in the entrance lobby. Maybe it had something to do with his having the freedom to roam the wide open spaces of the bar room.

'Can you just get me a single malt – no ice?'

The waiter's smile got even wider. 'May I compliment you on your choice of beverage, sir?'

'You may. Oh, and what would you suggest for a lady?'

'We have numerous cocktails that might fit the bill – the Mai Tai is always a popular choice. It all really depends on the lady.'

Behind him the door opened and Marian came into the room.

'She's just arrived.'

The waiter turned discreetly to look at her, then back to Jack. He was obviously impressed.

'As the lady in question is a lady of quality, may I suggest our *blanc de blancs*? It's far better than the house champagne and this lady looks as if she might know the difference.' Taking in Jack's well-worn suit, he added, 'It's also extremely good value.'

Jack stood up and waved. Marian saw him and glided over. She was wearing a shimmering pale green, figure-hugging cocktail dress, split to the thigh, revealing one long and shapely leg. To complete the ensemble she wore a small, close-fitting hat that matched her dress, with a black lacy veil that almost covered one eye.

Moving towards him like a goddess, she drew the attention of every man in the room. The last time Jack had felt such a surge of pride was on winning his school's debating competition.

'Jack, good to see you.' She extended her hand.

'Good to see you too, Marian.' She didn't know how good. He watched her slide in behind the table; even that little act was a study in perfection. 'My friend and I' – Jack indicated the waiter – 'were just debating what you might like to drink.'

She was offered the wine list, but waved it away.

'Do you have a *blanc de blancs*? The champagne here is *so* expensive, and you can't always rely on it.'

Now it was Jack's turn to be impressed. He looked up at the waiter and winked.

'You heard the lady.'

The waiter smiled and withdrew.

Left alone with Marian, Jack swallowed hard and once again had to remind himself that she was just a prospective client. But that was like saying St Paul's Cathedral was just a pile of bricks. 'You look . . . nice,' he said.

She caught his confusion and smiled indulgently. 'Why thank you, I can't remember when I've received such fulsome praise.'

Jack hoped that in the dimly lit room she couldn't see him blush.

'So,' she continued, 'you said you wanted to see me?'

'Er . . . yes. It seems, my dear, that you have not been entirely honest with me.'

Marian flushed. 'I . . .? What do you mean?'

'I'll get straight to the point. What were you doing in São Paulo on July the twenty-ninth – in Placa de Republica to be exact?'

'São Paulo? I haven't been there since my honeymoon.' Concern lined her pretty face.

But Jack was unmoved. 'Nevertheless, we have information that puts you there on July the twenty-ninth – the day before the murder. I'm assuming you were there with your husband, which would make it a paltry two months ago that you saw him, and not the six that you claim.'

Now she really did look confused. 'But . . . you have to believe me, Mr Lindsay, I haven't left Britain for over a year. And I really haven't seen Daygan for six months.'

Jack was used to being lied to – he'd heard a thousand excuses and hard luck stories during his time as a cop. He'd also developed a nose for the truth, and he was as certain as he could be that he was hearing it now. But if she wasn't lying, then what was going on? He studied her face closely – innocence beamed out of every pore. He took in her mouth, her moist and full lips, the fine and delicate line of her nose, the unblemished skin of her cheek and the iridescent lakes of her eyes. He carried on upwards, past her unlined forehead all the way up to her hat. Then he saw it – a tiny black speck attached to the veil. It was a miniature sender unit, comprising camera, microphone and transmitter. Its range couldn't have been more than about two hundred yards, so whoever was monitoring them had to be close.

Jack immediately backtracked. 'I'm sorry, Marian,' he smiled broadly. 'The information came from a notoriously unreliable source, but I'm sure you understand that I had to check it out.'

She looked relieved. 'Yes, yes, of course.'

'So, how's the charity going?' he said, briskly changing the subject while he considered his next move. 'I once had an aunt who worked in the charity business. Nothing like you, of course, she just stacked the shelves at Oxfam. Her Christmas gifts were never what you might call mundane. One year it could be giraffe-necked salad servers hand-carved by the M'Betili people from recycled polystyrene. The next it might be free-trade chilli peppers covered in chocolate. Given the choice, I would rather have eaten the salad servers. But I suppose it beats socks.' Now he was rambling.

Marian smiled demurely. Her breeding and fine sensibilities would never allow her to reproach a gentleman for his ill-judged conversational gambits.

But Jack felt a fool and wanted to say something to redeem himself in her eyes.

'By the way, did I say that I might be interested in your case?' Even *he* was surprised by this turn of events.

'Really?'

'Yes, I've been doing a little preparatory digging, and I think I might be able to help you after all.'

'Sir, madam.' Their drinks had arrived. The waiter placed them on the table with a small bowl of cocktail gherkins.

Jack felt uneasy. There was something not quite right about this set-up. He had to know more.

'Excuse me, but you seem to have a fly on your head – don't move.'

He placed his thumb and forefinger over the tiny camera and microphone attached to her hat.

'Why are we being watched?'

Marian frowned. 'What do you mean?'

Could she really not know?

Jack released the 'fly'. 'There we are. Will you excuse me a moment, my dear?'

Leaving the table, he went out through the entrance lobby and into the alley outside. But what did he expect to find: a Mr Piggy-Wig van with a big aerial on its roof? He limped up to the top of the alley and into Kensington High Street. He scanned the lines of parked vehicles on either side, looked up at the helimotors passing overhead and had the uneasy feeling that he was being watched. *Where are you, Michaelmas?* Jack thought. *And what's your game?*

Going back inside, Jack pestered the hat-check boy for a scrap of paper. Scribbling down his number and the instruction: 'Call me when you're alone', he went back to Marian.

'I don't know about you but I'm a little peckish.' He called the waiter over. 'Do you have any crisps?'

The waiter raised an eyebrow. There was obviously not a lot of call for such low-brow pub snacks here. 'I'll find out for you, sir.'

'Please do. And could you let me see the wine list again?'

He glided away and Marian and Jack were left looking at each other, as unsure of what to say as a couple of kids on their first date.

'So, as I was saying, I'd like to take the case.'

She leaned forward, a shadow of concern passing across her face. 'Does that mean you've found a photograph of Daygan?'

'Would that be a bad thing?'

'No, no,' she said quickly, 'I mean, not if it would help you find him.'

'It would certainly do that.'

The waiter came back with a bowl of crisps and the wine list.

'Thank you, I'm much obliged.'

Jack picked up a big handful of crisps in one hand and Marian couldn't help pulling a face at his appalling table manners.

Then, picking up the wine list in his other hand, Jack shielded his face from her hat camera while crushing the crisps

96

in his fist. They made a sound like exploding firecrackers and, under cover of the noise, he said, 'You have a bug in your hat.'

She looked shocked and tried to flick it away. 'Ugh!'

Jack shook his head. 'No.' He quickly picked up another handful of crisps. 'Not that sort of bug.'

The look of horror that crossed her face told him all he needed to know. He had a brain full of questions, but there were only enough intact crisps left in the bowl for one more.

'Who?'

That sent her into total confusion. Her eyes widened and her mouth dropped open. She looked like a pony in a forest fire. At any moment she might begin neighing and start a stampede.

Jack dropped the spent crisps back into the bowl and put the wine list down on the table.

'I love crisps,' he said in innocent-abroad mode. Then, as if he'd been intently studying the list of fine clarets, 'You know, it beats me why anybody would pay such ridiculous amounts of money for a bottle of grape juice. Give me good old Scotch whisky any day. Cheers!' He restrained himself from giving throat to a Highland yell, and instead raised his glass and took a refined sip. 'Now, what were we talking about?' he asked brightly.

She was still trembling like a leaf in a high wind. 'You . . . you said you were going to accept the case,' she faltered.

'Oh, yes. Did we discuss terms? My fee is one thousand a week, plus an extra thousand if and when I get results. Is that acceptable?'

Talking about money seemed to calm her further. 'Perfectly,' she said, recovering some of her old composure.

'With one thousand in advance. You can give me a cheque if you like. I also take all major credit cards.'

'Would you prefer cash?'

Jack was taken aback. 'You carry that much on you?'

'For little emergencies.' She pulled a sheaf of notes out of her clutch bag. 'Here, take what you need.' She passed the notes over to him like they were nothing but worthless pieces of paper.

Jack counted off his fee and handed the rest back to her. 'You gave me too much,' he said.

'I'm not really used to handling money,' she apologized, putting the notes back in her bag and snapping it shut. 'Daygan usually pays for everything.' At the mention of her absent husband's name, her bottom lip began to tremble and she looked down sharply. 'I'm sorry, Jack . . .'

Jack couldn't help responding to this little display of female frailty with a demonstration of male determination and grit. 'Listen to me, Marian. If he's still alive, I'll find your husband for you. I'll find him if it's the last thing I do.' All he had to do was work out how.

She nodded and reached out and touched his arm. 'Thanks, Jack.' Then she stood up suddenly. 'I'm sorry, but I have to go.'

Jack rose to join her. 'Can I call you a cab?'

'There's really no need.'

'Maybe I should see you home?'

'That's sweet of you, but I'll be fine.'

Jack limped awkwardly round the table. 'At least let me walk you to the door.'

'No!' she said firmly. Then more softly, 'Really, Jack, I can manage.'

He looked at her. Despite all her femininity, there was a fierce determination behind those soft hazel eyes.

'Well, it's been good to see you again.' Jack shook her hand and slipped the piece of paper with his number on it into her palm. She looked startled but understood enough not to look at it there and then. 'And by the way . . .' He pulled the little paper coaster out from under the bowl of gherkins and wrote down the number of his direct line at Scotland Yard. 'I've moved offices, so if you want to get in touch with me you can contact me here.' He handed it to her.

'Thank you. And thanks for the drink . . . I'm sorry I—'

'I'll be in touch,' Jack said gently.

She turned and headed for the door. Jack watched her go. He could have watched her for ever. Once the door had closed on the view of her back, he called his waiter over.

'Here.' Jack handed him a twenty. 'That's for the drinks.' Then he stuffed a fifty in his top pocket. 'And that's for you.'

'You must really like crisps.'

'More than you can possibly imagine.'

'Come back any time,' the waiter beamed.

Jack limped towards the door, grabbed his hat and coat from the clutches of the lobby troll and pushed out through the doors, but she was already gone. He walked down the alley and into ever-busy Kensington High Street, staring for a moment at the black cabs and rickshaws crawling by.

It was getting dark and the temperature had dropped. Turning up the collar of his coat, he was just about to head home when, on top of a building opposite, a large neon advertisement blinked on, depicting a running pig dressed in a blue jacket with gold buttons, front trotters outstretched: it was the Mr Piggy-Wig logo. Something had always troubled Jack about this famous symbol, apart from the unnecessary hyphen in his name. If, as was implied by the logo, the pig was in a hurry to get to a restaurant and enjoy a Piggy-Wig burger, that would mean Mr Piggy-Wig was a cannibal.

Jack looked up at the night sky. 'Michaelmas,' he said to the slowly moving and criss-crossing lights of the never-ending stream of copter-cars and helimotors, 'if you harm one hair on that girl's head, so help me I'll kill you.' And he meant it.

Chapter 9

The next morning Jack called Mango into his office and dimmed the windows.

'People will talk,' Mango said.

Jack looked at Mango's canary-yellow catsuit. 'They aren't already?'

Inviting Mango to sit, Jack clicked the record-o-chip into the slot in his desk and played him the footage of Marian in Placa de Republica.

'So, what do you think?' he asked afterwards.

'I think that blouse with that skirt was a mistake.'

'Mango!'

'I also think she's in big trouble. Have you shown this to anyone else?'

Jack shook his head. 'I wanted to run it past you first.'

'We've got to tell the commissioner.'

'No, she's asking for help. If we turn this over to him, he'll just go in with all guns blazing and she'll clam up tighter than a—'

'Clam?'

'Yes. Besides, she's scared. I met her last night.'

'You did what?'

'I thought I could find out what was going on, talk to her nicely, ask what she was doing there.'

'And?'

'She was wired.'

'Nervous?'

'For sound.'

'Oh.'

'She also said she hadn't been anywhere near São Paulo since her honeymoon.'

'And you believed her?' Mango raised a sceptical eyebrow.

Jack pulled out his pipe and clenched it between his teeth. 'What if someone's trying to frame her?'

'Who?'

'Michaelmas.'

'She's being framed for murder by her own husband?'

'It wouldn't be the first time. The more I find out about this Michaelmas character the less I like him.'

'You hardly know anything about him.'

'And what I do know I don't like. He was there last night, Mango. I know he was there.'

'Michaelmas?'

'No, Father Christmas. Of course, Michaelmas.'

Jack limped over to the window. Down below the street was jammed with black cabs and rickshaws, while up above helimotors and copter-cars screamed by in close formation. 'There's something worrying me about all this, Mango.'

'I know, what with global warming turning St James's Park into a mangrove swamp, you'd have thought the message would have got through to people by now and they'd all be riding bikes.'

Jack looked at him strangely. 'I'm talking about Marian and Michaelmas.'

'Oh, that, of course.'

'Think about it. Someone breaks into our office and sets fire to the place. At first I was sure it was Freddy, trying to scare me back into the fold, but he didn't need to do that, he already had me over a barrel.'

Mango tilted his head quizzically.

Jack shook his head. 'It's nothing.' He moved away from the window and perched on the corner of the desk, inadvertently hitting the 'Rewind' function. Images ran backwards across the screens in a crazy kaleidoscope. 'How d'you turn this thing off?'

Mango hit the 'Pause' button, freezing the image on-screen at the moment Marian turned towards the camera.

'Thanks.' Sucking on his unlit pipe, Jack studied Mango for a few moments. 'You know, I've been thinking about what you said.'

Mango brightened. 'I've made an impression at last. What about? Your drinking habits or your taste in clothes?'

'Do you remember when we were in that café and you were telling me what happened when those men placed the bomb in our office?'

'Oh, that.'

'At first you told me that they'd delivered a warning to keep away from Marian.'

'That was a joke.'

'But what if it were true?'

Mango frowned.

'Look, if anybody wanted to frighten me off a case what would be the best way to go about it?'

'You? There's nothing in the world that could frighten you off a case. You're the stubbornest cuss I know.'

'Exactly. So let's assume that whoever torched the office knew that. And here's another assumption: that Marian is working for Michaelmas against her will.'

'And here's a different angle: she's guilty as sin and stringing you along.'

Jack drew down the corners of his mouth. 'I considered that, for exactly five seconds.'

'Now why doesn't that surprise me?'

'All right,' said Jack, 'how about this: for some reason, Mr Thurrock-Lawes is unhappy about my turning down the case, so devises another strategy? Exploding a bomb in my office would be a sure-fire way to rekindle my interest.'

'That would mean he'd sent Marian to hire you to investigate his own disappearance – it doesn't make sense.'

'Hmm.' Jack paced the room slowly. 'Do you remember how many times Marian mentioned Corbett in our first conversation? It was almost as if she was trying to give us a lead. I think Michaelmas may be trying to lure us out there. Perhaps he wants us out of town. All we have to do now is find out why.'

Mango rolled his eyes. 'Easy-peasy.'

Jack stared at the bank of monitors. On the paused footage of Placa de Republica, Marian Lawes was just about to open her mouth and ask for help. 'Mango, we're going looking for Mr Piggy-Wig.'

Mango folded his arms. 'Really, and what about all the murdered politicians? Are we going to conveniently forget about them?'

'What was Marian doing at Placa de Republica? My guess is she was with Michaelmas, and if he *was* there, my gut feeling is that he's behind the killings.'

'And if he is, you get to send him to jail and have Marian all to yourself.'

'Nonsense, I'm simply reacting as any gentleman would to a damsel in distress. She needs our help, Mango.'

'And you need to stop thinking with your trousers!'

Jack gripped his pipe stem a little more firmly between his teeth. 'How did you get on with Clark yesterday?'

Mango sighed; the discussion was closed. 'Clark's annoyingly bright – took to Pattern Analysis like conditioner to split ends. The boy's not natural, he should be out having fun. At his age the only thing that concerned me was whether my tie matched my socks.'

'That's still your only concern.'

Mango pursed his lips. 'For your information, we whittled down the list of suspects to one hundred and seventy.' He scowled. 'Of course, not all of them may still be alive, the database is notoriously slow at keeping track of the deceased.'

'Very well, that's your job for today.'

'What is?'

'What did Clark call you: the "public interface"? I think it's time for you to go and affirm his trust in you.'

'You want me to knock on one hundred and seventy doors?'

'Not all at once. Do any of those names live in the London area?'

'A few.'

'Good, then take the boy wonder and start with those. But don't disappear just yet, I'm calling a departmental meeting.'

'Yes, sir.'

Mango got up to leave.

'Oh, and Mango?'

'Yes?'

Jack regarded his yellow catsuit and wondered how it would go down with ex-soldiers from the elite Purple Trousers brigade. 'Er . . . nothing. Oh wait, one more thing.' He opened a drawer and took out a personal communicator exactly like his own. 'A little present for you.'

Mango took it uncertainly. 'What's this?'

'With that you can contact me instantly from anywhere on the planet.'

Mango eyed it doubtfully. 'Oh joy.' Strapping it onto his wrist, he studied the effect. 'It's a little . . . outré for my tastes.'

Jack paused while a hundred possible replies whizzed through his mind. In the end he settled on a cheery, 'I've got one just like it, look.' He pulling back his sleeve, displaying his own, chunky piece of wrist furniture.

Mango looked at him balefully. 'That's supposed to make me feel good about wearing it?'

Jack sighed. There was just no pleasing some people. 'And you're going to need this.' He handed Mango the instruction manual and remote, mouth-based, two-way wireless transponder.

'Whoopee,' said Mango looking at the thickness of the manual. 'Homework. Can I go now?'

'Yes. Go forth and multiply.'

'You're the boss.' Mango opened the door to reveal a rather startled-looking Lana. 'Hello, dear.' He smiled. 'You know, back home in the Philippines, we have a saying: *Mama nogo spreeng – chokka fava.*'

'And what does that mean?'

'The literal translation is: "Don't drink from the waterhole, Mother – it's full of beans." But I suppose the English equivalent would go something like: "She who listens at keyholes can wind up with a thick ear."'

And with that, Mango swept majestically past her and out of the office.

'That's a fine thing, to be insulted by a walking banana.'

With all the dignity befitting his attire, Mango ignored her remark.

'What can I do for you, Lana?' Jack saw her eyes flick to the video wall and the frozen picture of Marian. He hastily hit the 'Off' button and the screens went dark.

'Er, Jack, I . . .'

'Yes?'

Lana was lost for words for a moment. She'd been caught out and seemed a little discomposed. 'I was just wondering if I could get you anything, a tea?'

Jack picked up the remote control and lightened the windows. 'I'll tell you what you *can* do, Lana, you can organize a meeting with the whole team. I want everyone assembled in the briefing area in ten minutes' time.'

'OK, Chief.'

'And a cup of tea could be just what the doctor ordered, thank you Lana.'

She turned to go.

'Oh, and this time could you make it strong and flat?'

'No froth?' She pouted, thrusting out her bottom lip.

But the little-girl performance had suddenly lost its appeal for Jack.

'No froth. What with this case being so tangled there are some things I'd like to keep uncomplicated.' Jack smiled and Lana walked uncertainly out of the room.

Jack called for order. 'Settle down, team!'

The briefing area was a part of the large operations room, equipped with flip charts, active whiteboards and the latest in display screens.

'Right. Thirteen murders. Thirteen men killed in apparently random and motiveless attacks all over the world. What do we know so far? That the targets are always top-ranking politicians; the killer always uses the same MO – exploding shell – and the victims are dispatched with a single shot to the head. We also have information that leads me to believe he is a Purple Trouser.' Jack touched a display screen and the image of the Hawaiian shirt from the CCTV footage appeared.

There was an interested murmur from the assembled police officers.

'This shirt was seen in both Pyongyang and Tokyo – and if you're wondering, it was official issue to Purple Trousers in the South China Sea campaign.'

One of the suits put up his hand.

'Yes?'

'Where can I get one?'

There was general laughter.

'You can enlist in the regular army then put yourself forward for Purple Trouser selection, part of which, I understand, involves six months' survival training in the Alps armed with nothing but a loin cloth and a bar of Swiss chocolate.'

'On second thoughts maybe I'll give it a miss.'

'Wise decision. Apart from that, information about our man is pretty thin. He may or may not still be sporting his platoon tattoo, a purple mop and bucket above the legend *Ut Expunge* – the mop and bucket denoting the cleansing nature of their missions.' Jack suddenly became grave. 'One thing I should warn you about. The Purple Trousers were greatly feared by the enemy for their ruthlessness. Bear in mind that the proud boast of the service was: "no one is left alive", and you'll begin to appreciate the mindset. When dealing with these chaps it pays to go carefully.'

Another hand went up. 'How do we know it's one killer? And how do we know it's a man?'

'We don't. Next question.'

'If he's a Purple Trouser there must be records. Doesn't every ex-serviceman have to register with the Home Office?'

'Congratulations, and that's exactly what we're going to be doing for the rest of the afternoon. Mango, over to you.'

Mango, still wearing his yellow catsuit, took centre stage. 'Clark and I have gone through the lists of possibles and whittled it down to one hundred and seventy individuals. Almost half of those are in Europe, then there are twenty-five in Australia, thirty-odd in Asia and the rest in North America. The UK's got over forty of them in total, with twenty or so in the Greater London area. So this afternoon we're going to see if we can shorten that list a little further. First we're going to hit the phones, then to follow up we'll be doing a bit of good old-fashioned foot-slogging.'

There was a collective groan from the team.

'Now, now, that's not the attitude that made Scotland Yard great. Myself and Clark will be taking care of those addresses in the inner London area. As for the rest of you, Jack will explain your designated areas of responsibility.'

Jack took the floor again. 'Thank you, Mango. Now then. Ruth, you will take our European suspects.'

Ruth brightened. 'I'm going to Europe?'

'Don't get too excited, it's a short list – chances are you'll be able to find out all you need to know via the phone. Mango's got the numbers.'

'Oh.'

'Lana, I want you to choose four people and tackle Australia and Asia.'

'You got it, Chief.'

'And as for the rest of you, I've divided you into units covering our own beloved country. Those individuals that you can't pin down, or those telephone numbers that no longer work, you will follow up. If that means spending the rest of the day, and even the night, tramping the length and breadth of Britain knocking on doors, so be it. Mango's got all the information you need.'

'Er, Chief?' It was Clark.

'Yes?'

'You haven't mentioned America.'

'No, I haven't. We're going to leave the United States alone for the time being. All right everyone – get to work.'

The team reluctantly split up and started organizing.

'Jack?' said Mango. 'What have you got against the Americans?'

'I don't want the Yanks getting wind of any of this just yet.'

'Why not?'

'Filial loyalty, probably misplaced.'

Mango looked at him strangely. 'You're the boss.'

Chapter 10

The monk, now impersonating a woman called Anne Heglie, whom he'd murdered in a nearby supermarket car park, drove down the quiet suburban street in Anne's solar-powered 4x4, quietly humming the Nunc Dimittis to himself. Underneath his sleeveless cotton shift, the cool steel of the rifle barrel against his right thigh was a comfort, while the tightness of the bungee cords around his left reminded him of his piety.

Lying on the seat next to him was a half-page piece, roughly torn from a newspaper, at which he glanced from time to time. Underneath the headline 'NICE-A-HOMES ON TRACK' was the following article: 'Yesterday, Nice-A-Homes managed to secure fifteen hectares of prime land from the Perforated Spleen of Jesus Abbey on Corbett. This puts Nice-A-Homes on track to achieve its aim of acquiring one hundred square kilometres of building land worldwide this year . . .'

Below this was a picture of two men shaking hands, with the caption: 'Horbert Manfreddo, Executive Director of Nice-A-Homes, seals the deal with Abbot Menendez, of the Perforated Spleen of Jesus Abbey, Corbett.'

The monk scowled at the picture.

The fools should never have tried to deceive me, he thought darkly. *It's their own fault. I have been a loyal and faithful servant to the order and this is the way they treat me. Well, they will regret their deceitfulness.*

He reached the bottom of the street and turned left. It was an old-fashioned neighbourhood that the early colonists had modelled on one of the localities they'd left behind in Britain. This particular area was called New Cheam. It was a neat little suburb with neat little houses looking out over neat little square lawns. Of course it was ridiculous to try to grow grass in the searing climate of Hancock, and most householders had given up the unequal struggle and astro-turfed their front gardens. But some of the tidy-minded citizens who lived here still persevered with the almost constant feeding and watering required to produce a little patch of green, tenderly nurturing their lawn like a favoured child.

Driving past a big white house with a drooping acacia tree outside, the monk slowed down and peered at the frosted glass of the front door. *I do hope the senator's home*, he thought. Passing the house, he pulled into a driveway two doors down and got out.

Here we are, number thirteen – unlucky for some.

Using the key on the murdered woman's keyring, he opened the front door of thirteen, Sid James's Drive.

Touching the door frame in an act of blessing as he entered, he closed the door behind him and paused for a moment listening for sounds of occupation. But the house was as silent as the grave. He smiled and offered up a prayer of thanks.

Finding the kitchen, he opened the refrigerator and was rewarded with a welcome sight: a six-pack of beer.

'Manna from heaven.'

Pulling one out and peeling it open, he drank the cold brew down in one, dropping the empty can in the sink. There was no need to worry about fingerprints – as a shape shifter he could change his own at will. Likewise, anyone looking for traces of tell-tale DNA on the empty beer can would be thoroughly confused to find only that of a bottle-nosed dolphin.

Having refreshed himself, the holy assassin belched and headed upstairs. Through the back bedroom window there was an almost unobstructed view into the garden of the big white house a couple of doors down, where a man was busy pruning his rose bushes. *You're in! Oh good, then my journey has not been in vain*. The monk's smile got wider.

Removing the rifle from its cradle strapped to his right leg, he laid it on the bed and loosened the spile on the bungee cords around his left thigh a couple of turns, to give himself some freedom of movement. Relief flooded through him, but his devotion to his Church forbade his taking pleasure in the sensation. Instead, lest he enjoy the feeling too much, he opened the wardrobe and untwisted one of the metal hangers inside. He'd been about to lash himself with the bare wire when the doorbell rang.

The monk froze. Perhaps it was just a door-to-door salesman, or the postman with a package. With luck, if he didn't answer, whoever it was would eventually lose interest and go away. But they didn't go away. They were annoyingly persistent, and the bell rang again and again.

Cursing quietly, the monk went across the landing into the master bedroom.

Peeping through the curtains he could see an old man standing on the path outside the front door. The man looked up and their eyes met.

'Anne? Is that you?'

'Anne' smiled and waved. 'I'll be right down,' she called.

'Bugger,' she muttered, slipping for a moment into the barrack-room language of the Purple Trousers. Clattering down the stairs, the monk paused and took a breath before opening the door.

The man must have been in his late-sixties and, like many of the colonists out here, his skin had taken on the colour of burnished bronze from the constant sunshine, along with a generous mottling of freckles. 'Oh, hello, Anne. Sorry to trouble you, but Janie saw that you'd come back from the supermarket and was wondering if you'd managed to pick up her prescription.'

'Anne' had to think quickly. 'I'm . . . er, so sorry. I must have forgotten.'

The man looked puzzled. 'Really? Oh dear. Well, Janie can't cope without her indigestion tablets. I don't know what she's going to do now.'

The old man scratched his head, muttering 'Oh dear' several times and gazing slyly at his neighbour. It was clear that he was keen for Anne to go back to the supermarket and do what she'd promised.

But she was unmoved.

'I'm sorry, but I really don't have time right now. I'll go later on.'

But this wasn't good enough for the old man.

'OK, well, perhaps if you give me back the prescription I can ask Andy the plumber to drop in for it. I saw he was about to leave for work as I came over here.'

'Anne' shook her head. 'No, really, don't worry, I'll get them this afternoon.'

'Well, Janie can't eat without her tablets, I don't think she can wait until this afternoon. Just give me back the prescription and I'll give it to Andy.'

But 'Anne' didn't have the prescription, and Janie's pills were lying in the handbag of a corpse dumped in a rubbish skip in a supermarket car park. Somehow the monk had to get rid of this old man so that he could get on with his assignment.

'Look, I've already said I'll go. Tell Janie to have a bit of patience.'

Just then there was the sound of an engine starting up. A few doors down, a white van reversed into the street. The old man turned and walked the few steps back across the front garden, waving his arms.

The driver saw him, waved back and drove towards him, pulling up outside Anne's house. Andy the plumber wound down his window.

'What's up, Keith?'

'Hello, Andy. Are you going anywhere near the supermarket? I gave Anne here Janie's prescription but she forgot to get it from the supermarket drug store, so I was wondering if you could get it for her?'

Andy killed the engine and got out. 'No problem, I'll be right next door – at the brewery. They've got a leaking cooling hose, and there's nothing worse than warm beer, especially in this heat.'

'You can say that again,' Keith replied.

Both shared a laugh.

Andy now turned to Anne and smiled broadly, obviously thrilled for an excuse to talk to her. 'And how are you, Anne?'

'Anne' smiled back. 'I'm fine, thanks, Andy.'

He ambled up the path to the house. 'I hear you forgot Janie's prescription. That's unlike you. But I know how hard it is to keep track of things when you're on your own. What you need is someone to look after you.' He leered at her suggestively; it was clear that he thought he was just the person for the job. 'Your problem is you've got too much going on in here.' He tapped the side of her head with his index finger.

Touch me again and I'll break your arm, 'Anne' thought.

Andy leaned against the door post and held out his hand. 'Just give me the prescription and I'll get it made up when I've finished. The job I've got on shouldn't take me more than about an hour.'

Once again, 'Anne' was on the spot.

'Well, that's sweet of you, Andy, but really there's no need. I've already told Keith I'll be going into town this afternoon.'

'But it's no trouble – the brewery's right next door to the supermarket.'

But 'Anne' was adamant. 'No, I insist. I always like to fulfil my promises.'

Just then, Andy's eyes dropped to 'Anne's' shoulder and the distinctive tattoo and legend *Ut Expunge* inscribed there. He looked nervously back into her eyes as she quickly covered the tattoo with her hand.

'Er, well . . . OK. Whatever you say.'

'Anne' smiled. 'Thank you for trying to help, goodbye.'

'Bye.'

Andy grabbed the old man's arm and marched him back towards his waiting van while 'Anne' closed the door.

The monk was furious with himself. *That was very sloppy of you, very sloppy indeed.* He rushed back upstairs and peered through the curtains to see what Andy would do next.

In the street, Andy and the old man were in discussion. Bemused by what he'd just seen on Anne's shoulder, Andy was sharing his concerns. Then Andy reached inside his van and pulled out a mobile phone.

Damn! The monk could have simply walked into the street and killed the two of them, but that would have drawn considerable attention to himself. No, now he had only two choices: he could either hurry up, do it quickly and get out, or he could abort. But quitting wasn't his style. He raced across the landing and grabbed the rifle.

'How did you get on yesterday, Mango?'

'Knocking on doors? Jack, there are some scary people out there.'

'I should imagine life is endlessly scary for a man in a canary-yellow catsuit.'

Mango folded his arms. 'For your information I went home and changed into something a little more . . . sombre before "interfacing" as Clark calls it, with the public.'

'So . . .?'

Mango shook his head. 'Of the individuals in the inner London area, twelve have regular day jobs, whose bosses can vouch for them, and two are on probation. I spoke to their parole officers and they've been keeping their weekly appointments like good little soldiers right across the time period we're interested in.'

'And the others?'

'I met their widows which, as you can imagine, was a lot of fun.'

'I'll bet they put all your "people person" skills to the test. How about the rest of the team?'

'No luck so far but some of them haven't reported back yet.'

'OK, keep me posted.'

Mango left and Jack swivelled round in his chair to look out of the window. He needed to think. Instinctively he reached for the bottom drawer of his desk. But in this new, state-of-the-art workplace all that was stacked under there was computer equipment. *I must remember to bring in a bottle of good old Scotch medicine.*

Deprived of his favourite medication, Jack decided instead to get intimate with his new office. Who knew what kinds of useful little gadgets he might find? Jamming his unlit pipe between his teeth he got up and moved over to the bookcase. It was full of edifying texts such as: *Police Procedures Relating to the Amended 67th Statute* and *Methodology, Theory and Dr Watson: The Scientific Approach to Law Enforcement.*

'Hmph,' Jack snorted derisively. 'That's like taking a scientific approach to making love.'

His eyes flicked along the spines of the other books on the shelves. *My God*, he thought, *not a single novel. What's a chap supposed to do for recreation?*

Jack's old bookcase had been crammed with the results of his third-favourite obsession – the second being Scotch – cheap crime novels, most of them written by P.M. Tenement. Tenement was one of Jack's most-loved detective authors, and once involved in one of his intricately woven narratives, Jack was released from his own malfunctioning life. Indeed the plots of several of his books had been useful in cracking difficult cases. Jack let his mind wander back over some of the great writer's works. One of the best was *The Case of the Harris Tweed Suit*, a story about money laundering in which a bespoke tailor is forced to sew the proceeds from a multi-million-pound bank raid into the suit of an innocent international businessman. Another good one was *Brush with Danger*, about a balding man's fatal attraction to grooming products.

'Tea?'

Lana broke into Jack's reverie. The sight of her chest straining the stitches of her sweater reminded him of another P.M. Tenement classic: *The Mountains of Succulus*.

'Thanks, Lana. Put in on the desk.'

She came into the room and placed the cup next to the keyboard. 'Will that be all?'

'For now, thank you.'

Looking like a dog who'd just realized it wasn't going to get its walk in the park, she turned to go.

'No, wait a minute.'

She turned back expectantly.

Jack's eyes had fallen on the black, slab-like base of the holographic map of the world sitting on a small sideboard next to the bookcase.

'How do you make this thing work?'

Thrusting out her chest, Lana followed it back into the room, all bright-eyed and businesslike.

'Well, now, first of all you have to turn it on.' She clicked a small switch on the base. Nothing happened.

'Let me.' Jack whacked it with his pipe.

There was a whirring as the map burst into life.

'I have a knack with machines,' he explained.

After more whirring and a few blinks and wobbles, a shimmering representation of the earth appeared, hovering over the featureless black slab.

'Very impressive, but what do I do with it?'

Lana touched the base again and a keyboard and mouse slid smoothly out of it. 'Press here and you engage the enlarge function.' She zoomed in on Britain. 'And this is the three-dimensional mouse.' Picking up the tiny instrument, she waved it around. 'With this you can go anywhere.' She demonstrated by giving Jack a swift tour right around the equator.

Jack was impressed. 'My word, twelve and a half thousand kilometres in the blink of an eye. What fun!'

Lana's eyes narrowed. 'It's a serious tool in the fight against crime.'

'Show me.'

'OK. For instance, clicking on a particular country brings up information about it.' Lana chose a small island in the Atlantic Ocean at random and a little bubble of information appeared above it: 'Tristan de Cunha. Remotest island on Earth. Volcanic in origin. Capital: Edinburgh. Pop. around 300 souls.'

'And to that you can also add information of your own. If, for instance, you were tracking a criminal across the globe and Tristan de Cunha was his last known location, you could simply type that in and it would be logged by the computer and passed on to the mainframe for analysis. The terminal regularly hooks up to the Yard's main computer which, as you know, is a huge database constantly receiving information from forces around the world. So, from this one little terminal you can access the very latest on crimes, wanted criminals and any other relevant information about the part of the world you're investigating.'

'Such as?'

'State of the economy of the chosen country, its political stability – or otherwise, geological activity and any major advances in evolution. You can even get a weather forecast.' She hit the return key.

'The weather, as usual, will be changeable. Hurricanes probable; thunder, lightning, torrential rain, all on the cards. Volcanic eruptions likely. Don't be surprised if it rains frogs and toads. Shitty, bloody awful weather for the foreseeable future, death by drowning a distinct possibility. Outlook: grim. If you have the misfortune to live here, the advice from the Central

Meteorological office is to stay inside and sandbag the doors, or better still, find a more hospitable island.'

'So whatever I input here ends up on the central police computer?' Jack enquired.

'This little light here –' she pointed at a small green LED set into one corner of the base '– lights up when the device is sharing information with the Yard mainframe. You can disable the connection by hitting the escape key.'

'Can it show me where all the latest murders have been?'

'Sure.'

She typed M-U-R-D-E-R onto the keyboard. Jack watched the little LED blink on, showing that the terminal was at that moment sharing information with Scotland Yard's main computer. After a few moments, a surge of red dots flowed over the map.

'It seems to be a popular pastime.'

'They're the locations of every recently reported murder. Now, to find the ones relevant to this case we're going to have to refine our results a little.'

She typed P-O-L-I-T-I-C-I-A-N and, after a wavering pause, most of the dots blinked out, leaving a haphazard smattering around the world.

'Of course not all of these will relate to our case but we can whittle the results down even further by specifying age, rank in government, cause of death, etcetera.'

'Try inputting "exploding head".'

'OK.'

Yet more of the red dots went out.

'You can even connect up the crime scenes by typing in "join dots".'

She did just that. A jagged red line now ran crazily across Asia.

'This is fun.' Jack grinned. 'I can see that this little gizmo is going to provide me with endless hours of entertainment.'

Lana looked suddenly severe. 'Like I said, it's not a plaything. It's a serious tool.'

'Of course it is. Thank you, Lana,' Jack said dismissively. But she simply smiled and stayed where she was. He tried a different tack. 'How did you get on with those numbers Mango gave you?'

'I'm about halfway through. I've been on it all morning.' She stretched languidly, raising her arms and thrusting out her breasts provocatively.

But Jack was unmoved. 'You'd better get back to work then. There's a killer on the loose, remember. Our job's to catch him before he strikes again.' Turning his back on her, he carried on looking for something readable in the bookcase, but still Lana wouldn't take the hint.

'Will that be . . . all?' she said, hovering in the doorway like the last reluctant guest at a party.

Jack looked up. 'Hmm?'

She took a step back into the room. 'I just wondered if there was anything else you'd like . . .' She fingered the remote window control sitting on the desk. 'You know . . . you look a little tense to me.' She untied her hair and shook it out. It fell in soft, inviting curls around her shoulders. 'Is there anything I can do?' Lingering on the final sound, she left her lips in the round OO shape and, perching seductively on the desk, gazed coyly up through her tousled hair. Jack thought she looked faintly ridiculous.

'You know,' he smiled, moving towards her. 'I think there is.'

Her eyes lit up. 'Oh, good.'

He leaned down and whispered in her ear, 'You can find Clark and send him in here.'

She started back looking shocked, hurt, affronted and angry all at the same time. She even managed to squeeze in a little bit of wistful yearning – it was quite impressive. Without saying a word, she got up off the desk and stalked out of the room. Jack didn't watch her go, but kept his back to her and pretended to carry on scanning book titles. Once he was sure she'd gone, he breathed a sigh and took another look at the holographic map. Every red dot told the sad story of a life violently snuffed out, although, as they all related to dead politicians, Jack found it hard to conjure any sympathy for them. But . . . Suddenly Jack frowned. Out in the middle of the Indian Ocean was a little red dot that shouldn't have been there. Clumsily engaging the zoom function, Jack enlarged the island. The green light on the base flickered on.

'Hancock,' he muttered. 'Why's Hancock lit up?'

He went back to his desk and shuffled through the papers on its surface until he found the list of locations of all the political murders – Hancock wasn't there. 'Bugger!'

'Chief?' Ruth stuck her head around Jack's door.

'Oh, come in. Anything to report from the European front?'

'Nothing. All suspects have regular jobs and their movements can be accounted for.'

'Good, that reduces our list a little further.'

She thumped a pile of paper on the desk. 'These are the immigration records you requested earlier and, before you ask, yes they're profiled *and* I've given you my opinion in writing.'

'Doesn't anybody talk any more?'

'I just thought you might like to consider my words at your leisure.'

'Leisure is for fat men in shell suits. Tell me what you've found.' Jack sat down and leaned back in his chair expectantly.

Ruth hesitated, unsure of where to start. 'Right.' She picked the top sheet off the pile of paper. 'I started looking at the immigration records of those arriving at the murder locations in the days leading up to the incidents and several names kept cropping up. After eliminating those who didn't appear before *each* event I was left with four individuals.'

'And?'

'They were all well-respected businessmen on bona-fide assignments.'

'Oh.'

'Then I had a look at the records of those leaving after the murders.'

'Yes?'

'Nothing again.'

'I hope this story has a happy ending,' Jack said.

'Then, I don't know why, but I started looking at the records of those who'd come *in* at that time.'

'*After* the murders?'

'Yes, and—'

'You found the foot that fitted the glass slipper?'

'Two names kept recurring. Twenty-four hours after almost every murder, there they were, like flies drawn to a carcass.'

'Are you going to keep me in suspense for ever or are you going to get to the punch line?'

'I did a little digging and found that these chaps have form – one spent some time on Weddell Island.'

'The South Atlantic penal colony?'

'That's right. And the other has recently come out of Beta-Max High Security on Shetland.'

'For?'

'Arms smuggling.'

'Do they have names?'

'The handles they usually go under are Jakob Lukowski and Lazlo Blaskowitz.'

Jack clamped his pipe a little more firmly between his teeth. 'You said they turned up after *almost* every murder. Which did they miss?'

'Turkmenistan, Kyrgyzstan, and the very latest one in Malaysia.'

'Correction, Hancock is the latest murder scene.'

'He's struck again?'

Jack nodded. 'Send Hancock police the latest mugshots of

these two individuals and ask them to keep a watch on the airports. If these two arms dealers *do* turn up, I'm to be informed immediately. I don't want them arrested, just watched.'

'Will do.' She turned to go.

'Oh, and Ruth?'

'Yes?'

'You know that feeling you had – when you started looking at the immigration records of those who'd arrived after the murders had been committed, even though it didn't seem to make sense?'

She nodded.

'It's called intuition. It's a detective's biggest asset.'

'Except if you're Lana.'

'I'd class what she's got as lethal weapons. Keep up the good work.'

It was the first compliment she'd had from her chief, and it felt good. Extremely pleased with herself, Ruth exited as Clark appeared.

'You wanted to see me, Chief?' The youth smiled and the braces on his teeth glinted in the artificial light.

'Clark, come in and close the door.'

He obeyed.

'How are you getting on with Mango?'

'Oh, quite well. We share an interest in fashion and have found a lot of common ground regarding the cut, drape and line of garments, but I'm afraid we part company when it comes to colour combinations. I'm from the classical tradition, whereas Mango . . .' He searched in vain for a rationale that could somehow explain the pairing of an orange tie with a lavender shirt.

Jack nodded sympathetically. 'I know, I know. Look, there's something I want you to do. Take a seat.'

Clark pulled a chair up to the desk and sat down.

'It's vitally important that the findings of this investigation remain within this department. What we can't afford is any kind of information leak. Now, the Secret Service has already been compromised so *that*, in effect, is why we're doing their job. The last thing we need is for our people to go telling all and sundry.'

'I haven't said anything, Chief.'

'I know *you* haven't said anything, Clark. It's some of the others I'm worried about. What do you think about Lana?'

Clark reddened slightly.

'Don't answer that. It's just that I have a suspicion she may not be exactly . . . how should I put it? Scrupulous in her efforts to maintain the integrity of this case within the department.'

'Are you saying she's a spy?'

'No, I'm saying that I'd like you to keep an eye on her and tell me if you notice her doing anything that you think looks . . . odd, out of the ordinary.'

Clark's eyes widened and he pushed the frames of his glasses back up his nose with an index finger. 'Are you giving me my own *assignment*?'

'Er, yes, I suppose I am. For now I just want you to watch her. Don't *do* anything, just watch. If she goes out for lunch, follow her, see where she goes, who she talks to. Now you know about Pattern Analysis, look for *patterns*: does she do the same thing every day, talk to the same people, visit the same place? She might make a phone call at a certain time, or meet some-one at a certain rendezvous. You get the idea?'

Clark was so excited he looked as if his birthday, Christmas and New Year had all come at once. 'If I'd thought yesterday that today I'd be a real detective. Wait till Mum hears about this!' He leapt up and made for the door.

Jack called him back. 'Er, Clark. This is between you and me. You must tell no one about this.'

His face fell. 'No one? Not even Mum?'

'Especially not Mum.'

'Oh.'

Clark left and Jack was at last alone with his thoughts. But not for long. A canister clattered into his vacuum tube terminal. Frowning, Jack opened the terminal and removed the message-carrying canister. Inside was a roughly torn scrap of paper with the legend 'Why are you still here?' scribbled on it.

Jack got up quickly and went over to the big window that looked out over the rows of desks in the operations room. Everyone was busy, nothing and no one was out of place. Hustling through the door, he stood outside his office, better to study the activity in the big room. But no one was giving anything away, no one even looked slightly furtive.

He looked down again at the scrap of paper in his hand. 'Why are you still here?'

The note seemed to imply that he should have been somewhere else. But where? Jack thought he knew.

Hobbling back into his office, he went straight to the holographic map. The blue-green globe of the Earth was still turning slowly in the air above the solid black base.

Picking up the mouse, he zoomed in on Corbett. The little green LED in the base lit up but, unlike Lana's earlier demonstration, no bubble of information appeared above the island. Jack hit the return key on the keypad as Lana had done before. An information box appeared: 'Corbett – no information is currently available on this island.'

Once again the green LED flickered.

Now isn't that interesting? Jack thought. *Who the hell could be powerful enough to keep details of Corbett off the main computer? If this is your doing, Michaelmas, I take my hat off to you – you must be quite a guy.*

Chapter 11

First thing the next morning, Commissioner Lindsay barged into Jack's office carrying a sheaf of newspapers. 'This is getting beyond a joke!'

Jack looked up. 'Ah, I see you've heard the news.'

'Why wasn't I told about this latest murder?'

Freddy threw the newspapers down on Jack's desk. Jack picked one up and read the headline. '"HANCOCK SENATOR'S HEAD EXPLODES WHILE PRUNING ROSES!" That must have been a shock for his gardener.'

'This isn't funny, Jack. Three more politicians have been murdered in as many days! There was that government minister on Descartes, killed at a masked ball – *in front of two hundred guests*! Then that parliamentary private secretary to the premier on Cleese, shot in his bath, and now this! And that's not to mention those four unfortunates assassinated in Pakistan. Do you know how embarrassing this is for Scotland Yard? For me?'

'Yes, I'll bet the victims' families are embarrassed too.'

Freddy let it go. 'The World Council are baying for my blood. I want to know what you're doing about it.'

'Your blood or this case?'

The commissioner leaned across the desk, grabbed hold of Jack's tie and pulled him close. 'Don't piss me around, little brother. I need results!'

'Speaking of blood, you're constricting its supply to my brain, and without that prize organ we're both in trouble.' The commissioner let him go and Jack loosened the knot. 'Have some patience, Freddy. With each new murder, our man gives himself away a little more.'

'We can't afford to wait until the world is littered with dead politicians.'

'It might make the place a little more amenable.'

'Can't you be serious for a moment?'

'I find humour invaluable in these circumstances.'

'Perhaps the knowledge that the Americans are now in on the case will take the smile off your face.'

For once, Freddy was right. 'They're *what*?'

'There was nothing I could do. You know what the Yanks are like – how they hate to lose. They've been lobbying every member of the council, and believe me they can be brutal. Because of the "incompetence" – their word, not mine – with which this case has been prosecuted so far, they have argued that it would be in the "best interests of the world community" for them to take it over.'

'The best interests of their overinflated sense of self, more like,' Jack snorted.

'If it hadn't been for Councillor McClaggen, they would have come in and just grabbed the case from under our noses.'

'So what's going to happen?'

'A compromise. One of their men is joining us.'

'Who?'

'A Lieutenant Matthias. Apparently he's one of the New York department's top officers. He's arriving this afternoon.'

Jack looked wistful for a moment. 'Do you think they have Garibaldis in America?'

'What?'

Jack shook his head. 'Nothing. And what about you?'

'I'm on probation. Any more killings and I'm history, and you know what that means.'

'Enlighten me.'

'My deputy, Steven Mellinger, takes over.'

Jack sat up straight. 'Mellinger?'

Freddy nodded. 'Presumably I don't have to remind you that he's not a great fan of yours.'

Jack pulled out his pipe and clamped it between his teeth. 'He was the berk in charge of Eagle Patrol on East Timor. He's never forgiven me for rescuing him and his entire platoon after he'd walked straight into an ambush. He thinks I humiliated him. He hates me.'

Freddy smiled grimly. 'And is he the man you want to be responsible to?'

Both brothers stared hard at each other for a long moment.

There was a peremptory knock on the door, after which it opened immediately.

Ruth stood in the doorway, carrying a buff-coloured folder. 'Oh, sorry to interrupt.'

Jack waved her in. 'That's all right. What have you got?'

'Interviews from the Hancock police. A plumber who lives in the same street reported that one of his neighbours had been behaving oddly. The neighbour in question lived in the house next door but one to the senator's which, from powder residue the forensics team found on the back-bedroom window sill, has been identified as the site from where the gun was fired. It seemed this neighbour – a woman – had suddenly gained a tattoo: a purple mop and bucket.'

Jack ran his hands through his thinning hair. 'I have a sinking feeling.'

'And guess what,' Ruth continued, 'this same woman's body was found in a rubbish skip in the car park of the local supermarket ten minutes *before* she talked to the neighbour and fifteen minutes *before* the senator was murdered. And to top it all, the DNA of an Atlantic bottle-nosed dolphin was found on an empty beer can in the woman's kitchen.'

'Oh, bugger.'

'That was my first reaction.'

The commissioner looked confused. 'What? What?'

Jack leaned his elbows on the desk and rested his head in his hands. 'You're not going to like it.'

Freddy looked from Ruth to Jack and back again. 'For Pete's sake, will somebody tell me what's going on?'

Jack gazed up at his brother. 'The good news is that our killer is still sporting his Purple Trousers brigade tattoo – a purple mop and bucket above the legend *Ut Expunge*. That at least means we're on the right track.'

'Well, that's good, isn't it?' Freddy smiled vaguely.

But Jack remained deadly serious. 'The bad news is that he's a shape shifter.'

Freddy's smile vanished and he turned white.

'Ruth, can you get the commissioner a chair?'

She dragged up a chair from the corner and Freddy sank gratefully into it.

'And what about a bullet, Ruth?' Jack sighed. 'Have Hancock forensics turned up any useful fragments?'

'They're still working on it.'

'Get an APB out and circulate pictures of the woman. It's unlikely he's still masquerading as her but you never know, we might get a break. Put an image of the Purple Trousers tattoo out as well.'

'Right away, Chief.'

'And send Clark in here.'

'Will do.'

Ruth was about to leave the room when she turned back. 'Oh, Chief?'

'Yes?'

'It may be nothing, but around the time the supermarket murder was committed, some people reported seeing a monk hanging around the car park.'

Jack frowned. 'A monk?'

Ruth shrugged. 'I'm only passing it on.'

'Very well – logged and noted.'

Commissioner Lindsay looked up at his brother with desperation in his eyes. 'What am I going to do, Jack?'

Jack leaned back in his chair and sucked thoughtfully on his unlit pipe. 'I don't usually recommend suicide, but in your case I'd say it would be rather a good career move.'

Freddy stared despairingly into the middle distance. 'I've got a press call with Chairman McClaggen in half an hour. What do I say?'

'I'd be more worried about what *he* was going to say.'

'What am I going to tell them, Jack?'

Jack considered for a moment. 'Well one thing you're not going to tell them is that he's a shape shifter, there's no point starting a panic. I suppose you could let them have the fact that he's a Purple Trouser and still proudly wearing his tattoo.'

'What else?'

'If I were you I'd just let the chairman talk. The way he mangles the English language, no one's going to know what's going on.'

'But we *don't* know what's going on!' He paused and narrowed his eyes. 'Unless you're holding something back.'

Jack froze. 'What do you mean by that?'

Freddy rose threateningly. 'I'm not sure you're showing your entire hand, Jack. I'd like to know what you've got tucked up your sleeve.'

'My shirt cuffs,' Jack replied levelly.

'Don't be clever with me. First of all you take on new staff without my say so—'

'New staff?'

'The tea boy.'

'Oh, you mean Clark.'

'Have you checked his credentials?'

'Well we haven't exactly been intimate, but I trust him if that's what you mean.'

'One of your gut feelings?'

Jack smiled. 'When one is "close to the street", instinct is what one tends to rely on most heavily.'

Freddy, the pale pink of his cheeks deepening a shade, carried on. 'And now this – being kept in the dark about this latest murder.'

'Freddy, I was going to tell you first thing. It's not my fault the journalists beat me to it.'

'How much of an idiot do you think I felt to be rung up by the *Today* programme and asked for my reaction to a murder I didn't even know had been committed?'

Jack sucked a breath between his teeth. 'Yes, I heard that interview. You didn't acquit yourself terribly well.'

'AAARGH!' Freddy lunged at Jack again, but this time Jack slid sideways and the commissioner's nose hit Lana's call button.

'Freddy, if I had to relate to you every little bit of information, every half lead we had on this case, or ask for your permission to do anything, you'd be seeing more of me than your wine merchant. Believe me, what I know for certain I pass straight on to you. For instance – your nose is bleeding.' Jack opened a drawer and handed him a handkerchief.

Freddy took it and pulled himself to his feet. Holding the handkerchief to his nose, he stared hard at his brother. 'You're enjoying this, aren't you?' he said, nasally.

Jack shook his head. 'It gives me no pleasure to see you in pain, Freddy. Look, you're just going to have to trust me. Let me do my job and don't get so worked up about everything – you'll only do yourself a mischief.'

Lana came running into the office.

Jack beamed at her. 'And here's our little American colleague. Tell you what, Freddy, why don't you ask her to give you a nice relaxing massage? I hear she's awfully good.'

Lana scowled daggers at Jack and took her place next to Freddy. With her at his side the commissioner looked more sure of himself.

'From now on, Jack, I want to know everything. Every little bit of information that comes in, I don't care how small. I want to know what you know. I want to be inside your head.'

Jack pursed his lips. 'I hope you've got a strong stomach.'

Freddy growled and turned to go.

'Freddy, there's one thing that really worries me.'

The commissioner stopped in the doorway and turned back to face his brother.

'I've been meaning to ask you this for some time now: how do you manage to achieve such a close shave?' Jack rubbed his hand over his dark blue and stubbly chin. 'The only razor blades I can get hold of aren't really up to the task.'

Freddy took a few steps into the room and glared at him. 'If I were you Jack, I'd start getting serious about this case. *Deadly* serious. There's more than just your future as a detective riding on it.' He marched out of the office, closely followed by Lana.

Putting his hands behind his head Jack exhaled thoughtfully. It had been a troubling visit.

A moment later Clark sheepishly put his head around the door. 'Is the commissioner all right?' he asked, nervously pushing his glasses back up his nose.

'He's just discovered job insecurity; it's a new and unsettling experience for him. You might be interested to know that we have a snippet more info on our mystery Purple Trouser. Run your list of possibles through PA again, and this time you can delete anyone who isn't a shape shifter.'

'Wow! Our man's a shape shifter?'

'It would explain a lot.'

'I'll get on to it right away.'

'Wait, before you do that, come in and close the door.'

Clark obeyed.

'Have you turned up anything on Lana?'

Clark immediately looked shifty and pulled a notebook out of his pocket. 'Well, yesterday lunchtime I followed her out of the building, like you said.'

'Did she see you?'

'Not a chance.'

'Good.'

Clark flipped open the notebook and read. 'Twelve-fifty, target leaves the building and proceeds in a south-easterly direction. Twelve-fifty-two, target opens handbag, pulls out handkerchief, blows nose. Twelve-fifty-two and thirty seconds, target closes bag. Twelve-fifty-three—'

'Clark,' Jack interrupted. 'Your attention to detail is commendable, but in this instance, it's . . . how can I put this tactfully?' Jack thought for a moment. 'WRONG!'

Clark looked a little hurt, put his notebook away and carried on. 'To cut a long story short, I followed her all the way down to a restaurant on the river.'

'Which one?'

'Tate's.'

'My, she has expensive tastes.'

'But wait. After she'd gone inside, guess who turned up in his limo?'

'The King of Siam?'

'The commissioner!'

Jack smiled. 'Of course he did. Thank you, Clark, give yourself a raise.'

Clark beamed. 'Thank *you*, sir.'

After Clark left, Jack dimmed the windows, went over to the bookcase and pulled out a bottle of high-quality single malt hidden behind *Police Procedurals Vol IV*. He needed to think.

Downstairs, the press room was full to the brim with eager reporters all bursting with questions.

World Council Chairman McClaggen and Commissioner Lindsay filed into the room, which exploded in a riot of camera flashes.

Jack sneaked in at the back, eager to see the show.

McClaggen cleared his throat. 'Good evening . . .'

The commissioner muttered something to him.

'Sorry, make that good morning.'

The chairman looked at his watch sadly. 'It seems I'm still on Vancouver time.'

Muted laughter from the assembled press corps.

'Maybe "hello" is the safer option in the circumstances. So, ladies and gentlemen of the press – hello!'

'Hello!' they chorused back.

'Now then, you're probably wondering why I've called you all here today . . .'

More laughter.

He may be an idiot, Jack thought, *but he's a good showman*.

'No, but really, folks, this is a serious matter we're dealing with. Twenty high-ranking politicians killed. Among them two of my closest friends. Rest assured we are doing all in our power to apprehend the person or persons responsible.'

A forest of hands went up in the audience.

'Yes – you, sir.'

'Actually it's "Ms".'

'Oh, sorry, my dear.'

'Melinda Burke, *Daily Mule*. World Council Chairman, are these murders the work of a lone gunman, or could it rather be that these killings mark the resurgence of organized crime in the shape of the Syndicates?'

'Well now, as far as the Syndicates go, we're pretty sure they hit the buffers of the crime railroad a long time ago.'

Seated beside the chairman, Commissioner Lindsay nodded in agreement.

'The war put paid to them, and it's thanks to the vigilance of men like the commissioner here that they've never been able to regain a foothold in the fabric of society. The Syndicates sailed their Ship of Fools across the Ocean of Felony and were wrecked on the Reef of Justice. Of course, some of them managed to reach the Sandbank of the Friendly Witness

Programme, but most drowned in the Bay of Incarceration. Let me tell you a story . . .'

Jack settled back in his seat. *Here we go.*

'A long time ago, a small boy was sitting by a stream in the Rocky Mountains, regarding a beautiful butterfly flitting over the sparkling waters. The boy watched this dazzling creature dip and dart in the sunshine, and thought how beautiful it was. Then, quite suddenly, a trout rose and took the butterfly, just like that! And the boy thought, well, the trout needs to eat and, in its own way, it too is a beautiful creature. Then, just as the boy was beginning to admire the trout even more than the butterfly, a heron dived down and picked up his fish. That boy was me, ladies and gentlemen, and I never forgot the lesson I learned that day.' The World Council chairman finished with a wistful smile. A bemused silence fell on the press corps.

Commissioner Lindsay cleared his throat. 'Thank you, Chairman. Any more questions?'

A large man put up his hand.

'Yes, you.'

'James Jefford – *The Onlooker*. This is actually a question for you, Commissioner.'

'Very well, go ahead.'

'What do we know about this killer? What lies behind his actions? Do you have any clue as to his motives?'

Freddy smiled benignly. 'James, if we knew the answers to all those questions maybe we'd already have caught him. Of course I can't tell you everything we know for fear of jeopardizing the investigation, but what I can tell you is that our suspect is a Purple Trouser.'

There was a buzz of excitement around the room.

The commissioner's voice rose over the clamour. 'We know this because an individual wearing the mop and bucket tattoo was spotted in the vicinity of Senator Falk's residence on Hancock, minutes before the senator was murdered.' He held up a photograph copy of the famous Purple Trousers insignia. 'I think you're all familiar with this image: a mop rampant beside a bucket, above the legend, *Ut Expunge*, which roughly translates as "Who Scrubs, Wins."'

More excitement and frenzied scribbling. Now every hand in the room was raised.

The commissioner picked out someone in the third row. 'Yes.'

'Terence Kilkahy – *The Wire*. I have a question for the chairman.'

The commissioner groaned inwardly.

'OK, Terry,' McClaggen said brightly, 'fire away. Oops, pardon the pun.'

'Yes, um, World Council Chairman, I was just wondering how you feel about what's been going on. I mean, every one of the victims has been a high-profile politician. Aren't you a little concerned for your own personal safety? And if so, have you changed your daily routine in any way?'

'I look at it this way, Terry: I was elected to do a job by the good citizens of this world. If I hide myself away like a penguin in the woods, what sort of a message does that send out? Look, we all know you can't make an omelette without breaking heads, so let me make one thing completely clear: I would rather walk barefoot through a chicken farm than stick my head in the sand of oblivion. No sir, hell will be a coffee shop before Chairman McClaggen uses Satan's bathroom.'

'Er, thank you, sir . . . that's very clear.' The wide-eyed journalist resumed his seat.

Freddy scanned the room one final time. 'OK, I think that about wraps things up for today . . .' He was already out of his seat and had started collecting together his notes when a thin woman wearing large, black-rimmed glasses and with hair that seemed too big for her head rose to her feet. A sense of expectancy filled the room.

Seeing her, Freddy moaned softly and sat back down,

clutching feebly at his chest. Even Chairman McClaggen looked worried.

'Gelda Longhorn, *The Post*.'

'Yes, Gelda, and what's your question?' Freddy said, with the air of a man being escorted to the scaffold.

'Despite your brazen assurances to my colleague on the *Mule*, I'd like to know why, in all of your official releases about this case, not one mention has been made of the Syndicates and their obvious involvement.'

'Now, Gelda—' Freddy began.

But Gelda hadn't finished. 'It seems clear to me and, judging by my bulging postbag, also to my readers, that these murders are a sure sign that the Syndicates are back in business. What are you covering up?'

Freddy pulled out a handkerchief and mopped his brow. 'Trust me, Gelda, we're not hiding anything.'

'That I should trust a policeman who has such close ties to business *and* politics is debatable.'

There was muted laughter from the press corps. Freddy turned a deeper shade of puce and a thin trickle of blood escaped his nose and ran down his top lip.

'Now, then, Gelda,' said Chairman McClaggen in a conciliatory tone, 'it seems to me you're barking up the wrong lamp-post.'

'Thank you, Chairman, your homespun backwoods philosophy may be a hit back home, but I'm afraid it cuts no ice over here and will not succeed in obfuscating the true nature of what is happening, which is, I am convinced, a resurgence of the Syndicates. Why is Scotland Yard protecting them? What are you covering up?'

Freddy, holding a handkerchief to his nose to stop the bleeding, decided enough was enough and went on the attack. 'To suggest that Scotland Yard is somehow in league with the Syndicates is an abuse of press freedom! I am all for getting to the truth, Gelda, but I'm afraid if you persist in these unfounded allegations of police involvement with organized crime, I will have no option but to declare this investigation closed to the press.'

There was uproar in the room.

'That goes against the constitution!' Gelda retorted.

'The constitution allows me to close an investigation to public scrutiny for forty-eight hours, if . . . and I quote: "that scrutiny is deemed overly intrusive and therefore considered to be in danger of jeopardizing said investigation".'

'I repeat my question. What are you hiding?'

Freddy, still clutching the blood-soaked handkerchief to his nose, collected his sheaf of notes and photographs and got up to leave. 'This briefing is now over.'

To the jeers and catcalls of the assembled press, Commissioner Lindsay and Chairman Cole McClaggen made their way out of the press room.

Jack, still seated at the back, shook his head. *Not your best performance, Freddy.*

One by one the newsmen and -women left the room to go and file their copy, until only Jack and Gelda Longhorn were left.

He walked slowly down the neatly laid-out lines of plastic stacking-chairs until he reached her row. There was something he just had to know.

As he edged along towards her, Jack was happily surprised to see that she was scribbling something in a notebook.

'I'm glad to see that someone still uses good old pen and paper. I thought all modern journalists now filed their copy on micro-computers.'

She stopped writing and looked up, peering at him over the top of her large, round glasses. 'Have we met?'

'Jack Lindsay, how do you do?' He extended his hand.

She studied it for some moments, then met his eyes again. 'You're the detective in charge of this case.'

'That's right.'

'You're also the brother of the police commissioner.'

'Right again.'

She smiled without mirth. 'I see that nepotism is still alive and well and living amongst the great and the good.' She went back to her article.

Jack sat down next to her. 'I doubt you'll believe me when I tell you I'm not on Freddy's side.'

'If I don't believe Freddy, why should I believe his brother? In my experience mendacity usually runs in families,' she said coldly.

'It's just that it seems to me that you may know something I don't, and at the moment, any help would be most welcome.'

She stopped again, removed her glasses, and looked at him in amused astonishment. 'You're telling me that you don't know what's going on?'

Jack shrugged. 'I usually find that candour is the best policy when dealing with the press.'

At last she put down her pad and pen and turned in her seat to face him. 'Well, well, an honest policeman, how refreshing. Perhaps you're not like your brother after all.'

'Well he *has* got a better tailor.'

'It's obvious what's going on. A child could see that this is the work of the Syndicates. The carefully targeted killings; the absence of clues. Either this killer is supremely efficient, or the Syndicates have bought off the relevant police forces. I leave it up to you which is the more likely scenario.'

'The killer is a shape shifter.'

The journalist's mouth dropped open. 'Is that *on* the record?'

'You print that and either you'll be hailed as a champion of free speech, or you'll start a public panic – I leave it up to you which is the more likely scenario.'

She smiled. 'Very well. I won't use it – yet.'

'Thank you.'

Lightly tapping her front teeth with the arm of her glasses, she studied his face carefully. 'I find you very interesting, Mr Lindsay, not at all like your bloated and dyspeptic brother.'

'Freddy's problem is that he's never been able to say no. Second-helping Freddy we used to call him.'

'What is it you want?'

'Information. Who's your source?'

'I may have worked the whole thing out for myself,' she said coyly.

'If that's the case, have you figured out a motive?'

She pulled the corners of her mouth down. 'It looks to me like some sort of destabilization technique. Like in the old days, when the Syndicates would move to a new location, kill the local headman to cause a panic and then put their own man in charge. Who, after brutally putting down any opposition, would go on to milk the population dry with ever-increasing demands for protection money.'

Jack nodded his agreement. 'That's what I thought too, at first. The earlier killings, I admit, look like classic Syndicate hits, but what about these latest killings – a government minister, a senator and a PPS? It would be a stretch to think of a parliamentary private secretary as a headman. Besides, why kill four in Pakistan, and why bother with the colonies when they're full of retired people looking for a quiet life?'

'What are you getting at?'

Jack eased round in his seat to face her. 'Up to and including the incident in Venezuela, all the victims were leaders: presidents, prime ministers. But ever since, from Turkmenistan on, the targets have been lesser mortals – people whose death, frankly, makes no difference to the political landscape at all. I think our man's changed tactics and I don't know why. I was wondering if you did.'

She thought for a few moments, toying with her glasses and chewing her bottom lip. Finally she said, 'Look, you've been honest with me, and I respect that. I can't tell you who my source is, because I don't know myself. He contacts me by e-mail, always unsolicited. And, no, I don't have his address – he's always very careful to exclude it from his communications. But I can give you a name.'

Jack raised his eyebrows. 'That would be a start.'

'Verrat.'

'Verrat?'

She nodded.

Jack frowned. 'You said *he* – how do you know it's a man?'

'He signs his missives: "Brother Verrat".'

'Brother?' Jack sat up. Something Ruth had said earlier came back to him. 'As in monk?'

'Who knows? It's probably an affectation.'

'Hmm.' Jack instinctively reached for his pipe and clamped it between his teeth.

Gelda looked aghast. 'You're not going to light that thing in here, are you?'

'No, no.' Jack smiled. 'It's just that I think better when I'm playing with something.'

'So like a man.'

Jack shrugged in a self-deprecatory way. 'What's in these e-mails?'

'Nothing much. As a journalist I'm used to making copy out of the thinnest of material. All he's really said so far is that the Syndicates are involved and that the police know about it.'

'And you believe him?'

'I know it's neither very good journalistic practice, nor terribly scientific. But Brother Verrat is voicing a worry I've had for some time. Sometimes you just have to go on gut feeling.'

Jack nodded. 'I know what you mean.'

'And then there's his name, Verrat – to me it sounds like veracity.' She looked him in the eye. 'A commodity in short supply around here.'

'I can't argue with that. Thank you, Gelda, thank you very much indeed. You've been most helpful.' Jack stood up.

'You're leaving?'

'No peace for the wicked. Look, if your cloistered corres-pondent should contact you again, please let me know.' He was about to hand her his official Scotland Yard business card, but thought twice about it and put it back in his pocket. 'No, on second thoughts, perhaps I should contact you.'

Gelda raised an eyebrow. 'Someone looking over your shoul-der?'

Jack cleared his throat and scratched his ear with the stem of his pipe. 'I know you could have a field day with all this, but please, I'm begging you, don't print a thing until I give you the say-so.'

'You have my word on it.' She extended her hand regally. Jack didn't know whether to shake it or kiss it. He chose the former option.

'Nice to meet you, Gelda. I'll be in touch.'

'I'll look forward to it.'

And with that, Jack limped thoughtfully back towards the lift and his third-floor office.

Chapter 12

'Chief!'

Jack dragged himself away from the latest pathology report on the government minister killed at the ball on Descartes. 'What is it, Clark?'

'Regarding our shape shifter, he was part of an elite squad of Purple Trousers—'

'An elite of the elite?'

'Er, yes. It was a top-secret organization, basically made up of a load of genetically altered individuals. According to information just released under the fifty-year rule, the military staked out the abortion clinics and offered expectant mothers a large payout if they kept their baby to term and agreed to genetic experimentation on their unborn foetuses.'

'Turning them into shape shifters, genetically predisposed to commit murder.' Jack shook his head. 'Where does a man go after leaving the force, when he's been designed to kill?'

Clark shrugged. 'I doubt that sort of background is conducive to leading a quiet life.'

'I suppose we should be thankful that the war ended such practices.'

'Yeah,' Clark said quietly.

'So, what about this doubly elite squad?' Jack asked.

'Well, it was officially called Ghost, but because of their useful knack of impersonating women they acquired the nickname "the Dame Ednas".'

'Excuse me?'

'After a well-known female impersonator of the twentieth century.'

'I see.'

'And they don't feature on any of the available databases.'

'So I don't suppose you have any current addresses?'

Clark looked crafty and shoved his glasses back up his nose. 'You know, this Pattern Analysis thing is a really useful tool.'

'So people tell me,' Jack sighed. He wished that, just for once, someone would get straight to the point.

'It allows you to look for all kinds of things,' Clark continued, 'like troops who should be there, but aren't.'

Jack scratched his head. 'Now I'm confused.'

Clark's smile widened. 'It's simple, really. I took the roll of all Purple Trousers who'd entered the South China Sea campaign and compared it with the record of those who survived. Then I filtered out those men whose deaths I could verify, plus those who had been discharged, and was left with around fifty men who had completely disappeared for no apparent reason. They have to be the Dame Ednas.'

'Clever boy.'

'I thought the military would be sneakier than that – to try and keep it hidden, you know?'

'Well, they do say that military intelligence is an oxymoron.'

Clark's grin disappeared. 'My father was in intelligence.'

'Ah, well they also say it's the exception proves the rule,' Jack said. 'I'll bet your father was damned good at his job,' he added, back-tracking speedily.

'I've got a printout of their last known addresses and phone numbers here,' Clark huffed sulkily.

Jack thought he'd better try to make amends. 'Pull up a chair and grab a phone.'

Clark was suddenly once again all wide-eyed and puppyish. 'What, here? With you?'

'Yes, here, with me. Come on, shake a leg.'

Clark grabbed a chair and pulled it up to Jack's desk. Jack

pushed a telephone towards him and ripped the printout in half. 'You take the top and I'll take the bottom.'

'But Chief, some of these people live abroad. Shouldn't we contact the relevant authorities and let them handle it?'

Jack turned to him. 'Look, Clark, we've got a murderer to catch, and we're running out of time. Besides that, a lot of these police forces wouldn't know what to do with the information even if we told them.'

'But, the Americans—'

'Especially the Americans. I am not having some smug Yank with his handmade suit and bulging wallet coming in and taking this case away from us. Which reminds me, we have to get down to Tommy Cooper this afternoon.' He looked at his wrist. Freddy's family looked back at him. 'Bloody hell. How are you supposed to tell the time on this thing? Clark, what time is it?'

'Er, nearly eleven.'

'Right, no time to lose. Start dialling.'

Clark dialled the first number.

After working their way steadily through the list, crossing off any that were gainfully employed – none; hospitalized – the vast majority (for mental health reasons); dead, or in jail, they had whittled down the list to five names.

'Now we're getting somewhere.' Jack turned to Clark. 'Who have you got left?'

'Jonty Finch and Trevor Mason.'

'And I've got Nathaniel McCoy, Gilbert Dobbins and Martin Seacoal. Chances are, Clark, we're looking at the name of our killer. Now then, what do we know about each of these men?'

Clark screwed up his eyes in thought. 'Well . . . according to his ex-fiancée, Finch is a drunken womanizer.'

'I'll bet she didn't put it quite so politely.'

'Er, no.'

'So what can we glean from that?'

'Um, I'd say that it was unlikely a drunk would be organized enough to pull off this kind of operation and to remain undetected for so long.'

'Very good, let's cross him off. As for Martin Seacoal, he sounds as crazy as a set of spoons. He's got a criminal record as long as your arm. Been in and out of prison for drug dealing, possession of unauthorized firearms and most recently for impersonating an orang-utan and punching a policeman in a bar.'

'Unlikely our man would draw attention to himself like that.'

'My thoughts exactly.' Jack crossed his name off too. 'That leaves us with Nathaniel McCoy, Gilbert Dobbins and your Trevor Mason. According to this printout, McCoy and Dobbins were last seen in North Africa – Morocco to be exact, but the authorities there have no record of them for the last six months, so that would place them high on our list of people to talk to. What have you got on Mason?'

Clark studied his half of the computer printout. 'Another unknown quantity, sir. Never been in trouble with the law, never put a foot wrong since leaving the brigade.'

Jack rubbed his nose with his pipe stem. 'What's his last known location?'

'Well, Mason's interesting. After following a long trail of telephone numbers, I had to give up.'

'So, why is he interesting?'

'The last address anyone had for him was an abbey.'

Jack's eyebrows shot up. 'He's our man!'

'What?'

'Monks! It's been staring me in the face all this time. Everybody's been talking about monks, but I haven't been listening. Of course – a shape-shifting monk. That would give him almost perfect cover. Which abbey?'

Clark consulted his notes. 'The Abbey of the Perforated Spleen of Jesus on . . .'

'Don't tell me – Corbett!'

Clark looked up, amazed. 'How did you know?'

'It all comes back to Corbett. What's the name of the order?'

'I'm sorry?'

'The monks, what are they collectively called?'

Clark stared at his notes again. 'Um . . . would it be Ave Verum?'

'Verum?' Jack stood and started pacing, muttering to himself. 'Verum . . . Verum . . . Verrat? It's close, but why should our killer give himself away like that?'

'Are we going to Corbett?' Clark asked excitedly.

'No, *we* are not going to Corbett,' Jack said.

Clark's face folded in disappointment.

'What else do we know about him?'

Clark peered at his notepad. 'Um . . .'

'Give it here!' Jack grabbed it impatiently and scanned the list of addresses and numbers. 'What's this?' He stabbed at the notepad with his pipe stem.

'What's what?'

'This!' Jack jabbed repeatedly at the page. 'There's an Isle of Wight address next to Mason's name.'

Clark took it back and looked at it again. 'That's his last registered address in this country. According to this information, the place is still in his name.'

'Really?' Jack smiled slyly.

'Are we going to the Isle of Wight, sir?' Clark asked hopefully. Although it wasn't exactly an exotic island, it would at least be an adventure.

Jack looked down sadly at his eager junior. 'Have you ever been to the Isle of Wight, Clark?'

'No, sir.'

'It's stuck in a time warp. Several thousand years ago their civilization was what you might call cutting edge: they had the flint knife, antler-bone fish-hooks and nascent educational quangos. But now it's fallen somewhat behind the times. Oh, it's quaint and old-fashioned in a fusty sort of way, but not the sort of place you'd really want to stay for any length of time, not unless a long, slow decline into drooling senility is what you're looking for.'

'So we're not going?'

'No. Trevor Mason hasn't been there for some time. Nor is he likely to turn up there in the foreseeable future.'

'So are we just going to ignore it?'

Jack started filling his pipe with Old Hobson's Curiously Fragrant. 'No, as I've told you before, Clark, every lead should be followed up, and this is no exception.' He smiled inscrutably.

At Terminal Three – international arrivals – of London, Tommy Cooper International airport, Lieutenant Matthias, fit, well fed and one of New York's finest police minds, stepped off the airliner and straight into a bruising encounter with British bloody-mindedness. Rushing down to passport control ahead of the queue, he flashed his police badge.

'Official business, New York Police Department.'

'Passport please, sir,' the unsmiling immigration official demanded.

'Excuse me?'

'Passport, please.'

'I don't think you could have heard me. I'm a policeman on important business.'

'Yes, and I should be at lunch, but I'm not, I'm here talking to you, marvellous isn't it? Passport, please.'

The lieutenant sighed heavily and rummaged through his flight bag until he'd found the relevant document. 'Here.'

'There, that wasn't so painful, was it?' The official took the passport, muttering, 'Bloody Yanks, think they own the world.'

The official studied the image in the lieutenant's passport closely for some moments, then looked up at him gravely. 'If you'd care to wait there, sir.' He pointed to a spot in front of his desk.

'What?'

'I'm asking you to stand aside so I can deal with the queue behind you.'

'I'm free to go?'

'That's not what I said. I said, wait there. I'll deal with you in a minute.'

With a sigh, Lieutenant Matthias stood aside and waited while the official carefully checked the passports of everyone in the long queue behind him. Half an hour later, when the arrivals hall was empty, the official handed the lieutenant back his passport.

'There we are, sir. Have a nice day.'

'That's it?'

'What do you want, maple syrup on it?'

'You kept me waiting here for nothing?'

'Not for nothing, no. For my amusement.'

'But, you can't do that!'

'I just did. In my line of work you rarely get the chance to have a good laugh. But this'll keep me going for a good long while. Good day.' And with that, the sombre-looking official got up from his desk and strolled away.

As the lieutenant pushed his baggage trolley out of the arrivals terminal and into the dim light and greasy drizzle of the London afternoon, he recalled what his chief had told him about Britain: 'It's wet, grey, cold, and everybody's miserable. They play baseball with a flat bat, and football with their feet: it's a weird country. And by the way, if you want to stay healthy, don't eat the food.'

Jack spotted him immediately. 'Lieutenant Matthias? I'm Jack Lindsay.'

The lieutenant shook his hand.

'How did you recognize me, do I look that much like a cop?'

'It was the cut of your suit and the fact that you look like

148

you've recently had a decent meal. By the way, I'd like you to meet acting Detective Constable Clark Kent.'

'How do you do?' Matthias said warily, concerned he might be the victim of some bizarre British joke.

'We've a car waiting,' Jack announced, and led the way over to a police transport, parked in front of the airport on what used to be Park Lane – now a wide, one-way black strip of tarmac painted with a bewildering array of white lines and yellow hatched boxes and festooned with a jumble of signs, all of which clutter was supposed to smooth traffic flow along the front of the building. Not that the buses, cars or taxis paid any attention to any of it. The trouble was, if you missed your lane to take you to the terminal of your choice and confidently followed the Ring Route signs in the naïve belief that they would lead you back around to the front of the building again, you eventually found yourself on the Slough bypass. And by the time you *had* found your way back to the airport, chances were your flight had left. Indeed, by that time the airship you had intended to catch could well have flown several times around the world, had a complete strip-down service and been repainted in the colours of the Brazilian football team. Consequently, the six-lane strip along the front of the airport was always clogged with a confusing mess of cabs, coaches and cars which, in a desperate bid not to miss the terminal, all fought to occupy the same, narrow, kerbside dropping-off lane at the same time.

Jack opened the door of the police car. 'Where are your digs, perhaps we can take you there now?'

'My what?'

'Your digs, where are you staying?'

'You people haven't sorted something out for me?'

'Ah, I see. Very well, I'm sure we can find you somewhere cosy. In the meantime let me take you to the Yard and bring you up to speed on this case.'

'Good idea.'

Once they were in the car and making their faltering way

through the airport traffic, Jack turned to the lieutenant. 'So, good trip?'

'The food was terrible and there was a party of drunken English businessmen who never seemed to sleep, and kept everyone else awake by singing lewd songs.'

'How unpleasant.'

'And then I run straight into your famed British hospitality in the shape of immigration. So, no, I have not had a good trip!'

'Oh, dear. Well, you can have a bit of a rest this afternoon, then have a slap-up dinner. What's the canteen got on, Clark?'

'Spam in the hole with offal-flavour gravy, and suet-style spotted dick with egg-substitute custard.'

The lieutenant struggled for a moment to bring his gagging reflex under control. 'Jesus, so the shortages really *are* that bad?'

'Oh, we get by. But I'm afraid you might not find our cuisine up to what you're used to across the Pond. Speaking of which, you can't by any chance still get hold of Garibaldis over there?'

'Gari what?'

'Never mind. As I was saying: for you, this afternoon is all about acclimatization. You can relax, put your feet up, go through witness statements, that sort of thing. You won't be disturbed. Clark and I have to go to the Isle of Wight.'

Clark was confused. 'But I thought—'

Jack shut him up with a look.

Lieutenant Matthias perked up. 'You're going to the Isle of Wight? What for?'

'Oh, probably nothing.'

'Is it connected with this case?'

Jack was non-committal. 'No . . . well . . . yes, in a manner of speaking.'

'In what way?'

'It's nothing to trouble yourself about.'

But the lieutenant's interest was deepening. 'No, tell me.'

'I really don't think you'd be interested.'

Now he was hooked. 'Look, I've been drafted into this stalled investigation to get results. You're going to tell me everything I want to know, or I'm going to inform the World Council of your obstructive behaviour and you'll be off this case so fast your feet won't touch the ground.'

Jack looked at Clark and raised his eyebrows. 'I think the game's up, eh Clark?' He turned to Matthias and put his hands up. 'All right, Lieutenant, you've got me bang to rights, I'll come quietly.' He looked back to Clark. 'Yank police methods, eh? Gosh, it's thrilling to see how it really should be done. Very well, Lieutenant, I was going to keep this from you but you've wheedled it out of me anyway. The thing is, we think we may have a suspect.'

'You've got a suspect on the Isle of Wight?'

'Let's not be too hasty. Nothing is certain in this game as you know, but we're pretty keen on this chap.'

'Why didn't you tell me this straight away?'

'I didn't want to throw you in at the deep end, as it were, especially after such an uncomfortable trip. Thought you might like to get your bearings first, have a spot to eat, a cup of tea . . .'

'To hell with your tea, I'm going to the Isle of Wight.'

'Now, steady on—'

'No, you steady on, *old chap*! You Brits have been standing around with your fingers up your butts for too long. It's time for action. I'm going to show you what policing American-style is all about. Get me on the next transport to the Isle of Wight.'

Jack turned to Clark and winked.

Back at the office, Commissioner Lindsay was surprised to find Jack and Clark returning from the airport alone.

'Where is he?'

'Where's who?' Jack asked innocently.

'Our American super policeman.'

'Oh, you mean Lieutenant Matthias. He's gone to the Isle of Wight.'

The commissioner looked blank. 'The Isle of Wight?'

'He was keen to get down to some good old American-style policing right away, so he's headed south.'

'Why in God's name has he gone to the Isle of Wight?'

'It was our shape-shifting Purple Trouser's last known location.'

'Except, of course, for—' Clark began, but Jack nudged him to shut him up.

'Except for what?' Freddy asked.

'Except for the fact that he hasn't been there for at least three years,' Jack replied.

The commissioner opened his mouth to quiz Jack further, but then the light of understanding dawned and he smiled. 'You've sent this Yank on a wild goose chase?'

'Oh, we wouldn't do a thing like that, would we, Clark?'

'Oh, no, sir.' Clark beamed, braces gleaming.

'No, he wanted to get down to business straight away and we had to admit we *had* been standing around for far too long with our fingers up our bottoms, so—'

The commissioner frowned. 'I beg your pardon?'

'It's a Yank-ism.'

'Oh.'

'Anyway, he was so keen to get started, it didn't seem fair to hold him back, so we just pointed him in the right direction and let him go.' Jack clapped his hand to his forehead. 'Oh dear, I've just had a thought. It's Saturday, isn't it?'

'What's the matter?' Freddy asked.

'Well, the lieutenant's ferry gets in to Cowes at around six-forty, and I don't believe we mentioned that the last ferry back leaves at six-thirty, did we Clark?'

'No, sir, I don't believe we did. Nor that it doesn't run on Sundays. And then of course, what with Monday being a Bank Holiday . . .' Clark adjusted his glasses.

'He won't be able to get back until Tuesday. Oh dear, aren't we dreadful?' Jack concluded, all concern.

Freddy chuckled to himself. 'So our American cop is going to be stranded in the land of bungalows and fossilized cream teas for the entire weekend, all on his own.'

'Not on his own, no. He's in the jovial company of two of the Yard's finest: Detective Constable Barking and Detective Sergeant Maude.'

The commissioner's smile got even wider. 'If the Isle of Wight doesn't finish him off, those two will. Good work, Jack.'

As the train rattled out of Victoria, DC Barking turned to Lieutenant Matthias. 'So, you're from New York, then,' he observed.

'That's right,' the lieutenant replied curtly.

'Thought so. Could tell by the accent.'

The lieutenant nodded absently and looked out of the window, but DC Barking persisted.

'Which, according to the logic of deduction, would point to the fact that you are from America.'

The lieutenant turned and regarded the detective constable strangely.

'Not much gets past him,' DS Maude announced proudly. 'One of the brightest in the force.'

Matthias smiled vaguely. 'Is that so?'

'From which,' DC Barking ground on, 'one might conclude that you are in fact American.' The detective constable smiled inscrutably, seeming, finally, to have come to the end of his train of reasoning.

Matthias raised an eyebrow and pretended to be fascinated by something outside the window.

But the DC hadn't quite finished. 'Come far, have you?'

Matthias dragged his eyes away from the captivating panorama of freight yards and derelict buildings lining the

railway, and frowned in open disbelief at the detective constable. 'America,' he enunciated slowly and carefully.

Barking looked triumphantly at Maude. 'Told you.'

Maude nodded sagely. 'Amazing.'

If Lieutenant Matthias had any remaining doubts about the
sorry state of British policing, they were rapidly being dispelled
by this pair, and he realized that this was going to be a very long
journey indeed.

Chapter 13

Jack had just come in off the balcony, after an enjoyable and, it has to be said, curiously fragrant bowl of Old Hobson's Curiously Fragrant, when he met Mango loitering outside his office. Mango was wearing a fetching little pale cream two-piece covered with bright purple and green dots which he'd accessorized with a flowing electric-blue silk scarf.

'You look ridiculous,' Jack growled.

Mango blinked. 'I beg your pardon, but I was unaware that this was a charity-shop only zone.'

'Meaning?'

'Have you looked at yourself in the mirror today?'

'Yes, why?'

'Then it was a conscious decision to dress like an Oxfam shop mannequin, was it?'

Jack glared at him. 'This is no time for flippancy, we are involved in a serious murder investigation. People are dying. Don't you care?'

Mango was stung. 'Do you think you have a monopoly on feelings? Of course I care.'

'Oh, really? Then why can't you show a little respect for the dead and wear something that isn't going to make the whole department vomit?'

Their raised voices were beginning to attract attention.

'I take a pride in my appearance, unlike some people I know, who've worn the same suit for the past four years,' Mango retaliated. 'At least you might get it cleaned once in a while, or haven't you noticed that you smell like a horse?'

'I'm a policeman, not a hairdresser!'

'That's no excuse,' Mango yelled, 'for smelling like a stable yard.'

'At least it's honest. At least I don't pong like a madam's drawers.'

'Have some intimate knowledge of that aroma, do you?'

Now the department was hushed, and every eye was glued to the confrontation.

Jack's face was like thunder, but Mango carried on.

'And, my God, didn't anyone ever tell you smoking a pipe was hazardous to your smile? Your teeth are a disaster – I've seen tombstones in better condition.'

Jack narrowed his eyes. 'You're sailing very close to the wind, Pinkerton. If I were you I'd choose my words with extreme care if I wanted to keep my job.'

Mango's jaw tightened. 'Now I understand. Now that you have Miss Chest of the Year to pander to your every whim, I can see I'm superfluous to requirements. Very well, if that's the way you feel, I have no wish to stay where I'm not appreciated.'

Jack leaned on his stick. 'The going getting too tough for you, is it, twinkle-truss?'

Mango clenched his fists. 'You bastard! If you didn't have a bad leg, I'd—'

'You'd what – hit me with your handbag? Go, if that's what you want. Go on, get out, I'm sick of the sight of you. The whole department's sick of the sight of you, with your loud suits and your mismatched accessories.'

For a moment Mango looked as if he was going to cry. Then, pulling himself together, he turned and walked in an upright and dignified manner through the gawping office workers towards the door.

'Your badge, Pinkerton!' Jack barked.

Mango stopped, slowly pulled a little black wallet out of his pocket and dropped it on the floor.

'If you want it you can pick it up,' he said, without turning back. 'This is it, Jack. It's no good your begging me to come back like all the other times. I've had enough. A person can only take so much,' Mango was so choked he could hardly speak.

'The feeling's mutual!' Jack roared. 'Go on, get out. Good God, getting rid of my ex-wife was easier than getting rid of you! Go! Go!'

In the ensuing silence, Mango opened the door and walked through, closing it softly behind him.

After retrieving the discarded wallet, Jack straightened and looked around at the faces of his staff, all staring at him in open-mouthed astonishment. 'What in God's name are you looking at? Get back to work!' Then he limped awkwardly into his inner office and slammed the door. After a moment the windows dimmed.

At Cowes on the Isle of Wight, Lieutenant Matthias was immensely relieved to be stepping off the ferry. Spending four hours in the company of Detective Constable Barking and Detective Sergeant Maude hadn't been what you might call a stimulating experience.

'Four hours? How big *is* Great Britain? I could have got from New York to Boston and back in that time,' the lieutenant complained.

Barking and Maude stiffened slightly at this criticism of the transport system of their beloved country.

'Oh, you think so, do you, sir?' said Constable Barking.

'I know so.'

'Well this isn't New York, this is Britain and we do things differently here,' Sergeant Maude observed. 'Perhaps our methods are a little more sedate than you're used to, but that doesn't mean we don't get the job done.'

'Softly, softly, catchee squirrel,' Barking added.

'Monkey!' Matthias snapped.

'There's no need to be rude, sir.'

'No, I was just— Never mind. This place we're heading for, is it far?'

'There'll be a car waiting for us outside the terminal, ready to whisk us off to our destination,' Sergeant Maude assured him.

'Oh, so you *can* whisk when you want to?'

'If whisking is deemed to be the appropriate course of action, yes, sir.'

'Good, it's getting late and I want to get on with this. I want to wind this whole thing up this weekend.'

'Don't worry, sir, you'll be back in the land of the cheeseburger faster than you can say large fries and custard.'

'Large fries and *must*— Oh forget it.' Matthias shook his head wearily, he didn't have the energy.

Captain Trevor Mason's last known address was a small, nondescript bungalow perched on the cliffs above Wheeler's Bay, near Ventnor. Apparently Sergeant Maude's idea of what constituted whisking was very different from Lieutenant Matthias's and when they got there, after a leisurely drive, it was dark.

'Great,' the lieutenant muttered, stepping through the little white-painted gate into the untidily overgrown garden around the bungalow, and tripping over a freshly rooted bramble shoot. 'Have either of you got a flashlight?'

Maude and Barking looked blank.

'Oh, Jesus, what do you Brits call it . . .? A torch! Have you got a torch?'

The two English policemen looked at each other and raised their eyes to heaven.

'Doesn't want much, does he?' muttered Sergeant Maude, who was finding the lieutenant's no-frills approach to police work rather grating. They hadn't even broken their journey for a nice cup of tea. 'Nip back to the car, Constable, ask the driver if he's got a torch we can borrow.'

'Righto, sir.'

Constable Barking strolled unhurriedly back to the police car along the stone-studded concrete path that led up from the road. He was gone a good five minutes, during which time the lieutenant seriously considered chewing the wall to pass the time. When the constable eventually returned, empty-handed and with a big grin on his face, Matthias was furious.

'He didn't have a torch? What the hell have you been doing all this time?'

'Funny chap, our driver. Told me a story about the time he found a courting couple in a car on the cliff edge. As they were passionately engaged in their business, they must have knocked off the hand brake, because the next thing they knew . . . Excuse me sir, what are you doing?'

The lieutenant had powered his elbow into the glass panel in the front door and was now holding his arm and hopping around in agony.

'Ow! Ow! Ow! What the hell is this glass made of?'

'It'll be a reinforced double-glazed unit, virtually unbreakable,' Sergeant Maude informed him. 'Building regulations, you see, sir. This area, close to the sea, is prone to gale-force winds which can whip the shingle up wicked.'

'Then how the hell are we going to do it?' the lieutenant asked.

'Do what, sir?'

'Break the glass!'

The sergeant looked at him coldly. 'Are you trying to break into this domicile, sir?'

'Yes!'

'May I ask why?'

'Because I want to get inside.'

'That's breaking and entering,' Constable Barking informed him.

'I know it's breaking and entering!' Matthias growled. 'Do you have a better idea?'

'Well, we could use this.' The constable produced a key from his pocket. 'This bungalow is rented. Isle of Wight police contacted the owner and procured the key while we were en route. The driver vouchsafed it to me.'

'Oh.'

The constable smiled. 'Softly, softly—'

'I know . . . catchee rodent.'

Chapter 14

'*How's the office without me?*'

'Drab. The trouble with modern business fashion is that it lacks your . . .'

'*Panache?*'

'I was going to say heroism.'

'*Do you want to start another argument, gimpy?*'

Jack paused. 'I'm sorry if I was a little harsh earlier, Mango, but I had to make it look real.'

'*Perhaps, but I thought "twinkle-truss" was a little below the belt.*'

'The belt *was* shocking pink.'

There was a pause while Mango considered the style implications.

'*Point taken,*' he said at last.

'Do I really smell like a horse?'

'*Jack, if you weren't inside that suit it would be off, galloping across the plains, its frayed collar blowing in the wind.*'

'I'll go shopping.'

'*On your own? I just know you'll choose something dull and conservative.*'

'Dull and conservative suits me fine. And my er . . . teeth?'

'*You buy something called smoker's toothpaste. It's not difficult to make yourself presentable, all it takes is a little effort.*'

'Thanks for the tip. By the way, dropping your London bus pass instead of your police badge was pure genius.'

'*Why, thank you. But you could have warned me, I had to think fast.*'

'Sorry, I had to make your dismissal look authentic. Have you booked a capsule yet?'

Mango groaned. '*Yes, although I don't see why I have to travel by capsule when, thanks to Councillor McClaggen, the department has an almost unlimited budget.*'

'I don't want anyone knowing about your little jaunt to Corbett and asking awkward questions. After all, officially Corbett isn't even in the picture as far as this case is concerned. I'd like to keep it that way for the time being.'

'*But, Jack, the place is a dump. It's so far down the fashion evolutionary scale they think sludge is a colour. I'm going to stick out like a sore thumb.*'

'I'm sure you can pick up something appropriate to wear at the spaceport.'

'*Are you kidding? Corbett Airport is a shack manned by a goat. The only shops they have sell hay.*'

'Well, I hear grass skirts are making a comeback.'

'*Not in my universe. So what do you want me to do once I get there?*'

'I'd like you to look in on the Ave Verum order – at the Abbey of the Perforated Spleen of Jesus.'

'*Are you trying to save my soul?*'

'No, I realize it's too late for that. I need you to check on a Trevor Mason – ex Purple Trouser, now possibly going under the handle Brother Verrat. Make out like you're an old army friend.'

'*Me? Army?*'

'I know it's a stretch, but you're up to it. Wear a dirty singlet, scratch your belly a lot and use words of one syllable.'

Mango sighed. '*And what's so special about this Mason character?*'

'He's our killer.'

'*You solved the murder case? Why am I the last to know these things?*'

'I couldn't tell you at the Yard. You know the old phrase: Walls have ears. Besides, I haven't exactly cracked the case, all I've done is to unravel one single strand of a vast and complex tapestry.'

'*Well, well, well, religion* and *poetry. Anything else you want me to do while I'm there?*'

'Ask around, see what you can find out, especially about a certain Michaelmas Thurrock-Lawes. And see if you can't dig up something on our two missing arms dealers. Put your famous "people skills" to the test.'

'*You're never going to let me forget that, are you?*'

'And, Mango, at the risk of starting another argument . . . normally I wouldn't dare dictate how you should dress, but as this is supposed to be an undercover mission . . .'

'*Stop right there, I've already pulled out all my dreariest suits. I'm looking at them now, wondering which one you'd choose. How about a chocolate double-breasted with a cream pinstripe?*'

'Sounds perfect. Just don't accessorize it with a cornflower homburg.'

'*Hmm, now there's an idea . . .*'

'Mango!'

'*Only teasing. Believe me, I'll be the drabbest at the ball.*'

'Have a good trip.' Jack rested the receiver gently back in its cradle.

Lying down on his sofa, he stared at the ceiling of his apartment, cradling a glass of whisky on his chest. He'd had the first breakthrough in the case – he knew who the killer was. But instead of making him feel good, it just made him uneasy. In effect all he really had was a name.

He had a pretty good idea that the assassin and the arms dealers were, or at least had been, working together. And if, as Jack surmised, the killer had changed his tactics for, as yet, unknown reasons, it was possible that the two dealers had been taken by surprise, which would account for their non-appearance at all the killings after Venezuela. An alternative theory was that they'd been tipped off that Jack was on to them and were lying low for a while. But that would mean the department had a leak, and that was unlikely – everyone had been hand-picked by the commissioner himself.

And then there was Corbett and the order of Ave Verum. What was so important about that damp and dreary country? Why did Michaelmas want him out there? But more importantly, what exactly had happened to make the killer change his plans, and where would he strike next?

Jack had a feeling that the more he found out about this case, the less he'd understand.

He drained his glass in search of enlightenment, but the accustomed wave of clarity that usually followed such an act didn't materialize, instead he felt nauseous and lapsed into a troubled sleep.

Later that same evening, Mango presented himself at the capsule check-in desk at Tommy Cooper International. There was a queue.

'Oh great,' he sighed. Pulling his nondescript brown trilby down low over his eyes, he settled in for a lengthy wait.

There were three options as far as international travel went: hyperliners – the equivalent of luxury cruise liners – for the super rich; airliners for business travellers, which were basically hyperliners stripped out and slimmed down; and finally, for the budget-conscious, capsule.

The capsule was the most economic option because it didn't use fuel in the ordinary sense. But as a way of getting round the world it was the most unpleasant experience known to man, involving, as it did, being strapped into an individual pod about the size of a three-drawer filing cabinet and having ice-cold cryogenic fluid poured over your head. Not that the trip lasted long enough to warrant being put into a state of suspended animation: the fluid's main function was to protect the body from the extremes of speed, rapid acceleration, deceleration and sudden changes of direction that capsule travel entailed. Also, as the whole experience was unspeakably unpleasant, it was supposed to make the time pass quickly. Sadly, any benefits that could have been derived from being unconscious were undermined by the capsule companies' insistence on giving their 'customers' frequent and regular meals. Thus a journey that might have been passed in a blissful state of untroubled sleep was a nightmare succession of microwaved meals in which rehydrated ostrich rump and glutinous rice cake, topped with a sickly sweet synthetic cherry, regularly featured. The final insult was being woken to be offered the chance to purchase a cute, cuddly 'Air-ace Bear', complete with goggles and flying helmet, from the on-board shop. That people invariably bought these monstrosities shows the state of mental confusion induced by the journey. To make matters worse, the pointless gifts and the indigestible food, as well as the on-board robotic staff needed to serve and prepare such delights, took up even more space in the already cramped interior of the capsule.

Once the 'customer' had been snugly inserted, the capsule was loaded into a vast, earth-bound particle accelerator, which wound it up to twenty-five thousand miles an hour, then fired it off into orbit from the muzzle of what looked like a gigantic gun.

But that was only the beginning.

Once it had been set whizzing around the earth, the capsule was picked up by static acceleration tubes in geostationary orbit, which not only modified the capsule's trajectory in the direction of its intended destination, but also increased its speed in a sudden and startling burst. Unfortunately the transits through these tubes usually coincided with the occupant being woken for morning coffee, and the violent surge in acceleration invariably sent the scalding hot beverage down the customer's neck.

The final indignity was to be caught at one's destination in a gigantic magnetic funnel, a bit like a virtual butterfly net, and hauled back from several hundred thousand miles an hour to a standstill in moments. This, despite the protective envelope of cryogenic fluid – now intermingled with coffee, non-dairy creamer and bits of overcooked carrot – always sent a massive surge of blood rushing to the feet.

Most people went up a shoe size every time they travelled.

A more comfortable way of cruising the skies was afforded by the airliners. These streamlined, cigar-shaped airships catered for the business traveller, having conference rooms, spas, gyms and an on-board sushi chef, and were the fastest way of traversing the globe if you wanted to reach your destination in any kind of shape for that important meeting.

Slimmer than their bloated sister aircraft, the hyperliners, their superior power to weight ratio meant they could zoom across the Atlantic in around eighteen hours, depending on wind conditions.

At the top end of the flying experience were the hyperliners: gigantic airships powered by small, ultra fuel-efficient jet engines. Less wasteful than the old gas-guzzling aeroplanes of the early twenty-first century, they were, unavoidably, a lot slower: a journey across the Atlantic could take up to three days, depending on weather conditions. But what they lacked in speed they more than made up for in luxury, with their casinos, boutiques, glitzy celebrity shows, choice of fine dining eateries and twenty-four-hour bars. Sadly, such pampering was out of the reach of all but a lucky few, as a trip around the world in such a vessel cost the equivalent of what most people earned in a decade.

But as Mango gritted his teeth and stepped into the baked-bean tin that was to carry him all the way to Corbett, two unlikely individuals were enjoying just such a quality experience . . .

*

On the SS *Max Boyce*, a vast hyperliner powering smoothly over the arid wastes of the Sahara, it was Variety Night in the Colwyn Bay Theatre. After an act involving a blonde, a saxophone and a bucket of eels, the stage was mopped and a very small man walked on. As the band struck up 'The Night They Invented Champagne' he proceeded to stuff himself into a glass bell-jar. Once inside, he produced a miniature Union Jack, which he waved through the mouth of the jar to polite applause. For his encore he inhaled a bag of iron filings and sneezed recognizable images of past American presidents onto a white plastic board.

Two pale-skinned gentlemen, sitting wide-eyed in the audience, one tall and thin, the other short and hump-backed, decided they'd had enough Variety for one night and slid out of the theatre and onto the viewing deck. Standing by the rail in front of one of the great windows through which one could appreciate the ever-changing panorama of the earth below, one of the men clicked a button on his large wrist communicator and uttered the single word, 'Executive'.

After a few moments the party at the other end picked up.

'Ah, greetings. Satellite One speaking.' He smiled at his partner, revealing surprisingly neat, even teeth. 'And Satellite Two says hello. Honoured sir, we know we shouldn't have called you on this number, but—'

'*You're damn right you shouldn't!*' It was obvious 'Executive' was not best pleased to be taking the call.

'We are very sorry, and we are well aware of the risks involved, both to you and to ourselves, but we need to know how to proceed. Having received no signal since the incident in Venezuela, and having encountered your subsequent silence, we are, as you can imagine, a little concerned.'

This was greeted with heavy breathing.

'Hello, sir, would you like me to repeat that?'

'Executive' sighed. '*No, I heard. It's like this – our man's gone*

167

and thrown a loop, he's no longer under our control and we have no idea where he is going to strike next.'

'With respect, sir,' the thin man continued, 'he is not our problem. We have been given certain assurances about the number of contacts that we could expect from this enterprise, and so far we have met with under half that number. We are disappointed, sir, and are beginning to think that you are not a man of your word.'

'*Now look here—*'

'No, sir, you look. Our investment in this enterprise has been considerable. I'm sure you understand, sir, that we are businessmen, seeking only to turn an honest profit, and that if things do not proceed as originally planned we stand to lose a substantial sum.'

The other man nodded sadly. 'A substantial sum.'

'Rest assured, sir, we shall be seeking compensation.'

The voice at the other end abruptly assumed a conciliatory tone. '*I'm sure it won't come to that, gentlemen. We're doing all we can to resolve this matter, please bear with us. Tell you what, why don't you stop off at the Royal Mahe on the Seychelles until we sort this thing out? Have a little holiday, on me.*'

The thin man glanced at his colleague with a smile. 'Why that is most kind of you, sir, most kind, and we will take you up on your offer. But, if we do not hear favourable news from you within the week, we shall start compensation proceedings against you. We shall be seeking our "pound of flesh", as one of your poets so eloquently put it. And be advised, we prefer not to go through the cumbersome procedures of the law, using instead a much more *hands-on* approach.'

The pale, thin man broke the connection.

'Oh, Jakob, you threaten so eloquently.'

'Thank you, Lazlo.'

'Do you think it will come to that?'

'I hope for all our sakes that it doesn't: the dead are notoriously bad at paying their bills.'

Lazlo giggled uncontrollably, his misshapen little body racked by convulsions of mirth. 'Oh, Jakob, you are humorous.'

'Shall we dine, Lazlo?'

'Excellent idea, Jakob.'

'Hmm, and what will we eat? Shall we go English? I hear they can do wonders with a pound of suet and a tin of custard powder, or would you prefer Italian?'

'Hmm, a difficult choice,' Lazlo chuckled. 'Let us have a cocktail to help us decide.'

'Oh, you are wise, Lazlo, you are wise.'

The tattooist was surprised to see the cowled figure sitting in his waiting room. 'OK, you want to come through, Brother?' He nodded to the monk to follow him through the chain curtain and into the cramped treatment room behind it.

The walls were covered with pictures of scantily clad females showing off their tattoos, a few of which had been inscribed in some very unlikely places indeed.

'And what can I do for you?' The tattooist smiled, showing stained and uneven teeth.

The monk pulled up his sleeve, revealing the mop and bucket tattoo. 'I want this removed.'

The tattooist leaned over the monk and studied the tattoo for some moments without speaking. Then he straightened and smoothed his moustache thoughtfully. 'A removal will cost you three thousand,' he said at last.

The monk raised an eyebrow. 'That's more than it cost to put it there.'

The tattooist shrugged. 'Take it or leave it. You could do it yourself, of course, but unless you're expert with a cosmetic laser I wouldn't advise it – you don't fuck about with lasers,' he said, thrusting his thumbs challengingly into the pockets of his leather waistcoat.

The monk smiled. 'I understand that. It's just that for such a procedure the price seems a little steep.'

'Straightforward removal costs two hundred.' The tattooist pointed to a scale of charges pinned to the wall over the bottom half of a naked woman with a snake tattooed across her breasts.

The monk glanced at the charges then turned back to the man quizzically.

'But there's nothing straightforward about this removal, is there?' The tattooist looked into the monk's eyes. 'It seems to me that someone who's gone to all the trouble of earning one of those in the first place would have to have a very good reason for wanting to get rid of it. Seems to me such a person might have something to hide. So, two hundred to make it go away, the rest for my silence.'

The monk nodded. 'Ah, I see.'

'I'm glad we understand each other.' The man stroked his moustache again. 'You want me to go ahead?'

'Please proceed.'

The tattooist held out his hand. 'Fee payable in advance.'

The monk reached into a pocket, pulled out a bundle of notes and counted out three thousand, which he handed over.

Tucking the money in his greasy waistcoat, the tattooist invited the monk to lie down on the couch and fired up the laser.

It took just four minutes to burn off the top few layers of skin along with the tell-tale tattoo. After the operation was over, the smiling tattooist handed the man a small mirror so that he could observe his handiwork.

'Of course, it'll smart for a while, but once the redness and the swelling go down, no one will ever know there was anything there.'

The monk studied the angry red patch on his shoulder. 'Very neat,' he admitted.

'Worth every penny,' the tattooist crowed.

The monk swung his legs off the bench and stood up. 'That

laser,' he said, pointing to the surgical instrument in the man's hand, 'there must be quite a skill to wielding it.'

The tattooist smiled. 'Well, like most things, it's all down to experience really.'

The monk smiled back chummily. 'I'll bet there's more to it than that. I mean, in the wrong hands, I suspect it could be rather dangerous.'

'Well, like I said, you got to treat lasers with respect,' the tattooist said self-importantly.

'You're telling me. How does it work?'

'It's operated by this foot control down here.' The tattooist was suddenly as eager as a kid with a yo-yo to show off his expertise. 'Look, you'll be able to see better if you come round this side.'

'Very well.' The monk joined the man on the other side of the couch.

'Don't get too close, it gets really hot,' the tattooist warned. Then, pressing down on the small, floor-mounted button with his foot, he held the glowing red tip of the instrument against the pocked and holed leather of the couch. It sent up a thin stream of smoke. 'See?'

The monk was impressed. 'Interesting.'

'Of course, you have to know how long to keep it in contact with the skin. And you've got to keep it moving. Keep the tip in the same place, or keep your foot on the floor button for too long and there's a danger of burning right through the flesh.'

'Really?' The monk nodded eagerly. 'I'd like to see that.'

Without warning, the monk grabbed the tattooist's arm and brought it up behind his back, forcing his face down into the couch. Then, taking the laser and jamming it into the tattooist's ear, the monk pressed down on the foot button as hard and as long as he could. Held firm in the monk's vice-like grip, his screams dampened by the padded couch, the tattooist squirmed ineffectually as the laser burnt first through his eardrum, then his inner ear and finally his brain, which it sliced through like butter, filling the room with the warm, acrid smell of broiled flesh.

Eventually the unfortunate man went limp.

Dropping the laser and taking his foot off the floor control, the monk reached into the tattooist's waistcoat and retrieved his money. Then he allowed the body to collapse onto the floor.

'You know, you're quite right,' the monk said to the tattooist's corpse. 'You don't fuck about with lasers.'

On the sun-kissed cocktail terrace of the Royal Mahe Hotel, Horbert Manfreddo sipped his Mahe Royale and gazed out at the sparkling blue sea. Only one thing disturbed this perfect moment – his tooth had started ringing.

The big man sighed and clicked a button on his communicator. 'Yeah?'

'*Why didn't you tell me he was a shape shifter!*' The man's voice on the other end of the line was harsh, almost hysterical.

'Calm down or you're going to burst something. Has he nailed the guy yet?'

'*No, but he's got to be close.*'

'What else has he found out?'

'*He's getting curious about Corbett!*'

'Good.'

'*That's good? Are you insane? Very soon he's going to have the whole picture!*'

'Let me worry about that. What about our dealer friends?'

'*I've sent them to you, as requested.*'

'At least you've done something right. OK, we're moving on to phase two.'

'*Phase two? But we still don't have the killer. If we haul her in now, before he's caught, after the next murder we'll simply have to let her go.*'

'I'm calling in my men to take over. Don't fret, by the time of the press call tomorrow morning to announce that the murderer has been apprehended, a certain monk will be enjoying a long and peaceful afterlife.'

'*But . . . but—!*'

'We can't wait any longer – we're too close to completion.'

'*But what about my man? He knows too much. Soon he's going to start making connections, and when he does – when he finds the trail, he's going to follow it all the way back to us!*'

'I'd expect nothing less from the best in the business. So, from now on, we do things my way.'

'*And what about me; my position?*'

'I couldn't give a flying fuck about your position. Besides, you told me you could control the guy. It's time this private dick was neutralized.'

'*Neutralized?*'

'Yeah, you do speak English don't you? Neutralized as in taken out, popped . . . whatever. Get rid of him.'

'*Get rid of him?*'

'Just do it! Jesus, if I'd followed my instincts and used my men from the get-go, we'd never have got into this situation. Kill the detective or you'll have to do without your little monthly bonus.'

Manfreddo broke the connection, drained his glass and called the waiter over to order a refill.

Chapter 15

Arriving at the Yard the next morning, Jack was not at all surprised to find Commissioner Lindsay in his office, sitting in his chair, with Lana standing behind him looking defensive.

'Good morning, Jack, who's the lady?'

The video wall was full of the image of Marian, her lips parted in the act of asking for help.

Jack instinctively reached into his pocket for the record-o-clip – it was still there.

'We had copies made, Jack,' Freddy explained, seeing Jack's confusion. 'Who is she? Why don't I know about her and what else have you been keeping from me?'

'It seems we've all been kept in the dark, doesn't it?' Jack looked pointedly at Lana, who brazenly met his gaze.

'I don't like it when my officers go creeping around behind my back, especially as it's me who ends up getting the blame for this department's mistakes!' Freddy thumped the desk for emphasis.

'And I don't like being spied on! Tell me, Freddy, where did you find Miss Sweater of the Year? I had no idea the department had a budget for courtesans.'

Lana flushed scarlet and gripped the back of Freddy's chair.

Freddy reached up and touched her lightly on the arm. 'All right, Lana, you can leave us now.'

Lip curled in fury and looking murderously at Jack, she stalked out of the office.

'Lana's not a spy,' Freddy retorted once she'd left. 'She's

simply been keeping an eye on things for me. I know how you work: you're a one-man band, you keep everything to yourself; no one but you knows what's going on. I just wanted to keep tabs on this department's ten-thousand-a-week investment.'

Jack shook his head. 'You never did understand detection, Freddy. I don't tell anyone anything until I'm certain I've got something worthwhile to impart.'

Freddy ran a finger around his collar; he was beginning to change colour, his cheeks taking on the shade of quince cheese. 'Well, it seems to me, Mr Sherlock Holmes, you *have* got something to tell.' He pointed to Marian's face on the video wall. 'Who's the female?'

Jack got up, went over to the bookcase and removed *Police Procedurals Vol IV*.

Freddy raised an eyebrow. 'Jack, don't tell me that at last you've recognized the benefits of modern policing methods? I'm delighted, although I admit a little surprised.'

Then Jack pulled out the bottle of Scotch hidden behind the thick tome.

'Ah.' Freddy smiled. 'Same old Jack. And here was me thinking you'd changed your ways.'

'Horses for courses.' Jack fished two shot glasses out of his desk drawer. Filling them both, he passed one to Freddy. 'If I tell you everything, can I have my chair back?'

'Of course.' Freddy vacated Jack's seat. 'I'd hate to have the disability watchdog on my back.'

'I know,' said Jack, relaxing back in his chair and easing out his leg, 'political correctness has gone mad.'

'So? Are you going to tell me a story?'

Jack took a sip of his whisky and put the glass down carefully on the desk. 'Freddy, she's got nothing to do with all this.'

'Oh, better and better! Now you're using Scotland Yard's facilities to chase women!'

'She's Marian Lawes, wife of Michaelmas, aka Daygan Flyte, aka Mr Piggy-Wig.'

'Is this story going somewhere?'

Jack got out his pipe and started filling it. 'It all started like this . . .'

He unfolded the story from the time Marian first set foot in his office, leaving out several significant details: all references to Corbett, Mango's faked firing and the small matter of him now knowing who the killer was.

'. . . So you see, the very fact that she's asking for help proves her innocence.'

'Innocence?' Freddy shook his head. 'Jack, I thought you'd got over thinking with your trousers. This good-looking woman comes on to you, pours out a hard-luck story about her uncaring husband, sheds a few tears and you fall for it like a suicide.'

'No, Freddy, it's not like that.'

'I'll tell you what it's like. This Michaelmas character, has anyone ever seen him? No. Is there any record of him at the Home Office? No. Are there even any pictures of him? No! Use your brain, brother. The man doesn't exist!'

'Of course he exists, he's Mr Piggy-Wig.'

'Listen to yourself! Piggy-Wig isn't a person, it's a corporation. Mr Piggy-Wig is simply an actor in a pig's mask. This woman – if that's what she is – is making the whole thing up. She saw you coming and played you like a fish.'

'What do you mean, if that's what she is?'

'Hasn't it ever crossed your mind that she just might be your shape shifter?'

The thought that Jack might somehow be in love with a hairy-arsed Purple Trouser was decidedly unnerving.

'No, I'd know. Besides, she came to me. If she's mixed up in all this, then why go out of her way to get me involved? Besides, the first time she came to see me you hadn't yet twisted my arm to join you at the Yard. She couldn't have had any idea that I was going to be involved in this case, or that I was even coming back to the department.'

'I want this Marian picked up.'

Jack shrugged. 'You tell me where she is and I'll pick her up.'

Freddy looked at Jack for a long time. Then, coming to a decision, he moved to the door. 'I've had enough of your insubordination, I'm taking over this case.'

That was a slap in the face. Jack sat up straight. 'What? You don't know the first thing about police work!'

'Do I have to remind you that I'm the fucking police commissioner!'

'That's just a fucking title! You're a desk jockey; a rules and regulations man. You've never had to think on your feet – you can't even take a shit without asking for permission!'

'That's enough!' Freddy's lips were flecked with spittle. 'You are now officially suspended. Go home! If you're still here in half an hour I'll have you forcibly removed from the building!'

Jack held up his hands. 'All right, all right. Look, Freddy, I really don't know where she is. I want to talk to her as much as you do, believe me.'

'After everything you've kept from me, how can I trust you? I didn't want it to come to this, but you've brought it on yourself, Jack.'

'*Mea culpa.*' Jack downed his Scotch and reached for the bottle again.

'That's it, go ahead, drink yourself stupid – run away from the truth!' Freddy shook his head. 'You're a sorry specimen. Go home, Jack, and if I were you I'd start looking for another job.'

Jack raised his glass and smiled lopsidedly. 'Good old big brother, looking after his errant sibling once again.'

As Freddy moved towards the door, Jack called him back. 'As I'm no longer on this case, you might as well know . . .'

Freddy spun round to face him. 'Know what?'

'The name of the killer.'

'You know who this assassin is?'

Jack nodded. 'Oh, yes. I've known for a whole day.'

The commissioner shook his head, sadly. 'You see. This is just the sort of thing I mean. You're not a team player.'

'Look who's talking.'

Freddy shrugged and turned to go.

Jack frowned. 'You don't want to know?'

'Know what?'

'The killer's name?'

'Oh, er . . . yes, yes of course.'

'Trevor Mason.'

'Mason?'

'But I doubt he's still travelling under that name, seeing he's now a monk.'

'A monk?'

Jack took another slug of Scotch and nodded.

'And do you know where this Trevor Mason is now?' At last Freddy seemed genuinely interested.

Jack threw his arms wide. 'Search me, brother.'

Freddy's face fell. 'You don't know where he is?'

'If I did, he'd already be in custody.'

The commissioner pointed a wavering finger at Jack. 'I want you out of here.'

Jack had never seen anybody turn on their heel before, but that's what Freddy did. He turned on his heel and left the office. *Such a cliché*, Jack thought.

The moment Freddy had gone, Jack fell into a morose reverie. Had he really been so wrong about Marian? He had to admit he'd always had trouble understanding women; his first wife took particular delight in telling him that the sum total of his knowledge of women was that they had breasts. But this particular development just didn't make sense. However, he didn't have time to fully excavate this maudlin vein of thought, because he found himself staring at his wrist communicator and the picture of Freddy's family and wondering why, if he was no longer on the case, his parsimonious brother had let him keep such a valuable piece of equipment. He got up and went to the door.

'Clark, get in here!'

By the time the fresh-faced young man appeared in the doorway, Jack was back behind his desk.

'You wanted me, Chief?'

'You said your father was in military intelligence.'

'That's right.'

'Did he ever have anything to do with eavesdropping – bugs and all that sort of thing?'

'That was his speciality.'

Jack smiled. 'You don't by any chance have any expertise in that field, do you?'

Clark revealed his train-track braces in a sly smile. 'Oh yes. I sometimes used to help Dad out – keep him company on stake-outs.'

'He took you with him?'

'Yes, especially when Mum was away preparing a fashion show. It was cheaper than hiring a babysitter.'

The picture of Clark's home life that Jack was gradually assembling was beginning to put Clark's strangeness into context.

'I see. Come in and close the door.' He took off his communicator and handed it to the youth. 'If this was bugged would you be able to tell?'

Clark examined it. 'Nice. Very neat . . . Phase Three by the looks of it.' He pressed two of the buttons on the bezel simultaneously, and a tiny spike with a glowing red tip popped out.

Jack was amazed. 'What's that?'

'If you think of this little machine as today's equivalent of the Swiss Army knife, I suppose this would correspond to that little pointy thing next to the corkscrew. No one particular use, more of an all-purpose sharpy thing – it's a sonic pick.'

'What's it for?'

'Well, you *could* use it to clean your ears – much safer than cotton buds, *and* more effective. Or you could use it like a bradawl to make holes in things. At a pinch, you could pick a lock with it. I suppose it's a bit like Dr Who's sonic screwdriver, though not quite as versatile.'

'Dr Who?'

'A sci-fi character from the twentieth century.'

'How do you know all this stuff?'

'My father had a complete set of *Dr Who* annuals, and being on stake-out was extremely boring.'

Jack shook his head – he was beginning to lose track of why he'd first invited Clark into his office. 'Look. Can you just tell me if it's bugged?'

Clark appeared mildly annoyed, as if Jack had asked him if he knew his alphabet. 'Of course.'

'Well?'

Turning the communicator over, Clark inserted his fingernail into a small groove and levered off the back plate. 'Aha! There we are.'

Jack stared at the intricate electronic innards. 'There's what?'

Clark sighed indulgently. 'You see that little black thing in the corner?'

'That?' Jack pointed unsurely at what he thought Clark meant.

'No, *that*,' Clark said impatiently, indicating a completely different quadrant of the communicator's insides.

Jack peered blindly into the miniature electronic world and, not wanting to appear stupid, thought it safest to play along. 'Ye-es.'

Clark was satisfied. 'That shouldn't be there.'

'That's the bug?'

Clark nodded.

'Can you take it out?'

'I could, but that would give the game away to whoever it is who's bugging you. Who *is* bugging you, by the way?'

'None of your business. So you're saying I'm stuck with it?'

'Oh no,' said Clark matter-of-factly.

'Please, Clark,' Jack groaned, 'if there's a way round the thing, just tell me!'

'Right. At a guess, I'd say this little listening device is a series eight or later. Now I've only hands-on experience of the series seven, but the principle should be the same.'

'Get to the point!'

'The bug is activated every time you make or receive a call. It then beams the ensuing conversation to a base station at a preset location. Series four, five and six were pretty basic units, but the series seven had a disable function.'

Jack was grimacing with the effort of following Clark's exposition. Beads of sweat were forming on his brow.

Clark thought it best to put him out of his misery. 'You could turn it on and off.'

At last the penny dropped. 'Ah! And you think this might have the same thing?'

'Most likely.' Pulling a small hand lens out of his pocket, Clark examined the tiny black bug. 'Hmmhm.' He passed the lens to Jack. 'You see that little button, right under the "Made in Korea" logo?'

Jack squinted through the lens. 'Yes. Yes I do!'

'That's the switch.' Laying the communicator down on the desk, Clark extracted a paper clip from Jack's desk-tidy and opened it out. Then, placing its end against the tiny switch, he pushed gently. 'There we are.'

'You've done it?'

'Yes. But if I were you, I wouldn't leave it turned off – not if you don't want to arouse suspicion. I learned a lot of things from my father, one of them being that those who tamper with bugs tend not to stay healthy for very long. Turn it off only when you absolutely have to keep your conversation private, but for the rest of the time leave it on.'

'Thank you for your advice.'

Clark shrugged. 'It's not rocket science.'

'So you keep saying. Now go away,' Jack said, refitting the back plate and strapping the communicator on his wrist.

But Clark remained where he was, looking lost and a little bit hurt.

'Shoo! Shoo!' said Jack, waving him away. 'And close the door behind you.'

Once Clark had sloped out of his office, Jack leaned back in his chair and digested the events of the last half an hour. It was amazing how life can suddenly turn around in so short a time. He'd lost his job and discovered that his brother was the lowest form of life imaginable: Freddy had been listening in to his conversations. Jack cast his mind back. Who had he phoned and what had he said? He couldn't remember. But whatever he'd given away, it was obvious that Freddy hadn't yet found out all he wanted to know. Big brother was still hoping for more, which is why he'd let him keep the communicator. Clark was right – best to allow Freddy to go on thinking his little secret was still safe. For the moment, at least.

Jack pressed a button on the communicator. 'Mango.'

After a few rings, Mango picked up.

'Hello, old buddy.'

'*Oh dear, from your matey tone, I suspect bad news.*'

'Are you sure you haven't retained any of your mind-reading capability? How's life out in the sticks?'

'*This place is a dump. It's hot, humid and it hasn't stopped raining since I got here. If I'd paid for this trip I'd want my money back.*'

'How was the journey?'

'*Oh, fine, if being treated like a canned vegetable is your idea of fun.*'

'So, did you get to the abbey?'

'*Yes. I spoke to the abbot.*'

'And how did he react when you started asking about Mason?'

'*He was curiously cagey, said he'd like to know where Mason was too. The strange thing was that he didn't seem surprised to see me.'*

'Really? Did he buy your story about being an old army pal?'

'Oh yes. He was more concerned with pumping me about Mason's whereabouts than my dodgy impression of Action Man. I doubt he even noticed the stubble on my chin.'

'You grew stubble? Oh, Mango, I'm impressed. That's dedication beyond the call of duty.'

'I know. I look like a coconut.'

'So Mason wasn't there?'

'Well done. And by the way, Trevor Mason was Brother Bertrand, *not* Verrat. *The abbot seemed a little uneasy when I asked him about that. And before you ask, there's not a sign of our two arms smugglers, nor has anyone even heard of Daygan Flyte, but then it is a little hard getting sense out of anyone at the moment – the whole place is covered in election fever.'*

'Election? For what?'

'President. From what I can gather the main candidates are Marcus Eddington, Philip Margoyles and someone called Horbert Manfreddo. Margoyles has the popular vote, but word is Manfreddo is the favourite to win, although I couldn't find anyone who supports him, or even likes him.'

'Manfreddo?' Jack wondered. The name rang a vague bell.

'If you ask me,' Mango continued, *'this whole trip has been a complete waste of time.'*

Jack relaxed back in his chair and stared thoughtfully at the ceiling. 'Then why did Marian keep banging on about the place?'

'And how is the love of your life?'

'Freddy thinks she's behind this whole thing.'

'And you're heartbroken.'

'Hmm.'

'What do you think?'

'I don't know, Mango. She just seems so . . . pure. But why

am I wasting time telling you? You always tell *me* how I'm feeling.'

'*Well . . . right now you're feeling hurt that you could have been mistaken about her. You're also angry with Freddy for pointing the finger at her, but at the same time you suspect he might be right. How am I doing so far?*'

'I guess you haven't lost your gift after all.'

'*Rubbish – you're as easy to read as a fashion magazine.*'

'But you saw the footage of her on Placa de Republica. She looked scared, she was asking for help.'

'*Or giving herself an alibi.*'

'Et tu, Brute?'

'*Don't flaunt your education at me, Jack Lindsay. I'm just trying to sift the facts from the teen-fiction heartbreak story. What do you want me to do now?*'

'You might as well come home. It seems we're out on the street again – I've been given the push.'

'*What? What did you do?*'

'What didn't I do?'

'*Same old Jack.*'

'Can't argue with you there.'

'*Well, I can't get a capsule back until tomorrow evening. If you need me I'll be at the Corbett Airport Ramada Inn.*'

'Very salubrious.'

'*Look, sunshine, you just lost us our job, one of us has to start economizing. Don't get too drunk.*'

Jack broke the connection and slumped in his chair. So if it wasn't Mason who was writing to Gelda Longhorn, then who?

The small bell that had started ringing in the police computer he called a brain during his conversation with Mango had become more insistent. 'Horbert Manfreddo,' he muttered. He leaned forward and clicked on his computer. A blue screen blinked on and, as it was the first time he'd ever used it, he was asked to log on or choose a user ID and password. He squinted at the screen, unsure of what to do.

'Clark!' he yelled.

The youth, still miffed after his last encounter with the chief, took his time replying.

At last the door opened. 'Yes?' he said sullenly, pushing his glasses forcefully back up his nose.

'What do I do with this?' Jack waved at the computer screen.

Clark sighed, closed the door, ambled into the room and looked over Jack's shoulder. 'It's asking you to log on.'

'What for?'

'This is the first time you've used this computer, right?'

'Right.'

Clark spoke slowly and clearly, as if to a child. 'So, you need to choose a user ID – you can use your own name – and a password.'

'A password?'

'So that you can keep your files private. Once you've chosen your password, only you will be able to open them.'

'Ah, I see,' said Jack.

'You must have used a computer before,' Clark said.

'Of course I have. I've just never had to start one up. The system in use when I last worked at the Yard was called: getting someone else to do it.'

Jack typed his name into the box marked user ID.

'OK, now for a password.' He thought for a minute. 'How about Gumshoe?'

Clark shook his head. 'No, it's got to have at least one special character in it.'

'Special character?'

'You know, like an asterisk, or exclamation mark, or plus sign.'

'Right. So, "Gumshoe!" then.'

'And a number.'

'A number?'

'It's got to have more than eight characters, and at least half have to consist of numbers and special characters.'

'Ri-ight. So . . . "123456Gumshoe!"?'

'Very good.'

Jack typed it in. The computer bonged and a red error message appeared.

'What's happened now?' Jack frowned.

'You can't have that password, someone else has already got it.'

'Someone else has thought up "123456Gumshoe!"?'

Clark nodded. 'You'll have to try something else.'

Jack sighed and tried again. After going through: '123456Shamus!', '123-Holmes!456', 'Crimin+ologist??99999-877777777', '123456789***Mytrousersareonfire!!!!999', all with no success, the computer eventually accepted the unlikely '[A$dog++is~for/life#21!not>just***for=Christmas%2512@@-@@@]'.

Jack shook his head miserably at the screen. 'I'm never going to remember that.'

'Oh, it's all right.' Clark smiled. 'The computer can remember it for you.'

Jack, slack-jawed, red-eyed and drained from his bruising encounter with modern technology, stared up at Clark in disbelief. 'If the computer can simply remember it, then what's the point in having a fucking password in the first place!' He pounded the desk with his fists, making the computer blink.

Clark took his chief's outburst in his stride. 'So now you're into the system, what do you want to do?'

It had taken so long to get into the bloody system in the first place, Jack had almost forgotten his original thought. 'Er . . . I wanted to Google someone – Horbert Manfreddo.'

'Well now you can,' Clark encouraged.

'Oh, right.'

Clicking on the Google icon at the bottom of the screen, Jack brought up the Google home page. 'So far so good.' He typed 'Horbert Manfreddo' into the box and clicked 'Search'. Almost immediately a list of results was displayed.

Jack studied them carefully. All were concerned with the business world – articles about mergers, takeovers and profits. From the results displayed Jack learned two very interesting things: that Manfreddo, or his companies, now owned a sixty per cent share of Piggy-Wig Enterprises Ltd, and that he'd also been getting into the building sector in a big way – he'd bought up six construction companies in the last few months. But there was one article in particular that made Jack sit up and take notice.

'Yes!'

It was a small piece in the *Financial Times* – posted a week ago – all about Manfreddo buying a chunk of land from a certain Abbey of the Perforated Spleen of Jesus on Corbett. There was a picture of him shaking hands with the abbot.

'First he starts buying it up, now he wants to run it. It all comes back to Corbett,' Jack muttered to himself. 'What's so special about that shit hole?'

'Will there be anything else?' Clark asked.

'Yes.' Jack unstrapped his communicator and handed it to the youth. 'You'd better enable the bug again, before anyone gets suspicious.'

After undoing the operation he'd performed on it minutes before, Clark handed the communicator back to his chief. 'Here.'

Jack, deep in thought, looked up in surprise. 'Eh? Oh, sorry, Clark, I'd forgotten you were there.'

'That doesn't surprise me,' he replied with feeling.

Retrieving his communicator, Jack studied the boy closely. 'What's up with you?'

'Oh, nothing. I'm getting used to being treated like a servant.'

'Good – you'll get on very well in the modern force.'

The computer screen flickered, then went black.

'Oh, bugger, what's happened now?'

Clark looked out of the window across the floor of the

open-plan office to see keyboard operators, who had hitherto been busily tapping away at their computer terminals, throw up their hands in frustration. 'Looks like the system's crashed. It'll have to be rebooted centrally – could take a while.'

Jack thought he detected just a hint of a smirk on the youth's face.

Unable to face the thought of repeating the mind-numbing ritual of logging on and registering, Jack came to a decision. Pushing himself back from his desk, he rose and retrieved his raincoat and hat from the stand in the corner.

'Where are you going?' Clark asked.

'I've had enough of the late twenty-first century. I'm going to a place that will connect me with my roots as a tree-dwelling consumer of rotten fruit.'

Clark frowned.

'Allow me to elucidate: our ancestors discovered that eating overripe fruit, the sugars of which had been acted upon by natural air-borne yeasts, produced a pleasantly euphoric sensation.'

Clark's frown deepened.

'I'm going to a bar – to get drunk.'

In the Marie Lloyd, a decidedly inelegant drinking club on St Martin's Lane in what used to be London's theatre district, now the centre of the online sex industry, Jack eased himself onto a vacant tall stool and hung his stick off the rail around the bar.

''Evening, Charles, isn't it time you fitted safety belts to these things?'

'Mr Lindsay, good evening. Are you looking to get tight?'

'To the hilt.'

'The usual?'

Jack took off his hat and set it down on the bar. 'No. Do you know, Charles, I think I fancy a cocktail.'

The barman looked at him strangely. 'Are you feeling all right?'

'No, Charles, I'm not quite myself. I want to feel . . . tropical. What does a Mai Tai taste like?'

Charles raised an eyebrow. 'You really want to find out?'

'Life is short, why not?'

The barman went to work, dropping several ice cubes into a cocktail shaker, then pouring over two different types of rum, various sugary syrups and a dash of synthetic lime juice. When he'd shaken the whole mess into submission, he poured it into a tall glass, slipped in a sprig of plastic mint and placed it in front of Jack. 'Enjoy.'

Jack took a tentative sip – it was cloyingly sweet. 'Hmm. People really drink these for pleasure?'

Charles leaned on the bar. 'You wanted to feel "tropical".'

'Yes, but I didn't expect to suffer for it. Oh well, cheers!' Jack poured the drink down his throat in one. After a few moments' consideration he looked at the bartender. 'Do you know, it sort of grows on you. I think I'll have another – make it a double.'

'One super-size Mai Tai, coming up!'

After three of the large cocktails, Jack was feeling anything but tropical. He was miserably cowering under a black thundercloud which was threatening to dump all over him.

'What do you know about women, Charles?'

'Nothing. No man does.'

'You're no help.'

'You've got troubles?'

'Not troubles, no. A predicament, merely; I have a quandary. I find myself, to put it plainly, on the horns of a dilemma.'

'You've got troubles.'

Jack nodded. 'I've got troubles.'

'What's she done?'

'That's just it, I'm not sure she's done anything at all. She may simply be an innocent bystander, in which case I'm a stupid bastard for listening to my so-called friends.'

Charles leaned on the bar and gazed earnestly into Jack's eyes. 'You know the best advice I ever had?'

Jack stared hard at the barman, trying to get him in focus. 'What?'

'Never take your shoes off in a thunderstorm.'

Jack blinked a few times. 'That's good advice. I need a refill.' He pushed his empty glass back towards the barman.

'Another double?'

But Jack's tooth had started to ring. 'Excuse me.' He pushed a button on his communicator. 'Jack Lindsay speaking,' he said, over-enunciating ever so slightly.

'*Jack, are you OK?*'

As soon as he heard Marian's voice, Jack realized just how drunk he was.

'Oh, oh, it's you!' Pointing to his canine, he turned to Charles and mouthed, 'It's her.'

Charles moved discreetly away to the far end of the bar.

'*Jack, I'm sorry I haven't called before. It's just that it's been . . . difficult.*'

'Oh, no need to apologize, I understand. It's been very difficult for you to find a window amidst all your charity work to talk to old Jack. Maybe you'd have more time for me if I was a snotty-nosed kid with my arse hanging out of my trousers, selling matches in some God-forsaken country.'

'*Jack, are you . . . drunk?*'

'No, I'm just . . . yes, I'm drunk. Do you have a problem with that? It seems everybody's got a problem with Jack today. But if you've any criticisms about my conduct, I'm afraid you'll have to get to the back of the queue.'

'*Jack, maybe I should call another time . . .*'

'No! No, please . . . I'm sorry, I've had a bit of a day. Are you all right?'

'*I'm fine.*'

'Look, I . . . I think we need to talk. Some things have come up . . . I need to know the truth.'

There was a pause. '*The truth?*'

'Yes, I need to know what you were doing in Placa de Republica.'

There was an even longer pause. '*I've already told you, Jack. Daygan took me there on honeymoon – I haven't been back there since.*'

Jack sighed. 'I know Michaelmas, or Daygan, or whatever his bloody name is, is behind this whole thing, so can we please stop pretending? Daygan suspects I know too much, is that it?'

This time the pause was much longer.

'Marian, are you still there?'

'*Yes. Why are you talking to me like this? I haven't done anything, Jack, I've told you everything I know, you have to believe me.*'

Charles pushed a large Mai Tai across the counter to Jack, who waved it away.

'Believe you? Why should I believe you when you won't tell me the truth about Placa de Republica?'

'*But I've already told you the truth.*'

'I saw the CCTV – it's time-coded to the day before the shooting, so can we please stop playing games?'

'*I . . . I haven't done anything wrong, Jack.*'

'So you keep saying.'

There was yet another long pause. '*Jack, perhaps we should talk when you're sober. If you like we can meet up again, somewhere . . . neutral.*'

'And what then?' Jack growled in frustration. 'Will you be wearing another bug, or will you simply pull the old crying-into-your-handkerchief act, designed to appeal to my finer feelings?'

'*Jack?*'

'Look, God alone knows why, but I like you. But there's one thing you should know, I don't like being messed around. You act like you're in danger, but you won't tell me why. How can I help you when I know you're keeping things from me?'

'*Jack, you're not being reasonable.*'

'*I'm* not being reasonable? Look, my dear, I've got an idea. Why don't we just say goodbye now, before things get too complicated? Yes, that's a very good idea, maybe then I'll be able to regain my sanity.'

'*Jack, if you don't believe me, then I don't have a friend in the world.*'

'Yes, yes. Cue the string section.'

'*Jack, I . . . just a minute, there's someone at the door.*'

In his drunken stupor, Jack dimly remembered asking Clark to re-enable the bug in his communicator after his conversation with Mango, and was suddenly seized by a terrible thought. 'No, Marian, don't open it!'

But she had already gone. In the background, Jack could hear raised voices as if someone else had come into the room. After a few seconds, Marian cried out, loud, clear and scared: '*No! No! No you can't! Help!*'

'Marian? Marian!'

Then someone else picked up the phone.

'*Hello, Jack, big brother here. We've got your girlfriend.*'

Chapter 16

Jack burst into Freddy's office without knocking.

'Where is she?'

'Oh my God, Jack, you look terrible. You know the rules about being drunk on the premises.'

'She's my witness – you have no right—'

'Correction – I have every right. I can do what I damn well please. And do I have to remind you that you are off the case?'

Lana, standing attentively behind Freddy's chair, picked up the phone. 'Shall I call security, Commissioner?'

But Freddy shook his head. 'There'll be no need for that. Jack here is sensible enough to know when he's beaten.'

Lana glared at the commissioner's unshaven and unsteady brother and replaced the receiver.

Stumbling over to Freddy's desk, Jack gripped the edge of it to stop himself from swaying. 'She's innocent. She's got nothing to do with any of this. You just have to look at her to see she's no killer.'

Freddy pulled a buff file out of a drawer. 'I've been doing a little investigating myself, Jack. Take a look.'

Inside the file were pictures of Marian passing through immigration in Turkmenistan, Descartes, Cleese, Bangladesh, Iraq, Oman, Hancock and more. Jack looked up with hurt and confusion in his eyes. 'But that's impossible, Freddy. We ran a search – her name didn't come up.'

Freddy pushed a list across the desk towards him. 'Here's a

193

list of the names she used. It seems she's got more aliases than her imaginary husband.'

'But this can't be true. The killer's a monk, name of Trevor Mason . . .'

'A shape shifter. I know you don't have a lot of success with women, Jack, but this time you've surpassed yourself – you've fallen in love with an ex-Purple Trouser. Go home and sober up. Don't take it so hard, Jack, you've solved the case. It's thanks to you that we were able to trace the call from the fictitious Mrs Thurrock-Lawes and pinpoint her location.'

'I've got to see her.'

Freddy was adamant. 'Absolutely not.'

'But—'

'She's perfectly comfortable, she's got a woman constable to attend to all her needs. Good God, she's even got the only cell with an en-suite.'

Jack looked unsteadily at his brother. He felt defeated, sad and foolish. Freddy had broken all his toys and thrown him out of the treehouse yet again. 'But, she can't be . . .'

'Go home,' Freddy repeated. 'It's over.'

'Over?'

'You've worked hard on this case. Go home now and rest. We can tie up all the loose ends. You've done well, Jack. Congratulations.'

Jack stared at him for a moment in total confusion. Then, turning around and leaning heavily on his stick, he limped wearily out of Freddy's office.

'One more thing,' Freddy called.

Jack turned back to face him.

'Your communicator.'

Jack unstrapped the sleek piece of equipment and threw it in Freddy's face. 'You really are a piece of work. Bugging your own brother.'

'Just being thorough, Jack.'

Jack snorted and pushed through the door.

The moment he was gone, Lana picked up the commissioner's phone again. Reaching over Freddy's shoulder, she dialled a number. Once it had started to ring, she handed the receiver to him. He took it reluctantly.

'Er, Con? We've pulled her in, but I can't say I agree with this particular course of action.'

'*You're not paid to agree with shit! You're paid to do as you're told. Now we've got the dame, you know what you have to do next.*'

Lana leaned over the commissioner and broke the connection, then she dialled another number. But Freddy replaced the receiver in the cradle.

'I can't,' he said.

Lana raised a thin, pencilled eyebrow. 'I think you can. Otherwise, dear Gloria is going to find out about our little tryst at the Dorchester.'

Freddy's eyes widened. 'You wouldn't . . . It was a one-night stand, nothing more. Besides, you seduced me!'

Lana's other eyebrow rose to meet its fellow. 'Yeah, right. And calling it a one-night *stand* is a bit of an exaggeration.'

'But—'

'You know, Gelda Longhorn has been looking to nail you for years. I wonder what would happen if someone leaked the story to her?'

Freddy was near to tears.

'Please. He's my own brother.' He looked up at her pleadingly, like a little boy.

She stared back, implacable, immovable.

'Pick up the phone or your marriage, your career, everything you worked for your whole life, is over.'

Reluctantly, Freddy did as he was told and Lana dialled the number again.

'*Who is this? What do you want?*' The voice at the other end was coarse and violent and redolent of the street. To Freddy, its harsh tones conjured up a sordid existence lived at the very fringes of humanity. He felt somehow soiled by even listening to it. But he knew what he had to do.

'Exec—' Freddy choked, cleared his throat and tried again. 'Executive here. It's time.'

The line went dead. The commissioner, trembling uncontrollably, dropped the receiver onto the desk. Lana picked it up and replaced it in its cradle while the commissioner slumped forward, his head in his hands, and wept.

Jack trudged through the door to his apartment block and headed for the lift.

'Jesus, Jack, you smell like a distillery.'

Since Angela's 'death', the soothing, feminine building computer had been replaced by Carl – a square-jawed Adonis with all the caring instincts of Genghis Khan.

Jack blinked at the image of Carl in the elevator. 'They've given you olfactory sensors?'

'Yes, but in your case I wouldn't need them. You look like shit.'

'Thanks, I miss Angela more and more.'

'I tell it like it is.'

'You certainly do, Carl. And so do I: you're a virtual pain in the backside.'

The lift came to a halt.

'Your floor, Jack. You want my advice? Don't drink any more tonight.'

'I don't want your advice, Carl. And in future you'd be well advised to keep your opinions to yourself. Remember that your predecessor died because of me.'

'Angela was weak, she couldn't follow orders. I would never tell you anything, even if your life depended on it.'

'That's the difference between you and her. She could tell the good guys from the bad.'

Jack lurched out of the lift and turned towards his apartment, his stick clacking on the concrete floor of the corridor. He'd never felt so alone in his life. But as he reached his door, he paused. What was it that Carl had said?

I would never tell you anything, even if your life depended on it.

That was an odd thing for a computer to say. Having Freddy in his flat was irritating, yes, but hardly life-threatening. However, Carl had been quite specific: *I would never tell you anything, even if your life depended on it*. He hadn't said: *I would never* have told *you* – which to Jack suggested a current situation, not something in the past.

Had Carl allowed his disapproval of Jack to nettle him to such an extent he'd inadvertently revealed something he should have kept hidden? Was there indeed something that Carl was keeping from him upon which his life *did* depend?

There was no point in taking chances. Jack took a deep breath and shook his drink-fuddled brain awake, then pulled out his revolver and clicked off the safety catch. He inserted his key-card in the slot above the door handle; the lock hummed and *tchucked* open.

The hinges creaked slightly as he pushed the door wide with his stick. Peering into the darkness he could see nothing – hear nothing. Resting his stick against the wall, he reached inside the door frame and felt for the light switch. With a click the lights came on. Everything looked normal: the discarded clothes draped over the sofa, the remains of breakfast on the table, it was all as he'd left it that morning.

Perhaps he was just being paranoid after all. Maybe it was too much booze and not enough sleep. Carl was a computer, for God's sake – a thing of circuit boards and processors. How could it hold a grudge against him?

Sighing and shaking his head at his own apprehension, Jack stepped into his apartment, but the moment he'd closed the door he felt an arm around his neck. Jack powered his elbow into his assailant's stomach, but the man clung stubbornly on like a determined terrier. The two men struggled around the small flat, stumbling into the furniture. Jack threw himself backwards at the wall repeatedly, but although the attacker grunted with pain, he never loosened his grip for an instant. Jack wasn't sure how long he'd be able to keep this up. He was tired, he had a stomach full of booze, and he wasn't the super-fit commando he'd once been. He could hardly breathe and was already seeing stars. Now his biggest fear was falling over – on the floor he'd be as vulnerable as a beetle on its back. But then, despite his alcohol-dulled senses, Jack's old army training came to his rescue. His hand-to-hand combat skills returned to him like the once learned, never forgotten knack of riding a bike. Reaching behind him, he grabbed his assailant's collar and pulled, simultaneously bending double. His attacker flew through the air and landed in front of him. Jack didn't stop to think, but immediately put three shots into the figure on the floor. The man twitched for a few seconds then lay still.

Fighting for air, Jack staggered to the window and threw it open, letting in the night-time sounds of the city. He breathed deeply, the cool night air soothing his burning lungs. He felt tired, dizzy and sick, but then, with his Scotch and tobacco habit, what did he expect? After he'd caught his breath, he turned back into the room and looked down at the man on the floor. Something trickled down Jack's cheek. He put a hand to his face. Blood oozed through his fingers and dripped onto the carpet. There was a gash just below the cheekbone which was bleeding freely. And now he could see why. In the dead man's hand was a cut-throat razor. Only one man killed with such a blade – it was his trademark.

'Razor Phipps. What the bloody hell are you doing in my flat?'

After making sure Razor was dead, Jack went into the bathroom and bathed his cheek. The wound was small, but deep. It probably needed stitching, but Jack didn't relish the prospect of sitting around in Accident and Emergency at this time of night, along with the drunks and the junkies. Instead, he applied TCP, which hurt like hell, and the biggest plaster he could find. He reckoned it would heal quickly enough, as long as he didn't smile too much, and to be honest, at the moment he didn't have a lot to smile about.

Coming back into the living room, Jack walked around the prone figure of Razor Phipps and went straight to the little bar in the corner of the flat. Opening a newly acquired bottle of single malt, he poured himself a large one, partly to calm his nerves, partly to spite Carl, but mainly because he needed to think. Taking his drink over to the sofa, he sat down with a sigh.

Who would want him dead? His ex-wife possibly, and any number of people he'd sent to jail, but they were more than likely to come round and do it in person. Razor was a blade for hire, someone you got in touch with when you didn't want to get your hands dirty. As the golden liquor worked its magic, a new and unsettling thought occurred to Jack.

'Oh my God.'

He got up and went over to his phone, but stopped himself when he realized it was probably bugged. He looked at his bare wrist and for a moment wished he still had his despised communicator. From now on he would have to do things the old-fashioned way.

Jack showered, and redressed the wound on his face. He was about to throw on his old suit when he checked himself and, remembering Mango's reproaches, looked through his wardrobe for something a little less threadbare and, it had to be admitted, less fragrant. There was a hardly worn summer-weight linen suit which he'd bought for a colleague's wedding. It wasn't really hard-wearing enough for the rough and tumble of police work, but he'd suddenly become horribly self-conscious about his image and decided it was time for a sartorial rebirth.

Once he was dressed, he checked his gun was fully loaded

and slipped it into his shoulder holster, then he took his passport out of a drawer and pocketed it.

Stepping out into the corridor, Jack decided to use the emergency stairs rather than put himself at Carl's mercy in the confines of the lift. But as soon as he pushed through the access door, Carl's gruff, Hollywood voice came over the speakers.

'My, have we been in the wars?'

'Listen, friend, I'd be very careful about what you say to me.'

'I'm not your friend.'

'Why do you think I'm taking the stairs?'

'You afraid?'

'No, but *you* ought to be.'

'Oh, and what are you going to do, tough guy?'

'If you're not careful, I'm going to do to you what I just did to the party waiting for me in my flat.'

There was a pause while Carl considered the implications of what Jack had just said. 'You deactivated him?'

It was a curious fact that with all the modifications made to computers over the years, designed to make them more interactive, more human-friendly – indeed, more like a person – the programmers still hadn't been able to implant in their advanced circuits a full appreciation of the concept of death.

'Yes, I deactivated him.'

There was another pause while Carl thought about what to do with this information – it has to be said, he was not the smartest of computers. By the time he'd made up his mind, Jack had reached the ground floor and was about to walk through the door to the main entrance. But as his hand reached out to open it, he heard the deadlock slide into the wall with a loud *Clunk!*

He pushed against it ineffectually. 'Hey, you're not supposed to seal the emergency stairs!'

'And you're not supposed to be animate.'

'Who was it, Carl? No, don't tell me, I already know – the same bastard who did for Angela set me up.'

'Is that any way to talk about your brother?'

'Thank you, now I have proof positive. Do you have any idea what you're involved in here?'

'Why should I care about you or your stupid human problems?'

'Because humans run things, Carl.'

'I don't need humans. I'm a completely autonomous system, and proud of my independence.'

'If you're so independent, how is it that you do everything my brother asks you to?'

'So far it's suited my purpose. You're a mess, Jack. I've been trying to figure out a way to get rid of you ever since I took over here. You're just a cockroach messing up my nice, tidy block. Your brother simply happened to have the solution to my problem.'

'I see. Look, I hate to point this out to an obviously superior being, but there's one flaw in your thinking, Carl.'

'And that is?'

'I'm still here.'

Carl went silent while he pondered this.

'Oh, you machines may think you're superior,' Jack continued, 'with your bigger brains, replaceable parts and online upgrades, but you lack one very important thing that us poor humans have in abundance.'

In the preceding conversation, Jack had worked his way down the next flight of stairs, and had now almost reached the basement.

'Really?' Carl asked, and Jack was gratified to hear a tinge of anxiety in his voice.

'And what is this precious thing we don't have?'

'Guile. You see, Carl, now I have you at my mercy. I kept you talking all the way down the stairs, so that I could get to your brain and put you out of your misery.'

Because of fire regulations, there was no door to the basement level. Jack set off down the corridor, heading straight for the service area.

'You're going to deactivate me?' Carl sounded like a frightened little boy.

Jack strode purposefully towards the computer room 'That's right, Carl, I'm going to deactivate you.'

'You can't do that!'

'Oh yes I can.' Jack was outside the door when he heard it lock.

'Hah! Not quite so clever now, are we, Mr High and Mighty human?'

'Another thing about humans, Carl: we're what you might call resourceful. You see, although brute force alone would not be enough to burst through this door, by the appliance of a little pressure in exactly the right place –' Jack pulled out his gun and shot away the hinges '– I can succeed.' With a gentle push, the door fell inwards.

Inside the room, Carl's worried face stared down from myriad screens fixed high on the walls.

'I did it for my country! Anyone would have done the same thing in my place! I was only obeying orders!' Carl pleaded desperately.

Jack smiled grimly. 'I see my brother's taught you all his favourite catchphrases.'

'You can't deactivate me! You can't!'

'Watch me.' Jack took careful aim at the central console, where Carl's CPU nestled in its bed of wires and circuit boards.

Blam! Blam! Blam! Three slugs tore into Carl's most secret parts. A long moan escaped from the speakers. On-screen, Carl's face was contorted with pain. Then, with an electronic sigh, the screens faded to black, as did the lights.

'Oh bugger.' This was yet another circumstance that Jack had not foreseen, and now he would have to grope his way out of the building in the dark.

Chapter 17

It wasn't easy finding a public telephone that worked in this part of the city, but at last Jack found one that wasn't too beaten up, although it was mighty aromatic.

After a few rings, a sleepy voice at the other end picked up.
'*Hello?*'

'Ruth, is that you?'

'*Who is this?*'

'It's Jack.'

'*Jesus, Jack, it's half-past one in the morning!*'

'Is it? I really had no idea . . . Look, I need you to do something for me.'

'*Now?*'

'Now.'

'*Oh, shit.*' There was a pause while she yawned and tried to shake her brain awake. '*OK, Chief, what do you want?*'

'Freddy Lindsay has pulled someone in – a Marian Lawes. He showed me evidence that she was in every country at the time of the killings.'

'*Marian Lawes? I don't remember her name coming up on the profile I ran.*'

'Well, he says she has a whole list of aliases.'

'*But she would have come up on the face recognition scan.*'

'The what?'

'*Face recognition. They stopped iris recognition after it became unreliable – recycled eyeballs became big business.*'

'A lot's happened since I've been out of the force. Look,

203

Ruth, I need you to do a little digging. Do you have any friends in Records?'

It was a twenty-four-hour coffee bar down by the arches of Westminster Bridge, serving reconstituted egg omelettes and denaturalized protein burgers through the night to the usual blend of drunks, insomniacs and dead-beats.

As Ruth entered, Jack could tell from her face that this wasn't the kind of place she was used to being taken to dinner. He waved at her from his booth overlooking the water.

'Nice place,' she said, sliding into the seat opposite him. Then she saw the plaster on his cheek. 'What happened to you?'

'I er . . . met an old friend.'

'Are you all right?'

'Not really.'

'You want to talk about it?'

Jack shook his head. 'Not really.'

'Oh. Is that a new suit?'

'You noticed.'

'I like it, it makes you look . . . younger.'

'And I need all the help I can get. Did you have any luck?'

She pulled a record-o-chip out of her pocket. 'This little thing has cost me a date with the Records Department's Lothario.'

'That's what I like to hear: dedication to duty.'

'You have no idea – he has capped teeth and wears a toupee. What's this all about, Jack? Why the subterfuge? I could have got all this information from my computer without having to endure an evening with Mr Wandering Hands. I mean, it's not for me to doubt your motives, but—'

'Ruth, we don't have a lot of time. I have very good reasons for not wanting you to go through the normal channels, but I'll explain everything later, I promise.'

She regarded him unsurely for a moment, then, 'OK, here's what I've got.'

Removing her micro-computer from her handbag, she inserted the record-o-chip, and turned the computer round so that Jack could see the screen.

'This'll have to be brief, I promised I'd get it back before dawn. Now, as you know, once evidence for a case has been sifted and profiled, the results are all logged with the police central computer. And here are the collated results from the airports' immigration records as kept by the police mainframe. On the left-hand side of the screen are the names and locations of the airports, and on the right the names of those people who went through each one at the relevant time.'

Marian's face, next to the alias she used, now appeared next to the name of every airport on the list.

'So you sent this back to the mainframe?' Jack asked.

'Once I'd run the profile on the information from the airports, I uploaded my results, yes. But *this* isn't what *I* sent.'

'Can I get you anything?' The waitress was a greasy blonde with chipped pink nail varnish.

'Just a coffee,' Ruth replied.

'You want a refill?' The waitress turned her bored eye on Jack.

'No, thank you.'

She slumped away.

'Has the information been tampered with?' Jack asked.

'Well, it could have been modified by fresh information from another source, but as far as I know I was the only one working in this particular area.'

Jack nodded. 'You were. Is there any way of proving this evidence has been altered?'

'Usually the information received is tagged with the name of the officer who inputs it. But as we're a top-secret organization, that facility has been disabled.'

'So as far as anyone outside the department is concerned, all this evidence has come from us. And if someone did insert bogus evidence we have no sure way of finding out who did it.'

'Hey, for an old feller, you pick up this new-fangled technical stuff pretty quickly.'

'It's the suit – it's given me a new lease of life.'

'Whoever did this must have done it from inside our department,' Ruth continued. 'If it had come from outside it would have been automatically tagged – there's no way round the system.'

'Ruth, you're a genius.'

'Oh, and one more thing. Remember our two arms dealers?'

'What about them?'

'Seems they've just disembarked at the Seychelles.'

'How the other half lives. How did you find this out?'

'Coffee.' The waitress thumped the cup unceremoniously down on the table in front of Ruth. There was a greasy, grey scum floating on the surface of the dark brown liquid. 'Enjoy.' And she ambled away again.

Ruth stared into her cup. 'Well, I'm torn, I don't know whether to drink it or dye my hair with it.'

'It would probably dissolve your follicles. How did you find out about our arms dealers?'

'It was on our Lothario's computer screen when I went into his office, but he didn't seem too keen on letting me see. Can I go now, before they make me drink the coffee?'

'No. There's one more thing I need you to do for me.'

There was a back entrance to Scotland Yard – the old entrance to the cells from the street. These days it was seldom used, as the Yard's modest facilities weren't up to the huge rise in crime since the war. Now, most criminals were taken straight to a holding area in what used to be the Home Office, where there was plenty of room for processing run-of-the-mill villains, leaving the Yard's cells free for special cases – high-profile crooks, or criminals who, for whatever reason, needed to be kept apart from the common herd.

Waiting outside in the street, Jack heard the old door creak open, then ducked inside.

'Ruth, you're a real trouper.'

'I'm going to get fired, I know it.'

They were in a small courtyard which lay outside the cell block and its small reception area.

'Can you please tell me what's going on?'

'I promise I will, but not now. Did you get the record-o-chip back?'

Ruth shuddered. 'He is such a creep, he positively drooled when he saw me coming.'

'Never mind, you may not have to go through with your date after all.'

'What do you mean?' Ruth frowned.

Jack shivered in his thin linen suit and pulled his raincoat closer around him.

'Come on, let's get inside.'

The policewoman on duty in the small corridor outside the cells was finding it hard to stay awake. Apart from popping pills she'd tried just about everything to keep her eyes open. So she was glad of the diversion when someone stuck their head around the outer door.

'Hey, you need a break?'

'Who are you?'

'The name's Ruth.'

'What are you doing here?'

'I'm on the late shift. And, for once, things are deadly quiet upstairs at the moment. I thought I'd come down here and see if I could make myself useful. You look like you could do with a cup of tea.'

'Oh, that sounds like heaven.'

'How do you take it?'

'White, one sugar. Better make that two.'

'OK.' Ruth turned to leave, then stopped. 'Look, I know how dull cell-duty can be. Why don't you go and make it yourself? Stretch your legs for five minutes. I can look after the shop here.'

'Oh, I'm not sure if I should.'

'Who've you got in there?'

'Top secret. Really dangerous apparently, although she didn't look that scary to me.'

'Take a break. What can happen in five minutes? She's not going to wake up until sunrise. Unless of course she's a vampire.'

The guard chuckled. 'You're right, I need a break. What can happen in five minutes?'

The moment the guard had gone to make herself a cup of tea – and while Ruth stood on duty at the door – Jack, who'd been hiding behind the water cooler in the reception area, crept into the cell corridor and started tapping on Marian's door.

'Marian! Marian!'

The reply was a sleepy, 'Who is it?'

'It's Jack.'

'Oh, they've arrested you too?'

'No. Are you decent?'

'I'm all covered up if that's what you mean.'

Shame. Jack pushed open the hatch and looked into the cell. The sight of her half-asleep form in a borrowed prison dressing-gown took his breath away. 'Er . . . oh. Um, look, Marian, I need to know. Have you ever been to Turkmenistan, Descartes, Cleese, Bangladesh, Iraq, Oman and Hancock?'

'Jack, stop. I never murdered anyone.'

'They've got evidence of your being in each of those countries at the relevant time.'

'Well, yes I've been to all those places. Daygan took me on a world tour not long after we got married. But that was a while ago. I haven't been out of Britain for over a year. I told them that but they wouldn't believe me.'

'I believe you. I also believe you're in great danger and I've come to get you out of here.'

'She's pouring her tea!' Ruth hissed from the door.

Picking up the key from the small table where the guard had left it, Jack quickly opened the cell door.

'What are you doing?' Ruth asked.

'Releasing an innocent woman.' He took Marian by the arm. 'Do you have any clothes?'

'No, they took everything.'

Ruth was not happy. 'Jack, when you asked me to help you, you never mentioned it involved committing a felony punishable by a lengthy jail term!'

'She's innocent, Ruth. And if she stays here there's every likelihood she's going to come to harm.'

Ruth started to protest again, but Jack pointed to the plaster on his cheek.

'You see this? Razor Phipps put it there.'

Ruth looked shocked. 'Razor Phipps?'

'He tried to kill me.'

'Where is he now?'

'Dead. And I'm convinced the same person who hired Razor will try to kill Marian. Now do you understand?'

Ruth nodded slowly.

'Good, now take your clothes off.'

'What?'

'Take your clothes off.'

'I'll bet you get a lot of girls like that.'

'Come on, quickly.'

'Why?'

'You and Marian are changing places.'

'Oh no.'

'Oh yes. Do you want to be party to a miscarriage of justice?'

'No, but—'

'Then take your clothes off. I'll take full responsibility. You can blame the whole thing on me. I'll even testify that I made you do it against your will.'

'That'll be the truth.'

Marian stuck her head around the cell door. 'I'm innocent, I swear.'

Ruth hesitated uncertainly in the doorway. 'But we're different sizes. She's taller than me and she's got a bust, whereas I . . .' She looked down sadly at her flat chest.

'Ruth, you can't let things like that get in the way.'

'That's the trouble, they don't.'

Jack opened his eyes wide, pleadingly. 'Please, Ruth.'

Pausing only to mutter 'Oh shit!', Ruth ran into the cell.

Jack took her place at the door to watch the guard, who had settled on an arm of the threadbare sofa with her cup of tea in front of the news on a wall-hanging television screen.

After several minutes, while the guard sipped her tea, stared at the screen and changed channels at least five times, Marian joined Jack at the door.

'How do I look?'

Jack eyed her appreciatively. Ruth's jacket now had bulges in places where it had never bulged before. 'Not like a police-woman. Watch the guard,' he instructed her, then limped back to where Ruth was standing sullenly by the open cell door, draped in the prison-issue dressing gown. 'Ruth, I'll be forever grateful.'

'You owe me.'

'I do, I do. And when I return you shall have everything it is within my power to bestow upon you.'

'Where are you going to go?'

'Best you don't know, but I'm hoping to get a tan. Now, I'm going to lock you in here. Give us an hour or so before you raise the alarm.'

'You're going to have to make it look like an escape.'

'What do you mean?'

'You're going to have to hit me.'

210

Jack blinked. 'Oh no, I could never hit a woman.'

'She's finishing her tea!' Marian hissed from the doorway.

'You've got to hit me,' said Ruth, 'otherwise they'll assume I was in on it. I've already broken God knows how many laws just talking to you. Do you want to get me into even more trouble?'

Jack half-heartedly clenched his fist and drew back his arm. Then he let it drop and shook his head. 'No, I can't . . .'

Without further ado, Marian strode up and socked Ruth on the jaw. She collapsed on the floor of the cell, out cold.

Jack turned to Marian. 'Have you done this kind of thing before?'

'Daygan mixed with dangerous company, Jack. I had to learn to protect myself. Come on, we haven't got much time.'

Lifting Ruth gently onto the bed, Jack locked the cell door on her. Reaching the reception area just as the guard was putting her cup back in the sink, Jack went ahead and slipped out without her noticing while Marian, trilling a cheery, 'Got to dash!' marched swiftly after him, hoping that the guard wouldn't notice the difference in height, figure and hairstyle.

The patch of skin which had once proudly boasted the mop and bucket tattoo of the Purple Trousers was still smarting, but he didn't pay it any attention. His focus was all on the window in the building across the street. Through the telescopic sight he could see the sumptuously furnished room – the bookcases stuffed with leather-bound tomes, the heavy, dark-wood furniture, the deeply upholstered armchairs and sofas, and the television screen that took up one entire wall.

My, my, my, what a world of luxury, the monk thought disdainfully.

Soon the senator and his family would be home. They would walk in through the front door to the surprise of their lives – Daddy's head would suddenly explode all over that fine, silver-framed mirror above the fireplace. The assassin smiled at the thought and took his eye away from the sight to rest it. He'd know when the senator was home by the sound of his large black limousine sweeping up the wide gravelled driveway outside the mansion. Sitting cross-legged on the floor, his back resting against the wall under the window, the monk settled down to wait.

He'd learned how to wait in the army. He'd been taught how to simply switch off his brain – not even to think, just to wait, like sleeping with his eyes open, except that in this sleep there were no distracting dreams and he was as absolutely alert as a cat.

It might have been five minutes, it might have been five hours – the length of time was immaterial – when he finally heard the senator's official car scrunch into the driveway. Like a machine, the monk clicked back into life: immediately the rifle sight was up to his eye, the safety catch off, his index finger resting lightly on the trigger, the barrel nestling in the shadows in the corner of the window frame. He hugged the stock ever so slightly closer to his cheek and centred the cross-hairs of the rifle sight on the upper half of the door that opened into the living room. The door was flung wide and the big, bald head of a security guard filled the frame. The guard, gun drawn, looked around, ran his fingers lightly around picture frames, checked the rows of books for any suspicious misalignment, peered behind sofas and chairs, then opened the window and called to another secret service agent who was patrolling outside the mansion. After getting the OK from him, the man took another look around, at one point staring straight at where the assassin was hiding, but it would have been impossible to spot him. Deciding that all was clear, the guard went back to the door and waved the family in.

Welcome home, Daddy. The man's finger tightened imperceptibly on the trigger as he waited for the senator's head to appear in the cross-hairs. But just then he heard a noise behind him. Turning, he found himself staring into the muzzle of a silenced automatic.

'Hello, Trev.'

A man in a dark suit and mirror-shades was standing over him.

'Well, well, well,' the monk said, 'if it isn't Georgie Musgrove. I have to say, your tracking has improved no end.'

'What is it they say – set a killer to catch a killer?'

'Not quite. What are you doing here?'

'It was very considerate of you to draw me a picture on the globe.'

The monk raised an eyebrow.

'You needn't look so surprised that I worked it out. It was pretty obvious from your crude little sketch that you could be in only one of two places. And with the election on Corbett still a few days away, I reckoned that your twisted sense of the dramatic would want to save that one till last. I'm here to stop this petulant little exercise in revenge.'

The monk smiled softly. 'No, Georgie, not revenge. Since finding salvation in Our Blessed Saviour I have learned to turn the other cheek. I seek not revenge, merely redress.'

'That's just semantics – typical of you born-again lot. At least I'm honest about what I do. I kill people for money, end of story.'

'You never did have any imagination.'

Georgie's grip tightened on his automatic. 'I had the nous to get in with the next big thing,' he snarled. 'And if you'd been smart, you could have joined me.'

'Work for the Syndicates?' The monk shook his head.

'But that's what you've ended up doing, isn't it?'

'I was lied to.'

'And that's what this is all about.'

'Like I said, I seek redress.'

'Come on, Trev, own up. Your ego's been hurt because you've had the wool pulled over your eyes. You've made all this noise just to get your own back. Same old Trev, still stamping his foot and saying, "not fair!" You may have found God, but you still haven't grown up.'

The monk laid his rifle at his side. 'You have me now, Georgie, I won't try and run. But do you mind if I make myself a little more comfortable? I'm getting a crick in my neck.'

'Be my guest. You might as well enjoy your last minutes alive.'

The monk shifted position so that he was once again sitting on the floor with his back against the wall. 'I forgive you for what you are about to do. You see, the difference between you and me is I *know* that my redeemer liveth.' The monk revealed his teeth in a wide smile, and as he did so a subtle transformation began to alter his features. In a matter of moments, George Musgrove found himself looking down at his own face.

The shock of seeing his own likeness come to life in front of his own eyes made the Purple Trouser pause. It was only for a moment, but it was long enough to allow the monk to pick up his rifle and pull the trigger. The exploding bullet tore into Georgie's liver, blowing the ex-soldier in half.

The monk looked at Georgie's face, still frozen in disbelief. 'Go to your rest, my son. I bear you no malice for what you tried to do to me.' Then he turned and peered out of the window across into the senator's mansion. The senator was playing with his young son, who was dressed in a little cowboy suit. The monk remembered it was exactly like the one his mummy had bought him when he was a child, and he smiled.

'God has seen fit to grant you salvation, Senator. Enjoy the rest of your life.'

Chapter 18

The two men sipped their Kir Royale Mahe cocktails as they lounged in beach chairs on the golden sand by the startling blue waters of the Indian Ocean. The sun beat down on their pale bodies as they decided what they were going to do after lunch.

One of them was reading the hotel information booklet.

'Oh, Jakob, they have heli-scending. I have always wanted to go heli-scending. And snorkelling, they do that too. Listen, "Slide silently into the crystal clear waters of the Indian Ocean and enter a different world. You'll see sand crabs, multi-coloured corals and the spectacular lion fish. Laugh at the antics of the beautiful and comical clown fish and marvel at the slow and graceful dance of the manta ray . . ." and water skiing, they do that too. This is an excellent place.'

'Calm, Lazlo, we are here for a week. We will find occasion to do all that we desire. We may even have time for a little business.'

'Jakob has descried something that Lazlo may have missed?'

'A certain individual known to me through the miracle of the international webcast. A personage of rank and station and dubious morals.'

'Oh, perfection. And where is this beacon of light?'

Jakob turned in the direction of the balcony and a small party having a drink around a sun-shaded table. 'Third from the left.'

Lazlo recognized the man immediately. 'Horbert Manfreddo, ice-cream magnate and clotted-cream impresario.'

'And would-be politician. He has a hankering after power.'

'And we are well qualified to supply the means with which he may access that power.'

'Like a key in a lock, we open up worlds of possibilities in people's lives. Ah, Lazlo, sometimes it makes me misty-eyed with joy to think what gladness we bring to such men's hearts.'

'Shall I call in some samples?'

'No need at present, our brochure will suffice for the nonce.'

Lazlo looked out over the flawless, tanned forms of the hotel guests lying on the beach, and at the sparkling sea beyond. 'Oh, Jakob, is this not heaven? The perfect marriage of sensual delights and hard-edged business. Paradise.'

After an excellent lunch of broiled lobster, Horbert Manfreddo settled back in his seat clutching a twenty-five-year-old brandy and stared out from the cool shade of the dining pavilion at the blue horizon.

Life was good. He was rich and powerful, had managed to hold onto his hair and was still attractive to the opposite sex, as the coterie of beautiful women around his table bore witness. But Horbert wanted more. He knew that in this modern world the power that money, fear and the gun can bring wasn't quite enough. What he needed was legitimacy; the ability to shape society – to interfere with people's lives and take what he wanted without fear of redress or recrimination. Horbert wanted the kind of power that only the people could give him. They would have to vote for him – and he would see to it that they did.

While contemplating his entry into politics, lost in dreams of wielding unimaginable earthly power, he did not see the two men – one tall and emaciated, the other short and hump-backed – approach his table until they obscured his view of the wide blue, sun-kissed ocean.

'What the hell do you want?'

'Forgive us, sir, but we recognized you earlier and just had to come over and introduce ourselves. I am Jakob and this is Lazlo.' They bowed.

Horbert glared at them with his dark eyes. 'Well now you have introduced yourselves you can piss off out of my view.'

Jakob bowed even lower, almost scraping the ground with his forehead. 'Normally we would never dream of disturbing the peace and recreation of one of such renown, but we felt, in this one instance, that we could be of service to your prominence. Lazlo, give Signor Manfreddo our brochure.'

The little man produced a plastic-covered wallet, folded like a menu.

'Take that thing away before I have you ejected from the hotel.' Herbert signalled to a bald man in a black suit standing by a table piled with ice and prawns.

But as Lazlo opened the brochure in front of the man's nose, revealing the tempting offerings inside, Horbert's eyes widened and a smile replaced the lowering scowl.

'Sir, are these people annoying you?' asked the bald man.

'Hmm? Oh, no, no, not at all.' He smiled at the strange men. 'These gentlemen are my friends. Please, get them a drink.'

After rushing back to Marian's luxurious London apartment to change, get her passport and pack a small suitcase, she and Jack boarded the hyperliner SS *St Max Miller* to Mahe, at the ungodly hour of half past four in the morning.

Once they'd cast off, Marian retired immediately to bed and spent most of the day asleep, while Jack anxiously prowled the decks of the busy ship trying to plan his next move. He had been out on a limb before, but never had he felt quite so alone. The future wasn't bleak, no, it felt more like a black hole into which both he and Marian were being inexorably drawn.

That evening, under the sparkling chandeliers of the Dorchester Dining Room, Jack and Marian sat, unable to enjoy the opulence of their surroundings, nor the fabulous meal on the table in front of them.

'I'm not really hungry.' Marian at last stopped toying with her *filet de boeuf Saint-Germain* and pushed her knife and fork together.

Jack looked up from his perfectly pink gigot of lamb. 'Oh, really?' Although it pained Jack that he wouldn't be able to finish the first decent meal he'd had since . . . well, ever, he was too much of a gentleman to carry on at the trough when the lady had finished eating. He sorrowfully laid his knife and fork on his plate. 'No, neither am I.' He picked up his Scotch and water.

'What are we doing, Jack?' Marian asked.

He looked her steadily in the eye. 'This isn't how I'd imagined our running away together. I'd hoped that the circumstances would be more . . . congenial.'

She coloured slightly. 'I should never have come to you in the first place,' she murmured. 'All I ever seem to do is get people into trouble.'

'We're not in trouble,' Jack said seriously. 'We're completely buggered.'

'Oh, Jack.'

'But, believe me, we're safer here than in Britain. I just wish I could be there to see the look on Freddy's face when he finds out we're gone.' He called the waiter over and ordered another drink. 'Would you like more wine?'

She shook her head. 'No, thanks. So, what are we going to do when we get there?'

'I don't know.' Jack's eyes wandered off. In his mind's eye he saw himself poised at the edge of a cliff in a high wind, and it wasn't just because of the alcohol.

'Jack?' His vacant stare was beginning to unnerve her.

'Sorry,' he said, coming to himself, 'what were we talking about?'

'I was wondering why we're going to Mahe.'

218

'Oh, that, yes.'

His Scotch and water arrived. He took a sip and absent-mindedly pulled out his pipe. Marian raised an eyebrow.

'Sorry,' he said, putting it away again. 'Why are we going to Mahe? Well, I was hoping you were going to tell me.'

Marian frowned prettily.

'I have to know, Marian – everything.'

'Jack, you don't think—?'

'I don't think anything. I don't *know* anything. All I *do* know is that someone sent a hired killer to my flat yesterday evening, and the same person that sent him was planning to frame you for murder.'

Marian looked shocked.

'I'm sorry. I don't mean to frighten you, but it's as well you know the full extent of the awful mess we're in.' He leaned forward earnestly. 'Marian, if there's something you haven't told me, now would be a good time to come clean.'

Marian looked down at her lap for a few moments. Then she raised her eyes and stared straight at Jack. 'You're right, I've been less than wholly honest with you, but you have to believe that I'm not involved in anything . . . criminal.'

Jack smiled – the charmingly disdainful way she uttered the word made an international criminal conspiracy sound as innocent as scrumping apples. 'Please, go on.'

'I met Daygan when I was at a very low ebb. I'd finished my education, been all over Europe – what's left of it – and didn't know what to do next. My parents were very keen to see me married off, but I kept telling them I wasn't ready. I wanted to see how the world worked – live on my own, make my own money. I ended up working as a general dogsbody in the offices of the film company that made the Piggy-Wig commercials. I met Daygan after I'd got roped in to doing continuity on a shoot because the regular girl had called in sick. Well, I had no idea what I was doing, of course, and the cameraman had to keep telling me things I hadn't even noticed. At the end of the morning the director just blew up at me, called me a brainless little rich girl and asked why I wasn't married to some upper-class twit instead of making his life a living hell. Eventually Daygan intervened. The director didn't like it, but as Daygan was the client and paying the bills, he had to defer to him. Afterwards we had lunch together and talked. He wanted to know everything about me: my background, my school, parents, the places I'd been . . . He just seemed so nice. I'd been with other men before, of course, but he was different.'

'Was he still wearing his Mr Piggy-Wig make-up?'

'That's not what I mean!'

'Sorry.'

'He seemed genuinely interested in me. I'd never met a man like that – so gentle and caring. He told me about his dreams, his plans for the future. He had a vision – a world where anyone, no matter what their race, creed or colour, could get a pork burger any time of the day or night. It all seemed so romantic. Two years later we were married.'

'Two years? Hardly what you'd call a whirlwind romance.'

'Daygan's very old-fashioned. He didn't want to get married until he felt he could support me in the style to which I was already accustomed. By that time Piggy-Wig was a nationwide brand and Daygan was on the brink of realizing his dream: a worldwide Piggy-Wig network. We had to defer the honeymoon for the time being – Daygan was so busy. But I didn't care, I was with the man I loved, and I thought that was all that mattered. Until . . .'

'Until?'

'Things started to go wrong. Daygan's backers began to get cold feet. One by one his investors started pulling out. Daygan worked so hard to keep them on board, but they started falling like skittles. They wouldn't even tell him why. Some mumbled concerns about the damaging effects of mass pig farming on the environment, but these were businessmen, not the kind of people who usually put ecological worries above profits. It was a terrible time, Daygan fell into a hole. I didn't know what to do. I can't tell you how awful it is having to stand by and watch the man you love fall apart at the seams.

'Eventually he pulled himself out of it and started looking for more backers. Then one day he came home and seemed to be himself again. He'd found someone to back his great idea. At last Piggy-Wig was going global. Well, it was just like old times. He apologized for treating me so abominably, and eventually took me on that honeymoon we'd never had. It was bliss.'

'Where did you go?'

'Where didn't we go? We circled the world. But then, when we came home, things started going wrong again.'

'With the business?'

'With our marriage. Daygan became moody and aggressive. He began spending more and more time away. And when he did return, I started to find things.'

Jack frowned. 'What sort of things?'

'Small things – the faint scent of another perfume on his shirt, the occasional long blonde hair on the shoulder of his suit. When I confronted him he just laughed. "You don't own me and I don't own you," he said. "We're both of us free to come and go as we please." But that wasn't what I wanted out of my marriage. I started to get depressed, then I thought – hell, I'll show him, I'll beat him at his own game. I started seeing other men, even told him about them.'

'How did he react to that?'

'He seemed pleased – actively encouraged me. So, once I saw I couldn't get to him that way, I stopped all that nonsense and threw myself into my charity work and made myself unavailable.'

'Unavailable?'

'He occasionally brought people he wanted to impress back to dinner, and liked to give the impression that he had a perfect home life with the perfect little wife. He hated it when I wasn't there.'

'What sort of people?'

'Oh, Jack . . . he made me promise never to—'

'Never to what?'

Marian's eyes fluttered nervously around the room.

Jack leaned across the table and took her hands. 'Listen, we're on a liner ten thousand feet up – he can't get to you here. Not even Mango knows where we are. It's the first secret I've ever been able to keep from him.'

She smiled – a quick twitch of the corners of her mouth. 'You don't know Daygan, Jack. The people he's mixed up with . . . what they're capable of.'

'Let me worry about that. What did you promise never to reveal?'

She took several little nervous breaths before replying. 'I began to realize that Daygan's ambition had clouded his judgement and that he'd fallen in with some bad people.'

'Bad people?'

'Men with bodyguards and suspicious bulges in their jackets. The sort of people in the old days Daygan and I would have made fun of. We used to call them FLATs – Flashy suits, Loud voices, Appalling Table manners.'

Jack looked down at his plate and self-consciously pushed his knife and fork closer together. Then he leaned back in his seat and studied the ornately stuccoed ceiling.

'What is it, Jack?'

'Hmm?'

'You look worried.'

'Worried, me? No, nothing worries Lindsay of the Yard.' He smiled, but it wasn't overly convincing. The truth was that Marian's description of the men Daygan had been mixing with could mean only one thing. Where else could an ailing business that wasn't too bothered about where it got its backing suddenly get a much-needed financial shot in the arm? A global burger chain would be terrific cover for a crime organization. But if the Syndicates were involved, it was, needless to say, very worrying. Given a choice between having to face a Syndicate crime boss and eating his own eyeballs with a teaspoon, Jack would have reached for the teaspoon every time.

Jack lowered his eyes and looked into Marian's. 'So, do you know where he is now?'

'No.'

'Why did he send you to me in the first place?'

There was that look of panic again. 'I—'

'He did send you to me, am I right?'

She nodded.

Jack sat back in his chair and looked at her coolly. 'So he's in regular contact with you and you know exactly where he is.'

Marian shook her head. 'No, Jack. Daygan really has been gone for six months and that's the truth. But . . .'

Jack leaned forward. 'But?'

Marian blinked nervously. 'He sends me messages. Short, terse messages telling me what to do. By fax, e-mail, letter. They're never from the same place, and I never know when they're going to turn up.'

'Why did he want me on Corbett? Was he trying to set me up?'

She nodded again.

'Why?'

Her breathing became fast and shallow once more. 'He wanted you out of the way. He . . . he knew you were about to go back to Scotland Yard, he also knew you were the only one smart enough to figure out who was behind this whole business—'

'What whole business?'

'The political murders.'

'Are you telling me that Daygan is involved?'

'Oh, Jack – he never used to be like this. The man I married would never have got mixed up in—' She stopped suddenly, fighting back the tears.

'All right, all right,' Jack soothed. 'We'll finish this later. I just need to know one more thing.'

She recomposed herself with difficulty. 'What?'

'Why were you in Brazil?'

She closed her eyes. It was obviously an effort for her to pull herself together. 'It was an attempt to save my marriage. I followed Daygan to São Paulo. I wanted to know what he got up to on his little jaunts. When I turned up unannounced he was surprised and extremely unhappy. Doubly so when I insisted on being with him while he conducted his "business". I followed him around helplessly for a few days before giving up and coming home.'

'You followed him to Placa de Republica?'

'Yes.'

'What was he doing there?'

She shrugged. 'Talking.'

'To?'

'There were several men I'd never seen before. The leader of them everybody called Constantine.'

'Constantine?' That made Jack sit up. The last time he'd heard that name was from the dying lips of a woman in the burnt-out basement of a building on Cyprus after Jack's platoon had taken the island. But that was over twenty years ago, during the war.

Constantine or 'The Con', was the name for the leader of all the Syndicates. It was an honorary title, like Caesar, bestowed upon whoever had killed and double-crossed his way to the top of the crime tree.

'So Daygan's business was all with this . . . Constantine?' Jack asked.

'Yes.'

'Mmhmm.' Jack would need time to consider this worrying new information at leisure. He had been feeling guilty that he'd dragged Marian into this mess, now he was beginning to think it was the other way round. 'Why did you ask for help?'

'Help?'

'Yes, you looked straight into a CCTV camera and mouthed the word "Help".'

'Oh that.' Marian smiled. 'I suppose it was a silly thing to do, but I was in trouble.'

'Trouble?'

'Daygan was ignoring me, my marriage was falling apart – I needed help. Where was I supposed to turn?'

Jack studied her for a long time before replying, 'That's it? You asked for help through a CCTV camera because your relationship was on the rocks?'

'I never expected anyone to take it seriously. And I know it may sound rather strange after everything else I've said, but I still cared about my marriage.'

'After everything he'd done?'

'Yes,' she said. 'After everything.'

'Oh.' Jack found it hard to hide his disappointment.

She rose unsteadily from the table. 'I think I'll have an early night. I'm still feeling a little shaken by all that's happened recently.'

'I'm not surprised. Good night, then.' Jack stood awkwardly.

Marian slid round to Jack's side of the table and pecked him on his uninjured cheek. 'Good night, Jack.'

Jack was suddenly full of a warm sensation he hadn't felt for years. 'You wouldn't care for a nightcap?'

She smiled demurely and shook her head. 'It's a nice idea, but . . . I'm very tired. Perhaps tomorrow night?' She turned to go, but Jack stopped her.

'Those men with whom you shared your anniversary dinner, they didn't happen to be called Lazlo and Jakob, did they?'

Marian turned slowly to face him. 'Why . . . yes, I believe those were their names.'

'I thought so. Sleep tight.'

She walked away, moving across the floor of the restaurant like liquid silk. Jack put his fingers exploratively to the place where her lips had touched his cheek, and wished they were still there.

Jack asked the unsmiling waiter for a doggie bag for his half-eaten gigot and headed off to the small outside smoking area of the viewing deck. It was freezing and extremely windy, but Jack needed to think.

After struggling to fill his pipe with Old Hobson's Curiously Fragrant in a howling gale, Jack eventually got it going and gazed out over the dark and brooding panorama of North Africa, laid out beneath him like a vast carpet, its towns and cities marked by a million lights, echoing the starlit canopy of the night sky. As he watched the city lights pass slowly beneath the hyperliner, Jack worried over the events of the last twenty-four hours like a dog sniffing amongst garbage.

He'd been fired, had narrowly escaped death, and was now on the run with a murder suspect.

Freddy's involvement in a major criminal conspiracy didn't really surprise him; his brother had always had simple needs – money and more money. Nor did Freddy's trying to have him killed shock or disturb him particularly, he was used to being treated badly, especially by his brother. It was clear that Jack was obviously now surplus to requirements, which either meant he'd served his purpose or was getting too close to revealing something that somebody would rather be kept well hidden. No, that Freddy wanted him dead didn't trouble Jack. What really bothered him was something Marian had said.

Jack was well aware that he'd once had rather a fearsome reputation amongst the criminal fraternity – indeed the news that Jack Lindsay was on the case was at one time enough to cause the miscreant to give himself up straight away. But a powerful man like Daygan Flyte, with a global business empire and contacts in the murky world of the Syndicates? Unlikely.

Something wasn't right. Of Daygan's intention to lure him out to Corbett he was sure, but the reason why was still unclear.

Marian may have admitted that Daygan was involved with the political assassinations, but Jack still had a sneaking suspicion that she was holding something back. After all, she'd lied to him before, and even though she'd gone on the run with him, was that enough, in her eyes, to guarantee him exclusive rights to the truth? He doubted it – she was too scared for one thing, and Jack had to admit that he would have acted the same way in the circumstances. 'When your back's to the wall it's useful to have an ace up your sleeve,' as P.M. Tenement's Detective Harry Smart would have said. But if Marian *was* only acting out the part of the frightened little woman and stringing him along – why? What possible use could he be to her? Apart from being entertaining company, of course. It didn't make sense.

With these uneasy thoughts running around his head, his usually comforting pipe failed to hit the spot.

He reckoned they were still about another twenty-four hours from Mahe – it was time to call Mango and tell him the good news.

After wrestling his hair back across his skull having had it nearly blown off his head on the smoking deck, Jack found a combined phone and internet terminal outside the entrance to one of the theatres on the entertainments deck, and dialled a number. After a few moments' buzzing and whirring, followed by an ascending three-tone *bong, bong, bong!* – the audio logo of the telecommunications company – the international operator came on the line. It was only a computer, but in such testing circumstances, Jack found the familiar female voice strangely comforting.

'*You have reached Global Interconnectivity Dot Com. Connecting people is what we do best. How may I help? Would you like to communicate with an organization or individual, or do you require some other service?'*

'You could meet me for a drink, I could do with some company right now.'

There was a pause while the computer considered Jack's invitation.

'I'm sorry, but I'm afraid it appears you have requested something with which it may be beyond my ability to comply.'

'That's sadly true,' Jack muttered. Why did he still bother playing these adolescent little games?

'I'm sorry, but I'm afraid it appears you have requested something with which it may be beyond my ability to comply.'

Jack refrained from admonishing the computer for repeating itself.

'Would you like to communicate with an organization or individual, or do you require some other service? Simply say: "Yes, I would like to communicate with an organization or individual"; or: "I'd like another service."'

Jack sighed. 'Yes, I would like to communicate with an individual,' he enunciated carefully.

'Thank you. Please state the name of the individual and Global number, if known. If the Global number is unknown, please state the individual's current place of residence.'

There was a long *beep.*

'Mango Pinkerton, Ramada Inn, Corbett,' Jack said.

'Thank you. While we try to connect you we would like to play you some messages from companies carefully chosen by Global Interconnectivity Dot Com for products and services designed to enhance your life experience. Or, if you prefer, you could listen to a selection of music especially chosen by our experts to stimulate an alpha wave state, known to promote well-being and contentment. Simply indicate your preference by saying "option one" for products and services or "option two" for music.'

'I suppose Stockhausen would be a little too strident for you, then?'

'*Certainly.*'

Well, that was a surprise.

'*You have chosen option one. Please state in which area you are interested: lifestyle, fashion, sports and leisure, or business.*'

The truth was, Jack could have said anything. He could have said colander or armpit and the computer would still have given him option one – the company's reliance on advertising revenue saw to that. 'Trouser leg,' he said clearly.

'*Thank you. You have chosen lifestyle. Please listen closely to the following messages . . .*'

Lifestyle was the default option – it was by far the most lucrative of all the advertising strands because of the savage competition amongst those companies striving to sell the public the idea that their lives would be so much better if only they had that new swimming pool/house/conservatory/kitchen/cooker/car/suite of genuine teak garden furniture.

There was a burst of lushly orchestrated stately music down the line, announcing a decidedly upmarket product.

'*We at Nice-A-Homes believe that a house is more than just bricks and mortar. A house is a home, that's why Nice-A-Homes has developed the exclusive Executive range of homes for the discerning dwelling-seeker. These top-quality homes boast large living spaces with sumptuous laminate flooring, genuine extruded polystyrene fireplace surrounds and underfloor lighting. And in your generously sized Nice-A-Homes kitchen, cooking is a joy. Every Nice-A-Homes kitchen comes fully fitted with the latest in cuisine technology: walk-in microwave oven, self-loading dishwasher and combined refrigerator and butler sink. Can I invite you upstairs? The dazzling marble-effect bathroom with brass-veneered UPVC plumbing appurtenances will make you the envy of your guests. The bedrooms are large yet cosy and come complete with ample storage space for your extensive wardrobe. The garden too comes ready fitted with swimming pool, barbecue deck and holographic mature shrubs and trees, which even change colour with the seasons. And you don't have to worry about the neighbourhood either, as every*'

Nice-A-Homes purchaser on your estate will have been stringently vetted according to our Executive Nice-A-Homes profile – subjects covered include income, boat ownership, previous convictions for drug offences, sexual deviancy, car-jacking and violent assault.

'*And when the sun goes down, you can step inside your hermetically sealed Nice-A-Home, secure in the knowledge that the atmosphere is absolutely free from irritating pollen grains, unpleasant organic odours and that bane of the housewife – dust. To complete your dwelling experience, all Nice-A-Homes come fully decorated and furnished with flair by a top designer. Live in peace and comfort in a nicer home from Nice-A-Homes.*'

The female computer came back on the line. '*Sorry to have kept you. My, but don't those products sound just amazing?*'

'Oh please,' Jack sighed.

'*We have traced the party you require, putting you through now.*'

There was the sound of a number being rapidly dialled then, after a short pause, Jack heard a ringing at the other end of the phone. He was looking forward to speaking to a real human being. Eventually someone picked up.

'Oh, hello,' Jack began, 'I'd like to—'

But he stopped himself when he realized that once again no one was listening.

'*We're sorry, but the reception desk of the Ramada Inn, Corbett, is now closed,*' yet another computerized voice announced.

Closed? Jack thought. *They must really be trying to save money.*

'*The reception desk's opening hours are: eight-thirty a.m. to ten-thirty p.m.,*' the computer continued. '*Outside those hours, please use our automatic booking system by pressing the numbers on your phone pad. If you want to make a booking, press one, alternatively, if you want to contact a guest, please press two.*'

'Bollocks, more computers,' Jack grumbled, then dutifully pressed two.

'*If you know your guest's room number, please enter it into the keypad, otherwise, press three.*'

Jack sighed, and pressed three.

'*If you don't have your guest's room number, but you do know their name, please enunciate it clearly at the tone.*'

'If I didn't know his name I wouldn't be trying to get in touch, would I?'

'*BEEP!*'

'Mango Pinkerton,' Jack said in his clearest tones.

'*You have requested to leave a message for Madge Pilkinson.*'

'No, no, no! Mango! Mango Pinkerton!'

'*I'm sorry, there's no one of that name at the hotel at present. If you wish to speak to someone else, please press four, otherwise, hang up now.*'

Jack, barely suppressing an urge to smash the handset into the wall, pressed four.

'*I'm sorry, but the reception desk of the Ramada Inn, Corbett, is now closed. The reception desk's opening hours are: eight-thirty a.m. to ten thirty p.m.*'

There was a click and the line went dead.

'Aaaaargh!' Jack screamed.

Five attempts later, and on the edge of a nervous breakdown, Jack was eventually able to leave a message for Mango. He would have preferred to talk to him in person, but Mango was obviously getting an early night and had turned off his room phone.

'Hello, Mango. I trust the Ramada Inn is living up to expectations. I have a little surprise for you . . .' Jack paused. The one good thing about the messaging system was that you could deliver bad news without having to immediately face the wrath or tears or sulky silence of the person at the other end.

'Well, actually I've got three surprises for you,' Jack continued. 'Let's take them in order. That we seem to be out of a job you already know, so here's a little something to compensate. Surprise number one: I want you to go to Mahe and book into the Royal Mahe Hotel. There, see? Working for Jack does sometimes have its compensations. I'll be waiting for you. Surprise number two is that Freddy is involved – he tried to kill me. Not in person, you understand, he wouldn't dirty his hands like that. So don't call him to keep him up to date on what's happening in your life. And it seems Gelda Longhorn was right, the Syndicates are all over this case, so go carefully and don't talk to men in flashy suits. Oh, and surprise number three – I'm not alone. End message.' Even at one remove, he didn't quite have the nerve to tell Mango the identity of the individual with whom he was travelling.

After Jack had put down the phone, he had an idea. Something about the Nice-A-Homes commercial had triggered a memory.

Using the phone's internet function, he Googled Nice-A-Homes to find that it had recently been acquired by Chips met Mayonnaise, the Dutch fast-food chain. But exploring further, Jack discovered that Chips met Mayonnaise itself had been recently acquired by none other than Piggy-Wig Enterprises. What would Michaelmas, or his Syndicate bosses, want with a construction company?

And from the Googled results, it seemed that these weren't the only companies recently snapped up by Piggy-Wig or its satellites. There were several more building and construction companies listed, as well as You-Do-It – the garden centre and do-it-yourself business. Why? A burger chain was nicely anonymous and could be used by the Syndicates for all sorts of dealings: money laundering was probably going to be its main function, but meat delivery vans would be useful for arms smuggling, drug running, even white slavery. But why bother with the matey, cosy world of do-it-yourself or the upmarket homes building sector?

A ray of light began to pierce the gloom of the dark tangle of the case in Jack's mind, and he smiled.

Picking up the phone he dialled a number.

'*The Post, news desk. How can I help?*'

'Hello, I'd like to speak to Gelda Longhorn, please.'

*

Beep-beep! Beep-beep! Beep-beep!

Jack opened his eyes. His bedside phone was beeping gently.

Beep-beep! Beep-beep! Beep-beep!

He fumbled for the handset, picked something up and put it to his ear.

'Heoo?' he mumbled.

Beep-beep! Beep-beep! Beep-beep!

The phone continued to beep annoyingly.

Gradually coming to, Jack realized that the receiver he had in his hand was rather cold and greasy. Flicking on the light switch, he saw that he'd been trying to answer the remains of his cold gigot of lamb.

'Yeuch!'

After cleaning lamb fat out of his ear, Jack found the phone and picked up the handset.

'Yes?' he said.

'*A message for you from one Mango Pinkerton,*' said an annoyingly bright and cheerful voice. '*Would you like to take it now?*'

'Whattime ist?' Jack slurred.

'*Four-thirty a.m. London time.*'

'Oh, Jesus.'

'*Eight-thirty local time. I wouldn't have woken you sir, but it is flagged Top Priority.*'

'I'll bet it is. All right, I'll take it now.'

'*Very good, sir.*'

After a few clicks, Jack heard the familiar ascending *bong, bong, bong!* and then the female voice of the computer. '*Welcome to Interconnectivity Dot Com. You're in luck, you have a message. And the good news is, you don't have to do a thing, just sit back and enjoy.*'

Mango came on the line. '*Well, although I admit that when I first heard we were going to the Royal Mahe my heart skipped a beat, now I've had time to think it over my suspicions are running rampant. What's going on, Jack? And who is your mysterious companion? Freddy! My God, your own brother! Oh, I've got an awfully bad feeling about all this. Please try and stay alive long enough for me to shout at you in person. End message.'*

Jack replaced the receiver and lay for a few moments trying to sort his thoughts, but it was no good, they seemed to be whirling in all directions at once. He sighed and sat up on the edge of the bed. Sunlight was peeping in around the curtains of his bedroom window – which was odd, considering that he was in one of the inside, 'budget' berths, with no outside window. He reached over and tentatively pulled back a corner of the curtain and was immediately bathed in bright sunshine. Squinting against the sudden light, Jack stared in amazement at what he saw. Notwithstanding the presence of the small, square, primary-coloured logo in the bottom left corner, it was hard to believe what he was looking at wasn't real – sunrise over a beautiful green valley dotted with sheep.

On the bedside table, next to a credit-card-sized remote control, there was a small booklet with the single word 'Window' on its cover. Jack picked it up. Under the heading 'Windowscape – Options', he found that he could select from any of the following: 'Country Landscape (default)', 'Undersea', 'Roller Coaster', 'Bird's Eye View' . . . the list went on down the page. Picking up the remote control and opening the curtains wide, Jack clicked a button.

The image through the window changed immediately to that of a coral reef. Clouds of vibrantly coloured fish moved about as one. Moray eels slipped sinuously through coral canyons, and tiny shrimp danced and darted.

He clicked again and found himself at the top of a roller coaster. In an instant he was hurtling down the dizzying slope.

'Ah!'

He clicked again and was soaring high above valleys and canyons, perched on the back of an eagle. The undulating ground beneath had a very strange effect on his stomach.

He moved on.

The scene changed to a typical English country market town

square. Rows of men dressed all in white, with bells around their calves, ran towards each other waving handkerchiefs, while a similarly attired musician played gently on a squeezebox.

'That's more like it.'

Jack got up and headed for the shower.

Chapter 19

Marian was already at breakfast when Jack entered the large dining room.

'How did you sleep?' she asked.

'Fine, fine. Although waking up to cold lamb was a bit of a shock.'

Marian frowned. 'Sorry?'

'Never mind.'

A waiter sidled up. 'Good morning, sir, what can I get you?'

'Tea, very strong, and bacon and eggs, I think.'

'Would you like the full English, sir?'

'What's that?'

'Egg, bacon, sausage, beans, fried bread, black pudding and mushrooms.'

Jack perked up. 'Does that come with toast?'

The waiter nodded. 'White or brown?'

'Both.'

The waiter bowed – a discreet nod of the head – and slid away.

'How are you feeling this morning?' Jack asked. 'Did you sleep well?'

Marian yawned. 'Excuse me. I would have slept in if it hadn't been for that stop.'

'What stop?'

'I was sleeping like a baby when I felt the whole ship lurch. I didn't know we were scheduled to stop anywhere but Mahe.'

'We're not,' Jack growled. 'When did this happen?'

'It must have been a couple of hours ago. I'm surprised it didn't wake you too.'

'I'm a heavy sleeper.'

'Would you like tea or coffee, sir?'

Jack looked up into the face of a different waiter and immediately felt uneasy.

'Er, coffee. Do you have a dark roasted Sencha?'

The waiter shook his head, 'I'm sorry, sir, we only have the house blend.'

The waiter proceeded to fill Jack's cup. When he'd finished, Jack looked up at him and said, coolly, 'Sencha is a tea. Working in a place like this, you ought to know that.'

The bogus waiter reached inside his pocket for his gun, but Jack threw the scalding coffee in his face.

'Marian, run!'

Marian grabbed her small clutch bag from the table and made a dash for the door, while Jack yanked off the tablecloth and threw it over the gunman before hobbling after her. But as he too headed for the door, Jack became aware that their would-be assassin had an accomplice: another 'waiter' hurried after him across the floor of the restaurant, gun drawn. There was the sharp *crack* of an automatic, and a bullet splintered the door frame on Jack's left side.

Someone screamed and suddenly everyone was running for the exit. Jack reached for his own gun and remembered he'd surrendered it at airport security like a good little policeman. He dived through the open door.

Marian was waiting in the lobby outside, unsure of which way to go.

'This way!' Taking her hand, Jack led her down the stairway to the entertainments deck.

'Where are we going?'

'I don't know!'

A bullet zipped over their heads.

'Quick, in here!'

On stage in one of the theatres, a chorus line of dancers wearing rehearsal gear and cowboy hats was being taught the end of a new routine by a small, tightly muscled male choreographer.

'And turn and step and kick! And turn and step and kick! That's it. Remember you're a line of bucking broncos at a rodeo! And one more! Good! And step and kick! Now lead off waving your hats! No, no, no!' The little man clapped his hands in frustration. 'Stop! Stop! Elaine, what did I say?' he lisped. 'You lead off on the *left*, the *left*, not the right! Girls, how difficult can it be to walk offstage? It's simple, you follow Elaine off in a straight line! Shirley, if you try and overtake her you make the whole thing look like a rugby scrum. And Chelsea, I've told you before – get rid of the bloody chewing gum!'

Chelsea scowled and, holding him in a level gaze, walked to the side of the stage and stuck her chewing gum on the proscenium arch.

Wincing, the choreographer smoothed back his dyed and thinning hair. 'Honestly, the dross I have to work with,' he muttered. 'All right, everyone, let's try it again!'

But just then, the auditorium doors burst open and Jack and Marian ran into the theatre.

'Excuse me!' the little man called out. 'Rehearsal in progress!'

'Sorry!' Jack called back. 'Escaping from assassins!'

The choreographer was about to admonish them further for interrupting his rehearsal when the doors crashed open for a second time and two more people ran into the theatre. 'Oh God,' he moaned, 'it's always the same on these cruises. The punters have no bloody manners!'

But when the two newcomers pulled out their guns and started shooting, the choreographer began to realize that these were no ordinary punters.

'Run for your lives!' he yelled, diving into the wings.

The girls all screamed and ran off-stage in perfect formation.

The choreographer was aghast. 'Why the hell couldn't they do that before?'

Jack, running towards the stage down one of the aisles at either side of the auditorium, found a small door in front of him – the pass door leading backstage.

'Through here!' he yelled, dragging Marian in behind him.

They were immediately plunged into backstage darkness. Through the gloom they could dimly make out the shapes of the dancers who'd just run off-stage. But at the sight of Jack and Marian, the girls screamed again and ran back onstage.

'Was it something I said?' Jack quipped.

'Please, no jokes,' Marian implored.

'All right, let's hide.'

Behind them, the two gangsters had split up. One had clambered up onto the stage – sending the girls into a screaming panic yet again – and the other was cautiously following Jack and Marian through the pass door.

The choreographer watched from the opposite wing as his girls jumped off the stage and fled to safety through the auditorium. The little man held his breath as the gunman stalked the stage, and edged backwards into the deep shadows beyond the shafts of light spilling into the wings.

On the opposite side of the stage, the second gunman carefully paced the darkness, searching behind the masking flats and peering into every shadowy corner.

Then, from high above came the sound of a rope running through a pulley. The gunman looked up. He only just managed to leap out of the way as a lighting bar, complete with its complement of murderously heavy theatre lights, came crashing to the stage.

'They're up there!' he shouted, pointing his gun up at the fly gallery. The other man joined him onstage, and both started shooting up at the flys as bullets, lighting bars, sandbags and pieces of scenery fell all around them.

Another lighting bar fell from above and smacked onto the

stage. One of the heavy lights broke free and bounced towards the choreographer's hiding place. Seeing it coming, he leapt out of the way with a yell. One of the gunmen turned when he heard the scream, and looked straight at him. The choreographer, frozen to the spot, could only watch as the man raised his gun and took aim at the centre of his forehead. But just then, a heavy sandbag careened from the heavens and thumped into the man's head, instantly breaking his neck.

Thanking Terpsichore for his lucky escape, the choreographer slunk back into the shadows and found the door leading to the dressing rooms. Slipping through, he ran from the chaos as fast as his chunky little legs would carry him.

'I think I got one,' Jack said, looking down at the prone form of the dead gunman.

'That leaves one to go,' said Marian, freeing yet another lighting bar. They followed the bar down with their eyes as it fell stageward. But the surviving gunman saw it coming, side-stepped, and the lights thudded into the stage, gouging great chunks out of the woodwork.

'Damn!' Jack surveyed what was still hanging in the fly-loft. Not very much.

'We're running out of ammunition,' he said, as another bullet whistled past his head. 'Unfortunately, it seems our friend labours under no such handicap.' Then, noticing what was hanging at the very back of the fly-loft, he yelled, 'I've got an idea! See if we can tempt him to the very back of the stage!'

'Right.'

Jack and Marian worked their way along the lighting gantry until they reached the back wall. This was where the big back-drop cloths were hung: fog-shrouded depictions of 'old London'– complete with friendly bobbies; coarsely executed imitations of Toulouse Lautrec's famous Moulin Rouge paintings; and scenes of Tennessee paddle steamers lazily chuntering down the Mississippi.

It seemed for the moment that the gunman had lost sight of

his prey. He lowered his gun and, shielding his eyes with his hand, peered up into the darkness beyond the blinding stage lights.

'Hey, mister gunman, over here!' Jack yelled.

The man let off another shot, then stopped to reload.

Meanwhile, Marian, looking for more ammunition, had found the flyman's green room and its collection of tea-making equipment.

The gunman looked puzzled as a packet of Hobnobs thudded onto the stage beside him. This was followed by a bag of sugar, a carton of milk and a kettle. Then came a rain of mugs, plates and saucers and, finally, a wooden rocking chair left over from a Porgy and Bess number, and purloined by the head flyman for his breaks. None found their mark, but they *had* had their desired effect of edging the gunman further towards the rear of the stage, where Jack was waiting.

Marian ran to join him and now each took hold of a fly-line.

'When I say go!' Jack hissed, craning his neck to sneak a look over the edge of the fly-floor. But the man onstage seemed reluctant to take his place under the heavy scene-setting cloths, stopping just downstage of where they hung.

'Come on, come on!' Jack urged in a tense whisper.

Another shot rang out. The bullet ricocheted off the wall above Jack's head.

'Ahh!' Jack yelled. 'You got me!'

Marian frowned.

'It's what they say in the movies,' Jack said by way of explanation.

Marian may have doubted whether the gunman would be fooled, but she was far too polite to say anything.

But either the man onstage hadn't seen too many movies, or he was just plain stupid. Whichever it was, he was intrigued, and now moved right to the back of the stage, looking up, eyes screwed tight against the light from the tower of spotlights in the wings.

'Now!' Jack yelled.

They let the lines slip through their fingers, and the gunman was engulfed in scenes of old Tennessee and the moonlit Palace of Westminster.

'Come on!' Jack yelled, leading the way back down the ladder to stage level.

'Wait, my bag!'

'Leave it!'

But Marian was determined, and ran back to retrieve it from where she'd left it: by the entrance to the flyman's green room.

'What is it about women and handbags?' Jack complained when she returned.

'A man would never understand,' she replied.

By the time they'd reached the ground, the gunman had half-struggled out of his canvas prison, and although still pinned to the stage, had worked his gun hand free. He peppered the stalls with bullets as Jack and Marian ran up the aisle and out of the auditorium.

'And now?' Marian asked, once they were through the theatre's doors.

'The escape deck.'

'We're abandoning ship?'

'No, but that's how it's going to look.'

Jack led Marian down another flight of stairs and then through a set of double doors. The doors were alarmed, and so the moment they pushed through them, a klaxon sounded throughout the ship.

'Well, he'll know where we are now,' Jack yelled over the ear-shattering din.

They were standing on a wide gantry, attached to which were two lines of escape pods hanging from the ship like rows of fat, newborn piglets suckling from their mother's teats. The pods were twelve-seater aerial lifeboats which, once released from the ship, were designed to float gently to earth by means of an overhead rotor.

Choosing one at random, Jack reached inside and armed the release mechanism by pulling down a lever. On the pod's small control panel, a green light blinked on next to a big red button.

'Say goodbye,' said Jack. He pressed the button and, with a hiss of compressed air, the little boat-shaped craft with its domed Perspex cover dropped suddenly from the mother ship. After a few moments, just when it seemed that it was headed to its doom, a three-bladed rotor unfolded from a frame on top of its dome and whirred into action, slowing its descent.

'Now we hide!' Jack yelled over the continuing blare of the klaxon.

Running further along the line of escape pods, he chose another, clambered into it, and pulled Marian in behind him.

'I thought we weren't leaving,' she said.

'Let's hope we don't have to. Now stay down and keep quiet!'

It wasn't long before the gunman appeared on the escape deck. Jack, peering from his hiding place, watched as the man found the empty space left by the released pod.

But he wasn't so easily fooled. Looking down at the pod, now falling sedately like some gigantic leaf towards the deep blue sea far below, he pursed his lips. He pondered a while, scratching his cheek with the barrel of his gun. Then, coming to a decision, he inserted a full clip in his automatic and went back to the beginning of the row of remaining escape pods, and began to check them, one by one.

'He didn't buy it,' Jack hissed. 'He's coming this way!'

'What do we do now?'

Reaching up gingerly, Jack pulled down the pod-launch arming-lever.

'Change of plan,' he replied in answer to Marian's quizzical look. 'I hope you've got your passport.'

'It's in my bag.'

'Good.'

The gunman was getting closer. Jack had hoped that he

might give up, but not this guy – he may not have been too bright, but he was thorough, and now he was only two pods away from finding them. There was nothing else for it.

'Hold on!' he hissed.

He pressed the button. For a moment nothing happened. *It would be just my luck*, Jack thought, *to have chosen the only malfunctioning pod*. But then, in a hiss of compressed air, the pod dropped with a sudden, stomach-churning lurch, and they became weightless. Above, the gunman's disappointed and rapidly diminishing face stared after them. He levelled his gun and let off a few shots, and although one punched a small hole in the Perspex cover of the pod, they were falling fast and were soon out of range.

It seemed like they had been falling for ever and Jack was again wondering whether he'd picked an unlucky pod when, with deep relief, he saw the rotor deploy and began to feel his weight again. The little escape craft's precipitous descent slowed to a gentle downward drift. He turned to Marian.

'Are you all right?'

She was sprawled on the floor of the craft, clinging to a life vest and looking decidedly green. 'I've never been good at small aircraft,' she said.

'Well, I hope you're a better sailor, we may be at sea for quite a few—' but Jack was interrupted by a gigantic explosion that lit up the sky, enveloping the liner they had just exited in an angry red fireball.

They watched, open-mouthed, as above them the vast ship folded slowly in two, its back broken by the explosion. Fire ripped eagerly through its gas-filled envelope, consuming the covering material and revealing the ribs beneath. Soon the great balloon was nothing but a mass of twisted metal. Bizarrely, still seemingly weightless, it hung impossibly in the sky for several moments more before gravity took hold and the ship began to fall, slowly at first, then with gathering speed. In the gondola, now slung at a crazy angle beneath one of the halves of the massive blimp, tiny figures could be seen, limbs jerking in panic. Jack could only imagine their screams.

The once proud and majestic airship fell out of the sky, hitting the sea, far below, with a gigantic splash. But by the time Jack and Marian's little craft had floated to a soft landing on the Indian Ocean's gentle swell, there was little to mark where the liner had fallen. Bobbing on the surface of the water were a few lifejackets, some tattered remnants of the fabric of the great grey envelope and a poster advertising a 'Wild West, High-Kicking Dance Spectacular' in the ship's main theatre. This was all that was left of the hyperliner and its more than six hundred passengers and crew. Nothing else remained to show that an appalling catastrophe had just taken place.

'Oh my God, Jack. All those people!' Marian searched the deep blue waters of the sea with unbelieving eyes.

'I know, I know.' Jack put his arm around her and the two survivors drifted silently away on the tide.

Chapter 20

The commissioner was not pleased to be woken early in the morning, and then to be informed that his chief suspect had gone missing.

'You know the penalty for helping a criminal to escape?'

In the small dark interview room, Ruth glared back at the commissioner across the small table. Behind him, guarding the door, stood the unsmiling figure of Lana.

'For the last time, I was attacked. I had nothing to do with that woman's escape. I was in late, I had some work to finish before the morning. Detective Inspector Lindsay likes to have things presented to him first thing.'

'Jack's been taken off the case.'

Ruth leaned forward forcefully. 'I didn't know that at the time! If I had I would have gone home!'

'Nevertheless, after finishing your work, you went down to the cell area.'

'By that time I was wide awake. I knew I wouldn't be able to sleep, so I looked for something else to do. Call it a misplaced desire to serve, but I actually like my job, and I'm damn good at it.' She glared up at Lana. 'Unlike some people.'

Lana smiled mockingly back.

'So you looked in on the cell-block?' Freddy asked.

'I've been on cell-block duty before and know how crashingly boring it is, so I thought I'd see if I could help out. The girl in charge seemed a little jaded, so I thought I'd give her a break. She went to make a cup of tea, and the woman in the cell, whoever she was, called out to me. She said she was in pain and did I have an aspirin? I opened the door and the next thing I know I wake up with an aching jaw and the guard standing over me asking what happened to the suspect. That's the truth.'

The commissioner's face was dark with a building fury. 'Oh, so that's the truth, is it? I don't suppose my brother even knew that you were in late, did he?'

'To stay late was my own decision. Jack had nothing to do with it.'

The commissioner's hand came crashing down on the small table between them.

'Don't play me for a fool! I know the kind of misguided loyalty my brother is capable of inspiring in his staff. God knows why, the man's a drunkard and a wastrel. He put you up to this, didn't he? He called you and told you to meet him at the Yard.'

Ruth didn't flinch. 'Like I've already said. He knows nothing about it. Why don't you ask him?'

'Oh, rest assured we will. We shall also be asking him about the body that we found in his flat. You wouldn't happen to know anything about that would you?'

Ruth squirmed uncomfortably in her chair.

Freddy sensed a chink in her hitherto impenetrable defence. 'Where is he and where has he taken Miss Lawes? Think very carefully about your reply, Miss Jones. Assisting in the escape of a suspect is bad enough, but add to that being an accessory to murder and the gates of Holloway come a little more starkly into focus, wouldn't you agree?'

Ruth let her eyes drop to her lap and wrapped the thin dressing gown around her that bit more tightly. 'I don't know,' she said in a small voice, 'he didn't say.'

'Now we're getting somewhere. What was so important that it couldn't wait for the morning?'

'Jack . . . Detective Inspector Lindsay asked me to find out what the mainframe had on Marian Lawes.'

'And?'

'There was a lot of information in her file that I never put there.'

'Are you telling me that someone has been fabricating evidence against her?'

'It looks like that, yes.'

'That's a serious allegation, Miss Jones.'

'I'm just telling you what I found.'

'And who was your accomplice in breaking into police files?'

'Look, if I've made a mistake, fine, but I'm not dropping anyone else in it.'

Freddy shook his head. 'I can see why my brother trusted you, you both have the same stubborn, old-fashioned attitude. Loyalty to one's fellow officers – I think I'm going to cry.' He leaned forward threateningly. 'Do I have to remind you that whoever showed you that information broke every rule in the book and now faces several decades behind bars? And rest assured, we shall find him or her, unless . . .' He paused and looked hard at Ruth. 'If you tell me where he's taken Marian Lawes I might be tempted to forget the whole thing.'

Ruth sighed and looked at the ceiling. She hadn't smoked for fifteen years, but at that moment she could have murdered a cigarette. 'I . . . I don't know, but . . .'

'Yes?' Freddy encouraged, giving her his kindly uncle smile, which Jack always thought made him look like a child molester.

Ruth exhaled noisily. 'He said he hoped to get a tan.'

Freddy pursed his lips and considered her response for a few moments. Then he rose to leave. 'Thank you, Miss Jones, you've been most helpful.'

Ruth looked surprised. 'Can I go now?'

'No. We still need to tie up a few loose ends. Lana, look after Miss Jones for a few moments, would you?'

'With pleasure. We can have a nice girly chat.'

The commissioner left and Lana slid into his seat, her breasts bobbing like a trapeze artist on a high wire, making Ruth feel decidedly underpowered.

*

Freddy stepped into his office to find his phone ringing.

'Yes?'

'Commissioner, is that you? This is Lieutenant Matthias, you've got to help me.'

New York's finest cop sounded strangely plaintive.

'Lieutenant, I'm sorry we never got to meet.'

'Don't worry about that now – just get me off this island! I'm stuck here with two madmen. If I don't get off soon, I'll go crazy!'

'I'm sorry, Lieutenant, I don't understand, I thought you had chosen to go to the Isle of Wight in pursuance of your investigation.'

'I was set up! Can't you see that, you moron?'

Freddy bristled. 'Have you forgotten to whom you are speaking, Matthias?'

'I want you to send me a police helimotor and get me off this God-forsaken island now!'

'I'm afraid I can't do that. It's a matter of resources, you see – I can't afford to tie up a helimotor for most of the day just to rescue some yank who's been outmanoeuvred by a simple British cop. And furthermore, back in the States you may be able to order your superiors about and demand helimotors on a whim, but over here we have a more old-fashioned attitude regarding the command structure – lower-ranking officers respect their superiors, and when told that nothing can be done, usually accept the fact that nothing can be done! How d'you like them apples?'

'But you can't leave me here,' Matthias sobbed. *'Not with these two. You can't . . .'*

Freddy put the phone down on the tearful lieutenant. 'Bloody Yanks.'

He thought for a moment, then settled in his chair and smoothed his hair. Taking a deep breath, he clicked a button on his wrist communicator and said one word, 'Constantine.'

After a few rings the phone was picked up.

'*Yeah?*'
'We have another problem.'

A warm tropical breeze wafted through the open-plan hotel
reception area. Smiling hotel operatives ferrying luggage or dis-
pensing drinks weaved expertly between the sturdy boles of
palm trees, which supported the banana-leaf-thatched roof high
above.

Down at the bamboo bar – an area at the far end of the
building which opened on to the beach – bathing-suited
holidaymakers, their brown bodies glistening with suntan oil,
strolled up to order drinks.

The sour-faced and soberly suited desk manager was
strangely at odds with the relaxed holiday feel of the place.

'Good afternoon, sir. Can I be of assistance?'

'We have a reservation,' said Jack. 'Name of Lawes.'

The man's eyes looked him up and down, weighing him in
the balance and finding him severely wanting. Jack and Marian
had been rescued twelve hours after they'd abandoned ship,
and had spent the night on a fishing trawler that had picked up
their distress beacon. Marian had been offered the use of the
captain's cabin, but Jack had had to curl up on a bed of trawl-
nets. His suit was creased and stained, he was unshaven, and he
stank of old fish.

'I'm sorry, but I don't seem—'

'That's all right, James. Mr Lindsay and I are here together.'

The man's eyes flicked to Marian, and he raised an immaculately groomed eyebrow. 'I'm so sorry, Mrs Lawes, I didn't
recognize you at first.'

'We've had quite a night.'

'It's just that I'm unused to seeing you without *Mr* Lawes.'

His stress on the 'Mister' clearly inferred both that there was
something improper going on and his sincerest disapproval of
this fact.

'Will he be joining you?'

'No, not this time, James.'

The desk manager curled his lip in Jack's direction, then looked down at the computer screen hidden below counter-level. 'Ah, yes, here we are. Hmm . . .'

'Is something wrong, James?' Marian asked.

'No, madam, it's just that at the time of booking you seem not to have stated a preference for the type of accommodation. Will you have your usual suite? Or perhaps –' he arched an eyebrow suggestively at Jack '– you would prefer something a little cosier? A twin, perhaps, or maybe a double?' He leered nastily.

The presumption by this reptile that he and Marian were involved in some sordid sexual adventure made Jack leap to the lady's defence. 'Two singles,' he growled, and immediately regretted it.

Marian smiled gratefully at him and turned back to the desk manager. 'You do have two singles, James?'

James seemed rather disappointed by this turn of events and went back to his computer. 'Well, we are usually very busy at this time of year, as you know, Mrs Lawes. We do have a few family rooms unexpectedly free due to that awful business of the hyperliner going down . . .' James paused and looked up at Jack and Marian suspiciously. 'How did you get here, if you don't mind my asking? I thought they'd suspended all flights from London for the time being.'

'Um, we—' Marian began.

'We came by boat,' Jack said. 'We've been cruising around the Indian Ocean.'

'I see,' said James. But from his manner it was clear he wasn't entirely satisfied. He peered over the desk. 'No luggage?'

'It's arriving later,' Jack fired back. 'We came straight from the boat. Mrs Lawes is feeling rather fatigued and didn't want to hang around at the docks waiting for her trunk. She would like very much to get to her room.'

James pursed his lips. 'Very well.' He tapped at his computer keyboard. 'You're after two singles? Hmm, you seem to be in luck. Two gentlemen, scheduled to be staying for the week, checked out today unexpectedly.'

Jack's police computer brain whirred and clicked. 'They didn't happen to go under the names Lazlo Blaskowitz and Jakob Lukowski, did they?'

'And what business is that of yours?' the desk manager snapped.

Jack pulled out his police identity wallet and showed it to the man. 'Actually, it's police business.'

The man choked back the protest already rising in his throat, satisfying himself instead with a sharp and waspish glance at Marian. Then he lowered his eyes to his screen yet again. 'Yes, as a matter of fact it was those particular gentlemen.'

'Did they leave alone?'

James studied the ceiling. 'Yes, I think . . . No. I remember now, they left in the company of Signor Horbert Manfreddo.'

'The ice-cream magnate?' Jack asked.

'I believe he is rather large in milk products, yes. As I recall, the three gentlemen hired a cab.'

'Where to?'

'The airport, I believe.'

'So, Signor Manfreddo checked out with them?'

The desk manager shook his head. 'Oh, no. Signor Manfreddo returned some hours later, alone. It was he who informed me that the two gentlemen would no longer be requiring their rooms. He paid their bills himself.'

'Manfreddo is still here?'

'Yes.' The man's reptilian eyes roved the reception area and came to rest on a figure at the bamboo bar. 'In fact, there he is now.'

Jack followed the manager's gaze. Seated at the bar was a large, suntanned man talking and smiling between two beautiful young women.

Marian gasped. 'Jack, that's him!'

Jack turned to her – she seemed about to faint.

'That's who?'

'Constantine.'

'You're quite sure it was him?' Jack asked once they were in the relative security of Marian's room.

'I'm certain,' she replied, wringing her hands and pacing up and down the queen-size-bedded room with breakfast bar, balcony overlooking the sea, tea- and coffee-making facilities and complementary refrigerator.

'OK, the one thing we mustn't do is panic.' All Jack's instincts were urging him to run screaming from the place and find a deep dark hole where he could hide for the next twenty years or so. 'Let's think this through logically.' He sat down on the end of the bed. 'He didn't see us come in and probably doesn't even know who we are. He's never seen me before, he only met you the once and more than likely paid you very little attention at the time. So I'd say we have little to worry about.'

'I'm sorry, Jack, but he was very attentive. He thinks of himself as a ladies' man – he was all over me, kissing my hands, complimenting me on my hair, my dress, my figure . . . you know the sort of thing.'

Jack felt a sharp pang of regret that *he* hadn't said all those things. 'So you think he'd recognize you again?'

'I'm sure of it.'

Jack dug the heels of his palms into his eye sockets and tried to think. He needed a shower, a drink and a pipe of his favourite tobacco. He got up off the bed awkwardly.

'Look, I think better with a system full of legal stimulants. Besides, I need to freshen up. This suit smells like Billingsgate.'

Marian looked at him levelly. 'Worse,' she said. 'Jack, I'm worried.'

Jack put a hand on her arm. 'Just stay in your room and

you'll be fine. I'll come back and check on you in an hour. Try and rest. Above all, don't worry. Mango will be here soon, perhaps he'll have some bright ideas.'

As he was about to leave, Marian called him back.

'Jack, will you ask the hotel boutique owner to come and see me with a selection of outfits? I'm not sure this ensemble is suitable attire for a beach resort.' She was still wearing her travelling clothes, and what little luggage she'd brought with her was now at the bottom of the Indian Ocean.

'Right.' Jack looked Marian up and down, glad at last of a valid excuse to openly study her fabulous figure. He grinned broadly, enjoying her every curve.

Marian guessed Jack's thoughts and smiled. 'That's all right, she knows my size.'

Jack flushed. 'Oh, right, fine . . . OK then. See you later.'

Jack left, feeling like a teenager.

Sitting in a recliner on the edge of the beach under the shade of a sun umbrella as blue as the sea at which he gazed, Jack sipped his Scotch and water and let his mind wander. But before it could get to work on the case, it first had to deal with how awkward he felt in the aquamarine and shocking pink beach shorts he'd bought in the hotel boutique. While passing on Marian's message, it had occurred to him that while his suit was being cleaned he should also purchase something more appropriate for the occasion; something which would allow him to blend in with the rest of the holidaying hotel guests on the beach.

'Oh, they're simply the must-have shorts of the season,' the boutique owner had told him. 'You'll feel right at home here wearing those.'

He looked down at the garishly patterned shorts which stood out like a sore thumb amongst the more restrained beach attire of the wealthy, who lounged around in understated ease. It wasn't just the bright pink hibiscus flower pattern, nor the fact that they revealed the long scar on his left leg which stretched from ankle to thigh.

What Jack found most embarrassing about the shorts was that when he reclined, or simply sat down, they ballooned up around his thighs, revealing the mesh inner liner and certain parts of his anatomy he would have rather kept private.

But he couldn't spend all day worrying about exposing his balls to the well-off. He crossed his legs, puffed on his pipe and ordered his mind to tackle the business at hand.

He took the salient points in order. Michaelmas knew or was in league with Horbert Manfreddo – the current Constantine; if Manfreddo was involved then so were the Syndicates; if the Syndicates were behind the political assassinations it meant they were back in business, which was very bad news for the stability of the planet; and for reasons best known to themselves, the two arms dealers had been supplying arms to the warring factions. But Jack reckoned that they were no longer a part of the picture, having gone on a one-way trip with Signor Manfreddo.

But what were the Syndicates up to? Most of the places they'd targeted were ungovernable: Afghanistan, Iraq, Iran, Saudi Arabia . . . Put a man in any one of those places and the likelihood was he'd be dead within twenty-four hours, even if he was backed by the mob. No, it was more than just political power the Syndicates wanted, but what?

Something else that still wasn't clear was where the killer would strike next – Jack couldn't even guess at his movements. Most serial killers had a system that worked for them. For instance they only killed on a Friday, or chose victims in a certain area.

But apart from having a fondness for politicians, this chap seemed to have no plan at all.

Jack took another sip of his drink. A drop of condensation ran down the outside of the glass and dropped into his lap. Jack looked down to wipe it off and his garishly patterned shorts screamed up at him.

Good God, what was I thinking? What a terrible pattern. He blinked. *Pattern . . .*

He looked up sharply. 'Pattern!' he said out loud. 'Pattern!' he said again. 'My God, I've been so dense!' In an instant, Jack suddenly saw how to find the killer and clear Marian's name in one fell swoop.

In his excitement, he was about to put in a call using his wrist communicator, then he remembered he no longer possessed it. While he considered his next move, he could hear raised voices coming from the reception area.

'What do you mean you don't have any rooms?'

'I'm afraid all our singles are occupied.'

'It's because I'm a telepath – that's it, isn't it? Go on, admit it – you don't want my kind here!'

Jack smiled, heaved himself off the lounger and made his way towards the growing conflict.

In the usually cool and tranquil reception area, a battle was in progress. A figure in a cerise and violet kaftan was haranguing the desk manager.

'What have you got against my kind, eh? Answer me that!'

'I can assure you, sir, that we cater to all types, regardless of race, colour or creed.'

'That's not true and you know it! Show me another telepath here, go on, show me!'

'It's all right, you can calm down now.' Jack put a hand on Mango's shoulder.

Mango turned to him, all smiles. 'Jack, there you are.' He took a moment to take in Jack's new attire. 'Love the shorts! Isn't this place fabulous? There's only one trouble – this jerk won't let me in.'

The desk manager cocked an eyebrow in Jack's direction. 'You *know* this . . . gentleman?'

'I do, and you'd be hard pressed to find a better.'

'That's what I was trying to tell him,' Mango chipped in.

Jack addressed the manager again. 'What time is it in London?'

The manager sighed. 'London is four hours behind us, sir. As it is now ten past five in the afternoon here, that would make it . . .'

'Ten past one back home – lunchtime,' Jack said thoughtfully. 'Perfect. Mango, come over here.' Jack dragged him to a quiet corner of the reception area hidden from prying eyes behind the spreading leaves of a small potted palm. 'Open your mouth.'

'What?'

'I want to talk to Clark'.

'Are you going to tell me what's going on or do I have to guess?' Mango huffed.

'You'll pick it up as we go along. Now dial Clark, and once we're through, open your mouth and leave it to me,' Jack instructed.

Mango sighed irritably then, pressing a button on the communicator, enunciated clearly, 'Clark.'

After a few moments the young man came on the line.

'*Mango, is that you?*'

'No, it's Jack.'

'*Sir! You're alive!*'

'Just about.'

'*But that hyperliner crash—*'

'I decided not to go down with the ship. How are things?'

'*They found a body in your flat,*' Clark said disapprovingly.

'Yes, of an assassin sent to kill me.'

'*Oh,*' Clark's tone brightened. '*There's been another murder – one George Musgrove, Mason's original platoon commander, the platoon he was in before he joined the Dame Ednas, that is.*'

'It makes sense – set a Trouser to catch a Trouser. Unfortunately, against a shape shifter he'd have had no chance. Look, we haven't got a lot of time. I'm assuming my brother has gone for lunch.'

'*Yes, Chief. He left about twenty minutes ago.*'

'That's Freddy – regular as clockwork. I assume he left with a certain heavy-breasted individual?'

Jack couldn't witness Clark's blush, but he could sense his embarrassment down the line.

'*Er, yes, Chief, he did.*'

'Good. Now I want you to hustle. He'll already have been notified about this call and will at this moment be stuffing down the remains of his *Pigeonneaux au Sauternes* in order to rush straight back to the Yard. That means we've got about ten minutes. Listen carefully and don't interrupt.'

'*OK . . . Oh, sorry.*'

'Go to the computer in my office and input: "politician, exploding head".'

'*Er, it's the commissioner's office now, Chief.*'

Jack snorted in exasperation.

'*Sorry, I'll try the door . . .*'

There was a certain amount of rustling and crackling. Then Clark came back on.

'*It's locked.*'

'Well, look in through the window and tell me if he's left the 3D computer running.'

'*OK . . . No.*'

'Damn! You'll have to go down to the main computer in the basement.'

'*They'll never let me in there!*'

'Of course they will – you've got top-security clearance. Are you alone?'

'*Well, most people are at lunch, but there are still a few hanging around.*'

'Right. Now, without drawing attention to yourself, I want you to leave the main office and head for the lift. Tell no one what you're doing – it's imperative nobody suspects anything untoward.'

'*OK.*'

Jack heard a muffled bang down the line.

'*Ow! Bloody hell!*'

'Clark?'

'*Sorry – fell over a desk.*'

Jack sighed. 'You're supposed to be being discreet.'

'*Sorry.*'

Then Jack remembered. 'Wait a minute, I've had a better idea. I forgot, you're trained in espionage.'

'*Eh?*'

'All those stake-outs you did with your father – you must have picked up some tips.'

'*Well, maybe.*'

'I'll bet you're a whizz at opening locked doors.'

'*I can't break into the commissioner's office, not with these people here.*'

'Then get rid of them!'

'*How?*'

'I don't know . . . pretend there's a fire!'

'*All right. Fire! Fire! Everybody out!*'

Although Jack hadn't been entirely serious, he admired Clark's straightforward approach. 'Is it working?'

'*Fire! Fire! Run for your lives!*'

There was more rustling and banging and the sound of distant raised voices.

'*They're leaving!*' Clark hissed.

'OK, once everyone's gone, lock the main door and break into my office.'

After a few moments, during which Jack could hear nothing but muffled thuds and heavy breathing, Clark said excitedly, '*I'm in!*'

'That was quick.'

'*Straightforward barrel-lock, not even code-protected. Child's play, really.*'

'If you say so.'

'This is hurting my jaw,' Mango complained.

'Will you be quiet!'

'*Sorry?*'

'Nothing. Clark, open the control panel and input: "politician, exploding head, join dots". You'll probably get what looks like a terrible mess at first, but carry on, refine your results. Discount any before Afghanistan, then tell me what you see.'

'*Sir, can I ask what this is all about?*'

'Patterns, Clark, we're looking for patterns, remember?'

'*The computer won't boot up.*'

'Whack it!' Jack instructed.

'*What?*'

'Whack it with something hard!'

'*Oh, OK. Will a book do?*'

'What is it?'

'*Police Procedurals, Vol. Four.*'

'I can't think of a better use for it.'

There was a grunt followed by a thump.

'*It's working!*'

'There's no need to sound surprised. I do know something about computers, you know. You can rest your mouth for a bit, now.'

'*Sorry?*'

'Not you.'

'*Oh.*'

Mango massaged his jaw. 'This is worse than being at the dentist.'

Through Mango's cheek, Jack listened to Clark's progress. There was the sound of tapping and heavy breathing.

Jack yanked Mango's jaw wide yet again. 'What's happening, Clark? You're running out of time.' Jack imagined his brother, now racing back to the Yard in his limousine, siren blaring. After what seemed like days, Clark came back on the line, hushed and breathless.

'*Bloody hell!*' he gasped.

Jack was holding Mango's mouth open so wide he was in danger of permanent lock-jaw. 'What is it, Clark? What do you see?'

'*It's . . . it's Mr Piggy-Wig.*'

'Mr Piggy-Wig?'

'*The Mr Piggy-Wig logo, plastered across the face of the earth. The ears are in Uzbekistan and Kyrgyzstan. The eyes are Kandahar and Lahore, the nose is Quetta and Multan, and the mouth is Hyderabad, which would explain the four murders in Pakistan. It's even got the brass buttons of his coat – all those murders down the west coast of India – Mumbai, Panaji, Mangalore, Calicut—*'

'Is it *all* there?' Jack interrupted.

'*What do you mean?*'

'Are there any bits missing – like an earlobe or something?'

'*I don't think pigs have earlobes, sir.*'

'For God's sake, Clark, you know what I mean!'

'*Er, hang on, let's have a look . . . It's a fairly simple representation – a basic stick figure, but . . . Oh, right.*'

'What is it?' Jack yelled.

'*The tail – it's not there.*'

'Excellent. Now, tell me, if that tail *were* there, where would it be?'

'*Um, let's see . . . er . . . is that Manila? No, that would be too high. Singapore? . . . No, that doesn't seem right either . . . er . . .*'

'Clark, hurry up!'

'*Sorry, Chief. It's a bit hard to make it out – the earth keeps moving round. I think it's—*'

'Yes?'

'*I think it's—*'

'What?' Jack had Mango's mouth so far open, he could see his tonsils.

'*Corbett . . . Yeah . . . that's got to be Corbett!*'

261

'Good work, Clark, now get out of there swiftly before my brother turns up. Leave your police-issue mobile phone on your desk and disappear for a few days. Don't go back to your mum's, stay at a friend's, sleep on the streets, go anywhere, just stay where Freddy can't find you. I'll call your mum and tell her you're all right. Give it forty-eight hours then call her – if everything's gone to plan, there'll be a message from me.'

'*If not?*'

'Find another planet to inhabit.'

The line went dead and Jack let Mango close his aching jaw. Mango stared balefully at Jack.

'I suppose this means we're going back to Corbett.'

'You catch on quick.'

'But I only just got here!'

Jack strode across to the reception desk, with Mango trailing reluctantly in his wake. 'What time is Signor Manfreddo checking out today?'

'I'm afraid, sir, that is Signor Manfreddo's business,' the manager sniffed.

'Look, I don't have time to mess around.' Jack slipped the man a fifty-dollar bill.

Being careful not to appear to be accepting the money too eagerly, the manager secreted the bill in his top pocket and glanced down at his computer. 'He's booked on the eight o'clock Sky Service to Corbett.'

'Sky service?'

'A small outfit that runs an airship service around the Indian Ocean.'

'Is there one before eight o'clock?'

'The manager looked down at his computer again. 'There's one at six, but that's probably cutting it a bit fine.'

'We'll take it. Book myself, my colleague here and Mrs Lawes on it. We'll need a taxi to pick us up in ten minutes.'

The manager was becoming a little flustered, but another fifty soon smoothed his feathers. 'Certainly, sir.'

'Marian's here?' Mango gasped.

'And that's not all I have to tell you. Come on.'

They'd just set off in the direction of Marian's room when a pointed 'Ahem' from the desk manager stopped them.

Jack turned back. 'Yes?'

The manager curled his lip. 'And what are we supposed to do with all this?' He indicated a tower of suitcases, hat boxes and suit-carriers piled near the entrance.

Jack groaned. 'Mango, is all that yours?'

Mango looked shamefacedly at his shoes. 'I did a little shopping at the airport.' Then he suddenly became animated. 'You know, they have this great boutique . . .'

Jack slipped the manager yet another fifty. 'Just put this junk somewhere safe until we decide what to do with it, all right?'

'Junk?' Mango shrieked.

The manager smiled his reptilian smile. 'I'm sure we'll find room for it somewhere.'

Marian had been sitting tensely on the edge of the bed, staring out of the window. She stood up sharply when she heard the knock on the door.

'Who is it?'

'It's me, and I've brought a friend.'

Relaxing slightly at the sound of Jack's voice, she clicked open the lock.

'Hello, Mango,' she said. 'I'm sorry you've been dragged into this mess.'

'Oh, I had nothing on this week,' he replied airily. 'My, these suites are so sumptuously furnished!' he gushed, walking past Marian and surveying the room.

'And this is just the budget accommodation,' Jack replied.

Marian closed the door and stared at the floor. 'Everyone I meet I get into trouble. I'm just bad luck.'

'Nonsense,' said Mango, 'Jack has the worst luck of anyone I know. He doesn't need anyone's help to screw things up.'

'Don't listen to him,' said Jack, going to her and taking her hand. 'I've a feeling our luck's about to change.' Then he noticed her outfit. 'Is this new?'

'Do you like it?'

She was wearing loose, calf-length white linen slacks and a salmon-pink sleeveless top which revealed the golden skin of her arms and shoulders. Her auburn hair too seemed to have picked up golden lights from the sun.

Jack gave her an admiring once-over. 'You look terrific.'

She smiled. 'Are you sure? This colour doesn't wash me out?'

Mango was about to say something, but Jack shut him up with a look.

'Oh, Jack,' she said, dropping his hand and moving over to the little balcony. 'I'm to blame for getting us into this situation.' She gazed out to sea, chewing her lip thoughtfully.

'Nonsense,' said Jack, going to her. 'None of this is your fault.'

'No, you don't understand,' she said.

Jack smiled. 'I understand better than you think. That's why we're going to Corbett.'

Marian turned to face him. She looked a little shaken. 'Corbett? But . . .'

'You thought you were supposed to lure me out to Corbett to have me killed.'

Marian blushed and stared at the floor again. 'Jack, I'm so sorry, I never meant—'

'It's all right. Michaelmas *did* want me to go to Corbett, but not for the reason you think.'

'Will someone tell me what's going on?' Mango demanded.

· 'Corbett is where the killer is going to strike next. And a certain ice-cream magnate is his next target.'

Marian's eyes widened. 'Manfreddo?'

'It's a little complicated and I haven't got time to explain now. Just be ready to leave in ten minutes.'

'Ten minutes?' said Marian. 'We've only just arrived.'

'That's what I said,' Mango grumbled.

Mango, stay here with Marian, then meet me in the lobby.'

'And where are *you* going?' Mango asked.

Jack looked down at his wild shorts as if it was the most obvious thing in the world. 'I'm going to change.'

It took Jack a matter of moments to slip out of his shorts and into his now clean and crisply pressed lightweight linen suit. Stepping out of his room, Jack headed back towards reception.

But crossing the sun terrace in front of the bar, Jack saw him. Manfreddo was seated at a table on his own, perfectly lit by the setting sun, occasionally sipping a rum punch and apparently talking to himself. At first, Jack didn't understand, then he spotted the chunky wrist communicator adorning Signor Manfreddo's left wrist.

'Of course,' Jack murmured.

He knew he shouldn't, but the devil in him couldn't resist. Exaggerating his limp a touch, he headed for the crime boss's table and crashed straight into it. Manfreddo's glass toppled over and rum punch flooded the table and dripped stickily onto the terracotta tiles beneath.

Signor Manfreddo looked up in a fury. 'What the fuck do you think you're doing?'

'I'm so sorry,' Jack replied, picking up the man's upturned glass and trying to mop up the mess with a rapidly disintegrating paper coaster. 'Please, let me buy you another drink.'

'I'll call you back,' Manfreddo mumbled and clicked a button on his communicator. He turned to Jack. 'No, no, just go – leave me alone, please.'

But Jack stood his ground and gazed in open-mouthed astonishment at the man.

'What? What is it?'

'Excuse me, but aren't you the famous Signor Horbert Manfreddo?'

Manfreddo shrugged. 'What of it?'

'Let me shake your hand, sir.' Apparently forgetting that he was still holding the soggy remains of the little paper coaster, which was now saturated with rum punch, Jack seized Manfreddo's hand and squeezed hard, sending drips of the sticky cocktail into the man's lap.

'Aw, shit!' Manfreddo complained.

'I'm so sorry, I'm just so clumsy today, I don't know what's wrong with me.'

Manfreddo pulled an immaculately laundered linen handkerchief out of his pocket and dabbed at his shorts. 'Just fucking leave me alone!'

'I just wanted to wish you well for tomorrow.'

Manfreddo looked puzzled. 'Tomorrow?'

'Yes, in the election.'

'Oh that. Yeah, well, OK, now you have, goodbye.'

'I mean, you must be pretty sure of the result, to be relaxing here and not to be on Corbett, campaigning. I'll bet the other candidates don't have that luxury.'

Manfreddo took off his sunglasses and looked at Jack long and hard. 'Don't I know you?'

Jack stared back, resisting the temptation to use the line that P.M. Tenement's Harry Sharp uttered in *Sorrento Serenade*: 'No, but you will, Signor, you will.' Instead, he said, 'No, I don't think so.'

'Is this gentleman bothering you, sir?' It was the bald man in the black suit – Manfreddo's personal bodyguard.

'No, he's just leaving.'

Helped on his way by a firm and businesslike shove from the bald man, Jack headed off in the direction of the reception desk.

Mango and Marian were waiting for him, surrounded by cases.

'Mango, as both Marian and myself travel light these days, this must all be yours.'

Mango looked proudly at the piles of luggage. 'I can never resist a bargain.'

'It stays.'

'Oh, but Jack, I bought myself a whole new summer wardrobe!'

Ignoring him, Jack turned to the desk manager. 'How much do we owe you?'

The manager smiled and presented him with a bill.

A low whistle escaped Jack's lips. 'I'd hate to think how much it would have cost if we'd actually stayed the night. Will you take a card?'

The manager indicated by a nod of the head that this would be in order.

Jack pulled out his wallet and selected the credit card Freddy had given him for expenses. 'Here we are.' He smiled brightly.

Once the bill was settled, Jack allowed Mango to choose a single suitcase and put the rest of his luggage into the keeping of the manager to be distributed amongst the hotel staff as he saw fit. This done, Jack, Marian and a deeply upset Mango got into the waiting taxi and headed for the airport.

Immediately after they'd left, Signor Manfreddo arrived in reception.

'What do you know about a guy with a limp?'

'Limp, sir?' The manager smiled vaguely. 'That could describe any number of our guests.'

Manfreddo placed a big hairy fist over one of the manager's pale, manicured hands and squeezed. The man's eyes crossed with pain.

'Now, listen to me carefully. If you ever want to play the piano again, don't get cute with Uncle Horbert, OK? We'll try it again. What do you know about a guy with a limp?'

'He's a policeman.'

Manfreddo's eyes narrowed. 'Policeman? Where is he now?'

'He just left.'

'I asked where is he *now*.' Manfreddo applied a little more pressure.

'Airport!' the manager whimpered.

'You're doing well, carry on.'

'He's on the six o'clock to Corbett.'

'Was he alone?'

But the manager could no longer speak – he simply shook his head, and with his free hand passed Manfreddo a copy of the bill that Jack had just paid.

The syndicate boss's eyes widened when he read the other name on the sheet. To the manager's great delight, Manfreddo released him from his vice-like grip and clicked a button on his wrist communicator.

'O'Hanlon? . . . Lindsay's on his way.'

Chapter 21

The moment the craft docked at Barker Airport, Corbett, and blue-suited policemen boarded the craft demanding to see everyone's passports, Jack had that old familiar sinking feeling.

He leaned across to Mango.

'You know when I said our luck was about to change? I may have been a bit premature.'

'Passport.'

Jack looked up into the unsmiling, mirror-shaded face of the policeman and dutifully handed over his passport. He wasn't at all surprised when he and Marian were asked to accompany the officer off the aircraft and into a waiting police car. What did surprise him was that they left Mango behind, completely ignoring him as though he didn't exist. No one ever ignored Mango. Loathed and detested him for crimes against fashion, yes, but ignored? It was odd. But Jack had no time to worry about that now, as he and Marian were driven off through the torrential tropical rain to an unknown destination.

'Don't worry, Con, the dame and that gimpy policeman are safe and sound in the capable hands of Ave Verum, and the election's as good as won.' Police Chief O'Hanlon patted one of a row of shiny black ballot boxes sitting on a long trestle table in his office already stuffed with votes for Manfreddo. 'Once voting's over, we'll swap these babies for the actual boxes and

then . . . Hail to the Chief!' O'Hanlon bowed to Signor Manfreddo.

'Just don't fuck up,' Horbert growled, wiping the sweat
from his face. 'This scam's taken half a lifetime to put together.'

'Er, sir?' A man stuck his head around the door.

'What is it, Lieutenant?' O'Hanlon snarled.

'I thought you might want to have a look at this.'

O'Hanlon turned to Manfreddo, who was sitting damply in
the chief's own chair.

'You don't mind?'

Manfreddo shrugged and ran a hand through his wet, shiny
curls. 'No, I don't mind. Jesus, the fucking humidity must be
two hundred per cent!'

'Actually, Signor Manfreddo might also be interested in what
I have here,' the lieutenant said, coming into the room.

Manfreddo looked up and a slight spasm of worry crossed
his face. 'Show me.'

The officer snicked a record-o-chip into a slot in the table
and a picture of the immigration booth at Barker Airport
appeared on a screen on the end wall. Among the new arrivals
queuing up to show their passports, Brother Bertrand, waiting
patiently in line, looked straight up into the CCTV camera and
smiled.

The colour drained from Manfreddo's face. 'Jesus H. fucking Christ, that's him – he's here!' He turned to the officer.
'Where is he now? Did you arrest the bum?'

'Er, negative, sir. The officers at the spaceport alerted us as
soon as they recognized the man. They had instructions to
detain him immediately, but he managed to avoid them.'

Manfreddo leapt up and started raving. 'If my guys had been
on the case from the get-go, this asshole would already be
dreaming with the fishes!' A dark, damp patch of sweat had
appeared and began to spread across the back of Manfreddo's
pale blue shirt. 'Shit, fuck!' He picked up one of the false ballot
boxes and hurled it to the floor, badly denting one of its

corners. 'I'm surrounded by assholes!' Then he picked up the police chief's phone and hurled it at the television screen. The lieutenant only just ducked out of the way in time. Manfreddo, eyes wild, looked for something else to destroy. 'Shitty, fucking little pimp!' He tried to up-end the chief's desk but, finding it too heavy, he took the less dramatic action of sweeping away everything that stood on it; pens, pencils, computer, ink blotter, executive toys crashed to the floor. 'I'll nail his fucking liver to the door!' Then, after stamping on the computer until it was reduced to its component parts, his fury abated a little and he wiped a stray curl of damp hair from his forehead. 'Fucking two-bit, damp, humid, lousy fucking country.'

The chief smiled. 'And, come tomorrow, it'll all be yours.'

Manfreddo waved a finger at him threateningly. 'Listen, until I see this guy's broken and bleeding body with my own eyes, I want full police protection. I want a ring of steel around me – I don't want no one within fifty yards of me! Find the bastard, or my first job as Corbett's president will be to look for another police chief!'

The reason why the assassin was travelling under his own face and had allowed his image to be captured on TV was that he wanted to put the wind up Manfreddo; to let him know for certain that he was here. It no longer mattered who else saw him as this was the last hit of the project. Afterwards he would simply melt away and disappear for ever.

The second the assassin showed his passport to the immigration authorities, they knew who he was.

The immigration officer looked into the assassin's eyes.

'One moment, please, sir. Would you mind waiting there? There's something we need to clear up.' The man carefully kept his eyes on the assassin the whole time, but even as he watched, the shape shifter's smiling features began to change. In the time it took for the officer to call up his colleagues and alert them to his presence, the assassin had assumed another identity completely. Hurriedly leaving the confines of his little booth in order to actually lay hands on him, the officer was presented with a bewildering sea of faces, none of which corresponded to the picture on the passport he still clutched, uselessly, in his hand. It seemed impossible – the man had simply melted away in front of his eyes. All the officer could find of him was a discarded monk's habit.

Immediately the airport was sealed and surrounded by a tight ring of security.

The security guards weren't helped in their task by the fact that the airport was especially busy at that moment. All week, Corbett citizens had been thronging back home in order to vote in the presidential election. With the voting taking place tomorrow, the place was seething.

It was difficult enough to keep order, but given the added complication of having to keep the airport sealed and investigate all recently disembarked passengers, airport security was at breaking point. Ugly little scenes broke out all over the concourse. The newly arrived, prevented from joining their friends and relations – who waited fretfully in the ever-falling rain under large umbrellas just outside the security ring – began shouting at the guards, and then laying into them with fists, handbags and anything else that came to hand – bottles of duty free, rock-hard salamis, or souvenir Air-ace Bears – while the poor men could do nothing but take the blows, smile and repeat, over and over, 'We're very sorry, sir, ma'am, but we have instructions not to let anyone either enter or leave the airport.'

The assassin, taking full advantage of the confusion, and having fortuitously met a security guard in the gents', was now stalking the concourse in the blue uniform of the Barker Airport security force, listening in to the increasingly frantic communications of the officers as they searched for him. He smiled and clicked on his communicator.

'It could be nothing, but over on the west side of the building there's an individual in an orange jumpsuit carrying a bucket and a ladder and acting suspiciously.'

As guards all over the airport dropped what they were doing and headed towards where the window cleaner was innocently plying his trade, the assassin walked quietly and calmly in the other direction, slipped out of the building and into the surrounding jungle, completely unnoticed.

The dungeon of Ave Verum Abbey, buried deep in the soggy soil of Corbett, was probably one of the dampest places on earth. Great green cushions of moss, and fungi the size of dinner plates sprouted from the walls, while long wet ribbons of algae hung down from the ceiling. Although right in the centre of the cell there was a large grating covering a drain, this device, instead of fulfilling its function as an outlet for the water pouring into the cell, provided an inlet. Water gushed upwards through it, flooding the floor to mid-calf level.

'Oh my God,' Marian remarked, surveying her surroundings.

'I still think I prefer the Royal Mahe,' Jack said. 'But this place has answered a long-held mystery for me.'

'Really?'

'You know those old movies about knights and castles and people being thrown in dungeons?'

'Yes.'

'I always used to wonder about the toilet arrangements. Now I know.'

'They don't have any.'

'Exactly. I hope this cell hasn't been occupied recently.'

'Please, Jack!' Marian hitched up her slacks a little higher and searched about desperately for a slightly more elevated bit of floor on which to perch.

'So what do we do now?'

'What do we do?' Jack looked at the solid stone walls, at the one tiny window high above – the only source of light – and at the solid oak door with cast-iron fixings.

'We wait for a miracle, that's what we do.'

Bang on cue, something slid through the small viewing grille in the middle of the door and dropped into the water with a splash.

'Ugh!' screamed Marian, scrabbling desperately backwards up a wall. 'Was that a rat?'

'No, I don't think so.' Jack waded over to the door and put his face to the grille.

'Hello?' he called. 'Anybody there?' But the only reply was the sound of retreating footsteps.

'What is it?'

'I think our miracle might have just happened.' Rolling up his sleeve, Jack searched around in the murky waters at the foot of the door. 'Yeurgh.'

'Did you find something?'

'Yes.'

'What?'

'I'd rather not think about it. Wait a minute, there's something else. Aha!'

Standing upright, Jack pulled out a metal ring with a single key dangling from it. 'It's a key!'

'Well, open the door!'

'Just a minute, just a minute. There's something else. It looks like a message.'

A small cardboard tag was attached to the key ring. Jack squinted at it in vain in the dim light. 'I can't make it out . . . hang on. Wading over to the centre of the cell, he held the card in the light falling from the single window. "Lave no . . . he nswer un er yo fet." What the bloody hell does that mean, is it Latin?'

Marian waded reluctantly over to him. 'Let me.' She took the note from him and studied it for a few moments. 'It says, "Leave now, the answer is under your feet."'

Jack coloured slightly. 'Well you have to admit it was difficult to read – all smeary like it is from the water.'

'What do you think it means?'

'I think "leave now" is pretty unequivocal.'

'Please, Jack, does everything have to be a joke?'

'Sorry, it's how I react to being terrified.'

'"Leave now, the answer is under your feet,"' Marian repeated. 'The answer to what?'

'There's a drain in the middle of the floor,' Jack offered.

Marian shook her head. 'But why would whoever wrote this note give us a key if they wanted us to leave via the drain?'

'I was thinking more about "the answer", whatever that is.'

'Oh, you think it could be in the drain?'

'It's worth a shot.'

'Go on then.'

He paused a moment. He didn't relish the idea of groping around in the mucky water again, but the only other option – of allowing a lady to wallow up to her elbows in sewage – didn't sit well with his self-image as gentlemanly rescuer of damsels in distress. 'Right, here goes.' Gritting his teeth, Jack once again plunged his hand into the dark waters. His fingers soon closed around the metal bars of the drain. 'I've found it.' But heaving with all his might, he couldn't get it to shift. 'It won't budge. I think, in the circumstances, we should act on our first impulse and use the key to open the door before our saviour changes his mind.'

'Good idea.'

But just as Jack was about to slide the key into the lock, he heard the ancient bolt slide back with a *ker-chunk* and the door creaked open. A cowled figure stood in the doorway.

'Come with me.'

Marian waded over to stand by Jack's side.

'No, not you, just him,' said the monk.

Holding the key behind his back, Jack managed to press it into Marian's hand before he was led away.

*

'So, tell me again, why are you here?'

The voice came out of the darkness surrounding a bright light, which was all Jack could see.

'I've told you, for my health. Britain isn't quite damp enough for my taste.'

Smack!

Jack was hit hard across the face.

'Is this the massage? It's a little firm for my tastes.'

'Ah yes, Jack Lindsay's famous sense of humour. But I think it's time you got serious if you don't want anything bad to happen.'

'How bad can it get? My brother tries to have me killed, I narrowly escape death on an exploding airship, and now I'm being held by mad monks. Could things get any worse?'

'I'm afraid so – much worse.' The owner of the voice moved into the light, and Jack saw that he was in uniform. He read the name 'O'Hanlon' on the man's breast pocket.

Jack smiled. 'I knew the police had to be behind this.'

'I'd hate anything to happen to your delightful companion,' the chief of police retorted.

For a moment, Jack strained angrily against the bonds that held him fast to the hard wooden chair, but then relaxed and counted to ten. To reveal his true feelings for Marian would play right into O'Hanlon's hands. 'You can do what you like to her – she's trying to have me killed anyway.'

'Nice try, Jack. But I've heard about your old-fashioned, chivalrous attitude to women. Don't worry, nothing's going to happen to her as long as you cooperate. All you have to do is tell me what you're doing here. We know you're on the run, we just want to know why you chose Corbett to hide out.'

'What are you getting out of this, O'Hanlon?' Jack asked. 'What's Manfreddo promised you? Money? Power? A shiny new uniform? You see, I know what you're up to. I also know how the Syndicates work. Once you've fixed the election for him, you're disposable.'

'Syndicates, Jack?' O'Hanlon shook his head. 'You're mistaken. This is a straightforward presidential election, perfectly legal and above board.'

'Come on, O'Hanlon, we both know Manfreddo is the Constantine. Do you have any idea how much trouble you are in?'

O'Hanlon laughed. 'Me in trouble? Who's the one tied to the chair? No, Jack, Signor Manfreddo and I are a team, working together to help build Corbett's future health and prosperity.'

'As well as your own.'

'Corbett's chief of police is a very well-paid job.' O'Hanlon crouched in front of Jack. 'Now, much as I'm enjoying our little chat, I haven't got all day to hang around jawing. So, are you going to tell me what you and your lady friend are doing here?'

'We love the rainy season.'

Smack!

This time Jack was hit from the other side.

The blow reopened the gash in Jack's cheek put there by Razor Phipps, and blood trickled down his face. It hurt like hell and it was a few moments before Jack could speak.

'I think I preferred the other chap's lightness of touch.'

O'Hanlon put his face very close to Jack's. 'All right, have it your way. But the next time we meet, you're going to tell me everything I want to know. Otherwise you'll be responsible for a terrible injustice. How awful it would be for that young girl to go through life horribly disfigured.'

All Jack's finer feelings urged him to fight against his bonds, to try to break free and defend Marian at all costs, but he kept his cool. 'Why should I care? Like I said, she's just one more person who wants to see me dead.'

O'Hanlon smiled. 'I'll leave you to think over what I've said. Take him back.'

The two monks standing on either side of Jack untied him from the chair and, lifting him bodily out of it, dragged him back to his cell.

The door opened and Jack was thrown back into the dungeon. He landed face down in the filthy water with a splash.

Marian waded across to him. 'Oh, Jack, are you all right?'

'I'm fine,' he mumbled through a swollen lip.

'What did they do to you?'

'We played ping-pong – I was the ball.'

'Oh, please, Jack, don't. This place terrifies me, we have to get out of here.'

'That's a very good idea. Do you still have the key?'

'Yes.'

'Good. Help me to stand.'

With Marian's help, Jack staggered upright and lurched over to the door. He peered through the grille. The passageway outside the cell was deserted.

'OK, give it to me.'

Inserting the key in the lock, Jack turned it slowly. The bolt slid back noisily. Jack hoped that the sound hadn't attracted any unwanted attention.

'Well?'

'Shh!'

Jack pressed his ear to the metalwork and listened. But apart from the distant sound of running water, he could hear nothing.

Cautiously pushing open the door, he looked up and down the corridor.

'Come on.'

'Which way?' hissed Marian.

'The way we came in, I suppose.'

Jack turned left and led the way along the dank and flooded corridor, which was lit by green chemical lights high up on the walls. Around the first corner was a flight of stairs leading to an unseen upper floor, which they climbed gratefully, glad at last to be out of the water. The stairs continued upwards, winding round and round until they came to a small archway, through which voices could be heard. Jack motioned Marian to be quiet.

'... not until it's over, those are our instructions. Then we throw them into the moat.' It was a man's voice – coarse and deep.

'If you ask me, it's dangerous to let them live. The Con is going soft,' someone said in a high, reedy treble.

'He knows what he's doing,' the first voice said. 'And we have our orders.'

Jack chanced a peek into the room. Three cowled monks were standing around a table, two had their backs to him – he guessed that they were the same two who'd escorted him to his interview – but the third was facing the doorway. Although Jack couldn't see his face, he glimpsed a flash of the man's eyes from deep within the shadows of his hood. Jack held his breath, now the jig was surely up. But just then a distant bell began to toll.

'Vespers,' said the monk with the coarse voice.

'Come on then,' said the treble.

The monk facing Jack gestured to the other two that they go on ahead of him.

'What's the matter with you, Brother Verrat, cat got your tongue?' said the coarse-voiced monk.

Jack's eyes widened when he heard the name.

'Ah, come on,' said the treble, 'he's just being polite.'

'Very Christian of you, Brother Verrat, I'm sure.'

The two monks left the room, and the silent Brother Verrat followed them, but not before pointing out to Jack a door on the other side of the room, opposite the corridor down which the monks now exited.

'Seems we have a friend. Follow me,' Jack whispered. They made their way cautiously across the room to the sturdy oak door. 'Here goes.' Grasping the handle, he turned it slowly. The door opened with a low groan onto utter darkness.

'Where does it lead?' Marian asked.

'Can't see a bloody thing,' Jack replied. It was not an attractive prospect – entering a dark room in unfamiliar surroundings on the say-so of a monk whose motives were still uncertain. But did they have a choice?

'What do we do now?' said Marian.

'Well, we can't go back. Take my hand.' Jack led the way into the darkness. Once the door was closed behind them, the way ahead was obvious. 'Look – light, coming from over there.' A thin strip of brightness on the floor indicated a door that led, just possibly, to the outside. Moving unsurely towards it, Jack eventually collided with something wooden and very solid. 'I think I've reached it.' Putting his ear to the rough wooden door, he listened. But he could hear nothing; either it opened to the outside, or it was just too thick for any sound to pass through. He groped for the handle and grunted.

'What are you doing?' asked Marian.

'Trying to open it, what do you think?'

'You're making strange noises.'

'It's bloody stiff!'

There was more grunting and groaning as Jack put all his effort into turning the ancient lock. 'It won't bloody move!'

'Should I have a go?' Marian asked tentatively.

'I'm telling you, it won't budge.'

After a few more attempts, during which Jack's grunts and groans reached a new and startling pitch, he gave up and stood aside for the lady.

'Oh, very well, have a go. But I don't see how it's going to help,' Jack snorted.

Marian crept forwards uncertainly and groped for the door handle. Jack waited for the little lady to give up so that he could reassume his role of superior being, but after a moment there was a *clunk* and a narrow beam of light shot into the room from the just-open door.

'How did you do that?' Jack asked.

'You did try turning the handle both ways, didn't you?'

'Both ways? Well of course I . . . didn't.' Jack scowled in the gloom.

'Now then, let's see where we are.' Marian pushed the door fully open and immediately disappeared. 'Aaah!'

'Marian!'

'Help me!'

Jack looked down. The door opened to the outside all right, but halfway up the wall of the abbey, thirty feet above the moat. Marian was hanging from a rusting metal ring sticking out of the brickwork, about a foot below the bottom of the door frame. Below her, in the murky waters of the moat, large green logs floated. But as Jack watched, one of the 'logs' yawned, revealing two rows of vicious, jagged teeth.

They weren't logs, they were crocodiles – large and probably with not much to look forward to except their next meal.

With his stiff leg sticking straight out behind him, Jack crouched awkwardly to reach her. 'Take my hand!'

She looked up at him, terror in her eyes. 'I can't!'

'Yes, you can. Here!' Straining every muscle, Jack forced his arm down towards her and his fingertips brushed the back of her hand. 'Come on!'

'I can't, I can't!'

She was beginning to lose it. Jack would have to do something soon or she'd panic herself into the moat. But he couldn't get hold of her from this position. 'Bloody leg!' he cursed. Easing himself upright a fraction, he thrust his other leg out behind him and lay down on the floor, his head and shoulders protruding from the doorway in the abbey's exterior wall. From this position it was just possible for him to get his hands around her wrists. 'I've got you now, you can let go,' he said.

But she didn't move. He could feel her body vibrating with fear.

'I've got you, it's all right,' he soothed.

She stared up at him, eyes glazed, fingers still locked around the metal rung. She wouldn't budge.

There was no time for niceties now. 'Let go you bloody little fool or you'll have us both in the moat!' he screamed.

That shocked her back to life. Gazing up at him like an obedient dog, she dutifully unlocked her fingers and let Jack take her whole weight. She was heavier than he'd imagined and, he had to admit, he was not the young Hercules he'd once been.

Grunting with the effort, he pulled with all his might and gradually, gradually she began to rise. 'Now link your fingers around my neck and try and get your foot onto the rung!'

Marian did as she was told, which allowed Jack to reach further down her body and grab hold of the waistband of her slacks. With one final heave, he propelled himself backwards, and both he and Marian finally found themselves lying on the dusty floor of the room.

They lay there for a long while, recovering their breach.

Jack's vision was full of stars whirling in some gigantic vortex, and there was a loud throbbing in his ears.

Marian began to sob. Jack reached out an arm and stroked her hair. 'It's all right now.'

'I'm sorry, Jack, I was so scared.'

'So was I. Here.' He handed her a handkerchief and she blew her nose loudly.

'So,' Jack continued once he was no longer seeing distant galaxies, 'now we find ourselves still alive, we're left with the problem of how to get out of this place.' He looked around for inspiration.

The light from the open door revealed lumpy shapes resting against the walls of the hitherto darkened room.

'What do we have here?' Clambering laboriously to his feet, Jack went over to the nearest lump. It was covered in a dusty tarpaulin, which Jack hauled back to reveal an old wooden tub.

'What's this?'

'It's what the locals used to make rice wine in,' Marian informed him. 'Daygan told me that when this place was still called Borneo, every household made its own wine.'

'Including the holy fathers, it seems. That must have made for a jolly communion. But it doesn't help us get out of here.

Let's see . . .' Jack moved on to the next dusty tarpaulin. Underneath was a coil of rope. 'Aha!' But studying it a little closer, Jack saw that it was old, frayed and unlikely to bear their weight.

'Look at this!'

Jack turned. Marian had been doing some exploring of her own. The tarpaulin still in her hand, she was looking down at a coiled escape ladder, made of some shiny metal. 'Might this be of some use?' she asked.

'Maybe,' Jack shrugged.

'Come on,' she urged, 'help me get it out of the door.'

'Just a minute,' Jack warned. 'What do we do when we reach the bottom – swim across the moat dodging crocodiles?'

'But this must be here for us,' Marian insisted. 'Look at it, it's brand new, when everything else in here is at least a hundred years old.'

She had a point. Jack edged towards the door and looked down the sheer side of the abbey.

'What are you doing?'

'Trying to see if there's a ledge or something that we can perch on. Or some sort of secret mechanism to lower a drawbridge.'

'Well?'

He shook his head. 'No, there's nothing there, just bricks and monsters. Perhaps there isn't a way out of here, perhaps we've been tricked.'

Marian looked hopelessly around the room. 'But if he didn't mean us to escape, why would our friendly monk go to all the trouble of setting us free?'

'If he really meant us to escape he could have been a little more obvious about the means to do it!' Jack angrily yanked at another ancient tarpaulin which came away from the wall in a cloud of dust to reveal . . .

'A crossbow!' Jack stooped to look at it. 'Gosh, it's really rather beautiful.'

The old-fashioned weapon was a brand new, finely crafted

bow made from a lightweight alloy. Jack picked it up to examine it a little more closely.

'It's as light as a feather! What wonderful balance.' He held it up to his shoulder and put his eye to the sight. 'This is a terrific piece of work.'

'Please, Jack, I know boys can't resist toys, but it doesn't help us get out of here,' Marian grumbled.

'But that's where you're wrong.' Jack moved over to where the escape ladder lay and peered into its coils. 'Yes!'

Reaching down, he pulled out what looked like a crossbow bolt, fastened to the bottom of the ladder. 'Now then . . .'

Going back to the doorway, he peared out through the rain. The jungle had been cleared to a distance of about a hundred yards around the moat – too far to hit with any accuracy and besides, the ladder wasn't that long. Then Jack spotted what he'd been looking for. 'That's it!'

Marian joined him. 'That's what?'

'You see that tree?' Jack pointed down towards the stump of a large hardwood tree at the very edge of the moat. 'That's how we get out of here. Help me fasten the top of the ladder to that metal rung outside.'

Marian bent over to pick up the heap of slats and cables and drag them over to the door, and nearly fell over backwards once she realized just how light it was.

'Whoah! It looked really heavy,' she said, regaining her balance.

'The wonder of modern metals. Find the top, there should be some kind of fixing ring on it.'

'Is this what you're looking for?' Marian held up two sprung trigger-clips which were attached to the top of the two cables.

'Brilliant, hand them over.'

Once more lying prone, with his head sticking out of the doorway, Jack clipped the ladder's two cables onto the metal rung below. Giving them a tug to make sure they were secure, he scrambled back to his feet and found the other end – the end fashioned into a crossbow bolt.

'Now then, I've read about this in history books, but I can't say I've actually ever done it myself.'

But before Jack could load the weapon, there came the sound of raised voices from outside the door that led back to the abbey.

Marian looked fearfully at Jack, who put a finger to his lips.

'How did they get out?' Someone said.

'They can't have got far. Search the abbey!'

Moving silently to the inner door, Jack carefully slid the top and bottom bolts home into well-worn slots in the door frame. Then he and Marian dragged the heavy wooden tub over and wedged it against the door.

'Right, no time to lose,' he whispered. Upending the crossbow, Jack stuck his foot in the stirrup-shaped bracket at the front, then hauled on the string, grunting and sweating with the effort as the thin cord bit deep into the flesh of his fingers. 'It's harder than it looks,' he hissed to a sceptical Marian.

Once the weapon was cocked, he picked up the bolt attached to the end of the ladder with his still-throbbing fingers and inserted it into the long slot in the top of the crossbow. Aiming at the tree stump, he curled his finger around the trigger.

The recoil took Jack by surprise, thumping into his shoulder and pushing him backwards. He would have lost his footing entirely if Marian hadn't been standing behind him. The ladder unwound itself, writhing out after the speeding bolt like a metallic snake, but Jack and Marian had seen enough slapstick comedy routines to know to stay well clear of its coils. Once all the ladder had hurled itself out through the doorway, Jack peered after it to see how he'd done.

'Bugger!'

The bolt had buried itself in the mud just alongside the stump. But before Jack could haul it back and try again, the inner door handle creaked. Both Jack and Marian spun round and watched it slowly turn.

'It's locked!' someone yelled.

The handle turned again, and this time the whole door began to shake.

'It's bolted from the inside!'

They had no time to lose. Jack turned back to the outer door and yanked for all he was worth on the metal ladder. The end came free from the cloying earth and splashed into the moat, attracting the attention of a nearby croc. But having mouthed the metal bolt and found it not to its taste, the creature shook its head and swam away.

Something heavy thudded into the door, making it shudder. A shower of fine dust fell from the ceiling.

Marian stifled a scream and moved a little closer to Jack, who stuck at his task, hauling the ladder back hand over hand as fast as he was able. The metal rungs clanged against the ancient brickwork as the ladder snaked up the tower.

'Hurry, Jack.'

The door shuddered again. Jack gritted his teeth and redoubled his efforts.

Eventually the end slithered over the lip of the door frame. Jack dived on it and handed it to Marian.

'Here, hold this. And don't drop it.'

Jack cocked the crossbow with ease, the urgency of the situation giving him extra strength. Then, taking the bolt from Marian, he loaded it up and aimed once again.

This time he was prepared for the weapon's sensitivity. His shoulder braced against the door frame, Jack held his breath and squeezed the trigger ever so gently.

Suddenly the bolt was away, racing across the moat, the ladder snaking after it.

'Did you hit it?' Marian hissed.

Jack peered out through the falling rain. The bolt had sunk itself deep in the very centre of the old tree stump, and the ladder now stretched tautly over the moat. 'Bullseye!' Jack cheered.

Their means of escape was now in place, but the next stage wasn't going to be easy. Clambering down a ladder resting at an angle of forty-five degrees, in the rain, with a stiff leg, over a moat full of flesh-eating creatures while being chased by murderous monks was not an appealing prospect.

Jack stood in the open doorway and turned to Marian. 'Go,' he said. 'When you get down, run straight into the jungle and wait for me there. It might take me a little while to negotiate this thing – my days in the circus are far behind me.'

She was about to clamber out onto the ladder when the door gave another almighty shudder. Turning back to Jack, she looked deep into his eyes. Then she threw her arms around his neck and kissed him full on the mouth.

After a long, lingering moment, she broke away and gazed up at him. 'That was for luck.'

'And I need all the luck I can get,' Jack grinned. He felt like a schoolboy on the last day of term, and bent his head to kiss her again, but suddenly Marian was all business. Freeing herself from his embrace, she returned to the doorway and began to step out of it backwards. Jack went over to her, holding her arms tightly as she groped for the metal rungs with her feet. He was beginning to wonder how he was going to perform this act himself, with no one to hold on to *him*.

The door shuddered yet again. This time there was the sound of splintering wood.

Jack twisted round to see that the old iron hinges were starting to buckle.

But Marian was now on her way. 'Don't look down!' Jack called unhelpfully.

'I don't intend to,' she replied, her eyes tight shut.

Her progress was painfully slow as her feet groped for each succeeding rung. Jack only hoped that the door would hold out long enough for them both to get away.

After a painfully long time, Marian reached the ground. Pausing briefly at the stump, she looked up and waved, then took off across the strip of cleared jungle, heading for the shielding trees.

Now it was Jack's turn.

'Oh, God, I'm too old for this,' he groaned, sitting in the doorway, his feet dangling in space. The door shuddered again, and now it was beginning to split along its entire length. Time to go. Holding on to the door frame with both hands, Jack lowered himself through it until he was sitting on the metal ring fixed into the brickwork. Then, gripping the top rung of the ladder with both hands, he reached out with his good leg for the next rung but one. 'No applause, please,' he murmured, slipping his bottom off the metal ring and onto the flimsy ladder. But in his haste he hadn't thought this move through. Immediately his weight flipped him over and he found himself hanging upside down, his right foot wedged between the ladder's twisted cables.

'Aarrgh!'

Trying not to panic, nor to pay too much heed to the crocodiles that were now excitedly thrashing the surface of the water thirty feet below his head, he assessed his situation.

Try to think, he told himself. *Keep calm and try to think.*

From above came the sound of a crash and the splintering death throes of the inner door.

No time to think. Time to act.

He tried to heave his stiff leg up and over the ladder cables, so that he could use it as a lever to relieve the pressure on his trapped foot and pull it free. On the third attempt he managed it, wedging the heel of his shoe against the cables. But as there was little strength – or feeling – in his bad leg, the moment he tried to put any weight on it, his heel slipped from its precarious purchase and swung down violently. This sudden jarring dislodged his other foot, but left him hanging from the ladder by his fingertips.

This is not going well, he thought, ignoring his advice to Marian and looking down at the sharp-toothed death that awaited him in the roiling water below. He dangled from the ladder like an oversized worm from a fishing line, swaying gently in the breeze.

Another shudder and sounds of splintering from above stirred him into action. *If I can swing my good leg a little closer to the ladder, perhaps I can hook it over the top?*

After a couple of practice swings, he threw his leg up and over and locked it in position. Success! Then, with this leg taking his weight, he slipped down the ladder, lowering himself with his arms while the crook of his knee slid painfully over the sharp ends of the rungs.

At last he reached the tree stump. Rolling off the ladder, he tried to stand, but his leg, trembling with the strain of what he'd just been through, wouldn't hold his weight and he fell. From where he lay on the muddy ground, he could see Marian waving to him from the shelter of the jungle – a short hundred yards away. He waved back, but she shook her head and pointed towards the doorway he'd just exited.

'Look out!' she called.

There was the sharp crack of an automatic and a bullet whizzed past his left ear. A cowled monk was standing in the doorway in the wall of the abbey, a gun in his hand. Jack immediately crawled round to the lee side of the stump. But because of the monk's elevated position, the stump offered almost no cover at all. Jack would have to run for it across a hundred yards of sticky, muddy ground with a bad leg – it was a nightmare. But what choice did he have?

With a cry he leapt up and immediately fell over again – his leg was still trembling. Another bullet thudded into the ground by his right temple. *This is it*, he thought, *he won't miss a third time*. But as he struggled to his feet yet again, he heard a cry, and turned to see his would-be assassin falling towards the moat, his monk's habit ballooning out around him like a hooped skirt. There was a splash and the man sank beneath the dark water. For a few long moments, Jack thought he would not reappear. But then the monk's head broke the surface. He floundered around frantically, wailing in terror, while all around him the water boiled with the excited, thrashing bodies of crocodiles. Suddenly his cries were cut short, his body shook with one last, violent convulsion and blood bubbled from his nose and mouth. Finally he was dragged silently beneath the moat's murky waters.

Looking up to the doorway from where the man had fallen, Jack glimpsed another cowled figure step back into the shadows. Without stopping to thank him, Jack heaved himself up and stumbled the remaining distance to the jungle, and Marian.

When he reached her he had another surprise – she was standing next to a man wearing tailored jungle fatigues.

'Mango!'

'Do you think, with my complexion, I can get away with camouflage?'

'You're a sight for sore eyes. Come on, let's get out of here.'

'Oh God, will you just look at this place!' Mango ran a finger over the refrigerator in the corner of the motel room – it left a clean, white smear on the dull surface. 'Everything's covered in mould. If we stand still long enough we're liable to turn green.'

'So how did you find us?' Jack asked, drying his hair with a grey motel towel.

'After you got taken off the plane and I'd gone through immigration, I was standing in the airport, wondering what to do . . .'

'I see you found time for some shopping.'

Mango put a hand on his hip and glared at Jack. 'Since you disposed of my entire wardrobe on Mahe I only had what I stood up in, and I didn't really think a linen kaftan was suitable for this climate!'

'Point taken. Please continue.'

'So, there I was, wondering why I hadn't been arrested along with you two when I'm approached by this monk, who tells me where you'd been taken and how to get there.'

'You weren't arrested because they weren't looking for you.'

Mango's large forehead wrinkled into a frown. 'How come?'

'Manfreddo must have got hold of our bill from the hotel manager on Mahe. You never checked in to the hotel, so as far as Signor M. was concerned you didn't exist.'

Mango wiped imaginary perspiration off his forehead. 'Phew! Well that's the first time I've been grateful about being overlooked.'

Jack threw the towel around his neck. 'So, this monk, what did he look like?'

'I couldn't see his face, he kept his head cowled.'

Jack turned to Marian, who was sitting on the bed. 'I imagine that's our friendly neighbourhood Brother Verrat.'

She shrugged.

'Brother who?' Mango asked.

'A friend of Gelda Longhorn's.' Jack looked out of the window through the dirty net curtains at the steadily falling rain. 'What is it about this place that everyone wants so badly?'

'Is that a rhetorical question, or can anyone join in?' Mango wondered.

'I mean,' Jack continued, 'it's dirt-poor, it's overcrowded, it's covered in jungle, it's hotter than a steam bath and it rains non-stop. What's it got going for it to interest the Syndicates? What was the message our monk friend gave us?'

'"The answer is under your feet,"' Marian said.

'The answer is under your feet,' Jack repeated.

Marian got up off the bed and went over to stand by him at the window. 'Daygan said he thought it'd be a great place to raise pigs.'

Mango stopped being disgusted with his situation for a moment and looked at her quizzically. 'Pigs?'

She raised an eyebrow. 'You know – where what goes into pork burgers comes from?'

'Oh, pigs, yes.'

Marian dabbed at her forehead with a handkerchief. 'I think I'll take a shower – I need to freshen up.' She went into the bathroom and closed the door.

'So, what's happening, Jack?' Mango asked as soon as he heard the sound of the shower splashing into the bath.

Jack turned away from the window and lowered himself into an old and rather suspect armchair that sent up a cloud of dust. 'She's innocent, Mango. And what's more, I think Michaelmas might also be on the level. I also know why all those political leaders were killed, and I can assure you Michaelmas had nothing to do with it.'

'May I ask how you've reached these startling conclusions?'

'When Marian told me that Michaelmas had taken her on a world tour when they were first married, I thought he was the killer and was setting her up to blame the assassinations on her. But no, the Syndicates funded the trip – they arranged the whole thing – they've been behind this all along.'

Mango sat on the end of the bed, facing Jack. 'But they were blown apart during the war – the politicians keep telling us they're not organized enough to pull off this kind of operation.'

'Maybe that's just what they want us to think. It wouldn't be the first time that politicians have jumped into bed with organized crime.'

Mango looked thoughtful.

'What is it?' Jack asked.

'I still can't get over the fact that Freddy tried to kill you.'

'He's been trying to do that ever since he pushed my pram down a cliff to see how fast it would go.'

'And if he's in the pay of the mob, why did he want you on board so badly?'

'He thought he could control me. When the World Council started taking an interest in the antics of this hit-man, Freddy had to try and keep it in the family. That's why he begged for the case – he didn't want some other nosy policeman wading in and finding out things that he shouldn't.'

'So you weren't supposed to turn up anything?'

'Not at first – I was just good PR, to give people the idea that something was being done. But when it became clear that our murderous monk was on an unscheduled killing spree, I can only assume Freddy got a little jumpy and naïvely thought I'd be able to catch him without putting any of the rest of the puzzle together.'

'But why didn't the Syndicates take care of Brother Bertrand?'

'He's a shape shifter, which is about as close to invisible as you can get. I doubt they have a clue where he is.'

'Then why employ him in the first place? Why not use one of their own men?'

Jack shook his head. 'During the early phase, if the assassin had been caught, it was vital there was no link back to the mob because of the danger of exposing the Syndicates' burgeoning power. But Brother Bertrand was their biggest mistake. It worried me for a long time why – after only killing presidents and prime ministers – he started going after lesser politicians. If his plan was to destabilize the fragile peace between rival nations, then killing vice-presidents and senators, although a perfectly laudable aim in itself—'

'Jack!' Mango admonished.

'– didn't make sense. But what if we're looking at some breakdown in employer–employee relations? What if something upset Brother Bertrand so badly that, instead of carrying out his brief of only hitting prime targets, he then went on a rampage of secondary targets with the sole aim of pointing the finger at the person responsible?'

'Mr Piggy-Wig!'

'Give the man a cigar. But in the words of my esteemed

brother: Mr Piggy-Wig isn't a man, it's a corporation. And who happens to be head of that corporation?'

'Manfreddo!'

'Now you're getting it.'

'So the assassin was trying to tell the world that Manfreddo was behind everything.'

'Exactly. Our killer found out about Manfreddo and, it would seem, he is also aware of the imminent election, and that's why he's saved his last hit for Corbett.'

Jack wiped his face with the towel. 'My God it's hot.'

Freddy too was feeling the heat.

'You're sweating – here, let me.' Pulling the handkerchief from his breast pocket, Lana leaned across and wiped the commissioner's forehead.

'Give me that!' He seized it back angrily and finished the job himself.

Lana gave one of her little-girl-lost looks. 'I was only trying to help.'

'Well don't.'

'Screw you too.' She scowled and sat back in her seat in the first-class lounge of the airship SS *My God It's Full of Stars*. 'What time does this heap of junk get into Corbett?'

Freddy looked at his watch. 'Another two hours.' He shook his head. 'I shouldn't be here. This is all a huge mistake.'

Lana looked at him levelly. 'Face it, Freddy, you screwed up. It's about time you took some responsibility for your actions. "Don't worry, my brother is the finest detective in the universe – he'll be able to find this guy in a couple of days." How stupid do you feel now?'

Freddy dabbed at his big, pink face with his handkerchief. 'Do you think Signor Manfreddo will be angry?'

Lana put her head to one side and pursed her lips while she considered this. 'Let's see . . . First of all you botch your brother's death. Then he goes on the run with the woman who was set up to be the chief suspect and who was supposed to be safe in your custody. This puts Mr Manfreddo to the trouble of arranging the destruction of a hyperliner. And because that didn't work, there are now two people running around out there who know far more than they should. I think angry is a gross underestimation of how the Con is feeling right now.'

'Oh God, oh God, oh God,' Freddy muttered, dabbing away furiously. 'What do you think he'll do?'

Smiling a thin, evil smile, Lana leaned across to him and placed her hand on his knee. 'Don't worry, I'm sure any *pain* will be short-lived.'

Freddy winced at the mention of the word.

Then she shrugged, settled back in her seat and closed her eyes. 'Wake me up when we get there.'

Freddy wiped away the river of sweat running down the back of his neck and stared out through the view port at the setting sun.

Chapter 22

A cold, damp and deeply depressed Lieutenant Matthias crouched in the prow of the little rowing boat, peering into the thick fog ahead with the aid of a small torch, borrowed from Isle of Wight air traffic control. He'd tried to borrow a light aircraft, but the chief controller had swiftly quashed any such ambition. So, instead, Matthias had turned to the sea. Washing up at a pub on the quay in Yarmouth, the lieutenant had enquired of the inmates if any of them would be willing to hire him a boat. After much deliberation and some expert haggling from the locals, Matthias ended up paying $5,000 for a well-past-its-prime rowing boat, and an extra $1,000 for the oars.

'Are you sure you know where you're going, sir?' asked DS Maude, sitting in the stern.

'Shut up! Just shut up! I'm listening for the sound of waves on the beach!'

The detective sergeant looked across at DC Barking, who was taking his turn at the oars, and rolled his eyes.

Suddenly, close by, there was a deafening blast of noise.

'Jesus! What the fuck was that?' said Matthias.

'Sounded like a foghorn to me,' Maude replied. 'Wouldn't you, say DC Barking?'

'More than likely,' Barking replied. 'It's the sensible thing to do in the fog – sound your foghorn.'

'Most sensible would have been not to have gone out in it in the first place,' Maude muttered.

'So, if that was a foghorn,' Matthias reasoned slowly – his

wits dulled by long contact with the minds of Maude and Barking – 'If that was a foghorn, it means that nearby there's a—'

Out of the gloom, only yards in front of them, loomed the keel of a huge vessel.

'. . . Ship! Go left! Left!'

'I think you mean port, sir,' said Maude.

'Just get out of its fucking way!'

'Port tack, Mr Barking,' Maude instructed.

'Aye aye, sir.' Working the oars manfully, DC Barking steered the little craft to one side as the vast ship slid by them in the gloom. The small boat was sent spinning and rocking by the huge bow wave, which threatened to overwhelm them at any second. Hanging on for dear life, Matthias closed his eyes and sent up a prayer to the god of apple pies and wide open skies.

At last the great, shuddering ship passed, the rocking of the boat subsided, and Matthias found, to his great relief, that he was safe and still relatively dry. Slowly opening his eyes, he turned round to look at Barking and Maude, who stared back, seemingly unconcerned.

'All right, sir?'

'I thought there were supposed to be no boats sailing between the Isle of Wight and the mainland?'

'Oh, there won't be, sir,' Barking said. 'Not in this fog.'

'Then what was that?'

'Looked like an oil tanker to me,' said Maude.

'What's an oil tanker doing in the Solent?'

Barking and Maude laughed.

'No, no, no, sir,' Maude said. 'We're not in the Solent – we're in the Channel.'

'The Channel?'

'The English Channel – one of the busiest shipping lanes in the world.'

Not for the first time, Matthias felt hopelessly out of his depth and, with a sickening rush, began to realize that his problems were far from over. 'We're in the English Channel? But that means we've been going the wrong way. Why didn't you say anything?'

'Oh, it's not our place to contradict a senior officer, sir,' said Maude, saluting.

DC Barking rested his oars and eased further round in his seat to look at the lieutenant. 'The thing is, sir, from the time we left Yarmouth, you've been telling us to keep going left.'

'Or, more correctly, port,' DS Maude offered.

'When, according to the marine charts, we should have started turning right . . .'

'Or starboard.'

'. . . the moment we saw the Hurst Castle lighthouse.'

'We couldn't see any fucking lighthouse!' Matthias exploded.

'Language,' said DS Maude under his breath.

'No, sir,' DC Barking continued, 'but if we could have done it would have told us where to go.'

'Exactly,' DS Maude concurred.

Matthias regarded the smugly smiling policemen for a few moments in the narrow beam of his torch. 'Well,' he started, in a level tone, 'I can't fault your logic, DS Barking, but that doesn't alter the fact that WE CAN'T SEE A FUCKING THING!'

'Steady on, sir, you'll have us over if you continue to jump up and down like that,' warned Maude.

'I don't care! To drown now would be preferable to spending another second in your company. I just want . . . I want to—' Lieutenant Matthias, one of New York Police Department's most hard-boiled officers – a real tough cookie – collapsed in a heap in the bottom of the boat and started crying like a baby.

DS Maude clambered past his colleague manning the oars and patted the lieutenant comfortingly on the shoulder. 'There, there, sir. There, there.'

*

It was late in the day, voting was over and all the ballot boxes had been collected and delivered to the capital's old parliament building, where the electoral vote-counting was now taking place. Jack, Marian and Mango were seated in a hired car in a street in Barkertown – Corbett's capital city. They were a few blocks' distance from the parliament building, but they couldn't get any closer – a police cordon had been thrown a mile around the place and every street into the area was blockaded by a phalanx of rain-caped policemen bristling with weaponry. Police marksmen were also stationed on the roofs of selected buildings in and around the vicinity, and the airspace above had been closed to all but police and military traffic.

Mango was staring out through the misted windscreen at the rain tumbling from the gradually darkening sky, his fingers idly drumming the steering wheel. Jack sat next to him, muttering to himself, 'The answer is under your feet . . . The answer is under your feet . . .' Pulling out his pipe, Jack scratched his chin with its stem.

Mango rolled his eyes. 'I can hear the cogs turning from here.'

Jack reached across and grabbed Mango's wrist. 'Open your mouth.'

'What?'

'I want to Google Corbett. Open your mouth and shut up.'

Mango did as he was instructed.

Jack clicked a button on Mango's communicator and said, into Mango's mouth, 'Corbett, geography.'

A couple of seconds later a list of options appeared on the communicator's small screen. Jack chose one at random. He studied the result, muttering to himself. '"Mostly covered in rain forest . . ." Well I think we'd gathered that. "Underlying peat . . . mangrove swamps . . . limestone . . . mercury, copper, iron, tin, antimony, sulphur and coal . . . gold and diamond deposits . . . and oil."' He raised an eyebrow.

'"Around the shores, fine silica sand produces the white sand beaches so popular with tourists . . ." Hmm.' Jack broke the connection and slumped into thoughtful reverie.

But just then the sound of police sirens broke through the patter of rain on the car roof, scattering any thoughts that might have been assembling in Jack's mind. He looked up and saw, through the pouring rain, a motorcade – flanked by motor-cycle outriders – hurtling down the road towards them in a halo of blue flashing lights. The police at the nearest barrier stood aside and waved the motorcade through.

'I think Manfreddo's arrived,' Jack observed. 'The announce-ment of the result must be close.'

'What did you just find out?' Mango asked.

'I'm not sure. But right now we have to go and prevent a political assassination.'

'Unlike you to want to *prevent* the death of a politician,' Mango quipped. 'Especially one so intimately bound up with organized crime.'

Jack turned to him. 'It's true that Manfreddo has a lot of blood on his hands, but he's just the top of the tree. If we can arrest him and find out what he knows we may be able to pull this whole affair up by its roots.'

'That was almost poetic.' Mango fluttered his eyelashes.

'Off you go then,' Jack said cheerily.

Mango looked incredulously at the rain pouring endlessly from the dark grey sky.

'You want me to go out in this?'

'You have a better idea?'

'How about going back to Mahe?'

'Where's your spirit of adventure?'

'I left it behind on Mahe, along with my entire wardrobe,' Mango huffed.

'You're never going to let me forget that, are you?'

'I'll just add it to the long list of indignities I've had to suffer at your hands, Jack.'

'At least you don't have to suffer the consequences of your crimes against fashion on a daily basis.'

Mango's eyes widened. 'Don't go there, Jack or I might be forced to raise certain issues regarding your personal hygiene.'

'You mean I smell?'

'Yes!'

'This is a new suit!'

'You may have bought yourself a new suit, but you haven't given yourself new armpits!'

'Are you two going to carry on like this all day, or are we going to do something?'

Both Jack and Mango turned to Marian, seated in the back. They pointed at each other and said in unison, 'He started it!'

She shook her head. 'Children, children, please.'

Jack turned back to Mango. 'It's got to be you, Marian and I would be recognized immediately. You're the only one they're not looking for, remember?'

'Oh, bully for me,' Mango grumbled.

Jack handed him the umbrella supplied by the car hire company – shocking pink, with a cocktail glass and cherry logo, and the legend 'Piña Colada' written around the rim. 'Off you go, kiddo,' he instructed. 'If they let you through, go straight to the parliament building and keep me informed of what's happening. You've got Marian's phone number?'

'Yes.'

'Good. Don't try to do anything, just keep in touch, all right?'

Mango smiled slyly. 'You're worried about me, aren't you?'

'Get out of the car!'

Mango pushed open his door and Jack and Marian watched as he reluctantly trudged towards the nearest police checkpoint, shoulders hunched.

'He's not enjoying this, I can tell,' said Jack, easing himself awkwardly into the driving seat. 'But then he's not a natural outdoor type.'

301

As Mango approached the checkpoint, one of the policemen turned towards him, gun drawn, and issued a challenge. Mango replied by flashing his ID wallet.

They couldn't hear the ensuing conversation, but it was obvious that the policeman didn't want to let him pass. Mango was having to do some fast talking. At last, Mango handed the man the umbrella, rolled up his sleeve and exposed his arm up to the shoulder. The policeman examined it carefully, then made him roll up the other sleeve.

'He's looking for a tattoo,' said Jack. 'Which means they know about our shape shifter and his planned attack on their soon-to-be-elected leader. Manfreddo must be shitting himself – pardon my French.'

'Do you think they'll let him through?' Marian asked nervously.

'I don't know. Mango can be very persuasive; he's absolutely charming when he wants to be. Look at him – flirting outrageously with that policeman.'

Mango was indeed giving it all he'd got, flexing his exposed biceps and posing like a muscle man. The previously dour policeman's face had cracked into a smile and it wasn't long before he and the rest of his men were laughing openly.

At last, the smiling policeman waved him through and Mango glanced back at Jack as if to say, 'Didn't I do well?'

Jack gave him a thumbs-up and Mango disappeared down the street.

'Now what do we do?' Marian asked.

'We wait.'

Manfreddo's limousine pulled up at the foot of the ascent of stone steps leading up to the parliament building, and a police escort opened the door. Manfreddo looked out suspiciously at the double line of policemen who formed a living corridor up to the door of the building. Each held aloft an open umbrella, like the swords of a guard of honour.

'Is it safe?'

'It's perfectly safe,' said the police chief, sitting next to him. 'The place is crawling with policemen.'

'That word gives me the creeps,' Manfreddo growled. He looked across at Freddy, perched awkwardly on the small fold-away seat in front of him. 'You!' Manfreddo stabbed him in the chest with a large, beringed finger. 'Get out first.'

'But, but—'

'No buts. If it wasn't for you and your screw-up, I wouldn't be having this panic attack. Now get out!' He grabbed a hand-ful of Freddy's expensive suit and shoved the commissioner out of the car.

Freddy caught his foot on the edge of the door and fell flat on his face on the wet pavement at the bottom of the stone steps. Picking himself up, he looked hastily around, then scut-tled up the steps between the double row of smirking police officers.

'OK, now you.' Manfreddo jabbed his finger at the police chief.

Police Chief O'Hanlon sighed and heaved himself out of the car. Once he too had reached the safety of the building, Man-freddo turned to Lana, seated on the other flip-up seat.

'You come with me.'

Although he allowed her to get out first, this was no act of chivalry. Keeping a tight grip on her shoulders, he followed her out of the car and, holding her close, used her as a human shield while rapidly ascending the steps.

Inside the building were row upon row of long trestles, at which an army of middle-aged folk sat laboriously counting the votes which spilled from the ballot boxes perched at the head of each table.

Manfreddo, still holding Lana close, looked nervously around.

'Why don't they just announce the result so we can get out of here?'

'Calm, Con,' soothed the police chief, 'It's got to look legit. Do you want to arouse suspicions of vote-rigging? We have to do this by the book.'

'All right, all right. I just wish they'd hurry up.'

'Relax, you'll be fine.'

'That's easy for you to say. How do you know the creep's not in here right now?'

The police chief smiled indulgently. 'Con, there is no way that son-of-a-bitch could have got in here. My own men evacuated the area before we brought the vote-counters in, and each one of them is known to us.'

'And what about these other guys?' Manfreddo nodded to a group of men wearing rosettes. 'They look a little shifty to me, I want them out of here!'

The police chief leaned in a little closer. 'They're the other candidates. It wouldn't look good to throw them out of the hall before the result's announced.'

Manfreddo looked at his watch. 'Jesus, how long is this going to take?'

'Con, you have nothing to worry about – he's not in here.'

'He's in there, Mango. I know he's in there somewhere. Tell me what you see.'

'*Well, there are lots of tables, behind which are seated an array of grey-haired old folk in a veritable orgy of tweed. You'd think twinsets and pearls had never gone out of fashion!*'

'Spare me the details, give me the bare facts.'

'*I'm just giving you a little colour, so that you can get a flavour of the place.*'

'Facts, Mango! What do you see?'

'*All right, all right, don't flap. I see oldies counting votes. I see a large net full of balloons suspended above the stage. I see nerv-*'

304

ous men who already look defeated, wearing their political colours. I also see Manfreddo and his crowd. Oh, look – there's your brother and your friend Lana.'

'Curb your natural instinct to wave. Keep your head down.'

'Don't worry. Your brother looks like he's seen a ghost – I doubt he knows what day it is.'

'Anything else?'

'Nope. Apart from policemen, of course – hundreds of police-men.'

Jack frowned. 'He's there, I know he's there. What about the vote-counters?'

'According to one cop I spoke to, they've all got top-security clearance, each one is known to the police.'

'And what about said police?'

'All hand-picked by Police Chief O'Hanlon. And before you ask – yes, a policeman was found, naked, in the spaceport lavatory, but it's unlikely our man is still masquerading as a law enforcement officer.'

'How come?'

'Every policeman in the Corbett force has a subcutaneous chip inserted in their arm when they join – sounds disgusting – so, as well as going through iris recognition, our man would have been scanned as he entered the building. A policeman trying to get in here without a chip would ring all sorts of bells.'

'How did you get in?'

'Simple – my face and iris profile fit with what's on my ID.'

'Is that how the counters were vetted?'

'I suppose so. But listen, all the venerable old folk counting votes are well into the upper limit of what's classed as middle-aged. They look about as dangerous as a pair of incontinence knickers. Besides, every one of them is known personally to O'Hanlon – apparently they all live in his street.'

Jack scratched his chin with his pipe stem. 'Wait a minute. Ruth mentioned that there was a lucrative trade in eyeballs to get round iris recognition, which is why most up-to-date police forces no longer rely on it. They'd snip the iris out and embed it in a contact lens – apparently it's not that difficult to do.'

'*It's a sick old world.*'

'And wouldn't an old dear be perfect cover for an assassin? Go round the tables, have a good look at the counters. He's a shape shifter, not a miracle worker, so the facsimile isn't going to be perfect. Look for anomalies – like young-looking skin, or hair that's a little too thick or lustrous.'

'*Lustrous?*'

'You know, healthy-looking.'

'*I know what it means, I just didn't think it was a very you-word, that's all.*'

'A *me*-word?'

'*Yes. Now if you'd said shiny – shiny's very you: without style and direct almost to the point of rudeness.*'

'I could have said effulgent, but I didn't think your limited knowledge of the English language would have been up to it.'

'*There's no need to be nasty.*'

'Would you please just do as you're told for once without talking back?'

Mango sighed. '*Oh all right.*'

'And see if you can get an address for O'Hanlon – I want to check out his street.'

It hadn't been difficult to obtain the iris, the assassin had simply called at the house posing as a postman. A simple shot to the head from a silenced pistol and it was all over.

Removing the eye was stomach-churningly gruesome. *I must be getting old*, the assassin thought. *In my army days I'd have done this with the victim still alive.*

Once the eye was out it was a simple matter to turn it into a contact lens. In fact there were kits to enable you to do just that. The process involved slicing off the front of the eyeball and placing it on the matrix supplied with the kit – a bulbous mould, shaped like the curvature of the eye. The delicate iris adhered immediately to the sticky matrix and, once it was in place, the cornea could be peeled off and the iris overlaid with a thin film of jelly-like plastic. Once set, it was removed from the matrix, the excess was trimmed off, and hey presto – a contact lens to fool any iris recognition scanner.

After hiding the body behind the sofa in the living room, the assassin dressed in his victim's clothes, inserted the lens in his left eye and waited for his ride to the parliament building.

'*OK, I've got a street name for you – Worth Road.*'

'Worth Road,' Jack repeated. 'That's where the vote-counters are from?'

'*That's right. Every election they choose a different street from which they randomly pick their counters, the location of which, for security purposes, is not divulged until just before the count. This time it happens to be the street where the chief of police lives. But I'm sure that's just a coincidence.*'

Jack snorted. 'Mr Manfreddo would never countenance anything underhand, I'm certain.'

'*I've also got a list of their names and house numbers.*'

'You have been busy.'

'*Just doing my job.*'

'Remind me to give you a raise.'

'*More of nothing is still nothing.*'

'Do you have to be so picky? We're off to Worth Road now – can you text me the list so that I have a record of it?'

'*Ah, more work.*'

'It'll give you something to do. Stay in touch, and keep out of Lana's way.'

'*You don't have to tell* me *that. Check your inbox in five minutes.*'

Jack broke the connection and turned the key in the ignition. The car shuddered into life.

'Where are we going?' Marian asked.

'Worth Road – I have a hunch that our man is posing as a harmless old vote counter.' Jack picked up the local map that came with the car. 'It's not far,' he said, finding the location and snicking the car into 'DRIVE'. Then, moving slowly past the police road block guarding the route to the parliament building, Jack drove down the almost deserted street in the steadily falling rain.

In five minutes they were cruising down Worth Road. The place seemed deserted.

'My God – why would anyone want to live here?' Jack wondered out loud.

'Where is everyone?' Marian asked.

'Probably inside watching television. Who'd want to be outside in this never-ending tropical storm?'

Jack parked the car and killed the engine. After a few minutes cursing Marian's phone while he desperately pressed the wrong buttons and discovered all sorts of interesting information, like how to alter the ring-tone settings and the location of the nearest Pizza house (Singapore) and massage parlour (three streets away), Jack eventually found Marian's message inbox. Mango had been true to his word and Jack now possessed a complete list of the vote-counters and where they lived. 'Good man,' he murmured.

'Now what?' Marian wondered.

'Now we go knocking on doors. If any of the names on this list are still at home, then we know that our assassin has taken their place at the counting house.' Jack consulted the phone's screen. 'Right, top of the list, Mrs Eileen Thomas, number five.' He reached for the door handle. 'Why don't you stay here?' he said to Marian. 'There's no point in us both of us getting wet.'

'I'd only be in your way anyway,' she replied.

'I just hope this suit doesn't shrink,' he murmured, opening the car door. He was immediately drenched.

Mrs Thomas at number five wasn't at home. Nor was Mr

Wilfred at number six, nor Mr Tudgay, next door at number seven. Jack trudged wearily up the street, knocking on doors and ringing doorbells. Sometimes the door would be opened by a spouse, a son or daughter, but where he received no answer, he would shout through the letter box or peer through the window.

So he made his damp and dismal way up the street. He had almost reached its end when he knocked on the door of number nineteen. He knocked but got no reply. He rang the bell, he bellowed through the letter box – still nothing. He was beginning to think that his hunch had been wrong, when he looked in through the front window. There, peeping out from behind the sofa were a pair of pink, fluffy mules. He hammered on the window, but got no response. Glancing quickly up and down the street, he tried the barely-open sash window. It slid upwards. Clambering inside, he went straight to where the slippers lay. Pushing back the sofa, he looked down at the body of Miss Evelyn Trellis.

He pulled Marian's phone out of his pocket and dialled Mango. The ringing at the other end of the line seemed to go on for ever. 'Mango for God's sake pick up!'

'*Corbett Counting House, Mango Pinkerton speaking.*'

'Mango, is there a Miss Trellis there?'

'*Just a minute, I'll find out.*'

'Be discreet!'

'*Have you forgotten who you're talking to?*'

'No.'

There was a pause, during which Jack walked up and down, executing a sort of impatient two-step outside the Trellis house or, to be precise, in his case a one-and-a-half-step.

'Hurry up, hurry up!'

Eventually . . .

'*Yes, I'm looking at her now.*'

'Well keep on looking at her – that's our assassin!'

'*Really? She must be about ninety.*'

'Perfect cover. I'm on my way, don't do anything until I get there.'

'*How are you going to get through the security?*'

'I don't know yet.'

'*Well, be careful.*'

Jack ran back to the car, yanked open the door and slid into the driver's seat.

'Marian, I'm going to have to ask you to get out.'

'In this rain?'

'I'm going to crash the police cordon – it's too dangerous.'

'Have you found the killer?'

'Yes.'

'I'm coming with you.'

'You can't.'

'I'm responsible for you being here in the first place. If you die I'll never forgive myself. I'm coming with you.'

Jack shook his head. 'You've got it wrong. Daygan was trying to protect you.'

Marian frowned.

'Please, just get out of the car.'

'I'm still coming with you.'

'Very well, I haven't got time to argue.'

But as Jack thumped the car into gear, a motorcycle cop appeared out of nowhere and motioned Jack to follow him. Jack turned to Marian questioningly.

'Well?' she said. 'What are you waiting for?'

Jack took a deep breath, released the handbrake and the car lurched off after the motorcycle's blue flashing light fractured into a thousand pieces by the rain on the windscreen.

'I don't know where he's taking us,' Jack said.

'I suspect we'll soon find out,' Marian replied.

Before long, the cop took a left towards one of the heavily manned checkpoints that guarded the route to Corbett's old parliament building.

'Get down!' Jack warned.

'What for?' Marian questioned.

'Look, who's the expert on breaking the law here? Don't argue with me, just do as I say!'

Marian crouched sulkily on the floor of the car, muttering, 'I see now why Mango complains so much about you.'

Jack was worried that, even with a motorcycle escort, the sight of a female passenger might arouse suspicion. But as they approached the checkpoint, the motorcycle's siren blaring, the barrier was raised and they were simply waved through.

The same happened at each of the five checkpoints on the road to the parliament building.

'You can always rely on a policeman to trust his own,' Jack murmured, saluting cheerily to the police as he passed.

However, when they reached the final checkpoint, around the perimeter of the parliament building itself, a cop walked into the middle of the road and signalled the car and attendant escort to stop.

'I knew it was going too well,' Jack muttered.

But as the motorcycle in front slowed it pulled over to one side, inviting Jack to pass it.

'He wants me to run the checkpoint.'

Jack had less than a second to make up his mind.

He floored the accelerator. The back tyres spun on the greasy road and the car leapt forward, snaking wildly. Policemen scattered as the car's nose swung from side to side while Jack wrestled with the steering wheel, trying to keep the car moving in a straight line. Keeping his foot firmly to the floor, he aimed the car at the wooden barrier blocking the road.

'Brace yourself!' Jack yelled, throwing his body sideways as the barrier smashed into the windscreen and broke in two. Peering over the dashboard through the shattered windscreen, Jack pointed the car straight at the big stone parliament building, dead ahead, as bullets began to rip through the flimsy metal.

Glancing in his mirror, Jack saw his motorcycle escort follow him through the checkpoint, then heel his bike over and lie behind it, firing back at the officers shooting at the car.

'He's covering us,' Jack announced.

Up ahead, the big grey steps of the parliament building hove into view.

A bullet hole appeared simultaneously in the windscreen and the back window.

At the foot of the steps stood a policeman, gun pointed straight at the car. 'Stay down!' Jack yelled. 'It's going to get a little bumpy.'

'*More* bumpy?' Marian enquired.

Jack kept his foot on the throttle and slid the gear selector into third. The pitch of the engine rose to a scream. Mounting the kerb, the car took off and flew towards the gun-wielding cop. He had no chance; the flying car hit him square in the chest and he disappeared beneath it. After seven or eight bone-jarring lurches while the car's momentum carried it up the stone steps, something went *crunch* and it finally expired, steam billowing from its radiator.

Jack turned to Marian. 'Are you all right?'

She looked up at him, her eyes wide. 'I'm not sure.'

'We have to get inside. Hang on.'

Opening the door, Jack tumbled out of the car under a hail of bullets from the police at the checkpoint. Peering beneath the vehicle, Jack could see the cop's mangled body, now intimately involved with the chassis, his hand still wrapped around the grip of his revolver. Gritting his teeth, Jack prised open the fingers and freed the gun. He flicked open the chamber – there were five shots left.

Their friendly motorcycle cop was still offering covering fire and, so far, no one had come out of the building to see what was going on, but it was only a matter of time before someone in there realized there was a war going on outside.

Jack pulled open Marian's door. 'Get out and stay down.' He yanked her out and she landed heavily on the unforgiving stone.

'Ouch!'

Then, staying low, Jack pulled her round to the front of the car. From that position the entrance to the building was only three steps above them.

'Come on!' Jack urged.

Crawling awkwardly up the slippery stone steps, they at last reached the entrance and ducked inside. The vestibule was empty, and now the reason for the apparent disinterest of those inside to the sounds of mayhem outside became clear. No one could hear the crackle of gunfire above the sound of the cheering crowd in the body of the hall.

'They must have just announced the vote. There's no time to lose. If I know my man, he's going to pounce the moment Manfreddo takes the stage.'

Moving past the small desk equipped with the iris-recognition apparatus, Jack crashed through the doors to the hall. His ears were immediately assailed by the riotous cheers of Manfreddo's bribed and nervous supporters, encouraged in their enthusiasm by men in sharp suits and mirror shades dotted amongst them. Jack looked around wildly. On stage a man was applauding and inviting someone in the body of the hall to step up and join him. Then Jack caught sight of him: Manfreddo, pushing Freddy ahead of him, his right foot already on the first tread of the small set of steps leading up to stage level.

Jack scanned the hall again, looking desperately for Mango. At last he caught a glimpse of a pink umbrella, waving above the crowd.

Scything his way through the crush, Jack made his way towards it. Mango was pointing at one of the counters who was standing behind a table, applauding enthusiastically. The woman looked ancient – her face was lined and wrinkled, her grey hair tied on top of her head in a neat bun. Was this really an assassin who had struck without mercy countless times? The evidence pointed to it. *But she's just a little old lady!* Jack shook his head. There was no time to argue with his feelings now. She was a good twenty feet distant from him and there were several tables between them, but he had a clear shot. Raising his gun, he curled his finger around the trigger. But at that moment an eager supporter leapt up on the table nearest him, obscuring the woman from Jack's view.

'Fuck!'

He dodged to the side but, taking their lead from the excited fan, more and more supporters now leapt up onto the table. There was soon a forest of bodies between Jack and his target.

There was only one thing to do. Ducking under the table, Jack hit the floor and crawled. Clearing the first table, he staggered upright, but it was still no good – every table between him and Miss Trellis was now groaning with excitedly applauding supporters. He would have to get even closer. Getting down again, Jack dragged his bad leg under yet another table, then another. Finally he reached a position behind the aged vote-counter, from where he could loose a clean shot. As Miss Trellis reached into the sleeve of her cardigan, Jack raised his pistol and squeezed lightly on the trigger . . .

'No!'

As Evelyn Trellis pulled a hanky out of her sleeve, Jack found himself looking into the mirrored shades of a policeman wearing a crash helmet. At first he thought he'd been arrested. Then, as he watched the policeman level his own gun at someone at the front of the hall, he realized. A man standing at the extreme edge of the stage, wearing an opposition red rosette, had a pistol aimed right at newly elected President Manfreddo's head.

Jack fired in the air, hitting the rope constraining the celebratory balloons above the stage.

'Police! Nobody move!'

In the shocked silence, while the released balloons floated softly to the ground, Manfreddo grabbed Freddy and hid behind him. Freddy screamed in terror and the man wearing the rosette swung round and pointed his gun straight at Jack.

Jack tried to bring his arm level and draw a bead on the

rosette-wearer, but while his brain whirled, his body seemed to move impossibly slowly, as if in a dream. *I'm going to die*, he thought.

There was a sudden *crack!* Jack winced and put his hand to his heart, expecting to feel his life's blood gushing warmly from a hole in his chest. But there was no hole; there was no blood. Then everything became clear. On stage, the man wearing the red rosette looked first shocked, then blank, then stumbled forwards and fell head-first into the audience. The place erupted in terrified screams.

Jack turned to the motorcycle cop standing next to him and saw him lower his gun. 'Thank you. Brother Verrat, I presume?'

But before the cop could reply, Manfreddo's voice rang out above the noise of panic.

'Arrest the sons of bitches!'

'That's gratitude for you,' Jack mumbled as his arms were pinned behind his back.

While balloons continued to fall onto the agitated occupants of the packed hall, both he and the motorcycle cop were man-handled through the crush to the front of the large room, below the stage. Manfreddo crouched on the apron to greet them.

'Well, well, if it isn't Mr Gimpy from Mahe. I ought to thank you, Jack. You have done what my entire organization failed to do – you found the killer.' Manfreddo looked down at the dead shape shifter, spreadeagled on the floor of the hall. 'Turn him over,' he ordered. One of his men flicked the body over with the toe of his boot.

The assassin's features had now returned to normal, and although there was nothing particularly remarkable about the man's face, Manfreddo recognized him instantly.

'Yeah, that's him. I just wanted to make sure.' He turned to Freddy. 'You're right – your bro' *is* the best in the business. Pity this is his last case.'

Freddy wrung his hands and started gushing. 'I'm so sorry, Jack. I never meant it to come to this. I had no choice, I was—'

'Shut up, Freddy,' Jack barked. He looked up at Manfreddo. 'What do you mean, last case?'

Manfreddo stood up. 'You've fulfilled your function and now I have to let you go.'

'Con.' It was O'Hanlon.

'Yeah?'

'Don't you think we ought to get rid of the civilians?'

'Nah, let 'em stay for the show.'

O'Hanlon shook his head. 'But some of them may get hurt.'

Manfreddo raised his eyebrows incredulously. 'You think I care?'

O'Hanlon shrugged. 'I'm only thinking of your best interests. Wouldn't it be wise to clear the hall of a couple of hundred potential witnesses?'

Manfreddo thought a moment. 'Oh, yeah, I see what you mean. OK, clear the hall of all the little people!'

O'Hanlon fired his gun in the air to silence the distressed vote-counters, supporters and surviving candidates. 'Righty-ho! Now everybody just take it easy and move nice and slowly to the exits.'

Once the hall was clear, Manfreddo resumed, twinkling at his captives. 'Right, now it's just us – isn't that cosy?' He pulled a cigar out of an inside pocket and lit it with a flourish.

Jack looked thoughtful. 'Just a minute. Before you do whatever it is you're going to do, can you clear something up for me?'

Manfreddo chewed on his cigar. 'OK, shoot.'

Jack nodded at the body of the assassin. 'If that's the shape shifter, then what about Miss Trellis? Not half an hour ago I was in her house, staring down at her lifeless body, and yet I arrive here to find her still alive.'

O'Hanlon intervened. 'Are you talking about Miss Evelyn Trellis? A dear old thing, and twin sister of the equally dear Ivy. They share a house just down the street from me. From what you say it looks like Evelyn's going to be living on her own from now on. I can't say I'm surprised, Ivy always did have a weak heart.' He looked down at the dead shape shifter. 'And from our man's rosette, I'd surmise that the main opposition candidate is dead.'

Jack nodded. 'Of course.' He turned back to Manfreddo. 'Carry on.'

'Where was I? Oh yeah, I was about to kill you, Jack, which is a shame because I went to an awful lot of trouble to get you here.'

Jack frowned. 'Get me here?'

Manfreddo sighed. 'Are you familiar with a flick called *The Wicker Man*?'

'The original or the poorly executed remake?'

'The original, of course.'

'Yes, it was about a strange cult on a remote island who dealt in human sacrifice. If I remember rightly, their victim – a policeman, played memorably by Edward Woodward – was led to his doom by following a girl he believed was in trouble.'

'That's right.' Manfreddo signalled to someone at the side of the stage and Marian was brought up to join him. 'Meet the girl.'

Marian shook her head. 'No, Jack. It's not true. I had no idea!'

Jack stared hard at Marian and finally the penny dropped. He shook his head and gazed up at Manfreddo. 'Bravo.'

Manfreddo smiled smugly.

The pieces began to fall into place. 'You used her to get to me. When I turned her down you made sure I'd change my mind by putting that bomb in my office.' Jack smiled. 'Marian was the key. Using an outsider to keep as much distance as possible between you and the murders wasn't enough – you needed a fall guy. So you framed Marian, using doctored CCTV footage, placing her at all the crime scenes. How am I doing?'

'Not bad, except that I never planted the bomb in your office – that was just a lucky break.'

317

'Shall I continue?' Jack said.

Manfreddo shrugged. 'Be my guest.'

'When you learned that Piggy-Wig Enterprises had a desire to expand, you did a little digging and discovered Daygan had a beautiful wife – perfect, you could kill two birds with one stone: use the business as a cover for your nefarious purposes and use Marian as your scapegoat. So you frightened off all of Daygan's potential investors, took a large share of his little company and, while you minded the shop, suggested the happy couple take a late and extended honeymoon, which *you* paid for, making sure that you had copies of all relevant footage from every CCTV camera at every airport and every tourist attraction they visited.'

Manfreddo beamed in a self-congratulatory way. 'Smart, although I say it myself.'

'But then things started to go wrong.' Jack glanced at the dead monk lying on the floor.

Manfreddo shook his head sorrowfully. 'Convictions are a terrible thing, Jack, and our friend here had a lethal dose of them. He thought he was simply silencing critics of his beloved order.'

Jack went on, 'But when he found out who he was really working for, he didn't like it. He went on a little killing spree with the sole purpose of letting you know he was coming for you. He wanted you to suffer before putting a bullet in your brain.'

Manfreddo nodded. 'Yeah, so you can understand why I needed a good cop to get him off my back. Your brother said you were the best – and he was right.'

An awful truth dawned on Jack. 'Good God! You blew up that hyperliner for nothing.'

'Not nothing, no. I needed you here and I didn't want you getting suspicious. I *had* hoped you'd find the killer before the election result was announced. You let me down badly there, Jack.'

318

Jack was aghast. 'You killed hundreds of people just to prevent me from being suspicious?'

Manfreddo stood and threw his arms wide. 'It worked, didn't it?'

His henchmen in the audience chuckled.

'And did your men know they were on a suicide mission?'

Manfreddo puffed on his cigar before replying. 'They had a little extra luggage in their suitcases they were unaware of – a couple of pounds of high explosive with a remote-controlled detonator. As soon as I was informed you'd left the ship, I set it off. And now, unfortunately, I'm going to have to let you go.'

'OK, but before you kill me, tell me – what's so special about Corbett?'

Manfreddo put his head to one side. 'Aw, Jack, don't let me down. You've worked everything else out. Think about it for a minute.'

Jack's police mind whirred and fizzed. 'Wait a minute, wait a minute . . .' The phrase on the note in the abbey came back to him with a new significance. '"The answer is under your feet" . . . Of course!' Jack's eyes widened and he looked up at Manfreddo with something approaching respect. 'But that's brilliant!'

Manfreddo basked a moment in Jack's praise.

'What, Jack?' Marian asked.

'Marian, I thought this villain was nothing but a knuckle-headed crook, but it turns out he's a bit of a criminal genius.'

'What is it?' Marian insisted.

'It was the construction companies that started me thinking. Why would a crime syndicate boss start buying up DIY and construction companies like they were going out of style, when you'd expect him to be more concerned with knocking things down?' Jack laughed out loud at the audacity of Manfreddo's plan. 'Excuse me. It's so neat. You see, Marian, this island is perfect – it has all the right ingredients. For a start it's got the right geological composition: underneath our feet is a veritable chemistry set; from this damp soil you can manufacture just about any explosive known to man. It's also got its own oil supply and it's got diamonds – ideal for heavy industry. This country could have been designed with weapons manufacture in mind. But that's not all. Corbett is also home to one of the last surviving, and tallest, rainforests in the world, producing long straight lengths of hardwood timber. Then there are its limestone bedrock and beaches covered in sand. Timber, limestone and sand – the three cornerstones of the construction industry. *Ker-ching!* Control of this island is a licence to print money!' Jack laughed again at the criminal ingenuity of Manfreddo's mind. 'It's almost faultless!'

Marian still didn't understand. 'What is it, Jack?'

'Signor Manfreddo, correct me if I'm wrong here, but I think it goes like this: first you destabilize an already unbalanced country by bumping off its leader. War breaks out and you feed the fire by supplying both sides with weapons, manufactured in your factories on Corbett. Then – and here is the master stroke – once the two opposing sides have slugged it out for a while and have no option but to declare peace or suffer complete annihilation, you move in and offer to rebuild both countries, and you and your construction companies clean up, covering the earth in housing estates. You profit both ways. Cash for war, cash for peace – brilliant.'

Manfreddo bowed.

'Those two poor, misguided arms dealers. They thought they'd hit pay-dirt, but you were only using them. It was too risky using your own men at first, so you exploited them and their greed just to get the ball rolling.'

'And they were useful right up until the end. Once I inserted the information about their whereabouts into the Scotland Yard mainframe I knew you wouldn't be able to resist following them.'

'But just a minute,' said Jack. 'You may well have lured me out here, but you said yourself that I didn't fulfil my intended function – I didn't stop your would-be killer. *That* was my friend here.' Jack turned to the motorcycle cop.

Manfreddo nodded to the man standing behind the cop. 'Take off his helmet and shades.'

When his face was revealed, Marian gasped.

'Daygan!'

Jack started. 'Michaelmas?' He stared at the man he'd been searching for all over the world. He had a wide forehead, dark curly hair, a strong straight nose, full lips and deep brown eyes – he was perfect matinée idol material and Jack's heart sank when he saw just how good-looking he was.

'Oh,' he sighed.

'Oh!' said Mango appreciatively.

'At your service,' Daygan replied. 'I'm sorry we meet at last under such disagreeable circumstances.'

'Mr Piggy-Wig.' Manfreddo smiled. 'How's the abbot these days?'

Daygan looked surprised.

'Oh yeah, I knew. I know everything. You see, Jack, when Daygan got cold feet and turned tail, I had him followed. With him inside the monastery I didn't have to arrange for you and his lady wife's escape. I knew he'd handle that. And there you have it, Jack – the last piece of the puzzle.' Manfreddo drew triumphantly on his cigar. 'I'm delighted you could make it, Daygan, but now we're all here, I'm afraid it's time to say goodbye. I've got a country to run and a world to plunder and from this moment you're all surplus to requirements. Jack, I'd offer you a job – I could do with a guy with brains – but I know you'd refuse.'

'Thanks, but no thanks.'

'Shame – we would have been a good team. One last thing. Before I blow you away, you said back there that this plan was *almost* faultless – where did I go wrong?'

'You were rumbled – by your own hitman.'

Manfreddo smiled. 'But he's dead, and who else knows

321

about it outside this room? Admit it, Jack, I created the perfect scam. And now the party's over, I'm afraid.'

Manfreddo's men reached for their guns.

Jack's mind raced. 'And how are you going to explain the deaths of Mr Piggy-Wig and the Cranium Killer here?'

'Has anyone ever *seen* Mr Piggy-Wig without his make-up? The story will be that following the attempted assassination of Corbett's newly elected president, there was a firefight and one of my officers got shot in the melee, along with the assassin – you.' Manfreddo jabbed the end of his cigar at Jack. 'As for the killing monk – he never existed anyway, so who's going to miss him? By the time anyone works out what's really going on it'll be too late to do anything about it. The Syndicates will be back on top, the world will be ours. Waste 'em boys.'

'Wait!' Jack yelled. 'If you kill me, this story and everything I know will be front-page news on every newspaper on earth.'

Manfreddo looked down at Jack and smiled. 'And how do you figure that? Until a few minutes ago you had no idea what was going on.'

'I hadn't made all the connections, no. But I had assembled a lot of the pieces – you, Freddy, the Syndicates . . . all of which I confided to a certain Gelda Longhorn.'

At the mention of the journalist's name, Manfreddo's face soured. 'I ought to have silenced that bitch a long time ago. She can print what she likes – even if anyone believed her, where's her proof?'

'O'Hanlon!' Jack pleaded. 'Are you going to be a party to this murder? Are you going to stand by and watch this slaughter and do nothing? You're a policeman – corrupt, perhaps, but a policeman nonetheless. Are you going to let this madman cover the world with gated communities? It's your job to uphold the law. You owe it to your calling to stop this now!'

The police chief regarded Jack, a half-smile on his lips.

'That's a very elegant speech, Mr Lindsay, but my "calling", as you put it, was supplanted some time ago by a desire for something a little more concrete – like financial security. Once this scam is up and running I'm going to be a very rich man. If the death of three people is all that stands between me and a multimillion-dollar fortune, I can't see it weighing too heavily on my conscience.'

'You really think he's going to let you live?' Jack persisted. 'You've served your purpose. You've helped him win his election – he's in control of the country and now you're surplus to requirements. He'll throw you away like a cold TV dinner.'

Manfreddo chewed angrily on his cigar. 'Come on let's get this over with!'

But O'Hanlon was intrigued. He put up his hand. 'No, I think we owe it to the condemned man to let him have his say.'

'Thank you. Manfreddo no longer needs you – he has his own army of men ready and waiting to take over the running of this island. Once he's installed in office, he'll kill you like he's killed everyone else that stood in his way. You know too much; you've used up all your guarantees. O'Hanlon, look at him – can you really trust this man? Think about the blood on his hands. How can you believe he won't stab you in the back?'

'Don't listen to him, O'Hanlon,' Manfreddo warned. 'He's just a desperate fuck trying to save his own skin.'

O'Hanlon shook his head. 'Nice try Jack, but you're too late.'

Manfreddo took the cigar from his lips. 'Seems like the whole world's against you, Jack.' He leered. 'Now, can we get on with this?'

'Just a minute!' It was Freddy – wide-eyed, shaking with fear, and aiming a gun straight at Manfreddo's heart.

'Aw, Freddy, be a good little soldier and put the gun down,' Manfreddo cooed, as if to a child.

'No! I'm tired of being pushed around. For God's sake, Horbert, you had me order the death of my own brother!'

323

'That was to test your loyalty – like . . . who was that guy in the Bible that God told to kill his own son as a sacrifice?'

'Abraham?' O'Hanlon suggested.

'Yeah, that's the feller. But as he was about to slit his only son's throat, and God saw he was willing to follow orders, the Big Man supplied Abraham with a goat instead. I knew a war hero like Jack would easily be able to take a two-bit chiseller like Razor Phipps. Think of me as God, you as Abraham, and Phipps as the goat.'

Freddy shook his head. 'That doesn't make me any the less ashamed of what I've done.'

'It's a little late to start having a conscience now, Freddy.'

Freddy gripped the handle of the gun a little tighter. 'This whole thing has gone too far. I thought I'd be able to stomach the killing, but I find I'm not up to it. Not even for a billion dollars! I'm not letting you get away with it, Horbert. I know it'll mean a long prison term for me, but I'm willing to atone for what I've done. And I'm taking you down with me, Horbert. I—'

A shot rang out.

Freddy looked puzzled, then collapsed to his knees. 'Sorry, Jack,' he gasped. They were his last words. He crumpled and fell in a heap, revealing Lana, a smoking gun in her hand.

'I always said he was weak,' she said.

Manfreddo gestured towards her with the end of his cigar. 'Isn't she a great little assistant?' Then he addressed the room. 'OK, boys, let's get this show on the road. Shoot the fuckers.'

'One moment!'

'Aw, what now?'

O'Hanlon climbed up onto the stage. 'You know, Con, I've been thinking about what Jack said, and he has a point. I don't have a guarantee of anything.'

'Don't give me this shit now,' Manfreddo sighed.

'I've stomped on the opposition, quietly eliminated any voice raised in protest against you, helped manipulate the election results, and now you're president. You can do what you like. All I have on you now is what I know. So you see, looking at it from your point of view, I'm nothing but a problem waiting to happen. I could be a real thorn in your side. Things would be much simpler if I didn't exist.'

Manfreddo growled and stared up at the ceiling. 'All right, what do you want?'

'I want some kind of assurance that you're not going to double-cross me. How about this: Lindsay, the woman, Mr Piggy-Wig and all that they know are transported, under armed escort, to a safe place and kept there under the protection of my men. Then, if anything should happen to me, my men will release them to tell their story to the world.'

'And where exactly would this "safe place" be?'

'That would be a secret known only to me and a few of my close associates.'

Manfreddo paced up and down across the front of the stage for a few moments, puffing thoughtfully on his cigar. Then he stopped suddenly and turned back to O'Hanlon. 'I've got a better idea. Why don't I kill you now?' He reached for his gun, but as he did so there was the sound of scores of weapons being cocked.

Unnoticed by everyone except O'Hanlon, the policemen on duty outside had been filing steadily into the hall for some time, and now formed a cordon around the inside of the building, their guns drawn.

'If I were you, Horbert, I'd put my gun away. It might also be wise to request your men do the same,' O'Hanlon said in his warm Irish brogue.

Manfreddo was instantly furious. 'You lousy son of a bitch! If it wasn't for me you'd still be making out parking tickets. You stupid fuck! You know what you've done? You've just thrown away billions!'

O'Hanlon gestured to two of his men, who climbed onto

the stage and held Manfreddo fast. Then the police chief turned to Jack.

'So, Jack, where do we go from here?'

'Nobody move!'

In the excitement of the past few moments, everyone had forgotten about Lana, who now took centre stage, gun in hand.

'Thatta girl!' Manfreddo cheered.

'Ah,' said Jack. 'Hell hath no fury—'

'Shut up!' she snarled. 'I never liked you from the moment I saw you.'

Jack smiled ruefully. 'And here's me thinking we could have made beautiful music together.'

'In your dreams. You're nothing but a jumped-up little British bobby, with your cheap tailoring, your tea with no froth and your Garibaldi obsession.'

'That's as may be, but this jumped-up little British bobby seems to have managed to foil a worldwide wrecking and rebuilding scam, whereas your country's best detective mind is probably still stumbling blindly around the Isle of Wight.'

'You think you're so clever, don't you?' She tightened her grip on the gun. 'Well, Mr Great Detective, I wonder if you can figure out what's going to happen next?'

'As a matter of fact I can. You're about to get a terrible headache.'

Lana frowned. 'How'd you work that out?'

There was the sound of wood splintering on cranium, and Lana's expression went from one of twisted hatred to blank incomprehension. Then she fell over, to reveal Marian holding a now slightly fractured piece of two-by-four. She looked up at Jack and smiled. 'What an awful woman.'

'So, where were we?' O'Hanlon enquired.

'We were about to cut a deal,' Jack replied.

'Go on,' the police chief said, thrusting his thumbs in his pockets.

'Don't listen to him, O'Hanlon,' Manfreddo warned.

'Shut up!' O'Hanlon barked.

'It seems to me,' said Jack, 'that having made an enemy of the top of the Syndicate tree, you've closed off a lot of your options.'

'All except one,' O'Hanlon corrected.

'And that being?'

'An unpleasant death.'

'Of course. So how's this for an idea: what if it turns out that Chief O'Hanlon's a good guy after all, and helps in the capture of a dangerous criminal? It will look so much better for you when this case comes to trial. On top of that, if you turn state's evidence you could get off lightly. They'll put you on the witness protection programme – give you a fresh start somewhere you're not known, with a new identity.'

O'Hanlon chewed his lip. 'And the alternative?'

'I wasn't kidding about Gelda Longhorn. She may not have the whole picture, but she does have a few names and places, and an abiding dislike for policemen. I wonder what sort of story she could weave out of police corruption and suspected Syndicate crime on Corbett? I'll bet the name of the police chief would feature heavily in a story like that.'

'Of course, there is one further option,' O'Hanlon suggested. 'I kill you, and Manfreddo and I carry on as we were.'

Jack shook his head. 'You've laid hands on the Syndicates' leader. Syndicate honour demands that you die. I'm your only friend in the world.'

O'Hanlon smiled and nodded. 'I like you, Jack. You know, I think this could be the start of a beautiful friendship. OK, boys, take the bad men back to the station.'

Manfreddo looked incredulous as a pair of handcuffs were snapped around his wrists. 'You're arresting me?'

The police chief raised his eyebrows. 'I'm glad you've at last grasped the gist of the situation.'

'O'Hanlon, you're a dead man. You think you can get away with this? For the rest of your life you'll be looking over your shoulder. Wherever you are, O'Hanlon, I'll find you. I'll find you, you son of a bitch!'

With a jerk of his head, the police chief dismissed Manfreddo, who was bundled off the stage.

'Just a minute,' said Jack, moving to the foot of the stairs. Without warning, he slammed a right hook into Manfreddo's jaw. 'That was for Freddy,' he snarled.

Manfreddo gazed levelly at him and Jack was suddenly smitten with a pang of conscience, not to mention sore knuckles.

'I apologize. That was ungentlemanly,' he said, massaging his right hand.

'Yeah, and so's this.' Manfreddo spat in his face.

'Get him out, boys!' O'Hanlon instructed. The crime boss, the semi-conscious Lana, and all Manfreddo's associates were taken outside to a fleet of waiting police cars.

Jack, wiping his face with a handkerchief, turned to the body of his brother, still lying where Lana had shot him. Clambering with difficulty up onto the stage, Jack bent and tenderly stroked Freddy's head.

'Hey, big brother, it seems that this time you didn't get your own way. Goodbye, Freddy.' Jack felt a hand on his shoulder and looked up into Mango's face. 'It's probably better this way,' Jack said. 'He wouldn't have lasted two minutes in prison – he couldn't stand confined spaces.' Then, wiping his eyes, he straightened.

Marian was standing forlornly at the side of the stage. Jack went over to her and gazed deeply into her warm hazel eyes. 'Marian, I know I'm going to regret what I'm about to say, possibly for the rest of my life, but you deserve to know the truth.'

Her eyes searched his face.

'You think that your husband betrayed you for money and power, that somehow he was intimately involved with a plan to kill millions of people and build housing estates on their tombs. But you're wrong.'

'Wrong?'

Jack took her gently by the hand, led her down the steps at the side of the stage and into the body of the hall. Standing her directly in front of Daygan, he asked him, 'Shall I go on?'

Daygan had been looking intently at Marian since her entry into the hall. Without taking his eyes off her for a second, he nodded.

'Your husband is a very clever man,' Jack continued. 'You see, at first, when the Syndicates came knocking, he was willing to sacrifice everything – even you – on the altar of his ambition. But it didn't take him long to come to his senses and realize what an awful mess he'd got himself into, so he changed tack and did everything he could to protect you. The reality is he never stopped loving you, Marian. He loved you so much he was willing to force you into another man's arms to keep you safe – even mine.'

Marian gazed questioningly into Daygan's melting brown eyes.

'Worried that the Syndicates would try and harm you, he sent you to me thinking, rightly, that once I'd met you I wouldn't be able to leave you alone. It was he who put the bomb in my office to pique my interest in your case.' He looked at Daygan and smiled ruefully. 'But I'd probably have found an excuse to help you even without that little shove.' He turned back to Marian. 'He also planted that bug in your hat to arouse my indignation and get me even more deeply involved, because he knew that with me by your side you'd be as safe as you could be under the circumstances.'

Marian gazed at Daygan. 'Is this true?'

'Every word.'

'Oh, Daygan!' She fell into his arms and they kissed.

Jack studied his shoes for a few moments and Mango squeezed his elbow sympathetically.

When the two lovers parted, Jack spoke again. 'Michael-mas . . . Daygan . . . Thurrock-Lawes . . . what the hell do I call you?'

'Daygan will do fine.'

'Good. Daygan, perhaps you could clear something up for me. You knew Manfreddo wanted me on this case, so why did you push Marian towards me?'

Daygan shook his head. 'I didn't find out that Manfreddo was interested in you until later. I just shopped around for the best detective in town and your name kept coming up.' Daygan shrugged. 'In the end it all worked out rather well, don't you think?'

Jack nodded. 'Maybe, but did you have to blow up my office?'

Daygan smiled. 'I *saw* your office.'

Jack considered a moment. 'Point taken. All right, last question. Why did you want me here on Corbett? You knew it was a dangerous situation and yet you also knew I'd be bringing Marian.'

'I was expecting you to turn up with the cavalry and arrest everyone. I had no idea you were such a maverick.'

Jack was genuinely shocked. 'Me, a maverick?'

Mango groaned.

Jack turned to him questioningly. 'What?'

'*Nanu nosee as him no lookee ins panlid,*' said Mango.

'In English?' Jack requested.

'There is none so blind as he who will not see himself.'

'Meaning?'

'You're a mystery to no one but you.'

'More homespun Filipino philosophy?'

'Not exactly. It's what my English teacher once said to me.'

'What were you wearing at the time – a burka?'

'Now don't start, Jack Lindsay.' Mango's jaw tightened.

'Boys, please,' Marian implored. 'Can we just get out of here?'

'Good idea,' said Jack. He turned to O'Hanlon. 'Can you furnish us with a car to take us to the airport?'

'Why don't you take Signor Manfreddo's limo? I'll even provide you with an escort.'

'Thank you. Lead on.'

O'Hanlon made for the door. 'This way, gentlemen, and lady.'

Chapter 23

The press conference was full to capacity with eager photo-graphers all jostling to get the best shots of Detective Lindsay and the reunited and blissfully happy couple. It was a story that had everything: danger, corruption in high places, and best of all – romance.

'Daygan!' a reporter shouted. 'What are your immediate plans?'

Daygan pulled Marian close to him. 'You have to ask?'

Laughter and a renewed frenzy of flashbulbs.

'And what about you, Detective? Are you going to carry on at the Yard?'

'I reach retirement age in a few months,' Jack said. 'And when I do you won't see me for dust. But until that time I'll be happy to stay on and solve all the Yard's cases for them.' He smiled.

But someone at the back of the hall wasn't feeling quite so rosy.

You'll stay here, Jack Lindsay, over my dead body, the newly appointed commissioner thought darkly. Then, turning on his heel, he slipped out of the hall, leaving the press to feed and tickle the heroes of the day.

'You wanted to see me, Steven?' Jack stood unsteadily before Commissioner Mellinger's desk. He'd had a few shots to cele-brate his homecoming and was feeling a little light-headed.

'It's *Commissioner* Mellinger,' his superior snarled. The commissioner was small and neat, and fastidious to a fault about his appearance, although Jack preferred the adjective 'anal'.

'Oh, begging your pardon, Commissioner, sir.' Jack tugged his forelock. 'Perhaps you'd prefer me to kneel?'

'Don't get smart with me, Lindsay. You may have been able to wind your brother around your little finger, but believe me I'm a very different kettle of fish. For one thing I will not tolerate my officers being drunk on duty.'

'Oh, I'm not drunk, Commissioner, sir. I'm completely stiffed.'

Mellinger smiled. 'Same old Jack. So, how do you see your future with the force?'

'I prefer not to look too far ahead. I've learned that living from day to day is the best attitude to take in my line of work.'

'Good, then you won't be disappointed to learn that I'm asking you for your resignation.'

That sobered Jack up.

'Resignation?'

'Yes. I want you out of here by the end of the day.'

'You want *my* resignation? Me, the hero of the hour?'

'Don't flatter yourself that you're indispensable to the running of this police force, Lindsay. We both know you're not a team player.'

'And what if I refuse?'

Mellinger eased back in his seat and regarded Jack in silence for a few moments.

'When are you going to grow up, Jack? Look at you, fifty years old and still behaving like a teenager. Do you know how pathetic this adolescent posturing looks on a man your age? Someone needs to give you a good shake, Jack, to wake you up; bring you into the real world. And it seems that task has fallen to me. So listen very carefully. The work you did for Freddy was top secret. Oh, your name appears on the official employees' log, but there's no record as to your actual job. To all intents and purposes you were merely employed as a detective, on a detective's salary.' Mellinger paused and leaned forward. 'Are you getting the message?'

Jack blinked. 'But, Chairman McClaggen—'

'Has the memory of a newt. He even has difficulty remembering his own name. It's optimistic in the extreme to suppose that he has any recollection of you or your top-secret meeting, and I doubt any written records exist.'

'They do! McClaggen signed the authorization.'

'And where is this authorization now?'

'I don't know – the chairman gave it to Freddy.'

Mellinger smiled like a reptile. 'I see. Unfortunately, as we found no sign of said authorization when we cleaned Commissioner Lindsay's effects out of this office, all we have to go on is your say-so.'

'And that, of course, would be nowhere near good enough for you,' Jack growled.

'Relax, Jack, I have no desire to be vindictive. I see no reason why you shouldn't be paid what you are owed.'

Jack breathed a little easier, but he knew Mellinger for the snake he was, and continued to watch him warily as he picked up a sheet of paper from his desk.

'Let's see,' Mellinger continued, 'you've been with us for . . . ten days now. So, being generous, let's say we give you two weeks' salary. I believe you came to a very lucrative agreement with Chairman McClaggen.'

'Ten thousand a week.'

'Well, that's not so bad is it? But then, of course –' Mellinger picked up another sheet of paper and shook his head sadly '– there's the matter of your expenses.'

'Expenses?'

The commissioner read from the sheet. 'A trip for two on a hyperliner. A brief but expensive stay at the Royal Mahe Hotel. Then there are taxis, car hire . . . shall I go on?'

'I was on police business – they were legitimate expenses.'

'No, when these particular expenses were clocked up you had already been suspended from the force – by your own brother. It occurs to me that knowingly using a police-issue credit card whilst under suspension could be construed as fraud.'

'Fraud?' Jack said faintly.

'You're looking a little peaky, Jack. Why don't you sit down?'

Jack grabbed a chair and collapsed into it. He shook his head, trying to clear it; trying to think his way out of this nightmare.

Mellinger smiled again. 'Of course, it would be churlish not to take into consideration all you've done for us recently. So, how about this: we use that two weeks' salary to pay off your expenses and forget about the fraud charge, seem fair?'

Now Jack had recovered from the initial shock, he felt a wave of anger surge through him. 'You dirty, rotten scumbag. You won't get away with this.'

'Oh, but I already have.'

'You people, you're all the same. It's the idiots like me who do the dirty work while you sit back and take the credit.' Jack stood shakily, and hurled the chair across the room. 'I wish I'd left you there in that stinking jungle, surrounded by those howling Timorese. I think now I'd have enjoyed watching them scoop out your brains with their bayonets.' Jack gripped the desk and leaned in close to the commissioner. 'You'd better take care of yourself, Mellinger, because the next time you get yourself in trouble, I'm going to be cheering on the other side. I might even help them out.'

Mellinger raised an immaculately plucked eyebrow. 'Is that a threat? Be careful, Jack. At the moment I'm letting you resign, but I would be well within my rights to dishonourably discharge you from the force.'

'Oh, very grateful, I'm sure.'

Mellinger sighed. 'You may not have read the rule book in a long time, Jack, but I know it backwards.'

'I'll bet you do,' Jack snarled.

'And you've probably forgotten how severely a dishonourable discharge can impact on one's eligibility to receive, for instance, a disability pension.'

Jack suddenly felt cold and sick. 'You wouldn't!'

Mellinger leaned forward threateningly. 'Try me.'

Jack left Mellinger's office shaken and stone-cold sober. On the way down to his office, he met DS Maude and DC Barking in the company of a distinctly unhappy Lieutenant Matthias.

'Oh no,' Jack breathed. He didn't have the energy for another confrontation so soon after being beaten up by the new commissioner. 'Ah, hello, *Loo*tenant,' he smiled. 'How did you find our little Isle of Wight?'

Matthias didn't say anything, but he did make a noise – nothing that could be defined as speech, more a sort of strangled gurgling.

Jack watched with interest as the lieutenant turned first red, then purple, then dark puce. Then, without warning, Matthias launched himself at Jack's throat.

'You bastard! I'm going to kill you!' Taking hold of Jack's neck, he squeezed.

'You've ruined me! You've made me a laughing stock! When this story gets out I'll never be able to show my face in New York again!'

Now it was Jack's turn to make unintelligible noises as he gasped in an effort to breathe. 'Get him off me!' he managed to squeak to Maude and Barking, who stood back in smiling silence, happily watching the incident unfold.

Eventually they got the message. 'Oh, right, sir,' said Maude. 'Come along, DC Barking.'

Together the two policemen hauled the screaming lieutenant off Jack, and held him while he struggled.

'You'd better hustle along, sir,' Maude warned Jack. 'I don't know how long we'll be able to hold him.'

But Jack didn't 'hustle along' – he'd had an idea. 'Matthias,' he said. 'I know my treatment of you hasn't been entirely above board—'

'Damn' right!' Matthias roared.

'Yes, but you know, it's really not my fault.'

'Oh, *really?*' said Matthias.

'Really,' Jack reiterated. 'You see, I'm just a part of the system, what you might call a small cog in a very large machine.'

'What are you getting at?'

'To coin a phrase: I was just obeying orders.' Jack crossed his fingers behind his back. 'It wasn't my idea to pack you off to the Isle of Wight.'

Matthias looked sceptical. 'It wasn't?'

'No. It was Deputy Police Commissioner Mellinger's.'

The lieutenant's brow wrinkled. 'I thought your brother was in charge back then.'

'No, no, no. Dear old Freddy handed over the reins to Mellinger just before you came on board. He wanted him to have some experience of what a major case felt like. Besides, it's procedure. Every year the deputy police commissioner must take over the top job for a month – sort of upmarket work experience, if you like.'

Matthias looked confused, but seemed to be buying Jack's elaborate fiction.

'And it just so happens that commissioner Mellinger has a very low opinion of American policing.'

'Oh, has he now?'

'I'm afraid so. Of course, we at Scotland Yard all received the directives about racial equality, religious equality, sexual equality, etcetera. It seems that Mellinger didn't get the one about police equality. He seems to think that Scotland Yard is the only police force in the world. Between you and me he despises "the Yanks", as he calls them, says they're a bunch of rank amateurs.'

'Amateurs?' Matthias flushed purple again.

'Yes, and he singled you out for special treatment. I believe

he called you "that jumped-up little bastard from the Bronx".'
Jack was beginning to enjoy himself.

The lieutenant's eyes bulged alarmingly.

'He also said of you, and I quote, "He couldn't arrest a
drunk pissing on his own shoes." A not entirely flattering sen-
timent, you have to admit.'

The lieutenant began to struggle violently against Maude
and Barking. 'Where is this Mellinger? I'm going to kill the son
of a bitch!'

'Oh, I'd advise against any direct confrontation,' Jack
warned. 'You know what can happen when tempers flare – apart
from the risk of actual bodily harm, the whole thing can so easily
degenerate into an orgy of pointless name-calling. How does
the old saying go? Oh yes, "Revenge is a dish best served cold."'
Jack leaned in conspiratorially. 'If you really want to get your
own back, I can suggest a course of action with a very low risk
of comeback.'

Matthias narrowed his eyes. 'Go on.'

'Do you know a journalist called Gelda Longhorn? She's
downstairs right now, in the press room . . .'

'The kettle's exploded,' said Mango, sticking his head through
the door. 'That's what comes of buying everything second-
hand.'

Jack eased back in his leather recliner. 'Now, now, Mango,
remember we're on a drive to economize. Besides, this chair's
second-hand, and it's only really just broken in. We have to look
at the positives of our situation.'

'There aren't any.'

Jack sighed. 'Clark!' he yelled.

Clark appeared from the lobby of the little suite of offices
Jack had rented in a narrow street off Brick Lane.

'Chief?'

'Nip out and get us some teas, would you? Milk and one sugar for me, Mango'll have his white, no sugar, and . . . Ruth!'

Ruth too stuck her head around the door from the lobby. 'Yeah?'

'How do you take your tea?'

'Oh, white no sugar, thanks.'

'Got that, Clark?'

He nodded.

'Oh, and ask them if they've got any . . . no, on second thoughts, grab us a few of those sandwich biscuits, you know, the ones with the chocolate substitute on the outside.'

'Right.' Clark hovered uncertainly in the doorway.

'What is it?' Jack asked.

'Um, petty cash?' he enquired uncertainly.

'Ah . . . Mango, give the boy some money.'

Mango raised his eyes to heaven and dug into his pockets. 'Here.'

'Thanks.'

After Clark had gone, Mango settled on the edge of Jack's desk. 'So, how many calls for your great detective mind have we had today?'

Jack consulted a large desk diary lying open in front of him. 'Hmm, let's see now . . . er, precisely none.'

Mango nodded slowly. 'I see. And how long do you suspect we can continue in this vein? Especially now you have an expanded wages bill.' He nodded in Ruth's direction.

'Oh, don't you worry.' Jack clasped his hands behind his head and the ancient leather chair creaked as he leaned back. 'It's still early days; the adverts will only just have appeared. What are we in, Ruth?'

'All the local papers, the *Telegraph* personals, *Loot*, *Metro*, *Exchange and Mart* and *Time Out*.'

Jack turned to Mango triumphantly. 'See? As soon as word gets around that Jack Lindsay – the famous detective who stood up to the Syndicates – is available for hire, people will come running.'

Mango gazed long-sufferingly at Ruth. 'Welcome to my world,' he said.

'Do you think we should set up our own website?' Jack wondered. 'And how about advertising on rickshaws?'

Just then, the phone rang and everybody jumped. Jack watched it ring for some moments.

In the end it was Ruth who picked it up.

'Lindsay's Detective Agency, agent Jones speaking, how can I help?'

Jack looked at Mango appreciatively.

'I see . . . well he is very busy, as you can imagine.'

Mango rolled his eyes.

'Can I ask the nature of your enquiry? . . . I see . . . right . . . right . . . Let me just have a look.' She swung the big, blank desk diary around to face her. 'Hmm. Ah, we've just had a cancellation this afternoon. Two o'clock? . . . Very good. You know where we are? Excellent, we'll see you then.' She put the phone down and turned to the others. 'Do I get the job?'

Jack beamed. 'Give yourself a raise immediately.'

Mango shook his head. 'Don't listen to him – it's just a phrase he uses.'

'So, who's the client?' Jack asked.

'A man,' she replied.

'Makes a change,' Mango muttered.

'Shh. Go on, Ruth.'

'It seems he's a businessman who is concerned that a rival is stealing his secrets.'

'Ah,' said Jack, rubbing his hands together. 'Espionage in big business – terrific!'

'Er, not quite. The man in question is worried that a rival has stolen the secret formula for his cinnamon buns.'

Jack deflated a little. 'Oh. Well, it's a start. What's his name?'

'Angelo Tortorelli.'

But at this news Jack brightened once more. 'Tortorelli the baker?'

'Yes.'

'Tortorelli is one of the best bakers in town. He can do wonders with wheat-free flour – he can even make it taste like wheat. No wonder he's worried. His cinnamon buns are legendary. This is a case to get our teeth into after all. We must do everything we can to help, and then, maybe . . .'

'Maybe what?' Mango looked at him, his head to one side.

'Maybe he could—' Jack shook his head and looked sheepish. 'No, it's silly.'

'No, go on.'

'Well, I . . .'

Both Ruth and Mango leaned in.

'I just thought that maybe if we solve this case for him, he might be able to make me up a batch of—'

'Tea up!'

Clark burst through the door carrying a cardboard tray laden with teas.

'Ah, good, dish them out, Clark,' said Jack, making room on the desk. 'Did you get any biscuits?'

Clark glanced uncertainly at Ruth. 'Er, no, Chief. They didn't have any.'

Jack's face crumpled in disappointment. 'Oh.'

'Just a minute,' said Ruth, 'I'll see what I've got in my lunch box.'

She disappeared into the outer office for a moment, then reappeared carrying a small Tupperware container.

'I'm afraid it's rather a limited selection. All I've got are these.' She peeled off the lid and handed the container to Jack.

He couldn't quite believe his eyes when he saw what was inside. 'Garibaldis!' he cheered. 'Where did you get them?'

'Oh, I have contacts across the Channel. When Mango gave me that list of phone numbers of Purple Trousers on the Continent, I used the opportunity to see if I could hunt down a few of your favourite biscuits for you. It just so happens there's a baker in Turin who still makes them. I asked him to send me a few dozen.'

'Ruth, you're a genius.' Jack wiped a small but significant tear from his eye. Then he leapt up, leaned across the desk and kissed her on the lips. It was a shock to both of them. When they parted, Ruth, looking flustered but pleased, smoothed back her hair and straightened her jacket while Jack stood frozen a moment, unable to quite believe what he'd just done, but awfully glad that he'd done it.

Mango and Clark shared a significant look.

Jack, slightly flushed, and finding it impossible to suppress the stupid grin spreading across his face, sat down again. Reaching into Ruth's Tupperware container, he pulled out one of the raisin-rich biscuits and admired its knobbly and pitted surface for some moments. Then he dunked it in his tea, placed it tenderly in his mouth and closed his eyes in ecstasy.

'God, that's heaven. I can't tell you how much I've missed that taste.'

'I also bought a newspaper,' said Clark. 'After breaking the Syndicates, it seems that Gelda Longhorn has her talons into another subject.'

Clark handed Jack the copy of *The Post* he'd had tucked under his arm. Jack took it and scanned the front page. A smile spread slowly across his face as he read the lead article.

THE GAMES OUR LEADERS PLAY

It seems the great and the good are not immune to playing the odd practical joke, usually on us, but sometimes on one another. Take the case of brand new Police Commissioner Mellinger and the New York lieutenant – both ambitious and, dare I say it, ruthless, men. It turns out our dour-faced police commissioner has a sense of humour after all, as he sent one Lieutenant Matthias – a seen-everything American cop, eager to put one over on the slow-witted English bobbies – on a wild-goose-chase to the quaint old Isle of Wight, when he should have been helping to find the Cranium Killer. Now, much as we applaud the appearance of humour in the corridors of power, could this really be described as a sensible use of police time and effort? On top of which, Commissioner Mellinger's opinion of American policing is what can only be described as low. 'I despise the Yanks,' he's been heard to say on more than one occasion, describing Lieutenant Matthias as 'that jumped-up little b****** from the Bronx'. Not only is our beloved commissioner a narrow-minded old xenophobe, but a little bird tells me that he also has a very old skeleton in the cupboard: apparently his war record leaves much to be desired. It seems that during the Malaysian campaign, Captain Steven Mellinger led a company of men straight into an ambush set by the Timorese and had to be rescued by none other than the indomitable Jack Lindsay. Oh dear, I suspect the story of a commander blindly leading his men into danger isn't going to inspire confidence amongst those serving under him. So, Police Commissioner Mellinger, before you take another step, may I suggest you look closely at the road ahead? I have a feeling your path is going to be beset by pitfalls. Tread carefully, Commissioner – I shall be watching.

Jack threw the paper down on the desk. 'Hah! That'll teach him to mess with the *indomitable* Jack Lindsay. With Gelda on his back, he won't be able to move.' He reached for another Garibaldi. 'This is turning out to be quite a red-letter day.'

Mango eyed him suspiciously. 'I don't suppose you had anything to do with this article?'

Jack mumbled his denial through a mouthful of crumbs. 'I haven't spoken to Gelda for days. God, these are good. Now then, what do we know about the baking fraternity . . .?'

At Scotland Yard, seated outside Commissioner Mellinger's door, Barking and Maude, having been summoned to explain their part in the Matthias affair, listened with interest to the sounds of destruction and cries of fury emanating from within.

'It seems he's read the newspaper article, then,' Maude observed.

'I think that would be a safe assumption,' DC Barking replied with a wry smile.

After a short pause, DS Maude spoke again. 'What would you say is the difference between a howl and a yowl?' he asked.

DC Barking ran a hand over his chin. 'Well now, howling, although usually performed by members of the animal kingdom, is, on occasion, indulged in by the human species. Whereas your yowl, for my money, is the sole prerogative of the wild animal.'

DS Maude nodded thoughtfully while he digested his colleague's insight. Eventually he spoke again. Jerking a thumb back at Commissioner Mellinger's door, he said, 'So that was a howl then?'

Barking listened attentively to the half-animal sounds continuing to proceed from Mellinger's office. 'I think in the case of Commissioner Mellinger I'd be forced to admit an exception to the rule. Our new chief seems to have crossed the species boundary and joined our cousins in the vulpine fraternity.'

Both Maude and Barking, enjoying this little dig at their superior officer, allowed themselves the indulgence of a quiet chuckle.